NEM

Book 4 of the Haunted Series

TONY MARTURANO

a Different Angle

Published in the United Kingdom and the rest of the world by a
Different Angle 2024
Cambridge, UK

A catalogue record for this book is available from the
British Library

ISBN - 978-1-7397694-8-2

This book is dedicated to…YOU.

Thank you.

AUTHOR'S NOTE

STUFF YOU MAY FIND INTERESTING, AND... OH, IMPORTANT BONUS CONTENT!

Hello, and welcome back to the Haunted series. Before you dim the lights and the shadows start to stir, allow me to share a few additional words with you.

SPELLING SOUVENIRS FROM ACROSS THE POND

I'm blessed to have a global readership – from the sun-soaked beaches of Sydney to the snow-capped peaks of the Swiss Alps, from the bustling streets of Tokyo to the serene landscapes of the Canadian Rockies. Whether you're reading this under the Northern Lights in Norway or in a cosy café in a small town in Vermont, you might notice a few differences in spelling throughout the book.

If you find yourself tripping over words like "colour" sprinkled with an extra 'u', or "realise" sporting an 's' where you'd expect a 'z', don't rush to adjust your glasses or your device's settings. Your spellchecker hasn't developed a fancy British accent overnight!

You see, I write in British English – the original recipe with all the extra letters left in for good measure. Think of it as the director's cut of the English language. Those additional letters aren't typos; they're just queuing up (yes, with an extra 'u') to add a dash of British charm to the story.

We're many nations divided by a common language but united by our love for a gripping tale. So, please consider these spellings as little souvenirs from across the pond.

BONUS CONTENT

I recognise that readers come to Marco's stories with different expectations. Some are eager to plunge straight into the heart of the new adventure, while others are curious about the quieter moments and the details. We've sought to cater to both by making a deliberate choice in how the narrative is presented to you. If you're one of those readers who enjoys the details – in this case, what happened in Marco's life following the events at Holt and Frost Lake Manor, between Cursed and Nemesis – please turn to the bonus content at the end of this book. These additional chapters are titled but unnumbered, setting them apart from the main narrative. They offer a deeper insight into Marco's journey, his healing process, and the steps that led him to where Nemesis begins.

However, if you're keen to dive straight into the suspense and thrills of Nemesis, feel free to continue reading from here. You won't miss any crucial plot points.

THE EVOLUTION OF THE HAUNTED SERIES

The story of Marco started simmering in my mind long before it ever saw the light of day. Psychosis was an idea that lingered for about a year before I penned the first few pages. I remember sharing those initial drafts with my sister. Her eyes lit up as she said, "Tony, you've got to write this book!" But I was deep into another project (Unspeakable), and so Psychosis had to wait its turn.

When I finally sat down to write it, the story flowed effortlessly. It was everything I had envisioned – intense, psychological, and deeply emotional. When both my sister and the focus group read it, it was everything they expected and more.

However, upon publication, Psychosis received a lukewarm response. It didn't resonate with readers as I'd hoped, and I'll admit, it was disheartening. Writing is always a labour of love, and this story of a man striving to fix others while grappling with his own demons was particularly close to my heart.

And so it was... until a year or so later, I was on location in Cornwall for a photoshoot. I was up in the early hours, prepping camera equipment, and I found myself thinking about a comment that was made by one of the Psychosis focus group members. I remember her telling me about how much she enjoyed the book but how she believed the book's ending very much lent itself to a supernatural theme. And so, I thought... what if... what if... there was more to the story?

So, I turned on my laptop and started tapping away at the keys, you know, just to see...

Haunted - book 2 of the series - was born. This time, the story took a different turn into the supernatural, taking Marco's psychological struggles and layering them with elements that blurred the lines between reality and the unexplainable.

Haunted struck a chord. It became an Amazon #1 bestseller for weeks. When the audiobook was released - amidst the challenges of the pandemic – it soared to the top of Audible's charts, sharing space with the likes of Stephen King and George R. R. Martin. It was surreal and beyond anything I had imagined. Not only that, but Book 1, Psychosis, was now viewed differently by series faithful who viewed it in a completely different light and adopted it, as they have the rest of the books that have now been optioned for film.

Whether or not the series will ever make it to the big or small screen remains to be seen. However, buoyed by your love for the series, I decided to continue Marco's journey with Cursed, completing what I now refer to as the Origin Trilogy. These three books delve deep into Marco's psyche, unravelling his past, his fears, and the events that shaped him - from the psychological unravelling in Psychosis through to the supernatural binding of Cursed.

After Cursed, I believed I had told Marco's story. So I returned to working on the demonological Sinister series – with another 3 more books.

But it would seem that many readers weren't done with Marco, often reaching out to ask if Cursed was truly the end of Marco and Buddy's story.

And so I began to wonder… WHAT IF…

What if the first three books marked the culmination of our exploration of Marco's personal story? What if, with his unique skills as a psychologist and the profound experiences he's endured, he is now poised not only to better help others but also go further and with Buddy set out to unravel the other mysteries of our world?

SAME SERIES. DIFFERENT STORIES.

With Nemesis, the fourth book in the series, we move beyond Marco's origin trilogy and embark on an exciting new direction. Each forthcoming book will introduce Marco to a unique and terrifying experience, plunging him into mysteries that defy explanation and challenge the very fabric of reality.

In Nemesis, Marco's journey to an isolated, snowbound island at the edge of the world doesn't mean he'll be alone – but that isn't necessarily a good thing. When fear turns to paranoia, who can you trust? And there's something truly horrifying out there in the snow. So, snuggle down, lock the doors (because you never know), and brace yourself – you're about to witness Marco's darkest nightmare yet.

Tony

PROLOGUE

The biting cold seeps into her bones, numbing her flesh and forcing her eyes open to a starless sky framed by the jagged silhouettes of naked trees. The ground beneath her is hard and unyielding, a thin blanket of snow crunching softly under her weight as she moves. Memories flicker and fade, fragments of a life she can't quite grasp. The world feels tilted; the edges blurring like a watercolour painting left in the rain.

She presses a trembling hand to her stomach as it churns and clenches. It's not hunger gnawing at her sides but something far more sinister – an omen, a warning that something is deeply amiss. She can feel it inside her – something foreign, something that doesn't belong – stretching through her with long tendrils of darkness, like an inky shadow staining her very being.

A surge of panic pushes her to her feet where she stands uncertainly, her body shivering violently, rebelling against the cold that is slowly numbing her fear and replacing it with an eerie stillness. Then she hears it, riding on the wind, accompanied by the sound of distant laughter. The sound spurs her forward, each step mechanical, like a marionette pulled by unseen strings. The snow crunches beneath her bare feet, the cold biting deeper into her skin as she trudges towards the orange glow in the distance.

Around her, the wind whispers through the branches of towering evergreens, their needles frosted with ice, shimmering under the weak moonlight, filling her nostrils with the scent of pine and damp earth.

She can feel it now, urging her forward to seek her kind as the warmly lit windows of the building draw closer and closer. But then the music, the festivities, stop suddenly, as if sensing her approach, leaving nothing but the wail of the wind and the pounding in her head. Still, she is here now. She is where she is supposed to be.

After hesitating for several moments, heart pounding in her chest, mind struggling to pierce through the fog, she steps forward and pushes on the doors, spilling light out onto the snow, spawning her elongated shadow.

The room is filled with people, each of their faces turning towards her in a mixture of shock and horror. They've been waiting for her. She tries to speak, to ask for help, but her voice is gone, stolen by the freeze. Instead, words that aren't her own spill forth, cold and detached yet filled with an ominous certainty: "You're all going to die here." The declaration hangs in the air, a grim prophecy that silences the room. Then, as darkness envelops her vision, her legs buckle, and she feels herself falling before being caught by strong arms as she slips into oblivion once more.

1

THE JOURNEY

SUNDAY. EARLY MORNING.

We left Cliffhaven under the cover of darkness – not by choice, but because of the season – which was probably for the best as we left behind the familiarity of my beloved southwest. Buddy is nestled by my feet, and I don't think I've ever been more grateful for the company of my trusty companion as we venture north.

As the train rumbles on, I find myself with my face almost pressed up against the window, like one of those sticky Garfield toys you see on car windows, listening to the hum and clatter of what will be our temporary home for most of the day.

You may remember from your last visit that I was considering a trip around Italy. No, please don't get excited – I didn't go on account of finishing my first book, *Psychosis* – yeah, can you believe that? I still can't – and building a new dream home called ANEW. And now, thanks to Frodo Aaron, I've abandoned my haven to embark on this bloody Lord of the Rings–like quest to a faraway land.

You remember him, right? Aaron Sinclair – former Marine, husband to my best friend. I tell you, that bloke never ceases to amaze me. He's like the wise Buddha of gays who has this uncanny influence over me. I imagine it's that laid-back demeanour of his. Nothing seems to truly rattle him, as I learned on the night of the restaurant incident. What, you don't remember that? Just as well. I'm reminded of it each and every time I do something stupid, which, I'm happy to report, doesn't seem as often these days. Although, I'm not sure if that's because I'm making good choices or because I'm actively limiting human interaction to just a few digestible portions each week. What do you think?

Don't answer that.

So, anyway, it's been just over a week since I received a letter and the pep talk responsible for us being here. To be fair, I was on the verge of needing medical intervention at the time. Don't worry. Nothing serious. The lads were staying over for the weekend, and Aaron had joined me on the morning run.

I can still feel the burn in my legs as we take a different route, leaving ANEW's boundaries and joining the public coastal path that runs the circumference of the bay. It winds through woodland, over and through cliff rock, eventually leading to Cliffhaven, a couple of miles away.

Below us, the ocean sprawls – a vast expanse of underdeveloped aquamarine, serene from afar yet deceiving. Closer, the surf clashes against the cliffs in a relentless ballet, waves thundering like the beating heart of the world itself. It's a reminder of nature's duality:

serene beauty intertwined with tumultuous force.

I stop and place my hands on my hips as I recover, sucking in the salty ocean breeze blowing at me. It's cold and invigorating.

It takes the American, Aaron, several more seconds to realise that I'm no longer keeping up with him. He stops and looks back at me sideways, squinting into the orange flare of the rising sun. "You okay?" he calls back between gasps.

"Yeah... just... admiring the view."

Buddy barks up ahead – *Come on, lightweights!*

Aaron walks back to me, panting, his short hair damp with perspiration. It's always interesting to me how the man, even after being out of the Marines for a while, still cuts his hair as if he's going to rejoin tomorrow.

"Wanna try that again?" he asks, casually stretching an arm behind his back and rotating his shoulders.

I sigh, look at him, and frown. "I'm good," I say.

He nods. "That's cool. So you're not thinking about Sarah or that letter you got out of nowhere. That's great," he says with a wry smile.

I chuckle. I forget how perceptive this bloke is.

"I'm okay," I say with a lift of the eyebrows. "Just a bit of a shock, that's all."

"Hell, yeah. Not every day your ex pays you a house visit with her new fiancé."

I groan. "Thanks for reminding me again."

"You're welcome."

I'm about to say something when my phone – that I don't normally answer when on a run – starts ringing. *Marco, there's a phone call from Eddie Chapman for you,* Holt announces through the earbuds in my ears – Yeah, I know, sounds a bit geeky, but that's what happens when you can pair your home AI with your phone. I am a bloke, after all, and by default, a big kid, remember – *Would you like me to take a message?*

"No, put him through, please, Holt," I say, looking in Aaron's direction and holding up a finger. I wait a few seconds, then smile,

"Eddie, good morning. Bit early for you, isn't it?"

"Not funny. I haven't had a good night's sleep since I was twenty, and hotel rooms don't make it any easier. Besides, you're up, ain't ya?"

"Yep. Got demanding houseguests." I wink at Aaron. "Wanted to get an early start on the day. Did you have a good time last night?"

"Yeah, good. But I think I'm gettin' a bit long in the tooth for this shit. The old champers plays havoc with the ol' lump of lead! Now I've got a noggin as 'eavy as a fuckin' anvil."

I chuckle. "Well, you need to treat yourself to a hotel fry-up and a cuppa before you hit the road. Maybe pace yourself next time. As you say, you ain't no spring chicken anymore."

"Yeah, hilarious. Listen, didn't get a chance to talk about it last night, but I've got the publisher breathing down my neck about this second book."

"Yeah, we didn't talk about it, Eddie, because I said I didn't want to this weekend, remember?"

"Yeah. But you also promised me some preview pages."

"Nope. I didn't promise you any pages."

"Yeah, you did."

"Bad signal, Eddie. Sorry, mate, you're... b...reaking... u...p."

"Marc, nobody falls for that shit, and don't you even think about hanging up on me—"

"Eddie... if you can hear me... as I said... talk tomorrow!"

"Marco!"

But I've already disconnected the call.

When I turn, I see Aaron looking at me with an amused frown.

I roll my eyes. "My agent."

He nods. "Yeah, I got that."

"He's like a bloody Rottweiler. Which is good when you're trying to secure a deal. Not so good when he wants something."

"You've started the next book, then?"

I shake my head, squinting into the rising sun. "Nah, wishful thinking on his part. On the other hand—"

"Man's gotta eat, right?"

I laugh. "Right. I told Eddie that I was thinking about it, but," I rock my head, "after building the house, I don't think it's any longer a case of if but when," I say with newfound pragmatism. "I'm in no hurry to relive what happened, but I know it makes sense."

"Well, you did an awesome job with the first one. No wonder they want more."

"Thanks, mate," I say. And it's genuine because despite what I keep hearing, I still struggle to see why anybody would want to read about me.

"So, when are you starting? Before or after your visit?"

"My visit?"

"Yeah, ya know, with your sister."

I groan. "I haven't even decided if I'm going yet. Besides, Samantha is my half-sister."

"Tomayto, tomato," he says. "The point is, what's to decide?"

"Well, for a start, whether or not I want to make a train journey that's going to take the best part of a day each way to the back arse of Scotland to attend a memorial for a man who's been dead for more years than he was an active influence in my life."

"You could fly."

"And put Buddy in cargo? No way."

"You could leave him with us. You know we'd love to house-sit," he says with a wink before jerking his head down the path.

We start to walk back. Seagulls call overhead. Crows caw from their perches on nearby trees.

"Did you know my dad had a brother?" he asks suddenly.

I look at him, surprised. "A brother? No, I didn't."

"Yeah. They were really close as kids – even joined the Corps together. Inseparable."

I glance at him, sensing there's more to the story.

"Then," he continues, "I don't exactly know why – I think I was about ten at the time – they had some kind of falling out. Stopped talking. Stopped calling. And, as you know, we moved around a lot, so they lost touch."

He pauses, his gaze meeting mine. "Then, one day, out of the blue, we get a call. My uncle was out in the field, chopper crashed – that was it. Just like that."

His voice takes on a sombre tone. "My dad took it really badly. You know, that was the first time I'd known him to cry. Not in front of me, of course. He'd never do that. We're not touchy-feely in our family. But I heard him, behind locked doors, when he thought I couldn't. And he was never the same since. I mean, although my little mind back then couldn't fully grasp what was going on, I knew then that something had changed."

I stare at him, wide-eyed, the weight of his story sinking in. "Too heavy for this early in the morning?" he asks, scrunching up his nose. "Yeah, I know."

I shake my head. "Just a tad; that's a bloody terrible story, Aaron. And I thought I was bad!"

He laughs but then steps forward, locking eyes with me in that intense way he does. "My point is, Marco... I know these people have been nothing but assholes to you."

"That's an understatement."

"Alright, dicks. But you know, this whole thing about starting anew... it's not just about the place, is it? It's about you, who you want to be now after everything you've been through."

Aaron's tone is earnest as he continues, "You've built more than just a house. You've built a life from the ground up, man. You've faced loss, betrayal, and unimaginable hardship, and you came out the other side. That's not just resilience; that's strength. You've found peace here," he says, looking at the majesty that surrounds us, "but there's something more you gotta build now." He takes a deep breath, turning into the wind and looking out over the ocean. "Reconciliation. Not just with your stepfamily, but with your past, buddy. Holding onto resentment would be like building walls in that new home of yours, walls that keep you from truly moving forward. You're richer in ways they'll never understand – you've got heart, depth, character, and a whole wealth of experiences that have shaped you. Made you who you are now."

I watch him place a hand on my shoulder. "You talk about finding peace, but it's not just a place – it's in here," he taps his chest. "I know you're a Brit, and this might make you cringe, but give it a second. Real peace comes when you let go of old grudges. Not peace for them, but for you. This is your chance to honour your dad. I know that's been eating at you. And who knows? Maybe you'll find the family you never really had."

I hesitate because I think I've got bloody goosebumps, but I'm not going to tell him that. "Shit, Aaron, I think you may have missed your vocation," I quip.

He shrugs and steps back. "You know, if we were having this conversation a few years back, I would probably be telling ya to avoid that shit. But now..." he breathes deeply and sighs. "After what you've been through. If you can survive that, then this'll be a walk in the park," he says with a shrug.

And he has a point. I just hope he's right.

The loud boom of a train passing in the opposite direction startles me back to the present.

That run was a week ago. Now, the greyscale daylight of a new cloudy day is busy processing the film negative of night into a landscape that forever morphs before my very eyes: from the lush, gentle hills dotted with quaint cottages and ancient ruins that whisper tales of yore to the rugged, untamed beauty of the north that stretches out like the pages of a storybook I've never read.

Then, as the aroma of freshly brewed coffee meanders down the aisle, the moving canvas subtly shifts. The undulating hills, a patchwork of greens and golds beneath the morning light, stretch endlessly. Small towns with their huddled cottages and spiralling chimney smoke pass by my window, reminders of the world stirring awake.

Rivers we cross glimmer like threads of silver, reflecting a world that's slowly coming into focus, not unlike how I'm feeling right now.

Buddy, ever the stoic companion, watches with a curiosity that I find enviable. His world is simpler, bound by the immediate and the tangible, while I'm lost in the abstract, pondering this journey's significance.

A brief pause in York is a necessary interlude, a moment to stretch our legs and breathe in the scent of the real world away from the confines of our carriage. The city, with its ancient walls and bustling streets, feels like a bridge between the old world we left behind and the new one the lies ahead.

As the train resumes its path northwards, snaking through the outskirts of the Lake District, the landscape transforms once again. I'm struck by the raw beauty of it all – the way the water touches the land, seamless yet distinct, like two lovers intertwined. The lakes, vast and serene, reflect the sky above, a canvas of blues and greys painted by the filtered light of the sun. The mountains rise majestically, guardians of the valleys below, their peaks occasionally hidden by low-hanging clouds.

Yes, I can hear myself – maybe I am becoming an author, after all, finding metaphor and meaning in the mundane. One thing's for sure: this journey, with its ever-changing backdrop, is not just a transition from the south to the north but also the metaphorical transition from what was known to the mystery of what's to come.

Scotland greets us with a grandeur that's almost intimidating. As the first sight of the Highlands pierces through the mist, it feels like we're entering a different world, one that's been lingering just beyond the threshold of my reality. The enormity of it all – the sprawling landscapes transitioning to ancient, brooding hills that swell into mountains under the waning light – renders my personal upheavals insignificant in comparison.

As we cross the Forth Bridge, the setting sun casts a golden glow upon the engineering marvel, arching boldly over the Firth of Forth that momentarily takes my breath away. It stands in stark contrast to the natural beauty I've been admiring, a testament to humanity's ingenuity amidst the wilderness. Buddy perks up as if sensing my awe, his gaze intently following mine out the window.

I'm aching now, literally. Nestled in the discomfort of my first-class seat – yeah, you heard that right, first class, because apparently, luxury equates to plush seating and complimentary snacks – I realise how much I loathe being confined. Here I am, surrounded by comfort, yet I'm fantasising about a bloody walk. No, the irony isn't lost on me. And yet, the yearning to stretch my legs, to feel the solid ground beneath my feet rather than the constant swaying of the train, intensifies as the day wanes. It seems no amount of plush upholstery can cushion the restlessness of the soul. That, or one could argue my so-called restlessness has little to do with my physical comfort and more with my mental discomfort about the purpose of my journey.

Then, finally, as night swallows the land, an announcement crackles through the speakers, signalling our arrival at Thurso train station. A wave of movement ripples through the carriage – zippers close, bags are hoisted, and anticipation hums in the air. I sit up, take a deep breath, and collect our things as the rhythmic clickety-clack of the train slows to a stop in front of a sign that reads THURSO.

Stepping off the train, the first thing to hit me is the biting cold. There's an icy chill sweeping across the platform, cutting through my blazer like a knife. The second thing, you'll be surprised to hear, is a certain sense of familiarity.

Do you remember when I described Porthcove train station as a hut in the middle of a field? Well, Thurso is a major upgrade, relatively speaking. It resembles a barn, complete with a couple of skylights piercing its roof. A small digital display shows the arrival and departure times and today's date, as well as confirms that it's cold enough to freeze a witch's tit in a brass bra: –1° Celsius. To be fair, there are several wood benches – perfect for parking one's arse while risking frostbite. Oh, and a green wheelie bin decorating one corner, complementing the rustic charm.

The place is deserted, as if souls are wary of venturing this far north, perhaps fearing a nosebleed from the altitude. My hasty research on the train revealed that Thurso, over 750 miles (about

1,243 km) from ANEW, is the northernmost town on the British mainland. Nestled in Scotland's Highland council area, it once throbbed with Norse power. It even features the ruins of a castle built in 1872. Winter temperatures seldom rise above 10° Celsius. This all leads me to wonder, *What am I even doing here?*

Even Buddy, usually the curious sort, isn't keen on Thurso. His bushy tail, usually a sign of his adventurous spirit, droops dismally as he heels close. I stoop down and give him a pat on the head. "Hey, we're good, Bud. We're good," I say enthusiastically, knowing he recognises the tone in my voice, but the dog looks up at me as if to say, *What have you been smoking?* Which, of course, prompts a welcome chuckle.

Stepping out of the station, past the futile whir of the overhead heating fan above the doorway, I'm greeted by yet another icy slap from the biting wind patrolling this place. I huddle into the thin fabric of my jacket, and as the doors pull hastily shut behind me, like a homeowner evicting a guest overstaying their welcome, I realise that this station is so small it may as well be a private dwelling.

But I think this is the main street, where bored, dry leaves skitter after each other over the wet, eroded tarmac. Potholes brim with rainwater, and vehicles trudge by, their exhaust fumes curling into the night. There's little else here but the cold and a forlorn road sign, *Lovers Lane*, affixed to a stone wall. Although any romantic notions are quickly dispelled, replaced by a sense more akin to a documentary on urban decay.

With my overnight case rattling behind me, I instruct Buddy to stay close as we trudge down the road in search of our lodgings for the night.

The Weary Traveller B&B marketed itself as being just a stone's throw from the station, but the reality proved to be a bit of a hike. After a short walk that feels much longer because of fatigue and the persistent chill, the building finally comes into view. It's fairly nondescript, wedged between two slightly more presentable buildings, as if it's leaning on them for support. Its exterior, a once cheerful shade of blue, now peels in surrender to the Scottish weather. The windows, dimly lit, offer a glimpse of warmth that seems almost reluctant to spill outside. A small, hand-painted sign hanging by the door boasts *Dog-Friendly Accommodations*, accompanied by a cartoonish dog that's seen better days.

But luxury isn't what we're here for. I need a place to rest, gather my thoughts, and prepare for what tomorrow brings. Besides, if the online reviews are to be believed, what The Weary Traveller lacks in kerb appeal, it makes up for in hearty breakfasts and strong coffee, which are precisely what I'll need to kickstart my day.

As we approach, the door swings open, emitting a blast of welcome warm air and the enticing aroma of baking, along with the faint sound of a radio playing some old tune that feels both comforting and out of place.

The innkeeper, a robust woman with wild hair and a toothy smile, welcomes us. "Come in. Ye must be Marco?"

I give the woman my best, yet no doubt weary, smile. "I am."

"Nae bother at all, we've got a snug wee room all ready for ye and your bonnie lad. And this fine chap," she continues, stooping to give Buddy a genial scratch behind the ears, "he can have the run o' the place. Ye both must be exhausted and hungry. Come in, come in," she says, waving us inside.

2

KIN

MONDAY

EARLY MORNING. THURSO, SCOTLAND.

It turns out that our room wasn't anywhere near as bad as I first thought; it was clean and the bed inviting, with all the facilities any traveller could want, including a lopsided table and chair by the window.

After a hearty supper and a shower, I was so tired I could have slept on a bale of hay. Thankfully, that wasn't necessary, and I actually slept well until I was wide awake at 5:00 a.m., ready for my morning run. Despite yesterday's mammoth journey across the length of the country, my body still wasn't convinced that I'd been crazy enough to bring us here, and by around 5:30, my mind began to agree.

I have no idea what to expect from today's meeting. In fact, I don't have any expectations at all, and yet, I can't help a dreaded sense of nervousness that I appear incapable of rationalising.

By 6:00, I was out of bed. By 7:00, I had finished a fairly decent shower, during which I spent the whole time asking myself what, exactly, I would be doing right now if I were back home.

At precisely 7:30, there was a tap at my door advising me that breakfast was ready. Yes, last night, I made the mistake of telling my friendly landlady, Fiona, that I had an early start. When she pressed me on the time, I plucked one out of the air. This became my wake-up call for breakfast, which was absolutely delicious if you ignore the whole *blood sausage* thing. No, can't say I'm a fan.

Buddy, on the other hand, had no complaints about his gourmet offering. He enthusiastically shared it with the resident canine crew, accompanied by a slurp of water that spoke volumes about his post-travel dehydration. After his morning bathroom break (which involved considerably less existential pondering), we retreated to our room.

By 8:45, I was surprised to feel the sun pushing in through the window. I was expecting a dreary day, but the sky is pale blue and dotted with fluffy clouds.

Now, just past 9:00 in the morning, I'm dressed in jeans, a white T-shirt, a sweater, and my trusty blazer, thanks to the lads – bless their sartorial wisdom – who insisted on "smart casual" for my meeting with my long-lost half-sister. Striking a perfect balance between confidence and relaxation had seemed like a tall order, but oddly enough, dressed and ready, it feels surprisingly right.

Checking myself in the full-length mirror hanging off the back of the door for what feels like the fifth time doesn't. It feels wrong in so many ways since I'm meeting a family member and not a potential lover. On the other hand, this person has never met me before, and I tell myself that it's only natural to want to make a good first impression.

The vibration in my pocket makes me jump. I've already spoken to everyone of note back home, so this is most likely my non-date. The text message I read confirms it.

Good morning. Hope you've had a wonderful journey. I'm here. Ready and waiting.

My half-sister, Samantha, isn't aware of my anxiety, that I hated the idea of stressing about the journey and getting here on time so as not to inconvenience her. Consequently, she thinks I am arriving in Scotland today.

Peeking out of the window of the establishment that's supposed to be just a stone's throw from the station, I twist my head, and if I angle it right, I can just about catch the faintest glimpse of the station's clock tower in the distance.

We make our way out of the B&B and, after thanking Fiona for her hospitality, step out into the early morning. The air hangs crisp, tinged with exhaust fumes. The winter sun, a pale actor phoning in a performance, casts a weak glow across the street.

There aren't many cars around here, so the black Range Rover parked across the road with its engine running and exhaust plume curling into the air quickly catches my attention. I watch the driver's door open, and a woman steps out. She's wearing sheepskin boots, a thick, stylish winter coat, and a fluffy hat, with tendrils of dark hair framing her face. She's a stranger, yet someone I've known of old. She's me. Or at least she reminds me of the female version of me, but more attractive – a young Demi Moore. In her thirties, maybe.

She's talking on the phone but ends the call as I approach. "Right, okay, gotta go. Please keep me updated," she says before sliding the phone into her pocket. Her smile is clearly forced, not for the caller but for me. In fact, those glistening hazel eyes look red-rimmed in the sunshine, like she hasn't been sleeping well or, dare I say it, crying. Not that it diminishes her beauty in the slightest. I hope she hasn't been crying. I certainly hope it isn't because of me.

Shut up, man! Even your thoughts are jabbering! Yes, I know I'm doing it, and I know why. *Breathe, just breathe.*

This woman could potentially be – because, let's be honest, she might just be some random stranger, and I could be making a complete tit of myself – the only living relative I have. That thought both excites and scares the crap out of me.

And yet, I'm making my way towards her, Buddy by my side. He seems happier now. His tail's up, and he's trotting towards the stranger like he recognises her.

She's looking at me curiously with what looks like a genuine smile on her face. Then she makes a show of looking at the train station exit.

I lower my head. "We got here last night," I say.

"You did?" She seems genuinely surprised. "You should have messaged me."

"I know, but it was late," I say with a smile.

"Oh, well… Welcome to sunny Thurso," she says with a shiver that transforms into a hesitant lift of her arms.

I think that was an offer of a hug. I'm not sure. Either way, what do you think my response is? That's right: I just smile like a complete muppet because Mr Gobby – that would be me – appears to have lost all ability to articulate.

After a few moments' hesitation, this woman, this stranger, takes the lead and throws her arms around me, her voice muffled against my arm as she says, "It's so good to meet you at last."

She smells pretty, like a bouquet of flowers – hyacinths, bergamot, and jasmine. The embrace lingers for a few heartbeats, as I imagine it might between siblings. That, or she needs it. Of course, I could be misinterpreting this since I don't have any direct comparison to draw on, except for the way David squishes and then deliberately slobbers over me, but that's a whole other annoying thing.

Then, as if reading my mind, she pulls back, a smile lighting up her face once more. "And who's this handsome fellow?" she beams.

"That's Buddy," I manage to say because the imbecile I've been reduced to can talk about all things dog, just not all things family.

"Buddy!" she exclaims, crouching down with a flourish and making a fuss over the dog, who, ever the tart, welcomes the attentions of this complete stranger with a flurry of excited tail wags. When she's finished, she says quickly, "Come on, we best go, or we're going to be late."

For what? I want to ask, but guess what? That's right. I say nothing because this person opening the back door for my dog, who jumps in as if he's made this journey a thousand times before, is, for all intents and purposes, my sister. And I can't stop gawking at her.

It's only when Buddy barks once – *Are you getting in or what?* – that I snap out of my daze and place my holdall in the footwell of the backseat. The car's interior doesn't appear to be as new as the sleek exterior suggests. The model's a couple of years old – at least, that's the impression I get among all the things I could be thinking about right now.

I climb into the passenger seat as our driver clicks her seatbelt. She waits for me to do the same, and then, with barely a glance in her wing mirror, she shifts the vehicle into drive, and we're off.

"So how was your journey?" she asks.

"Long," I reply.

"Yes, Cliffhaven must feel like a world away."

I pause because it feels odd to hear this stranger mention the familiar. "It does," I manage eventually.

Then we travel in silence for several seconds, except for the hum of the vehicle as our driver navigates turns and stops for pedestrians.

Then, suddenly, "Look, Marco. I know this must feel strange to you," she says, her voice laced with a hint of nervousness, and, I realise now, devoid of any discernible accent. "... It does for me, too. I went through all kinds of scenarios, all the things we might say to each other, but none of them seem appropriate right now," she says, pulling up to a STOP sign before turning to me and smiling. "But I'm glad you're here," she adds, looking back at the road, waiting for a car to pass before pulling out once more.

And so, I know what you're thinking: that my long-lost sis seems to be making all the effort here. And she is. I am aware of that. Just like I know that, as a therapist, dealing with awkward situations should be my forte. Well, I can assure you it is. Normally. But come on, this trip couldn't diverge any further from the bloody normal. I mean, I'm actually in Scotland, riding in a car with some woman who shares both my DNA and my surname. After all these years of feeling alone. And, may I add, she looks and smells good. Not in some weird, ew, sexual kind of way – that's just gross – but in a way that suggests she isn't some kind of mutant, some weird Battista extension of what my mind has conjured over the years, but a normal human being who looks like she has her shit together.

Of course, I have questions. Many, in fact. I just can't seem to process any of them right now.

We travel for a few more minutes before the car slows, then turns into a car park. "Great, we got here just in time," my half-sister says before pulling into one of the bays and killing the engine.

And so, it's very interesting to me that out of all the questions that I appear incapable of verbalising, this particular one should escape my lips with uncharacteristic bluntness, even for me. "What the fuck are we doing here?"

Outside, the sun, obviously unoffended by my previous comment, is getting its act together, irradiating the land with sunshine and colour, and glinting off the signs towering over us *Long-Term Parking* and *Ferry – Foot Passengers Only.* Beyond the signs, small fishing trawlers rock gently in the harbour, waiting for their next North Sea adventure. And beyond them, something larger....

"The ferry," Samantha says as if I've just asked a peculiar question.

"The ferry? To where?"

"Thistle Island," she frowns as if I should know what she's talking about. "You know, the memorial."

"Thistle Island? You didn't say anything about it being on an island," I say, as my heart pounds against my rib cage.

"Yes, the procession, you know..." she trails off, realising. "You don't know about the procession, do you?"

"Samantha, this is the first I'm hearing about it. Your letter said Scotland. Your messages talked about this place."

"Thurso? No. God, no. He would never have wanted it here." She thinks about this, then adds, "So you don't know anything about the island?"

"No. I haven't got a scooby."

I watch my sister's pretty face crease into a pained one. "I'm so sorry, Marco. I should have been clearer. I just assumed you knew."

"Knew what?" I ask, stifling the rising anxiety in my voice.

"Thistle Island. It's where we live. It's our equivalent of Dolce Vita," she says. Okay, now I feel like I am actually going to barf, just hearing the name of that place come out of this stranger's mouth.

Without even thinking, I yank on the door handle and tumble out into the cold air. The salty sea breeze should fill me with a sense of the familiar, but it doesn't. The tang is harsher, stronger here – a metallic bite that lingers on the tongue.

I reach out for the nearby stone wall to steady myself as memories of that night in Porthcove crash into me like giant waves, over and over. The cold. The turbulence. The freeze. The rhythm of the waves echoes in my ears: *air... water... air... water... air!*

A hand on my shoulder startles me. I turn to see Samantha; her face creased with concern. "Are you alright?"

I nod because it's difficult to talk with the lump of bile in my throat. Instead, I breathe. I breathe the bitter cold, foreign scent in through my nose and out through my mouth. *In through the nose and out of the mouth.* "I'm fine... I'm good. I just... the ocean and me, we don't get along ever since...." I leave the sentence unfinished because the less I think about that night, the better. Although I get the feeling that my host already knows what I'm referring to. "And, um," I gasp, struggling to catch my breath. "... I try to avoid the water."

"But don't you have a house overlooking the ocean?" she asks, obviously confused.

I look at her askance before straightening up to my full height once more. "Yes," I say bluntly. "Overlooking it. Not in it or floating on it."

She nods, although she still doesn't look convinced. "Well, we need to catch that ferry," she says, raising a finger in the ship's direction. "This is the first and last of the day to the island, and ah..." she hesitates, looking me over, "Is that what you're wearing?"

Actually, it isn't. I have a suit in my case, but I'm not explaining myself. “What’s wrong with what I’m wearing?”

“Oh, no, nothing. Nothing. It’s just, your jacket doesn’t look very practical. Fine down south, maybe, but it seems a bit flimsy for this climate, and it can get particularly cold around here.”

Spoken like a true Battista. I’m surprised she didn’t tack *just saying* to the end of that.

In any other circumstance, I’d probably find her bluntness amusing, but right now, with my heart thundering in my chest and cold sweat slicking my brow, well, not as much.

I haven’t been on a boat since that night in Porthcove. And there’s a good reason for that. Dr Holmes and I have discussed this ad nauseam, although it doesn’t really take a psychologist to work it out. I was almost drowned as a child – and again as an adult. It’s perfectly reasonable that I should develop some form of aquaphobia.

And yet, here I stand, discussing returning to water like a bloody lamb to the bloody slaughter.

Oh, shit. My chest is tightening. The world is shrinking to the frantic pulse in my ears.

Breathe, you fool. Breathe. You’re going to induce a panic attack right in front of her. Is this really how you want to be seen?

And yet, I’m struggling, now leaning on the car for support.

A loud, belligerent horn sounds, drilling through the air and my already frayed nerves. I continue to stare at my Timberlands on the wet tarmac, focusing on staving off an upchuck of this morning’s breakfast, but I can sense Samantha anxiously looking towards that sound.

The ferry. It’s going to leave without us.

Good! While you’re at it, ask her to take you back to the station!

The pressure is building in my temple, the hiss of blood rushing behind my ears, the pulse throbbing in my neck – and it’s cold, so bloody cold with this *flimsy jacket*!

Air… water… air… water! The loud rumble, hiss, and fizz of the surf fill my head before it’s drowned out by the deep bass of the ocean’s watery underworld. And then... light. Suddenly, breaking through the surface, warming my hand, spreading through me. Dark blue hues dissolving into golden sunshine.

Buddy nuzzles against my hand. His fur is warm despite the chill, and I cling to him, a furry lifebuoy in my sea of emotional despair.

It's because I'm cute and say cute things.

"Buddy...." I mutter.

And then, gradually, I hear another sound. Unfamiliar at first, but I realise that it's Samantha. She sounds worried. "Marco? Oh my God. Are you okay? Are you alright? Marc?"

I try to speak, but it comes out as a croak; my mouth is so dry, so I nod.

And this is it. Time to choose. Turn back and abandon this trip as a bad job, or get on that thing, assuming we're even going to make it on time now.

What would you do? And please don't tell me to "man up." I thought I had until this very moment.

Fuck.

The thought of clinging to a hunk of steel and floating across freezing waters fills me with dread so palpable I want to heave again.

The ship's horn blares once more as my half-sister slips a warm gloved hand around my cold fingers. I look at her; her smile is warm, sympathetic – as if she knows me, is familiar with my condition.

I allow it. I let her hurry Buddy, me, and my case through a maze of parked vehicles, weaving around puddles of water, right up to the gate, which is just being closed as we approach. A man in a fluorescent jacket spots Samantha and breaks into a welcoming smile. "Ye near aboot missed us," he says, swinging the gate open while giving me a curious glance.

"I know. Thanks, Andy," Samantha says, guiding me from the shore onto the gangway.

Shit.

Unlike me, Buddy has no qualms about boarding the craft. He hurries up the steps and across the gangway, his tail whipping against the biting wind that slashes across the water and into my face.

Although I'm barely feeling the cold now because my focus is locked on the water churning beneath us as the craft prepares to pull away.

Oh shit. Just as I'm giving serious consideration to turning back, I feel Samantha's reassuring hand on the small of my back, steering me through a door and, mercifully, out of the cold and into the warmer passenger deck.

There are rows of empty seats, giving the impression that this vessel is a charter of our own, save for a middle-aged couple in the corner eagerly gazing out of the window and a mature couple engrossed in a map spread across their laps.

The space is simple and functional, with a faint smell of diesel mingling with the sea air that seeps in every time the door opens.

I've decided, though, that if I keep my gaze on anything but the windows and the horizon, I'll be just fine. It'll just feel like a car ride. If I can ignore the swaying and the hum of the engine vibrating through the floor, a constant reminder that, like it or not, we're now at the mercy of the sea.

"I'll be right back," Samantha says. "Will you be okay?"

I nod but keep my gaze on the textured metal floor while holding onto the adjoining seat for support. "Okay. Won't be long."

Alright, so not my finest hour. But to be fair, I was pretty much broadsided. I thought I was here to attend my father's memorial. I had no idea we were going to end up on some kind of expedition across waters.

It's not like I didn't check. The first thing I did after reading Samantha's letter was look into her. I asked Holt to show me everything the internet had about my half-sister, but surprisingly, Samantha Battista didn't have much of a digital footprint. Holt's findings were limited. There were a few old articles, the kind that spoke more of my father, Roberto Battista, and his achievements than of his daughter. My father was a well-known figure in marketing circles – often referred to as a marketing maestro who once made waves in London with his innovative strategies.

Holt unearthed mentions of awards and accolades, fleeting

snapshots of success where Roberto was often accompanied by his two children: Samantha and his son, Roberto Junior. These glimpses into their lives painted a picture of familial unity, yet offered no real insight into the person Samantha had become.

All the articles were old, relics of a time when Roberto Battista's name was synonymous with marketing excellence. But beyond the glitz of awards ceremonies and the polished smiles for cameras, there was a void where Samantha's story should have been. No social media, no mentions of her achievements, her dreams, or her struggles – just a name that appeared as a footnote in her father's legacy.

Of course, Holt did suggest that she might have changed her name or married. Which is a possibility, of course. If it weren't for the book and the insistence of my publicist, I wouldn't have much of a digital footprint, either.

So what about Thistle Island? Samantha likened it to Dolce Vita, which, as you know, had a profound effect on me, not least because of its creepiness. My half-sister seems to know much more about me than I do about her.

Pulling out my phone, I'm relieved to see that the signal is still strong.

I tap a button and, after a beep, talk to my phone. "Holt, are you there?"

"Yes, Marco. How can I help you today?"

"Holt," I say in a loud whisper, glancing around at the few other passengers, "I need everything you've got on Thistle Island in Scotland."

"Thistle Island? One moment, please."

As Holt processes, the screen bursts to life with a digital mosaic of information and visuals. *"Thistle Island, with its dramatic cliffs and ancient landscapes, embodies the wild, untamed essence of the Hebrides, boasting a rich cultural tapestry,"* Holt narrates.

"The island spans three square miles, and – at last count – is home to 700 souls. Although small, it's a land of stark contrasts, from rolling hills to jagged cliffs. Its residents lead simple lives, far removed from the rush

of modern connectivity, making it a unique retreat for those looking to escape the digital world."

This lack of connectivity has, surprisingly, turned Thistle Island into a burgeoning tourist destination. Visitors are drawn to its shores for both the untouched beauty and the rare opportunity to digitally disconnect."

After the decline in Thistle Loch Foods, tourism has now breathed new life into the island's economy."

The on-screen slideshow of images continues: rugged cliffs enveloped in dense mists, a village that seems lost in time, docked fishing trawlers, and the Thistle Loch Foods logo.

"*The island has recently gained global media attention due to excavations uncovering evidence of a significant Norse heritage, sparking discussions about its historical importance. Would you like to read some articles?"*

"Yes, please," I say eagerly. But just as the circle in Holt's interface begins to spin once more, the door squeals open. Cold, fresh air rushes inside, followed by Samantha.

3

THE ISLAND

MID-MORNING

I've no idea why, but I make the action of returning my phone to my pocket appear casual as Samantha comes back, carrying Styrofoam cups. She hands one to me. It's watery chocolate. Doesn't taste of much, but it's hot, and a few sips in, my brain starts to thaw.

"Better?" she asks, studying my face with concern.

I nod, feeling the warmth of the cup seep through my fingers and into my bones. "Yeah, thanks."

Her expression softens. "Thought we were going to lose you there for a few seconds. You were looking a bit pale."

I manage a half-smile, still gripping the cup like a lifeline. "Yeah. Sorry. Just not a big fan of open water, in case I didn't make that abundantly obvious," I admit, rolling my eyes.

Samantha nods understandingly, holding my gaze for much longer than I expect, which, of course, prompts me to ask, "What? Weren't expecting a nut job?"

"No, it's not that," she says quickly, with another reassuring smile, but adds nothing further. Like she knows something but is reluctant to share.

I force an awkward laugh. "What is it then?"

Eventually, she gives me a reassuring smile and pats me on the arm. "Nothing at all. Just, despite everything, I'm really glad you're here."

Now, I know this is the part where I should say something trite, like *me too*. But I can't. My heart is only just starting to stabilise. Right now, I'm not particularly glad to be sitting on this boat on my way to a bloody remote island. So guess what? That's right. I nod.

When Samantha's gaze eventually drifts out the window, I make the mistake of following it to see the coastline of the mainland slowly recede into the distance until it becomes part of the vast expanse of the sea. And I must have a look on my face because my half-sister reassures, "Don't worry. We'll be there before you know it." She doesn't realise that, for me, that's part of the problem. I had no idea we'd be coming out here, and I'm finding that particularly unsettling.

On the other hand, the ferry ride appears to offer an opportunity for unique quietude. The soft lull of the waves, the occasional seagull cry, and the distant chatter of the few passengers create a natural backdrop for reflection.

Satisfied that I'm not about to make any more of a scene, Buddy flops at my feet. I reach down and stroke his head, finding solace in his presence.

"You two seem close," Samantha observes with a warm smile.

"Well, we've been through a lot together, haven't we, Bud?" I say, when there's a sudden squeal from one of the other passengers. And I don't know if I'm hallucinating, but I'm sure they just said something about a giant's thumb before rushing out the squeaky door, annoyingly leaving it ajar.

I catch Samantha's gaze. "The Old Man of Storr," she explains.

I cock my head, a silent question.

"It's a famous landmark," she offers. "Would you like to see it?"

"Um, no thanks, I'm fine where I am," I reply, my voice barely hiding the unease.

Meanwhile, my traitorous dog is back on his feet and barking at me, the sound reverberating around the space.

"No. No way," I say, which only prompts more barking.

"Stop it!" I order, looking around us.

Woof! Woof! is the reply, followed by the clacking of nails as the dog bounds for the open door.

"HEY, Buddy! NO! Get back here!"

"He obviously wants to see it," Samantha says, but I'm already on my feet, giving chase, heart engine firing up at the very thought of the dog ending up overboard or worse. Which is why I don't even hesitate to chase him back out into the cold.

I find Buddy, my unruly dog – you know, the one with those peculiar humanistic traits that spent most of the past few years creeping me out – sitting and waiting for us outside, like one of those eager children at a theme park.

"Seriously?" I say, scowling at him. His only response is to lick his chops.

I, on the other hand, now that the danger of dog overboard has been deescalated, become aware of the elements once more. Instinctively, I draw my jacket collar up, securing every button against the piercing sea air. The winter sun, obviously on reprimand for its lacklustre performance earlier this morning, has gone on indefinite leave.

The sky is now a canvas of menacing dark clouds with streaks of light breaking through, offering an eerie yet captivating backdrop to the majestic mountains rising high in the distance. Their silhouettes stand formidable against the brooding sky. The spectacle is awe-inspiring, a momentary distraction from the relentless churn of the water below.

"Blimey...." I gasp, scrunching my body against the chill.

Samantha, sensing my unease, launches into a captivating narration on local legends as Buddy heels beside me. If I didn't know better, I'd say the hound just did that on purpose to get me out of my comfort zone. He's now nuzzling my hand. *You still love me, don't you?* I just shoot him a glare.

"... And that towering column of rock over there? That's the Old Man of Storr, a fifty-five-metre-high volcanic plug. Legend has it that it's the remains of a giant's thumb." I turn to her. Her playful rise of the eyebrows and the twinkle in her eyes – green like mine in this light – disarm me, echoing my own sense of humour. In this moment, amidst the stunning scenery, I glimpse something more than a half-sister. I see my father's daughter.

As our ship slices through the water, Samantha's narration transforms into a tour of the spectacular Scottish landscape. She tells of the Outer Hebrides, a chain of over 70 islands off Scotland's northwest coast, where rugged mountains, moors, and pristine beaches create a landscape of stark contrasts and breathtaking beauty. Rich in Gaelic culture and folklore, these islands beckon both adventurers and those seeking tranquillity. She describes ceilidhs not just as gatherings but as vibrant celebrations of Gaelic folk music and dance, bringing life to these remote isles. As she speaks, the images she conjures – canoeing through serene waters, hill-walking under vast skies, windsurfing on the brisk Atlantic breeze, and unwinding by a warm peat fire – paint a vivid picture of a land steeped in history, tradition, and prehistoric relevance.

Despite the biting cold, I'm momentarily swept away by a sense of wonder. We're drifting into a realm where myth and reality blur. For a moment, my cynicism fades, replaced by awe at the raw beauty unfolding before me.

As we pass the Isle of Rum, Samantha declares that this landscape, standing as a stoic sentinel amidst the ocean's vastness, marks our journey's midpoint. But as mist engulfs the ferry, a familiar unease creeps back in. The calm is broken, at least for me.

Samantha's casual mention of our distance from both John O'Groats and Land's End – over 1,200 kilometres – only serves to underscore the isolation. I'm adrift in an alien world.

Forty-five minutes in, the mist's chill and creeping anxiety gnaw at me, tempting me back to the warmth of the cabin. But Samantha's voice cuts through my unease once more. "We should be there any second now," she says, with the wide-eyed enthusiasm of a horror movie victim. We drift into a mist that is thick and secretive, obscuring all sight and heightening the suspense. And I won't lie, I'm close to peeing my pants when she suddenly exclaims, "There!" I squint, seeing nothing initially, but her insistent, "There!" draws my gaze to the left.

Suddenly, Thistle Island emerges from the mist, reminiscent of a scene from a King Kong movie where Skull Island reveals itself. Shrouded in mystery and a natural – at least, that's what I'm telling myself – sense of foreboding.

As the mist lifts, a sprawling green landscape dotted with stark stone peaks comes into view. A cluster of stone cottages clings to the hillside. Beyond them is a dark line of trees, their branches reaching skyward as if worshipping the god-mountain towering over them.

"They used to be part of the village but have been converted to rentals. Now, city folk flock here in the summer to escape the digital grind," Samantha explains, her gaze lingering on the cottages.

"Why only during the summer?" I ask.

"Well, let's just say the winters out here aren't as welcoming as we are," she replies with a tone that suggests there's more to that story.

"So you own a holiday home on the island," I muse aloud.

She looks at me, hesitancy flickering in her eyes, and in that brief, revealing moment, realisation strikes me. I suck air in sharply over my teeth. "You own the island?"

"Dad formed a consortium to buy the place as a going concern," she confirms, somewhat reluctantly.

"A going concern?" I echo, my eyebrows arching in surprise.

"At its height, Thistle Island produced forty per cent of the fish supplied to supermarkets around Britain. You've heard of the Thistle Loch brand, right?" Samantha asks, a hint of pride in her voice.

"That's here?" I respond incredulously, my finger pointing towards the island as if trying to stitch reality with this new revelation.

She nods in affirmation.

I can barely believe it. My mind is a whirlwind of thoughts and memories. Thistle Loch, a staple brand akin to Birds Eye, always had a place in our freezer – Toby was obsessed with their fish fingers. But to think that my father might be in any way involved with the company... well, I had no idea.

Samantha continues, her voice a blend of pride and sorrow. "The brand really took off in the seventies, expanded globally. They built a processing plant here, on the other side of the island, and the workforce... huge.

"They even had a hotel for the executives, temporary staff, and frequent visitors. But like many businesses, they overreached, expanded too fast. Soon enough, they hit financial snags. Dad saw an opening there, and he took it.

"He and his consortium bought out the business, but during the process, they found out the island itself was in a rough state. No power. Islanders were leaving because of poor living conditions. And the Earl who owned it was broke.

"So they took over everything, worked with the islanders, started this massive project to make the island self-sufficient, inspired by the Isle of Eigg. But that focus... it cost them.

"By the time they turned their attention back, Thistle's market share was practically gone. Competitors had pounced on the opportunity, undercutting prices and securing long-term supermarket deals.

"It was a hellish time, particularly for Robert, who had only just joined the board. He felt like a failure in Dad's eyes. They fought relentlessly to keep it afloat, but they simply couldn't; the damage had been done. They were forced to sell what was left to a competitor. Now, the processing plant lies abandoned except for some local fishermen who banded together to buy their own trawler. They use a tiny part of the plant as a base.

"Dad was devastated. Because, after all, this place was more than a business to him; it had become our home." She pauses here, lost in thought.

It's clear to me now that she shared a bond with our father that I never did. I had imagined both my half-siblings were close to him, but I could see it now, not just in her words but in her face, that wistful way she looked when she spoke about him.

"What about the London properties?" I prod, careful to keep the bitterness from my voice.

"Gone. Sold to keep this place afloat." Her words hang heavy in the air.

Normally, I'd be dishing out comforting words by now, maybe even a hug. But the revelation of Dad's double life – Dolce Vita in the south with one family and this northern retreat, like a Scottish Balmoral – leaves me reeling and, yes, resentful.

The ferry is gliding into the bay now, the sea beneath us a mirror, perfectly reflecting the world above. Vibrant reds and terracottas mingle with faded greys on the cottages studding the hills, all clustered together as if sheltering from the cold.

Beyond the cottages, the hillside rolls upwards into a crescendo of pine trees, their deep green a defiant note against the encroaching winter. They remain lush and vibrant. The land seems to breathe, pulsing with the life of the isle. Rising above this verdant scene, the mountain looms – a king with its crown of mist and mantle of snow, standing as a watchful guardian of the island and its people.

The scene changes, however, somewhat dramatically as we near the dock. Fishing trawlers, like miniature islands ravaged by a storm, float haphazardly in the water. Some lie overturned, their wooden hulls faded and weathered, scarred by salt and countless days at the mercy of the elements. Others are partially submerged, masts tilted at impossible angles, like broken arrows piercing the water's surface.

My jaw clenches. "Not so welcoming now, is it?" I mutter, and Samantha's grim expression confirms my unspoken question.

"Remember when I said that the weather around here wasn't as welcoming as the people?"

"What happened?"

"We had a storm a couple of nights ago. Not that unusual this time of year. It was ferocious, though. As you can see, it devastated these trawlers. These are privately owned. Some are just leisure vessels. But others, those are working boats, how people make their living."

"That's awful," I say, unable to take my eyes off the devastation. "So is that it? What do these people do now?"

"Well, most of these will be insured, but nothing can be done with them until they've been assessed."

I follow her gaze. The sight of those wrecked vessels, tossed about like broken toys by some unseen giant, and the waves lapping hungrily against those broken hulls, a relentless drumbeat, sends another shiver through me, unrelated to the cold.

"Well, they're forecasting another in a few days. Complete with the first snow," she says, and my expression must react to that because she adds, "Don't worry. You'll be back on the mainland before then." She follows that up with a reassuring smile as the momentum of the ferry relaxes.

The dock that awaits us is unassuming, constructed of wooden planks, timeworn and weathered, mooring posts scarred by the hands and ropes of countless sailors across the years.

As the ferry edges closer, the outline of the high street starts to reveal itself. It's a stone-paved lane, cradled by a collection of establishments. It has the charm of a small village, yet something feels... different.

From here, I think I can spot a pub. Well, at least they've got their priorities sorted. Right now, I'm wishing I wasn't steering clear of booze because I could use a good stiff drink. Anything would do because the old butterflies are swarming in the proverbial belly.

I have no idea what to expect from this place. And what with storms and sunken bloody boats, I can't help but wonder if these are some kind of omen of what the hell's to come.

Let's not forget that I am going to be seeing my stepmother again after all these years. It's no secret that the woman couldn't stand the sight of me. Water under the bridge, or will she try to drown me in it?

I can still see her now. Primped blonde hair and her lips curling into a disdainful sneer every time I dared to share the same space. Except when my father was present, of course. Then she'd put that lopsided artificial smile on those pursed lips forever painted with that same washed-out pink, a touch too pale to be playful, a hint too bold to be genuine. She made it abundantly clear that I, the interloper in my father's life, wasn't welcome.

"Everything okay?"

Samantha's face comes into focus. "Yeah. Fine," I say.

"Ready?" she asks, nodding at the steps.

The ferry has docked. The gangway extended. We've arrived at the place my father secretly called home for years.

I make sure I don't look down but straight ahead as we cross the bridge from the ferry. Pointless, I know, considering that we've been floating on open seas for what feels like an eternity, but still, the feeling of land beneath my feet is surprisingly uplifting. It feels like I've been holding my breath this whole time.

Passengers have barely finished disembarking from the ferry when there's an efficient bustle around the cargo – the crew and islanders alike operate winches, a forklift truck, and dollies reminiscent of a Formula One pit team in waterproofs, their movements purposeful and brisk.

"Welcome to Thistle Island," Samantha declares, like she's suddenly embodied the spirit of Ricardo Montalbán from Fantasy

Island. I'm half expecting Tattoo to come running out from one of those buildings, yelling, *The plane! The plane!* If only.

The thought brings a faint smile. I know, but it's the little things right now. Anything to take my mind off where I have quite literally just landed.

The dock funnels us directly into the cobblestone high street, where the locals move with an ease that speaks of routine and familiarity.

"Morning, Gavin! Morning, Jennifer!" Samantha greets each person warmly. They respond in kind, their acknowledgement of me friendly yet reserved. I return the gesture, a bit clumsily – I am a Londoner, after all, though not completely alien to a place like this, thanks to my stints in Porthcove and Fawndale.

"This is obviously the high street," she narrates as we weave through people, Buddy by my side.

"It seems busy," I say.

"Yes. Mornings here are for personal time. The afternoons quieten down when everyone's at work."

"Work?" I echo, my curiosity piqued as we climb past more stone cottages towards a large, whitewashed building crowned with a red shingled roof that overlooks the harbour.

She smiles, leading the way. "Island work life is different. Mornings are for personal tasks, chores. Come afternoon, islanders turn to their jobs – baking, hairdressing – or contribute to island projects, like property repairs or signage services. On Thistle Island, community comes first."

To my right, the pub's aged wooden door swings open, releasing a burst of heat and a snippet of a folk song I've never heard before, laughter riding the melody out into the chilly air. It's a snapshot of communal life, where stories flow and troubles fade over pints of ale. I make a mental note – a visit might not only be inevitable but necessary, after all.

Next door, the fragrance of freshly ground coffee wafts from a café, mingling with the sea's briny scent. The large front window reveals a cosy tableau: patrons cradled by soft armchairs, some engrossed in books, others in hushed conversation, all surrounded by the steamy haze of their hot drinks. It's a haven of comfort, and I briefly envy their ease.

Up ahead, a chalkboard outside a small bakery announces today's special – "Island Berry Pie." The sweet, buttery aroma tugs at my senses and stomach. People step in and out, the door never quite closing before the next person enters, like a moving scene from an old postcard. The bakery and café blend into one.

"With the season over, work will soon begin on refurbishing the high street, individualising each store," Samantha narrates, as if she's just read my mind. "Now that tourism has become a big part of the island, we feel we need to better plan for the influx of people visiting us," she says.

On the opposite side of the high street is a small book and craft store. Its front display is a quirky mix of local history and maritime novels that beckon me. There's also a selection of hand-woven scarves, pottery, and confectionary carrying what looks like the island's signature motif.

"What does the thistle stand for?" I ask.

My tour guide smiles broadly, seemingly happy that I asked the question. "Oh, we've got a whole eclectic mix of flora and fauna here on the island. From endangered puffins to rare orchids. The island transforms in spring and summer. The meadows explode with colour, the thistles a stunning shade of deep purple," she says, a note of pride in her voice.

A bell tinkles as a middle-aged couple exits the shop, their laughter joining the lively hum of the high street. Samantha offers them a warm greeting, just as she's done with everyone we've passed. This island seems to run on smiles.

The steady thump of a hammer on a nearby roof and the rhythmic swish of a broom from across the way tell us that some islanders start their workday early, blending personal tasks with their jobs. There's a man sweeping outside what looks like a grocery store. "Good morning, Tom," Samantha calls.

"Good morning," the man responds, adding a nod in my direction.

We pass a post office, a souvenir store, and two buildings under restoration.

"Wow, there's a lot going on here."

"Yes. You'll find there's more to Thistle Island than meets the eye," she says knowingly.

I believe her. It may be cold – yes, I've been trying not to hunch the whole time – but there's a warmth here. It's woven into the cobblestones, the buildings, the smiles – the island's very pulse.

This small stretch of civilisation, sandwiched between the wildness of the sea and the quiet of the pines, feels like a world unto itself. And as we make our way through, I realise that, perhaps, this is exactly where I need to be – somewhere between the familiar and the undiscovered, walking a high street that's as much about the journey as the destination.

Samantha's smile suggests she's read my thoughts. "Beautiful, isn't it? I never tire of it." Her eyes sparkle, and her grin widens, making it clear that her question is purely rhetorical.

"How many people live here?" I ask, genuinely curious.

She tilts her head, feigning deep thought. "Not counting the three that are on the way, I'd say around seven hundred."

I nod, taking in her response.

The ferry's loud honk startles me, making Samantha smile.

"That's loud," I laugh, welcome heat rising to my cheeks.

"Has to be. The sound, or one like it, has echoed through the bay for generations. It's a signal to villagers that goods and people have arrived and a call to those departing to ready themselves."

"Does the ferry run at the same time every day?"

"Sort of. In the summer, it's two or three times a week. In the winter, it's only once or twice, weather permitting," she explains.

I can't help but wonder aloud, "Don't people feel isolated out here? I mean, it's stunning and everything, but..."

She gives me a look, one that says my city-slicker is showing. "We're islanders," she says with a touch of pride. "This is exactly how we like it."

I nod, acknowledging the sentiment. There's a certain charm to the isolation, a beauty in the self-contained world they've created. I should know.

My gaze shifts now to the grand church standing at the end of the high street. Its façade is made of weathered stone blocks, a stark contrast to the cheerful vibrancy of the shops. Its steeple rises into a sky of mottled blue and grey.

When we reach the church, the path forks. Left appears to meander towards the outskirts of the village, while the right leads us past several other buildings, including what looks like a community hall, and then begins to wind uphill. From here, we get a commanding view of the harbour below.

As we climb higher, the path diverges once more. Left continues up the hill to what I imagine is a coastal path to other parts of the island. The right path, however, leads us directly to a large, distinguished white building.

The view from here is absolutely breathtaking – spanning the ocean, the bay, the bustling dock, the rolling hillside, and the mountain.

Samantha gestures towards the building, catching her breath. "And this," she says with now familiar pride, "is the hotel."

4

REUNION

THISTLE ISLAND, SCOTLAND. LATE MORNING.

The imaginatively named THE THISTLE hotel is quite a handsome, white stately building, no doubt a vestige of grandeur on Thistle Island. Its architecture is a blend of traditional Scottish design with hints of Victorian influence evident in its gabled roofs and ornate façade.

The front door is a robust, panelled wood piece, painted a classic deep green with brass fixtures that gleam, albeit a bit weathered by the salty sea air.

Samantha eagerly leads the way down a central corridor.

We pass a cosy living area with a welcoming fireplace and plush sofas to our right, a library to our left, and, further along, a games room with a pool table in the middle and a playroom brimming with storage boxes and an elaborate train set.

"Hello?! Anybody home?" Samantha's voice carries through the hall, though it echoes back unanswered from the quiet expanse of the building before a small, joyful sound emerges from ahead.

"Mum!" The word is full of excitement as a boy, ten or eleven years old, rushes into view, grinning widely.

He has that mischievous sparkle of childhood still in his wide, ocean-blue eyes. He's wearing a hat and a leather jacket that's way too big for his slender frame, and his white t-shirt is peeking out from under his collar.

"My baby!" Samantha's voice mirrors the boy's enthusiasm as she enfolds him in her arms and plants kisses on his head, making him squirm.

"Did you miss me?"

"Yeah."

"Ye*s*. Did you miss me lots?"

"Yes," comes the boy's muffled reply from under his hat.

Needless to say, this youthful spirit instantly reminds me of my son, and I think my heart may have just stopped.

"What do I keep saying about wearing hats in the house?" Samantha playfully scolds, lifting the earflaps of the boy's woollen hat.

"My ears are cold," is his simple rebuttal.

... And now I'm reminded of my best mate, David. Only his ears are more like open taxi doors.

"And you're wearing Dad's jacket again."

"He said I could."

"Yes, but not in the house, silly. You'll feel no benefit when you go outside."

"But I love it. Makes me feel cool."

Samantha laughs.

The more I look at him, the more I'm convinced that this little boy, my nephew, bears an uncanny resemblance to Toby. It's not altogether unheard of, but the simple thought of them meeting in a different life and playing together fills me with overwhelmingly bitter sorrow.

I watch Samantha stand behind her son and turn him towards me, gently resting her hands on his shoulders. She whispers a prompt in his ear, "Hat!"

With a theatrical groan, the boy removes it, revealing a mess of tousled, honey-gold hair that looks like it's been styled by the wind itself. He gazes up at me with those round blue eyes, and my response is a grin. Words seem superfluous. The whole thing feels like a continuation of the surreal discoveries at Frost Lake Manor. The analogy might be clumsy, but it captures my disorientation perfectly.

"Luca, this is your Uncle Marco," Samantha announces.

"*Uncle* Marco?" The boy questions.

"Uh huh," Samantha affirms, sharing a look with me I can't quite decipher.

"It's a pleasure to meet you, Luca," I manage to say, way more formally than I intended.

My newfound nephew, still processing the introduction, offers an observation instead of a greeting. "You're really tall," he says.

Laughter comes easily. "Yeah, I get that a lot."

Buddy, ever the attention-seeker, barks, the sound reverberating in the spacious hall.

"Yes, alright. I was getting to you," I tell him. "This is Buddy... my pain in the ar... my mate."

My nephew's eyes widen. "Can I pet him?"

"Of course. He loves being the centre of attention."

Luca's tentative pat on Buddy's snout earns him a delighted lick, causing him to chuckle.

"Sam? Is that you?" A voice, distant yet distinctly memorable, drifts down the hallway. The sound instantly raises my hackles.

I turn to Samantha. "You invited everyone to meet us here?" I ask.

My half-sister cocks her head, lowers her voice. "Well, not exactly."

"What do you mean?"

She holds my gaze for a few seconds, hesitating before saying, "I didn't invite them. They live here."

"Live here? In the hotel?" I take a breath as if I'm going to respond to that but realise I can't. My mind reels – memories of my teenage years flashing, a bitter taste of betrayal rising in my throat. How could I allow myself to be duped so bloody easily? On the other hand, what did I expect was going to happen here today? It was obvious she was going to be here. Then again, I didn't expect to be ambushed so quickly. I imagined checking in, steeling myself, maybe nipping back to the pub for a pint or ten before the big reunion.

No such luck.

"I'm sorry. In hindsight, I probably should have mentioned it," Samantha says.

"Yes, you should have," I agree, forcing my voice to stay even because, after all, my nephew is now hanging on my every bloody word.

Shit.

"Sam?" That voice again. Belligerent. Grating – already.

Samantha looks at me expectantly. Seagulls squabble outside as if eager for a front seat to this shit show.

FUCK! I scream, but in my head, of course. Then I take a deep breath, swallowing the fire that is threatening to burn its way out of my throat. Heart thudding, I look up the corridor.

Samantha takes her cue. "Come on," she says to her son. "You can bring Buddy with you because I can't wait to hear what she has to say about that."

I want to question what she means by that, but she's already made an apologetic face, turned, and is walking up the corridor.

"Buddy. Come on," Luca encourages, following his mother while ensuring my faithful hound is in tow. Buddy complies with a knowing look back at me as if privy to secrets I'm yet to uncover.

I hang back, my flimsy, useless jacket suddenly feeling heavy and constricting.

A few steps up, Samantha turns towards a burst of light, and that clipped voice pipes up again. "Oh, there you are. I was wondering where you'd got to. I thought we were having breakfast together. Anyway, you should know that I've already talked to the reverend about the changes for the service, and did you know that—" Her words hitch, abruptly cut off by the sight of her grandson and then Buddy rounding the corner.

"What's this, and what's it doing in the house?" she demands.

But I don't let anybody answer. I step around the corner.

Okay... there's a lot to unpack here, so I'm going to start with the view because, well, it's stunning. That, and I'm not sure how to process everything else because I've just reached the shitty realisation that this is all much worse than I expected. I assumed my sister had simply failed to mention that she and the rest of her family had moved into the hotel where I thought I was going to crash, the place where I already planned to retreat if any of this particular mind trip became too bloody unbearable. But, judging by the stunned silence, I get the distinct impression that she actually failed to mention to anybody that she'd invited me here today.

Double fuck.

So yeah, the view is absolutely spectacular from here since almost the entire opposite wall is made of sash windows that offer an absolutely stunning view of the nook of the bay and harbour.

In front of this panoramic marvel, there's a banquet table. Or maybe it's a mishmash of bistro tables playing dress-up. Hard to tell. But it's decked out for royalty –crisp white tablecloth, a breakfast spread that screams "gourmet," and bread that looks so homemade it's practically begging for a butter bath.

A few minutes ago, I'd have been all over it like a rash. But I know now that this isn't a welcome feast but feels more like a trap.

This isn't Samantha's residence but my stepmum's. And there she is, like a queen bee surprised by a wasp at her banquet, sitting at the head of the table: Claudia.

She has changed little. Her hair's shifted from blonde bombshell to a dignified shade of white, but she's still got that timeless elegance. Her skin, a testament to years of privilege, still exudes a soft glow. As always, this woman didn't just sit down to breakfast; she dressed for it with a full slap of makeup, immaculate hair, and even a silk scarf – probably worth more than I spend on clothes in a month – with glittering gold motifs that catch the light just so.

Her startled expression, though – that's priceless. Clearly, like me, she wasn't expecting this little family reunion. Samantha's led me into what feels like a lion's den, and I'm not sure if I'm the guest or the meal.

Then there's a man at the end of the table. Early thirties, maybe. He's dressed in a black suit and tie and has hair so perfectly combed he could be a bloody mannequin. He pauses mid-bite, napkin dabbing at his lips, keen grey eyes darting between me and where I imagine Samantha to be standing. I may be wrong, but I think this man's my half-brother, Roberto. And he must think I'm less important than a stray hair on his immaculate suit because he doesn't even acknowledge me in any way; he simply turns his attention back to his food.

So what do you think the first exchange of loving words is after all these years of radio silence between me and Claudia? Oh, go on, give it a try. What do you think we say to each other?

Give up? It's easy. We say absolutely nothing. Instead, we both opt for a mutual nod of the head, her eyes skimming past me to Samantha standing behind me.

And those same words are now hanging in the air, heavy as the scent of the freshly brewed coffee. Oh, shit... I don't know what I'd give for a cup right now.

Mercifully, the tension is carved up by Luca, all youthful enthusiasm. "Grandma! Grandma! Look, it's Uncle Marco and his dog, Buddy." He's practically bouncing.

Claudia's glare melts into a manufactured smile, and her eyes shift from behind me to the boy in front. "Yes, I'm aware, darling," she says, voice laced with something that's not quite warmth.

"I know you don't like animals in the house, but can we keep Buddy in here? Please! Please!" Luca pleads, his eyes wide with that innocent charm only kids can muster.

Samantha intercedes. "Luca, why don't you take Buddy outside."

"Can I?" is my nephew's question to me.

Why bother? We're leaving now anyway is what I want to say, but instead, "Yeah. Sure. Just be careful." I don't even know what that last bit was for.

"Buddy... come on... come on, boy." And just like that, my nephew and my dog, nails clicking happily on the wood floor, recede back down the hall.

And so, the scene's set, the players are in place, and I'm bracing for a confrontation while considering how to excuse myself from the breakfast meeting from hell when Claudia clips, with a rise to her feet and a scrape of her chair, "Samantha, may I have a word?"

"Oh, Mum, can it wait? I'm starving," my half-sister says, but I feel it's for effect. She was expecting this, and as much as I hate that I have unwittingly become a pawn in her shitty game, I would say she's enjoying sticking it to her overbearing mother.

Me, not so much.

Which is why, when the stranger at the opposite end of the table dumps his napkin and stands with an "I'd like a word too," I take my cue. "Please, don't trouble yourselves," I say. "I'll show myself out."

I storm out of that place, slamming the door behind me. The cold air hits, a stark contrast to the tension inside. I feel like such an idiot. But then, what was I expecting? I have no idea.

I spot Luca, wrapped sensibly in a hat and coat, darting around a row of peculiar lavender bushes with Buddy hot on his heels, the dog barking playfully as they weave in and out of view. I swallow the flames still smouldering in my gullet and force a smile as I approach.

"Hey, Uncle Marco," my nephew greets me with a big smile that instantly warms my heart, not least because it reminds me of someone else.

Toby.

"Are you leaving already?"

I nod reluctantly. "Yeah."

"Didn't the reunion go well?"

The question takes me aback but brings a smile to my face. "That obvious, eh?"

"Mum didn't think it would. She says families can be complicated."

I breathe in to answer but think better of it. Instead, my attention is drawn to the cluster of purple bushes. With the renovations at ANEW, I spent a lot of time looking at shrubs but have seen nothing like these before. "These bushes look particularly colourful for this time of year," I say, mostly to steer us away from the family subject.

"Yeah, Dad made them," Luca responds enthusiastically, throwing the stick for Buddy once more.

"Made them?" I ask.

"Yeah. A hybrid," comes the proud response. "Dad made a cross between the island thistle and a common shrub. They stay colourful all year round."

For a split second, I think my nephew – who can't be that far over ten years old – is having me on, but then I meet his gaze and realise that he isn't. "Wow. That's clever," is all I can say.

"So your dad. He's what, a scientist?"

"Environmental scientist. He studies the ecology of life on the island."

"Oh, right... I didn't know that."

"Yeah! It's really cool. I think I want to be a botanist when I grow up. Did you know plants can talk to each other? Dad says that they are intelligent. They even communicate with each other through their roots. It's called... um... a mycorrhizal network! They even have superpowers; they can release chemicals to warn other plants about pests."

"I didn't know that either. You're pretty smart, aren't you?"

My nephew smiles, and I notice a sudden rouge on his cheek, a sight that makes my heart melt.

"Marco!" It's Samantha. I turn to see her rushing out of the house, coat in hand. "Marco, wait!"

"Come on, Buddy! We're leaving," I say suddenly. "It was great talking to you, Luca," I add quickly.

I turn to Buddy, but the dog has stopped and cocked his head as if to say, *Seriously, dude. Grow up.* "NOW!" I order.

"Marco, please..." my sister says, approaching us. "Luca, why don't you go play with Buddy."

"I... I am. I was."

"Don't bother. We're leaving," I say.

"Marco, please... I'm sorry. I know it must have felt awkward in there."

"Ya think?"

"It's really important that you be here."

"Why? so I can be made to feel like shit some more? No thanks. I knew it. I knew I should never have come."

"Don't say that. They'll come around."

"I came here for you, Sam. Not for her. And certainly not him. I don't even know him."

"Then stay."

"I can't. BUDDY, COME ON!" When the dog hesitates some more, I add, "NOW! I MEAN IT!" And he finally gets the message. Slowly, he makes his way over to me, tail between his legs.

"Marco, please reconsider."

I look at my sister. She seems genuine enough, but... "I can't, Sam," I repeat. "I'm sorry."

"Okay. Well, at least take this," she says, handing me the thick coat she's carrying.

"I don't want that."

"You do. It's freezing," she insists.

I look at the coat. We both know she's right. "Thanks," I say, taking the thing from her. "I appreciate it. Sorry things didn't work out. Come on, Buddy!"

With that, I turn and walk away.

5

THE PROCESSION

THISTLE ISLAND. EARLY AFTERNOON.

Up close, Thistle Island's church resembles one of those authentic centuries-old stone structures, its rough-hewn stones, weathered by time and the salt-laden breeze, telling a story of resilience – much like the island itself, I imagine. A series of worn stone steps, each smoothed by countless footfalls, no doubt, leads to the entrance.

Overhead, seagulls chatter as if amazed to see me pause at the bottom. Buddy obviously shares their amazement, sniffing the stone and then looking back at me as if to say, *Here? Really?*

I ignore him and allow my gaze to shift upwards, squinting in the winter sun as I survey the ancient structure towering over us. This is a place of worship, of faith, a sanctuary for those who believe.

But for me?

I've never been a religious man. It's not something that really figured much in my life. Not until I met Ellie's parents. They're borderline fanatical; at least, that's how they appeared to me. And yet, it's strange because, after we had Toby, I felt differently. That little boy was such a blessing that I felt compelled to give thanks, but to whom beyond his mother? An incorporeal being who allegedly lives in the sky, of course.

But then, after I lost my son... well, that changed everything. Any lingering notions I had of a benevolent deity, of a grand architect of fate, of fortune didn't just fade; they soured, turned to bile in my throat. Because no matter how hard I tried, I just couldn't get beyond that existential question: how could a just and loving God rip a child from us? Leave us with nothing but memories and a heart that felt so heavy it was surely turned to lead.

Yet now, here I stand. I can almost hear the whispers, the echoes of prayers and hymns within these walls, and I can't help but wonder if I'm even welcome here. After all the things I've said, the curses I've hurled skywards in my darkest moments, it feels almost hypocritical to even venture anywhere close.

That, and the fact that I've just imagined myself walking in and proceedings coming to a sudden scratching halt as all eyes turn my way. Not least those of the family I've never known.

Regardless, after taking a deep breath, I climb the steps and push open the heavy, weather-beaten doors, a little surprised by their weight. I can't help but wonder if this is a place of worship or a fortress designed to repel island invaders.

Inside, the starkness of the exterior gives way to an understated beauty. Stained glass windows, modest yet elegant, cast colourful patterns on the stone floor.

Interestingly, my prediction of the pub scene in *American Werewolf in London* doesn't materialise. Hardly anybody turns to look our way, with most people engrossed by the words of the man speaking from the altar.

The only people who do turn are an elderly couple. The woman smiles, whispers to her husband, who whispers to the person next to him, and suddenly, a pew-shuffling ballet unfolds to make room for me.

Shit.

Oh, well, I'm committed now; the old lady keeps grinning and waving her hymn book like one of those mechanical mannequins and is drawing attention.

Do dogs belong in church? Too late for second thoughts now.

I manufacture a grateful smile and file in next to my new friend, whose companion promptly hands me a hymn book.

Buddy's demeanour shifts. Head bowed, tail down, he wedges himself at my feet, finding a sliver of space between the pews.

And I feel it. It's a strange sensation that I don't think I've ever experienced before, except for maybe that night at the pub in Porthcove, but then, we both know that wasn't real. Was it? Either way, this... this is something else. It's a peculiar warmth, an odd welcoming embrace that seems to gather up the island's lost and wandering souls, of which I am now one.

The air hangs heavy with the scent of old wood and lingering incense, the kind that clings to the back of your throat. Polished wooden pews overflow, standing room only, as if the entire island has converged to pay its respects, a testament to my father's profound impact. It would appear that even here at the edge of the world, not unlike Porthcove before, his popularity, or perhaps the respect he commanded, is just as palpable in this silent, sombre gathering.

My gaze sweeps across the congregation, and I slip back into Toby's and my favourite pastime: weaving stories around the lives hidden behind these solemn expressions and the unexpected tapestry of colourful attire. There's a man with a wind-carved face and hands rough as shoreline rocks – a fisherman, no doubt. Tom? Jack? A fixture on a boat's prow, wrestling with nets and nature's whims.

A little further in, I spot an elderly woman, small glasses sliding down her nose – a schoolteacher, perhaps? Evelyn? Mary? Someone who's seen generations pass through her classroom.

Then, catching my attention, a pair of identical twins, their sharp suits ill-fitting in a rural chapel, looking somewhat out of place with their city polish. Lawyers? Accountants? Or maybe just heirs to a forgotten fortune, their identical watches glinting under the chapel's dim lights.

Amidst the sea of black and grey, a young woman with freckles and a shock of red hair stands out – an artist, perhaps, or a musician, her vibrant spirit undimmed even in mourning.

This sea of strangers, each a story I'm yet to learn, forms a backdrop to this solemn theatre as my eyes finally come to rest on the vicar and the large black and white image propped up on the easel next to him. My stomach lurches. There he is – my father, frozen in time, older than I remember. A man I should know, but don't.

He's wearing a beard the way he wore his business deals – thick, unyielding, and with a hint of wildness that suggests adventure. His hair, swept back with a care that is both casual and deliberate, gives him that air of effortlessness that I knew, all too well, was anything but.

This man, who I realise now is pretty much an older version of me, is clad in a dark suit that speaks of boardrooms and wine bars. And he's got that bloody half-smirk that I'm known for, as if privy to a secret punchline for a joke the rest of the world hasn't heard yet. His tie, a stark line bisecting his chest, is the only concession to formality. Everything else – such as the silk handkerchief just peeking out of his pocket – is a nod to the flair he thought he brought to life.

He's leaning slightly forward towards the camera, an approachable tycoon, if ever there was such a thing, and I can't help but marvel at the contradiction of it all. This is the man whose absence loomed over my childhood, yet here he is with this official portrait, standing watch over his own memorial, still commanding the room like some old-world captain of industry. It is so bloody quintessentially him, and as I sit here, I can't decide if the burgeoning weight in my chest is sorrow or just that familiar press of his larger-than-life legacy.

The vicar, a small, stooped figure with a voice that somehow fills the entire space, is speaking about Roberto, my father. Words like *pillar of the community* and *generous spirit* float around the room, settling on the ears of the mourners. And even after all this time, after everything I've learned, those words still seem alien to me despite the blood ties that bind me to the man being eulogised.

And yet, as I scan the crowd, I see faces seemingly marked with genuine grief, as if these people are all an extension of my family, assembled here to honour a man not out of some sense of duty or obligation but of love. It's a bizarre mosaic of emotions that reflects the complex web of relationships one man has left behind.

But then, on the other hand, I could be projecting all of this. After all, I've allowed myself to be lured out here to the back of bloody beyond without any kind of familiar tether. Everything here, ironically, even my family, is foreign to me, which means I have no choice but to take everything I see at face value.

It's impossible to dismiss the weight of a life's impact, how one person's existence can ripple through so many others' lives. As I sit here, in this ancient church, surrounded by people united in loss, I feel a tug of something – not quite belonging, but not entirely detachment either.

"... Go in peace. In the name of the Father, the Son, and the Holy Spirit, Amen."

And those words are our cue. I nod and smile at the couple next to me before hurrying out of the church as if my life depends on it.

I've barely made it down the steps when I hear a voice that makes me both smile and groan inwardly.

"Uncle Marco!" It's Luca, obviously.

I keep walking.

"Uncle Marco! Wait!" I'm just considering whether or not to keep going when the decision is made for me by the traitorous hound that turns and starts barking at my nephew. Yes. There's that word again, and it still feels strange.

"Uncle Marco!" Luca calls again, bounding up to us, eyes sparkling.

I turn, "Hey, Luca!" I say enthusiastically.

"I was calling you."

"You were?"

"Yes. Didn't you hear me?"

"No. Sorry mate. I didn't."

"Buddy did, though," he says, making a fuss of the little traitor.

"He certainly did," I say with a big, artificial grin.

"I thought you'd left for the mainland."

"Yeah. Me too. But I decided to stay one more day," I say.

"You missed the ferry, didn't you?" My nephew says, rubbing the furry tart's chin.

"Wow. Nothing escapes you, does it?"

He looks up at me. "Have you met my mum?" The line is delivered so deadpan that it makes me genuinely laugh as I am reminded of Toby. But the moment doesn't last long as I become aware of the tidal wave of village chatter rolling towards us. And I want to bolt, but I know that isn't going to be easy with Luca clinging to me like a barnacle.

And so, I brace myself as, one by one, the islanders, with their well-meaning banter that feels like sandpaper against my raw nerves, engulf us.

First, it's Mrs McKinnon, whose slender appearance belies her profession. "Hello, Mrs McKinnon."

"Good afternoon, Luca. Aw, what a beautiful service. Your grandfather would have been so proud," she says, glancing at me. Then, lifting the basket hooked onto her arm, she adds, "I opened the bakery early this morning to bake a batch of his favourite fruit scones," she says, her eyes roving over me.

"Oh, Grandad would be chuffed, Mrs McKinnon. He'd always say that they were his one true weakness," my nephew says with peculiar maturity. I exchange looks with him. Then he adds, "Have you met my uncle, Mrs McKinnon?"

"Your uncle?" the woman says, her thin eyebrows lifting, round eyes bulging behind thick spectacles.

"Yes, this is my Uncle Marco. Mummy's brother."

Half-brother!

"Marco? Oh, my goodness," the woman says, her delicate Scottish accent pushing through. "Your photo doesn't do you justice if you don't mind me sayin'. But you look the spitting image of him."

I just smile because I've been in this situation before. I hated it then, too, but what can I say? I'm a glutton for this stuff. Besides, I'm still reeling from the fact that this woman even knows who I am. And what photo?

"Good afternoon, Jenny, love," I turn to see that it's my elderly pew partner and the man I assume is her husband.

"Afternoon, Mr, and Mrs Harris," the baker responds in a loud voice. "How are you both doing today?"

"Well, mustn't grumble, Jenny. We're still here, which is all one could ever hope for," the old lady says before turning to me and smiling sweetly. "It was a real blessing," she says. "A real treat to see all of Roberto's children under the same roof. I know he would have loved it," she adds, touching my arm. Not unlike Samantha and Luca, she doesn't have any discernible accent besides sounding posh.

I nod, and guess what... that's right. I smile at her, too. The baker obviously agrees from the way she's grinning and nodding her head like one of those bobblehead dogs you can get for the car.

"Luca!" It's a familiar voice this time. And I look over to see that it's my half-sister hurrying towards us. "Luca, I said I didn't want you running off today."

"I know. Sorry, Mum, but I wanted to catch up with Uncle Marco and Buddy."

My sister is dressed in black but sporting a crimson scarf. Interestingly, Mr and Mrs Harris are also wearing black, but with matching yellow handkerchiefs. And I realise that the rest of the congregation is too, all dressed in black yet all adorned by one colourful item, be it a pair of gloves, a hat, an armband of fabric, or even multicoloured coats.

"Good morning, Jen, Mr, and Mrs Harris."

"Good morning, Sam. You must be thrilled to have both of your brothers together."

My sister glances at me, smiling broadly, "Yes, Mrs Harris. I certainly am."

"Your dad would have been so proud, Sam. It was a lovely service," says Mr Calloway, who I learn is a retired schoolmaster with a spine as straight as his moral compass.

"What a day of remembrance," remarks another rotund lady with wily brown hair, her multicoloured polka dot coat unwittingly playing host to a collection of cat hairs, each strand catching the light of the sun in a way that suggests her feline companions are never far from her, even in their absence.

I tune in to the hubbub of voices. A whole crowd has grown around us now, leading back towards the church. There must be at least five hundred people here, maybe more, and I'm starting to feel a little overwhelmed when I feel a small hand slip into mine. "Uncle Marco, we're walking together, right?" Luca's voice cuts through the noise, a simple question loaded with expectation.

And what can I say? I nod, although I have no idea what he means by walking together. On the other hand, his holding my hand sends a surge of memories of my little boy pulsing through me so powerfully that my knees go a little weak.

So, I distract myself with everything that is happening around us, and I don't know if I'm imagining it, but instead of dispelling, this congregation is growing from down the bottom of the high street up past the church and around us.

Then, in an almost biblical scene, the murmuring subsides and the crowd parts, making way for the vicar who, of course, is making a beeline straight for us.

Humble, with shoulders slightly bowed, no doubt from years of bending over pulpits and prayer books, he still moves with surprising sprightliness. His eyes, small and sharp, contrast with the warm smile he offers everyone, finally landing on me with gentle intensity. He's wearing a multicoloured bobble hat that tugs an instinctive smile from my face.

"Marco, I presume?" His voice, seasoned by countless sermons and funeral rites, carries a comforting timbre. "I didn't have the pleasure of welcoming you to our service today, but I was delighted to see you in the back row...."

This is where I miss the old me – the one who wouldn't give a shit. The new me just smiles inanely, like he's done something in his shorts and hopes nobody notices.

"... but there's no doubt that he was a figure of the community. Your presence here... it means a great deal to us, to all islanders."

I'm still not entirely sure what to say. The idea that my being here means anything to anyone feels a bit far-fetched, but hey, it appears I'm in the minority. "Thank you, Reverend," I say. "It's a... unique place you all have here."

The vicar smiles, a crinkling at the corners of his eyes softening his otherwise stern appearance. "Unique, indeed. Thistle Island has a way of leaving its mark on everyone who sets foot here. One can only hope that, in time, it might leave its mark on you, too."

Before I can respond, he turns to address the crowd. "Ladies and gentlemen, let us begin our march to the cemetery. We walk today not just in mourning but also in celebration of a father, husband, and pillar of our community."

There's a collective shuffling as the crowd begins to fall into a solemn procession, with the reverend leading the way.

That's when I notice several yards up ahead – somehow, and I have no idea how, but obviously by some other way – my stepmother and half-brother have managed to get in front of us and now appear to be waiting for the reverend and his flock.

Claudia is wearing a stylish black dress and red swing coat, like she's just stepped off the catwalk, while Roberto Junior, who, if I'm not mistaken still appears trapped in that perpetual state of discontent, is dressed in a black suit and coat with a blue scarf.

They are flanked by two uniformed policemen. One is all Highland stock, towering and broad-shouldered with tufts of ginger hair escaping from his hat, the other slighter and much less imposing.

As people greet us while filing by, we begin to take our place in the stream, expertly led by Luca as if he's done this many times before. Suddenly, the burly Highland cop steps out of line and approaches Samantha, his stern eyes locking on her.

"Sam, I need tae talk tae ye," he says, his voice a low rumble.

Samantha seems momentarily surprised by the approach before she shakes her head. "Not now, Sarge. We're in the middle of the procession."

"But it's important," he insists, his tone hardening.

She forces a smile, but there's a steely determination in her voice. "I said not now. This isn't the time nor the place."

For a moment, they stand locked in a silent battle of wills. The Highland cop's stern gaze doesn't waver, but Samantha's resolve is equally unyielding. Finally, she breaks the silence, her voice calm but firm. "We'll talk later."

With a reluctant nod, the cop steps back, though his eyes linger on her with an unreadable expression before shifting to me. His gaze runs me up and down, a look so cold and dispassionate that I half expect him to whip out a notepad and take notes on the most efficient ways to murder me.

Mercifully, he falls behind as we take the path out of the village, passing the rear of the hotel and up inland onto a coastal path that I imagine must run the circumference of the island. The views from here are spectacular, due in part, no doubt, to the waning strength of the afternoon sun that has dialled up the wintry saturation of mountain, hillside, and bay.

"Marco?" It's Samantha calling me.

"How's the coat?"

The coat is actually bloody glorious. I had got to the stage where I couldn't feel the extruding parts of my body, but this beast of a thing is something else. If it weren't for the lumps of ice that are my nose and ears, I wouldn't even be able to tell that it's still Baltic out here.

So I thank my sister. Tell her how grateful I am that she thought of me. That she foisted this coat on me and had slipped the note in one of its pockets, reminding me where the service was taking place. You believe that, don't you?

Of course, you don't. That's because you know me so well. My only response is to shoot her a glare.

"I know you're upset—"

"Upset? I'm not upset," I say, much more petulantly than I intend, eyes in front and on the scenery.

"What happened earlier is not what this is all about."

"I don't care. And shouldn't you be up in first class with your mother and brother?" I ask.

Samantha glances up ahead, then back at me and says, "You *are* my brother."

Okay. I didn't see that coming. And as much as my frozen mind scrambles for some kind of quip, I can't find anything. That statement may feel alien to me, but it's also, well... nice.

My sister, of course, in true Battista style, having discovered a weakness, ploughs on discreetly. "Look, Marco. I know I didn't go about this the right way," she adds quickly. I shoot her another look. "Okay, I went about it terribly, but I just knew if I didn't push you, then you wouldn't be here, and... and I know Pappa would have wanted you to be."

"Pappa?"

"That's what we called him."

"You spoke Italian with him?"

"Didn't you?"

I don't answer. I just simmer, and this is exactly why I wouldn't have had anything to do with this, as it's just one constant curtain-reveal of shit after another. Things that poor old Marco was deprived of. And I try not to feel resentful about it, but I bloody do because I was his fucking son too!

"Marco?" I turn and look at the woman that I want to dislike but find I'm incapable. "I read your book," she says. Her eyes emeralds in this light. Familiar. Like my own.

Yes, I'm focusing on that detail because the alternative is to absorb what this woman just said: that she has read my book – the summation of that awful time in my life, the things that happened to me during my childhood, losing my boy, the psychosis, and everything after.

Shit.

It's odd. Until now, if someone told me they read my book, I would feel a mild sense of pride. You know, like a recovering alcoholic who came out the other side and has written the proverbial book about it. But today it feels different. Personal. Like I've laid myself bare. Which, of course, also goes some way to explaining the sympathy in those eyes, the pain, the compassion.

I don't respond because there's a lump in my throat, and we're surrounded by people. Not least my ten-year-old nephew, who may be walking ahead of us with Buddy but remains nonetheless within earshot.

We've reached the crest of the hill now, and I have to catch my breath. The wind is stronger up here, yet bitingly fresh. It's a natural balcony with a stunning vista that's both wild and enchanting. To the right is an elevated view of the ocean stretching endlessly to the horizon and the island bay, which is a tranquil kaleidoscope of blues and greens merging with the dock, the village, and the church. Beyond are those quaint holiday cottages nestled in the hillside, specks of civilization amidst nature's grand canvas.

To the left, Thistle Ridge, the mountain, rises like an ancient guardian, its snow-dusted summit piercing the clouds. Below, a forest of verdant pine trees stretches towards and around its base, their needles shimmering in the breeze.

It's a humbling sight that dwarfs all the pettiness of sibling rivalry.

I glance at Luca, who has one hand resting on Buddy's back, and my heart skips another beat because, for a split second, I imagine he's Toby – my son – ever begging us for a pet dog.

Don't worry. I know he isn't.

I look at the woman who – regardless of my childish distinction that we don't share the same mother – I don't know if that's a blessing or a curse – is my sister. She meets my gaze as if she's just read my mind, and I scramble for something to say. Anything to dispel the moment. "What's that?" I ask, nodding towards a giant, gleaming structure nestled amongst the pine trees at the edge of the forest.

Samantha hesitates, as if reluctant to talk about it. "That," she says, "is the dome."

6

THE RITUAL

THISTLE ISLAND. AFTERNOON.

The dome, a botanical lab crucial to daily life on the island, is a research station where scientists study everything that lives here – plants, animals, insects, the whole ecosystem. This is their way of taking the island's pulse, as conservation is something they pride themselves on, especially since some endangered species live here.

"And that?" I ask, nodding up ahead. I'm referring to what looks like a tall standing stone to the side of the path.

"Well, Thistle Island has a very strong druid history. It's believed that this is where the druids appeased their gods, manipulated the weather, and transformed this land into the haven it is now," my sister explains, assuming the role of tour guide. "They did this by a series of rituals, some of which are still being observed to this day. This funeral walk is one such custom, practiced only for tribal leaders. It's a walk of remembrance, a time to reflect on the lives of those who have passed on to the other side, and the opportunity to give thanks to the gods and ask that they accept and watch over the spirits of those who seek to join them."

I look at her to make sure she isn't having me on, but she lifts her eyebrows as if to say it's true. And then, as if to prove the point, I watch the baker place a scone at the foot of the stone. Somebody else pours wine onto the earth. Others lay flowers.

"Each of these megaliths represents a different god. Mourners can give thanks to one or all of them on their way to the graveyard."

"Does that mean that...?"

"Yes. All of these people are here for Dad. He was loved by everyone on the island. Yes, he could get cantankerous. Swore like a trooper, but you couldn't help but love him. You remind me of him. I didn't realise how much until I saw your photo in the paper."

"So I keep hearing."

We come to a stop as Luca breaks from the procession, walks over to the megalith, and places what looks like a chess piece in the grass under it.

Then he returns to his mother, who gently rubs the hat on his head, then places a hand on his shoulder. I watch Buddy nuzzle him in that way he does when he senses something is off, before wagging his tail and coming over to check on me. "Everything okay?" Samantha asks her son.

"Yep," comes Luca's surprisingly sombre response while keeping his gaze lowered.

"You were close to Nonno, weren't you?" my sister asks her son, holding her arm around him. Luca nods. "They used to play chess together, didn't you?"

Another nod.

And just like that, it all feels real. The reason the whole island is traipsing cross country to the graveyard at the back of beyond. This is a funereal march, and as much as I wasn't feeling the weight of it until this moment, I am suddenly overwhelmed by it. Grief-stricken by the words I've thought but never shared. Luca's loss of a man who had obviously become his friend, and for my son, who was deprived of such an emotional treasure.

I touch my nephew's shoulder and then bend down to him. "Hey, have you tried playing stick with this guy yet?"

"No. I didn't know he could do any tricks."

"Tricks? Mate, he's a one-dog circus. That's all he ever wants to do. His favourite is fetching sticks. He'd probably even fetch a tree if I threw it."

I watch my nephew's face light up.

"Can we try it now?" he asks eagerly.

I look at the procession still shuffling by. "Well, maybe not right now. He might knock a few people over, and," I hold a hand to the side of my mouth and lower my voice, "between you and me, some of these people don't have much longer to go."

"Marco," Samantha hisses, though I catch the twitch of her lips fighting a smile while Luca goes for an all-out obvious titter.

"When we get back. Alright, mate?"

My nephew nods enthusiastically.

"Okay, now, let's get moving. We're getting left behind," Samantha says as a substantial gap has formed between the people in front of us and those behind.

"So, who are all these people? I mean, they can't all be native islanders, judging by the eclectic mix of accents, including yours."

She smiles. "No, all sorts live here. Some born. Others are transplants from all over, including us. We lived in London before we moved out here."

"Yes. I had to leave my school," Luca chimes in.

"Oh, right? Why's that?"

"Uncle Rob sold our house," Luca continues, "Didn't he, Mum?"

"*We*," my sister pushes in, "needed a change. And it just made sense to move up here. You'll understand that. You moved to the country too, didn't you?"

I nod, but I know my sister is deflecting by the way she pushed that subject right back onto me, and I can't help but wonder why. I want to press her further on it. It's only fair since she's already intimated how much she knows about me from reading my book.

But I don't get the chance. Our conversation is upstaged by the sound of rushing water. I look over to see a stream like a silver ribbon slicing its way down from the mountain and through the hillside. The crystal-clear water is a sight to behold as it tumbles over a series of rock pools before pouring through a natural aperture carved into another of those towering stone monoliths, gathering momentum as it plunges into a natural basin. The water resembles a bubbling cauldron before it calms, flowing serenely under a stone bridge ahead of us, then meandering towards the vast expanse of the ocean.

Samantha resumes her tour guide role. "This is Airmed's Tear. Legend has it that Airmed, an ancient healer, and herbalist, wept over the loss of her brother, and where her tears fell, these streams sprang forth."

I watch as the woman with the cat hair coat pauses on the stone bridge for several seconds before throwing something into the water.

It feels like my... *sister* is trying to make a point, but me, well, I just make a quip. "Wow. Airmed's in the waterworks business now? I hope she's charging for these miraculous plumbing services," I say with a grin.

"Funny you should say that," Samantha continues with a smile. "There are two more streams like this on the other side of the island. They supply all of our drinking water. And as the water flows down from the mountain, it is directed through turbines, generating clean, renewable energy for all of us. So, this ancient stream, once a source of myth and legend, now serves a practical purpose, intertwining Thistle Island's past with its present in a seamless blend of folklore and modernity."

"Is that right?" I say pensively, genuinely impressed both with the information and the way my sister dealt with my cynicism by reminding me she knows more about me than I first thought. ANEW uses the same renewable energy, and she could only have known that if she read some of the press articles in which it has been featured. She's definitely been doing her research, which is more than can be said for me. I smile and nod at her. *Touché.*

Then, I follow my sister – I know I keep saying that word because, well, it just feels weird – over to the bridge where we stop and gaze into the pooled water. And suddenly, it feels like one of those national minutes of silence where each of us stands with our heads bowed.

I sense people passing us – it doesn't feel intrusive but discreet, respectful of our time here. Similarly, Luca and Buddy have already crossed the bridge, so it's just Samantha and me.

I watch as my sister reaches into her shoulder bag and pulls out something wrapped in brown paper. She opens it to reveal what looks like a piece of cork. It's about the size of a large walnut, smooth and meticulously varnished to a soft sheen. It's a float, painted in a deep-sea blue, speckled with tiny white dots, reminiscent of a starry night sky. Around its middle is a thin, silver band, giving it a touch of elegance. At the top is a small, delicately carved anchor symbol. "Dad loved fishing," she narrates, raising her voice over the sound of the rushing water. "I was about Luca's age when we made this, and I've used it on every fishing trip since." She doesn't look at me, but by the tremble in her voice, I can hear she's getting emotional. "I miss him," she says.

It's odd hearing her speak these words about the man whose affections I've chased for most of my life. I should feel slighted, but I don't. She's grieving, and if anybody understands the overwhelming emptiness grief carves out of you, it's me.

"I love you, Pappa," she says, throwing the float into the water where we watch it bob for a short while before making its way under the bridge and out of sight.

A peculiar tightness forms in my chest. Samantha sniffs and looks up at me with a sheen in her eyes. "Marco. I really am sorry."

"For what?"

"For lying to you. Although, technically, I didn't lie. I just didn't tell you—"

"You lied, Sam," I interrupt.

She shrugs. "I did. And for that, I'm sorry, but I knew you wouldn't have come otherwise."

"Maybe," I say. "But that was my decision to make."

She nods. "You're right. But I needed to get you here."

"You said. But I don't understand. Why now?"

"I read your book..." she begins. I observe her, a knot forming in my gut.

"... and I just felt like I needed to set the record straight," she says as softly as she can, given the roar of the water.

I squint at her, fighting that instinctive urge to get defensive, since it's obvious she's going to say something about my book that I'm probably not going to like.

"I was just so sorry about what happened to you," she says, and from the continuation of that sheen in her eyes, I've no reason to think she isn't being genuine. This stirs something in me because I realise that nobody from this side of my family ever showed an interest in what happened to Ellie and me.

She places a reassuring hand on my arm. My immediate reaction is to shake it off as if through her touch she might read something in me. My pain. My grief. My vulnerabilities. I swallow hard as I feel the tide recede in my mouth.

"... In your book, you sound so angry. About Dad. And I felt you needed to know that you were wrong. He loved you, Marco. He loved you more than anything."

I scoff. "You're fucking joking, right? You brought me all the way here just to tell me that?"

"I brought you here because you needed to be here, today, and you needed to know that your perception of our father was wrong."

I nod, jaw muscles flexing. "Right," I slap my head, "I must have forgotten about all my fishing trips with the old man, all the chess games he played with my son, not to mention all the Christmases and birthdays where he acted like we didn't fucking exist."

I've obviously got that glare that I know I'm prone to when angry because I notice my sister flinch.

"You have every right to be angry," she says.

"Oh, do I? Thanks. Glad you approve."

"Dad wasn't perfect."

"Now there's an understatement."

"It was difficult for him."

"Difficult for him?!" I snap, then I glance over to make sure Luca didn't hear me, but he's busy, laughing, running in circles while Buddy chases him. I step forward and glower, "How the fuck did you think it was for me? Having to lie to my son about why his grandfather didn't give a shit about him."

"I understand—"

"No, you don't. You haven't got a clue what it was like for us—"

"Nor you for us!" she snaps before turning away from me. Then, after taking a beat, she adds, "They argued about you all the time. All the bloody time. To the point where it made me hate you! I hated you, and I didn't even know you," she adds, her last words softening.

I gape at her for several seconds.

She takes a deep breath before glancing over at her son and then looking up at me once more. "Look. I promise you... this is not how I wanted this to go. I... appreciate the pain you must have been in, Marco, and I can't imagine what it must have been like for you and your wife after...." She doesn't say the words, but another glance at her son tells me she's talking about Toby. "But this is why I wanted us to meet. Why I wanted you to know the truth and... if you chose to, give you the opportunity to pay your respects to Dad so that you, too, could get some closure.

"He wasn't a perfect man. Far from it. But who is? And maybe he wasn't strong enough to show it, but he loved you; of that, I am sure. They argued about you all the time, but my mum... she wouldn't have any of it. She said she was afraid of you, to have you in the house, and that you caused her to miscarry. From then on, it was a constant argument about who Dad chose to put first, and since he lived with her...." She doesn't finish the sentence.

Water churns. A lonely seagull calls overhead.

I say nothing. I can't. I mean, I know I played up as a teenager and was a shit to her, but I had no idea I caused that. Did I?

"... As it turns out, it had nothing to do with you. Dad had a gene deficiency. Later in life, he had some medical problems, and during that time, he learned that he shouldn't even have been able to father children. That's why he loved us all equally. We were his miracles." She has a hand on my arm once more. Her tone is soft, imploring. "It's why he gave you Dolce Vita, Marco. That place meant the world to him. He talked about it all the time. Of his time there with you. Of course, none of us wanted to hear it, but that didn't stop him. 'He's your family too,' he kept telling us, 'And I love him as much as I love you.' He always kept this with him."

My sister reaches into her bag once more, pulls out a 5x7 photo frame, and hands it to me. It's a selfie photo of my father and me! I look so bloody young with wild black locks! I must be in my teens still. My father, who I have to admit looks a bit like I do now, has his arm around me. It looks like we're on a boat. I can see it and part of the ocean in the background. My father is grinning from ear to ear, but me, I've got a lopsided smile. I do not look happy! And... oh, shit. "I remember that day," I say. "He picked me up from school in his new car and took me sailing, but I hated it. I was sick the whole time. I'd forgotten all about this." And yet, although I can still feel that queasiness now, that pissed look on my face does tug at the corner of my mouth.

I look at Samantha, who smiles at me encouragingly. Then she adds, "He kept this too." She reaches into her bag of mementos once more.

This time, she pulls out something that looks like it's wrapped in cloth. She unfurls it and hands it to me. It's a wooden fishing boat, a meticulously carved miniature, no bigger than the palm of my hand, crafted from rich, dark mahogany wood, giving it a timeless and classic appearance. The boat's hull is smooth and perfectly shaped, showing the skill and care taken in its creation. On its side, it has the name *Marco's Voyager* delicately etched in an elegant script. The sails are made from a thin, almost translucent fabric. The details are exquisite, down to the tiny ropes and the miniature anchor attached to the bow.

"Oh, my God," I gasp as I feel my stomach roll. "I'd completely forgotten about this," I say, turning the piece in my hand. "We made it when I came back from college. It was our thing. Our time together. But then I think it's also what started another argument. I wanted to keep working on it. Your mum wanted us to come inside. One thing led to another and..." I trail off here and look up at my sister as I build dams so that the mist in my eyes doesn't swell into tears.

Samantha nods at me, her face etched with compassion. "Dad always regretted not standing up to Mum. He just wanted to keep the peace and didn't want to risk losing us, but he tried to reconcile with you. He defied Mum, travelled to Porthcove, to Dolce Vita, because he wanted to arrange to see you and Toby. But then...." tears spill from my sister's eyes.

She doesn't need to finish that sentence because you already know as well as I do that my father, Roberto Battista, died alone in Dolce Vita of a heart attack.

I pull my sister into an embrace, grateful that the action ensures that she doesn't see the sheen of my own tears.

"I wanted you to know, Marco. I needed you to know," she says, her voice muffled against my coat.

We remain that way for a minute or so as the water rushes, crows caw, and the distant sound of Luca's giggling administers a tonic to our ears.

Eventually, Samantha emerges from the embrace, surreptitiously swiping at her tears before glancing over at her little boy. Then she looks at the boat in my hand and steps aside.

My heart pounds with the haste of the gushing water. This is my cue. My turn.

I look over the side of the bridge and into the churning trough. My sister, like the islanders before her, is keeping a healthy distance.

This is *my* moment. *My* grief.

Over the years, I've had mixed feelings towards my father. He, not unlike my mother, understandably, featured in a lot of my sessions with Doctor Holmes. If I had known then what I've just learned, things may have turned out differently. Who knows?

What I do know is that both my father as I knew him and the feelings that I coveted towards him are in the past. This is how it must be if I want to move on. If I ever want any chance of normalcy.

I hold the boat up, my fingers tracing the smooth wood worn from our hands. Childhood laughter rings in my ears, a flicker of warmth before the years of distance drown it out. Tears blur my vision, but I focus on the delicate sails, the words *Marco's Voyager* as I distil just some of the things that have led me here.

My grip loosens, a part of me wanting to snatch it back. But the boat falls, hitting the water with a plunk. It bobs, a lonely echo of everything that came before, teetering on the edge of the stream. Then the current begins to tug at it. Once... twice... pulling it towards the bridge's stony arch. And with each jerk forward, a knot in my chest comes undone, another emotional layer washed away until it disappears under the bridge.

7

THE OTHER SIDE

THISTLE ISLAND. AFTERNOON.

Yeah, so I bet you weren't expecting that, were you? If you were, you're more astute than I am. I had no idea a brisk morning walk would morph into a full-blown familial bloody therapy session.

Shit.

It's been a long time since I felt that raw – that vulnerable, yet oddly included. Maybe, if I dare let my mind wander that far, even a bit loved.

And so, we trudged on, moving across the island for another kilometre or so. The undeniable majesty of this place commands respect – it's a domain unto itself, both vast and sprawling. Encircled by the restless ocean, it stands as a bastion of solitude, as daunting as it is awe-inspiring in its seclusion. Its rugged elegance, a raw, and untamed beauty, humbles you, reducing your essence to a mere whisper in its grand narrative. Here, caught in the eternal ballet of earth and sea, one discovers a rare balance – feeling both insignificant and profoundly anchored.

Our trek took us around a wind farm, where a line of turbines stood like giants against the sky, their blades slicing through the air with a rhythmic *whoosh*. The gateway to the industrial side of the island.

We passed the other streams and hydroelectric dam, past a sentinel-like array of solar panels, and then, the imposing skeletal remains of the processing plant. With its own forsaken beach and port, it remained a spectral reminder of the island's faded glory.

Samantha shared more about its bygone vitality, how this was once the heart of Thistle Island where boats laden with a bounty of fish would berth daily, unloading their prized catch for the celebrated Thistle Loch products.

As we delved deeper, the remnants of industry yielded to a wild thicket. Ancient oaks and towering pines rose stoically, their fragrance filling the brisk wind that cut through the landscape.

Eventually, we reached the island's graveyard, nestled in a serene valley surrounded by an amphitheatre of trees – a picturesque place that, with its New Orleans–like arched iron gate for an entrance, reminded me of somewhere out of a Stephen King novel.

The graves lay scattered across the gentle slope, each moss-covered marker a testament to a life once lived in this remote part of the world.

Roberto Battista's grave – I don't know why I can't just say *our father's grave*, but I suppose that, like most things, it'll take some getting used to – was near the top of the valley, offering a view of the surrounding landscape, a fitting final resting place for a man who had once been so integral to the island's life. The headstone was simple yet elegant, bearing his name and a few words that encapsulated his life and legacy.

The reverend offered words of comfort and shared fond memories of Roberto. His speech wove tales of our father's life, his contributions to the island, and the memories he left behind. The wind carried his words across the valley, lending them a weightless, ethereal quality, underscored by the mournful cry of crows and the distant rumble of the ocean.

Standing there at the forefront as a member of his immediate family felt like an uncanny reverie. My sister – no longer half in any sense that mattered – was on one side, while my stepmother and half-brother stood on the opposite, a physical and symbolic divide. It was a stark tableau of life's tangled connections: united by our shared mourning yet still separated by an expanse of unspoken histories and half-healed wounds.

Despite my efforts to avoid it, I found myself stealing occasional glances at my stepmother. She remained stoic, betraying none of her internal turmoil, her grief, or her thoughts about my presence on the island. To be fair, she had already made her feelings towards me abundantly clear.

I toyed with the idea of approaching her after the service – not necessarily to make peace, but to express my regret for my part in how things had turned out between us. Yet, I quickly discarded the thought as vivid images of the service erupting into a family row before the entire village flooded my mind, which was the last thing I wanted. My hesitation, however, wasn't for my sake but for Samantha and Luca's. Knowing my sister had already gone against the matriarch and her son's wishes, I didn't want to exacerbate the situation.

I'll be gone tomorrow. It just isn't worth it.

But what of my stepbrother, my father's namesake? Well, he remained just as walled off as his mother, avoiding all eye contact. I concluded that it was probably for the best since there's a good chance that the man only has to look at me the wrong way now for me to want to put my fist through his face. Yeah. I didn't know where that came from either, but then I realised that the red mist of my dark passenger hasn't been seen for a while now. The beast in me may have calmed, but I don't think it's completely gone. And the thought of that often scares me because I know the trouble that it has got me into in the past.

I've already lost enough.

The walk back from the graveyard wasn't as sombre as the journey to it, but it remained nonetheless contemplative. The echoes of the service, the words spoken, and the emotions stirred at the graveside hung in the air, a shared experience that silently united us all. It was as though we were walking through a transition, leaving a part of our grief behind with each step as we moved away from the industrial relics of the island's bygone era.

As the expansive view of the bay opened up before us, the atmosphere subtly shifted. Laughter began to weave through our procession, gently at first, like a tentative ray of sunshine pushing through clouds. It signalled a change, a collective unspoken agreement that it was time to stop mourning the singular, suffocating blackness of death and start celebrating the vivid, diverse palette of life.

8

DARKNESS FALLS

THISTLE ISLAND. EVENING.

And so… what to do with good ole Marco?

Well, obviously, I couldn't stay in the hotel since it had already been occupied by enemy forces. The only place for me to spend the night is in one of the cottages.

Samantha resisted at first, but even she had to admit that it was the most logical conclusion unless I fancied shacking up with one of the locals. I know Miss Cat-Hair-Coat-Lady had given me the eye a few times. I bet she wouldn't have minded me staying the night.

Ugh. I just got an image of that.

Oh, come on. I'm not being unkind. I just have a type. You know that. Yes, I know it's superficial.

That said, after everything that happened, I've been celibate for some time now. It's been a case of securing my oxygen mask before helping others with theirs. Crap analogy, but I think you get my point. After Sarah, I want to be sure I have my head on straight before subjecting anybody else to me. So, when I say I want my next time to be with someone special, you believe me, right? Insert a most ironic wink here.

Anyway, as you know, I am a sucker for a killer view. And this cottage? It offers nothing but. From the tiny front windows, there are some seriously fantastic views of the bay. From the back, it's pine trees and the snow-capped mountain.

Stunning.

But here's the catch: I'd forgotten the whole point of these cottages. They are marketed on the very idea of providing an opportunity for occupants to disconnect from the electronic trappings of modern life. That means no electricity, no Wi-Fi, and no cell phone.

Shit. As you know from our experiences, isolation is in no way a good thing for me.

And, to make things worse, those enviable views I mentioned before include the village with its bright lights and merriment a kilometre or so's walk away.

Double shit.

But it's okay. It's alright. I'm fine. We're fine. This little episode is here for one night only, and even I can survive that.

Although you wouldn't have thought so, according to my sister. She insisted on filling the place with supplies, like I plan to be here for a week.

At one point, she actually mentioned her husband – husband? I didn't even know she was married. I mean, I assumed she was, based on my conversation with Luca. But I expected she might be divorced or something since I'm yet to meet the man, and he wasn't at the memorial today.

I brought up the topic, but she skilfully changed it. Instead, she started talking about the weather. Apparently, it's going to snow tonight, and she didn't want me to be unprepared. Unprepared? No, can't say I enjoyed the inference either. Nor the way my sister tends to avoid eye contact sometimes. There's obviously much more about this side of my family that I don't know, as shocking as that might seem, but I have to keep telling myself that we're not going to be here long enough to care about it.

Anyway, after fussing over me some more, Samantha drops the bombshell: there's a second part to today's memorial – a celebration of my father's life, taking place at the community hall. Apparently, everyone will be there. And from what I've learned about this place, when she says everyone, she means literally the whole island.

Samantha then told me it was really important that I be there. When that didn't work, she added that Luca would really like to see me. And when I continued to resist, she piled on how much it would mean to her too. And on and on.

She pretty much used the Battista charm to get her way. I've always been the one dishing out that kind of sorcery, so having it turned on me? Can't say I'm a fan. When I asked if other family members would be attending, she just gave me a look – of course they would. I told her I didn't want the whole thing to turn into something. She just smiled and told me it wouldn't because I would make sure that it didn't.

Right, so no pressure then. Or escape route apparently.

In reality, we all know that if I didn't want to go, I wouldn't. But it's a case of spending the evening in the company of a bunch of strangers or alone in that tomb-like cottage.

And so, after freshening up... when I say that, you know I mean it literally, right? That place is an icebox. The water's freezing! I thought I'd left that shit behind me at Porthcove, but apparently not. My shower hell appears to have been reincarnated into a sad over-the-bath job. And trying to wedge my six-foot-something naked arse under that trickle... not a good look.

Now, I'm trudging across the Scottish landscape, lantern in hand, as if I've just been time-machined back to medieval times – and guess what? It's snowing. That bitter cold wind is now carrying giant snowflakes across the water and hurling them at me.

Buddy appears unaffected, eagerly sniffing the path ahead like there's a pint with his name on it waiting at the other end. I considered leaving him at the cottage, but I don't know, something about abandoning him in that strange place just didn't feel right. That and the look he gave me when I dared to even suggest it.

On the bright side, my sister was right about this coat – it's lovely and warm. Smells, though. Not in a bad way. I think it's cologne. Faint. I assume it's my *brother-in-law's*. Yep. Still weird saying stuff like that.

I'm eager to meet this guy. Of course, when I made another attempt to find out more by asking Samantha if her husband was going to be there tonight, she just told me to worry about getting myself there by seven-thirty. I'm certain she's avoiding the topic. What I don't know is why... yet.

As I trek forward, the crunch of my boots against the freshly fallen snow feels like the only real connection I have with the world. The wind, bitter and unforgiving, rushes across the water and hillside with a ghostly howl, tugging at my coat and at the dim light of my lantern, causing shadows to dance creepily at the periphery of my vision.

The village, with its warm lights and the faint sounds of laughter and music, seems to be a world away, an oasis of warmth and life mockingly out of reach.

The surrounding blackness appears to be growing thicker now, the beam of my lantern a feeble defence against the encroaching gloom. With each step, the isolation deepens, enveloping Buddy and me in a silent world, save for the occasional distant cheer, distorted by the wind into something almost unrecognisable.

Suddenly, a sharp snap pierces the night. To my left, up on the hill, in the trees somewhere. A twig? A branch? I'm not sure. It's hard to tell.

I turn the useless lamplight in that direction, but it fails to penetrate barely a few feet into the blackness.

This is the one thing I miss about the city. The creature of the dark there has been tamed by the light. But in the country, it's left to flourish, burgeon, and thicken into walls of nothingness that press and squeeze on your chest until you can no longer breathe.

That's exactly how I'm feeling when a bone-chilling screech slices through the dark. An alien sound discordant with the natural noises of the night.

I spin in that direction, almost losing my balance, and listen, the lantern held high in front of me....

Nothing but the distant crash of the waves and the whoosh and rumble of the wind buffeting against my numbed ears.

Snowflakes whip and swirl around me as I tighten my grip on the flickering lantern, narrowing the world to a small circle of its glow. I pause, listening intently through the turbulence....

Nothing. The sound doesn't come again, but the silence that follows is just as chilling. Not an owl. Not a fox. Nothing.

We're alone out here with just this thin beam separating us from the vast, hidden wilderness, a realisation that sends a shiver down my spine that has nothing to do with the cold.

I've been in this situation before. And maybe that's part of the problem. The demons conjured by my mind are far worse than anything animal out there. Besides, if there were something stalking us, Buddy would have started—

Growling. I barely hear it at first. The din of the turbulence is frustratingly loud.

Oh, shit. That's not good.

"Come on, let's go," I say, without hesitation, starting forward on the path once more. Fast now. Boots thumping loudly on the snow, my focus on the lights in the distance and on the revelry I'm suddenly craving. Humanity. That's exactly what we—

I skid to a halt and spin around.

Woof! Woof! Woof!

Buddy – he isn't following. He's barking – sharp and angry, into the dark.

"Buddy! Come on. Come on," I call, but my words are snatched by the wind and dragged off somewhere into the blackness.

"BUDDY! COME ON! NOW!" I order, anxiety raking at my throat, eyes squinting into the swirling vortex of snow illuminated by the lamplight.

I can just about see him on the soft edges of light. Honey-gold fur ruffled in the wind. Ears up with one at half-mast. There's definitely something out there.

"BUDDY! Come on. NOW!" I order.

Finally, the dog turns. "Come on, let's go. Now!"

I start forward again, turning to make sure the dog is following me. He is. So I pick up the pace as the wind chases us, howling louder, as if frustrated by our escape.

The snow is falling much heavier now, each flake feeling like a cold finger brushing against my face, making me squirm because I'm under no doubt that there's something out here, stalking us from the black, watching us hurry across this frozen realm to what feels like safety.

By the time we make it to the edge of the village, the snow has transformed the world into a winterscape, already something like five centimetres high, and it's still falling. If this is what Samantha meant by a little snow, I'd hate to see what a lot is.

We've made it to the high street now, and I'm relieved to step under the bright light of one of the street lanterns. I know that makes me sound like a wimp, but you'll appreciate I'm not trying to impress anyone here. There was definitely something creepy about those pine trees. Buddy obviously agreed. Besides, we both know I've been in much more emasculating situations. Enough said.

Empty. The High Street's completely empty at this time of night, made eerier dusted in white. The fact that there's nobody out here at this time of the evening gives me pause. Do they know something I don't?

Of course, my thoughts instantly turn to previously enjoyed and now actively avoided horror movies, but I push the images from my mind and focus. This place isn't that big, but I still need a moment to get oriented. Okay. So turning right will take me to the ferry dock, and left leads up the high street and towards the church, so that means the community hall or room or whatever the thing is called is at the end of the street, turn right. I remember seeing the place once on our way to the hotel and again before we started our walkathon earlier today.

Besides, if I didn't know where I was going, all I would need to do now is follow the sounds of music notes falling around me like snowflakes.

Eventually, with the chill still clinging to me like a spectral shroud, I see the literal light at the end of the shadowy street emanating like an ethereal glow, promising a reprieve from the dark's eerie grip. I round the corner, and there it stands – the community hall. It's a brightly lit beacon against the bite of the night. The gothic-looking stone building was probably part of the church grounds or some grand estate, now repurposed for the people. The keeper of tales and history of Thistle Island, standing defiant against years of battling the relentless Scottish weather.

The snow is already painting it anew, softening its edges, draping over it like a cloak. But the warmth inside fights back, golden light spilling from the windows, casting a glow on the white blanket at my feet. The sound of life and laughter grows louder with each step, a symphony of merriment that feels worlds away from the dark quiet of the hillside.

I can hear it all before I even reach the door – the chink of glasses, the rise and fall of voices in song, the rhythmic tap of feet dancing to a fiddle's tune. *Seriously?* It's the sound of life. Unabashed. Unafraid. And it beckons me.

But I stand here for a moment, the snowflakes like falling stars, their cold kiss brushed aside by the warmth reaching out from the building. Buddy nuzzles my hand, dispelling the chill of my reaction to the isolation of the desolate cottage as I take a deep breath.

It's strange how easily one can be dragged back to a place of darkness. That's not where I am or who I am anymore. I've moved away from Porthcove and Fawndale, not just physically but mentally. I am no longer that man. And if there ever was a place for me to truly start believing that, it's here, at the edge of the world, at the commemoration of my father.

I think about what Samantha opened my eyes to today. This is my chance to accept and move on to another chapter, just as these island folk are demonstrating. There's a time to look back at the past with sombre introspection and another for thankfulness. I have mourned for my loss, but now might just be the time for me to start celebrating what was, and I can't think of any folk better than this lot to teach me just how to do that.

9

LOST AND FOUND

THISTLE ISLAND. EVENING.

As soon as I push open the sticky wood door to the community hall, the difference hits me like a slap in the face. The warm aroma of roasted meats and yeasty brews mingles with the hum of conversation and laughter. It's like stepping into a world alight with warmth and life, where the night's chill and my recent unnerving walk are instantly forgotten, replaced by the inviting embrace of a community in full swing.

The community hall is a rustic charmer, a far cry from its imposing exterior, dressed up for the occasion with strings of lights dangling from rafters and crisscrossing the stone walls, casting a warm, golden glow over the crowd and turning the simple space into something almost magical.

It's deceptively bigger than the frontage suggests, and I have no idea whether or not all the island's inhabitants are here tonight, but it certainly seems like it.

The clinking of cutlery draws my attention to a long table running the entire length of one wall, practically groaning with an eclectic mix of cellophane and silver foil-wrapped pots, pans, and dishes.

The sight makes my stomach rumble. When I glance down, I find Buddy looking up at me, licking his lips. "Don't you even think about it. You've had yours."

I packed a couple of rations of gourmet food and treats for the big guy intending to source more, if needed, when I got here, but Samantha brought some over with her food parcel earlier. When I gave her an equivocal look, she explained that it would otherwise go to waste.

Apparently, they had a dog called Rusty, but he's gone missing. Been over a week now. He was a senior, adopted from one of the older gents who passed away. Sam's theory is that he wandered off somewhere and didn't make it back. Luckily, they hadn't had him long enough for Luca to become too attached, but I guess that would explain his affinity with Buddy.

At one end of the room, elevated on a modest wooden stage, a group of locals, doubling as musicians for the night, command the room with a lively folk tune. A couple of basic spotlights, more warm than bright, hang above them, giving the musicians a soft halo that casts gentle shadows across their instruments.

A simple microphone stands before each chair, ready to carry the island's music to every ear. The musicians themselves, I imagine, are an ensemble of everyday faces transformed into the evening's stars. A fiddler, her bow dancing with precision; a flutist, his fingers moving in a blur; and a bodhran player, his beats the steady pulse driving the dance.

The dancers are an intergenerational tapestry, a little uncoordinated but full of joy as they appear to dance not for performance but for the sheer pleasure of it.

The room is buzzing with conversation, laughter, and the clink of glasses, a symphony of communal happiness.

And it would appear everybody has made an effort: dresses and ties, not in a formal, stuffy way, but respectful enough for the memory of the man who has everybody congregated here. This, of course, instantly makes me feel that I'm letting the side down with my jeans and black woollen jumper, but hey, I'm a tourist here. That's my excuse, and I'm sticking to it.

"Uncle Marco!" It's, well, I don't need to say who it is, as you will have guessed from that warm, smiley greeting.

My nephew has also dressed for the occasion. That mass of light brown hair that normally flops over those aquamarine curious eyes that belie his years has been tamed into a side comb, and he's wearing a shirt and tie.

He throws his arms around me like we haven't known each other for less than a day, and I tell you, that kind of love instantly thaws the ice that accumulated on my way over here.

I act casual, of course, because I don't want to seem overly familiar with a room full of people, but I close my eyes and lap up seconds like they are minutes as I am unavoidably reminded of the deliciously energising embrace of my little boy.

Of course, the moment is short-lived because, as always, I'm upstaged by the furry golden wonder at my heel. Buddy responds to Luca's affection in kind by licking him on the nose, prompting a fit of childlike giggles that are both a tonic for my soul... and a sharp reminder of what I've been missing – as if any were needed.

"Marco?" I watch a man in a tired grey suit walk up to me. "You made it. Welcome. Welcome. So wonderful to have you here." And it's weird because, for several seconds, I have no idea who this Cheshire Cat–grin of a man with small spectacles and thinning grey hair is. He sounds familiar and everything, but... then, just in time, I manage, "Reverend. I didn't recognise you out of your uniform," I say, shaking the man's hand.

"Oh, well, you know, even God resteth on that seventh day."

I nod, and then I'm just scrambling about for small talk material when I'm saved by the squealing sound of a microphone.

I look through the crowd to see that Samantha has taken to the stage. She's wearing a black midi dress with long sleeves that flows over her figure, highlighting her curves with a refined elegance. Her dark hair is styled fashionably, cascading around her face and over her shoulders, catching the light in a way that makes her eyes sparkle.

I have to admit, objectively and with all due respect to our familial ties, she looks stunning. There's an air of sophistication about her that seems to elevate her above the rest of the crowd. She commands the stage with a natural poise, as though she's born to be in the spotlight, perhaps even destined for office.

Beside her is that portrait of my father. In front of that is a small table with several glasses of alcohol. Obviously, an island thing.

"Ladies and gentlemen," my sister begins, leaning into the microphone. "If I could just have a moment of your time. I promise I won't keep you from the festivities for too long."

The room gradually falls silent.

"Today has definitely been an emotional day. For all of us, for many reasons. Not least the fact that we've all come together to remember a man whose laughter was as loud as the waves that crash against our shores, a man whose indomitable spirit was as unyielding as the stones of our beautiful island.

"My dad loved nothing more than a good knees-up, and I know he'd be over the moon to see each and every one of you here tonight, celebrating not just his life but the life of this incredible community.

"Five years ago, I stepped onto this island fresh from the city, and I'll admit, I was apprehensive. I expected isolation, long nights with no friends, no social life, and pretty much just the wind for company.

"But what I found here was something altogether different. From the very first day, you all welcomed me and my family with warmth and kindness. There was no adjustment period, no feeling of being an outsider. You made us one of your own.

"This island has a spirit, a heartbeat that you can't ignore. It's in the warmth of your smiles, the strength of your hands as you work, and the unbreakable bonds that we share. You've shown me that family isn't just about blood; it's about the connections we make, the support we give, and the love that we share with those around us.

"Tonight, as we stand together, we're not just neighbours, not just friends. We are one big, vibrant, and beautiful family. And I couldn't be prouder or more grateful to be a part of it.

"Like any family, we've had our share of troubles. When Thistle Loch closed down, it was a blow to us all. We lost jobs and that sense of purpose that comes from making something the world wants.

"And yet... this island, our people... we endured. We didn't just sit on our arses; we did what we always do, we adapted. We diversified. Our tourism industry is booming, drawing visitors from around the globe. And now, the notoriety that the dig is affording us is only going to increase that exponentially. And, of course, the prospect of this may concern some of us, but hey, it's a good problem to have."

My sister delivered that last line with a cock of the head and a smile that sends a ripple of laughter through the crowd. The room is captivated.

"... And that's not all. We've deployed remarkable technological advancements that have enabled us to transform what was once a rugged landscape into a beacon of green innovation. An achievement that didn't just power our homes; it set a global standard for how it's possible for communities to live in harmony with each other and the environment.

"And it's this hard work that has attracted not just tourists but major investors who want to work with us to nurture our beautiful island back to its former prosperity.

"So tonight, we're not just celebrating our past but also the visionaries who paved the way for our brighter, more prosperous future. Men like my father, Roberto Battista, who not only saw the potential in Thistle Island but also had the courage to dream big."

Samantha picks up one of the glasses from the table in front of the portrait, lifts it high, and says, "Here's to you, Pappa." Then turns to the rest of the room and shouts, "Here's to all of us!"

The room erupts into raucous cheers and applause, and naturally, I'm swept along by the infectious energy. I feel a twinge of pride for my sister, who, though I barely know her, has somehow – much like her little boy – managed to fix parts of me I didn't even realise were broken.

As the applause peters out, I watch the giant ginger policeman from the procession take to the stage. And by the way he's wearing that scowl and his neatly pressed uniform, I'd guess he isn't here to partake in the merriments.

He strolls over to the microphone and doesn't even have to speak for a hush to fall over the crowd. He leans in, holds out a giant hand towards Samantha, and growls, "Ladies and gentlemen, our mayor!" The applause instantly reignites, thunderous and loud.

Mayor?

The policeman waits with what I think are traces of a faint smile – at least I think it is, that or wind – for the villagers to express their adoration for their mayor before he leans into the microphone once more.

As the clapping calms, his eyes, sharp specks under the twinkling lights, sweep across the crowd before settling on the microphone once more. "I've got a wee announcement to make," he says, his voice as gruff as his appearance and his Scottish burr strong.

"First off, let's nae get too carried away wi' festivities, aye?" A murmur of laughter ripples through the room. "And secondly, just a wee reminder, the snow's comin' down thick, so please don't drink and drive," he adds, the corner of his mouth twitching into a wry smile. "We don't want any accidents, and I wouldn't want to turn this evenin' into a job for me, aye?" There are cheers and more laughter before the man nods and leaves the stage.

So I'm assuming that despite his imposing appearance, the local bobby actually has a sense of humour. If I remember correctly, Sam said that there were no vehicles on the island, so it's highly unlikely anybody's going to get into an accident.

The music has resumed with gusto, and since someone has conveniently distracted the reverend, I think now might be a good time to get a drink.

Now, as you know, I swore off booze a while back. No particular reason, you'll understand, except that I simply don't like the way it makes me feel. By that, I mean the hangovers that always barge in the next day and refuse to bloody leave. But tonight, well, tonight I feel like I could treat myself to a tipple. Maybe even partake in a glass of the local brew.

I'm considering this as I watch my sister make her way through the crowd, greeting and smiling at people before joining us. "So you got here okay?"

"Yes. No problem," I say, momentarily reminded of the trek over and dreading the journey back, only because you and I both know how suggestible I can be in the dark, and for good reason.

My sister nods, then turns to her son. "So what did you think of Mummy's speech?"

"It was awesome, Mum."

"Awesome? Really?" She says with a roll of the eyes. "I suppose that Americanism is better than nothing," she says, running fingers through her son's hair and then kissing him on the head, deliberately making him squirm.

And no, of course, I never did that to Toby.

"So mayor? I ask. Or is it mayoress?"

She smiles at me. "Mayor is just fine," she says.

"You kept that one quiet."

She shrugs, "With everything going on, it didn't seem that important."

I nod, absorbing her point. "Well, for what it's worth. It was a brilliant speech," I say as I feel heat suddenly rise to my face, thawing the numbness in my ears.

"Really?"

"Absolutely. It inspired me – and I don't even live here."

"Thanks," she says with a smile, her hand brushing my arm before she pauses, eyeing my empty hands. "You're not drinking?" Then, with a hesitant tilt of her head, she adds, "Oh, I'm sorry, do you... drink these days?" Her tone makes the word hang like it's a swear word or something. I keep forgetting that she knows more about me than I think, given that I decided to lay it all bare in a bloody book. See? Told you it was a bad idea. "Well, actually—"

"Of course, he drinks, Sam! He's a Battista, isn't he?" says a loud voice beside me. This is followed up with a heavy slap on my shoulder. It's Roberto Junior, in another stylish suit – though this one's likely blue, hard to tell in this light. But his tie has been loosened, hair dishevelled, face flushed. And those bleary eyes... I recognise that look all too well.

"Hi," he says, holding out a hand, "I don't believe we've been properly introduced. I'm Roberto Battista Junior, your *half*-brother."

It's weird. I haven't really heard this man talk before, but there's something about his Etonian pronunciation and the way he is making the very same distinction I did that puts me on guard.

I shake his hand. Even manufacture a smile.

"I just wanted to say sorry about before. I know I acted like a bit of a cock." Luca gasps and looks at his mum. "It wasn't on purpose. I was just broadsided, you know. On account of the fact that our sister, well, your half-sister, omitted to tell us she'd invited you up here to our little part of the world." His tone is loud, belligerent. "Isn't that right, Sis?" he asks, snaking a heavy arm around Samantha's neck.

My sister struggles to untangle herself while clearly trying to avoid drawing attention to us. "You're drunk, Rob," she hisses.

My half-brother laughs out loud. "Well, shit, Sis, nothing escapes you, does it?" He makes a show of thinking about his words, then adds, "Ah, well, actually, now that I think about it, some things do, though, don't they?" he says, giving her a knowing look.

My sister glares at him. I've no idea what that's about and don't want to know either. Just like I don't want to get into it with this prick. He's obviously drunk and looking to make trouble.

Shit. It suddenly feels hot in here, this coat suddenly much heavier, as I get a flashback of that night at Frost Lake Manor. I returned home at God knows what hour, after having a skinful, to find Sarah talking to her colleague. I behaved despicably.

And just like that, I feel like crap. Sarah, literally hundreds of miles away now because of me.

I casually pull at my jumper, releasing some of the trapped heat, then rub the back of my neck where it feels like the coat collar is cutting into me.

"Here you go," my half-brother says, handing me a pint of what looks like beer.

"No thanks. I'm okay," I say.

"Oh, go on," he says, thrusting the glass at me so fast that it spills over the side and onto Samantha's feet, causing her to yelp and leap backward.

"Oops," Junior says with an inebriated chuckle, putting an uncoordinated hand to his mouth while holding the glass aloft.

I glance at my sister, who is busy dabbing at her dress with a tissue, at the glass, and then at my brother, whose cheeks appear to be getting rosier by the second.

"No thanks," I repeat, flatly.

"What is it? Not feeling it? Something else, maybe? Jack Daniels, perhaps?" my half-brother adds with a knowing wink and a chuckle.

I look at Samantha, who meets my gaze. Has she been telling him about me? About my past?

The band is belting out a merry folk song, but I'm feeling anything but. Quite the opposite.

Growling draws my attention to Buddy, who's sidled up next to me, hackles raised, ears back. But I reach down and touch his back.

"What's this, then? Your support dog?" Junior sneers, eyes flicking between Buddy and me as another slosh of beer spills from his glass. "I've noticed he follows you everywhere."

Samantha steps forward. "Rob, stop it. You're drunk—"

Junior's grip tightens on her arm, cutting her off, eyes flashing with anger. "Don't tell me what to do," he hisses, leaning in closer. "Don't you ever tell me what to do again. Those days are gone, Sis. You made sure of that."

A bolt of anger shoots through me. "Let go of her," I order as quietly as I can, considering the din of the chatter and folk tune.

"Oh, isn't this sweet, Sam? Your handsome long-lost bro has ridden in on the ferry to save you."

"Let go of her," I repeat slowly through a clenched jaw.

My half-brother squares up to me. "Or what?" he demands, eyes bulging with hostility.

Samantha extricates herself from him, rubs her wrist, and says cheerfully, "It's fine. I'm fine. Really. I'm okay."

And yet, I appear to be locked in a stare-off with this belligerent prick. *Shit. Was I this bad?*

"Marco. Come on." I feel Samantha pulling at my arm, and it disarms me.

"No. No," Junior says quickly. "She's right. I'm sorry. I'm being a dick. Don't let me chase you off," he says, placing a hand on my arm. "Seriously, I'm sorry," he adds with a shake of his head. "Please. Let's just have a drink. Forget everything I said. I'm sorry. Okay. I'm sorry. Have a drink. Whatever you like. It's on me."

I glance at the hand on my arm and take a deep breath because, if I'm perfectly honest, I just want to deck this arsehole. But I know that will achieve nothing but embarrassing my sister, my nephew, and myself. He's too pissed to even care.

So instead, I want out of this place. I want out of here and to go home. I just want to go home. "I'm good. Thanks."

"What? You refusing to have a drink with your bro?"

"I don't drink anymore," I say, hoping he'll let it go.

"Oh, right, yeah. I'm sorry, mate. I'm sorry." I watch him smack his head. "It didn't even occur to me. I didn't realise. Sorry." And I think I've finally got through to him, but then he adds, "I get how booze must be a trigger for you now."

I feel the tension in my shoulders tighten. "What do you mean?"

"You know... after what happened."

"What happened?"

"Yeah... your son."

My gut churns. *Toby.*

"Rob...." I hear Samantha say as there are cheers from the other side of the room. Shoes scuffling. People dancing. All oblivious to what's taking place over here.

"You don't know what you're talking about," I utter.

"Oh, I'm sorry. Was I misinformed? I thought that's how your son, what was his name... uh... Toby. I thought that's how he died – because you were, you know...." He doesn't finish the sentence. He doesn't need to. Instead, he looks at Samantha with confusion, as if seeking clarification from her.

God help me, I don't even think. I lunge forward, grab the man by the collar, and start shaking him, his head jolting back and forth like a ragdoll. The attack is ferocious, primal as I scream into his face, "DON'T SAY HIS NAME! DON'T YOU EVER SAY HIS FUCKING NAME! YOU HEAR ME? IF I EVER HEAR YOU SAY HIS NAME AGAIN, I'LL FUCKING KILL YOU!"

There are gasps all around as drinking glasses are knocked out of hands, and a bottle smashes loudly on the floor. Then the chatter in the room, like an auditory Mexican wave, dies down. Seconds later, the music falls out of tune and to a stop.

"MARCO!" It's Samantha. Her voice is loud, desperate, and way past discretion.

I hold my brother, muscles taut, jaw flexing, and look into his glassy eyes where I expect to see fear, bewilderment, anything. But there's nothing. It's vacant but for a lazy half-smile.

He wanted this. He wanted me to revert to type, to appear unhinged. And I just played right into his hands.

I remain that way for several seconds, hot breath flaring in and out of my nostrils until I become aware of the hushed voices growing and reverberating around me.

Eventually, I release the stranger who is my half-brother, and under what must be the gaze of the entire village, I call to Buddy.

I turn and make for the exit when I hear him shout after me, "Tough talk for someone who spent the best part of three months in a mental institution paid for by the wife he murdered!"

Oh, fuck. And that's it. Suddenly, that familiar red veil falls over my eyes, and I can see nothing else but the need to feed the beast that is my dark passenger.

I turn back, and in just a few strides, I am grabbing my half-brother by the scruff of his neck once more with my left hand while slamming my right fist into his nose. The first time, there's a sickening yet familiar crack of cartilage. The second, I land while letting go.

The impact catapults Roberto Junior into the same crowd of people who scatter, allowing him to crash to the floor in a heap, blood instantly leaking and pooling around him.

I watch him writhe and wail in pain, surrounded by gasps and more screams. And yet, I'm ready to go back for more. I want to sink my boot into his crotch and stomp on his ribs.

But just as I'm about to do so, my nephew steps in front of me, his eyes wide with fear. "Uncle Marco, please. Stop! Please, don't hurt my uncle!" he cries, tears streaming down his face.

"Marco, for God's sake...." Samantha says, stepping beside her son.

Movement behind her makes me look over to see Claudia, my stepmother, gaping at her stricken boy on the floor and then up at me. Her face is ashen, her eyes wide and nostrils flared with hate as she snarls, "You..." Just as it did many years before, her disdain burns through the red mist, leaving nothing behind but my shame.

I look at my nephew crying into my sister's side and then at my sister. "I'm sorry," I murmur before I turn and make for the exit once more.

But before I can reach the double doors, they fly open, admitting a flurry of snowflakes that dust the threshold with a ghostly white veil.

The cold bites into my exposed skin, a stark contrast to the heat still coursing through my veins.

The room, only moments ago filled with shocked murmurs, falls eerily silent, the previous clamour dying down as if sucked away by the freeze.

And there, framed by the swirling snow, stands a naked figure that seems almost otherworldly. A woman. Her bare skin, the colour of moonlight, is goose-bumped from the cold. She is shivering violently, teeth chattering, shoulders hunched, arms wrapped tightly around herself as if to hold together a body threatening to come apart. Snowflakes glint in her lanky brown hairlike jewels of ice.

For a disorienting moment, I think I'm hallucinating, but then she speaks, "Y…you're…all going to die here."

"Amy?" Samantha's voice cuts through the silence, not just incredulous but laced with a haunting mixture of hope and fear.

My sister's words break the trance. I rush over, quickly shrugging off my coat to wrap it around the shivering stranger as she collapses into me.

10

FROSTNIP

THISTLE ISLAND INFIRMARY. EVENING.

I can't say I'm a fan of Thistle Island's ban on combustion engine vehicles because it meant I had to half escort, half carry the naked stranger across precarious ice patches to the infirmary, which is the best part of a ten-minute walk from the community hall.

On the bright side, the snow dump is on a break, leaving behind just the occasional flurry and that restless wind-turned-artist that is now building ice sculptures across the land. I'm reliably informed that this interlude is going to last for a day or so, which is great because, for a shocking moment, I had visions of us being marooned on this rock for a second more than necessary, and, you'll appreciate, I'm eager to get Buddy and me away from here as soon as possible.

I know that sounds selfish, but, well, you saw what happened back there. This whole family thing, I'm no good at it. Not to mention my whole trying to focus on a new calmer, quieter life. So far, I've decked my half-brother, reinforced my stepmother's loathing, terrorised my nephew, and alienated the indigenous population of an entire island. And that's omitting the whole naked-woman-wandering-around-in-sub-zero-temperatures thing.

Yeah. I think it's fair to say that this is a whole new level of drama, even for me. That ferry can't get here soon enough.

In the meantime, I barged through the infirmary doors as if it were my life that depended on it, prompting automated lights to flicker to life.

The place was desolate but warm, and we'd barely arrived when an officious-looking woman clutching a white coat emerged from one of the back doors. She and the pungent scent of hand sanitiser led us down a short corridor to a small ward.

The space is functional, with four beds lined up against one wall, each meticulously made with crisp white linen. I lifted Amy onto one of them. A nurse instantly wrapped her in a silver blanket while the officious-looking doctor ordered us to wait outside in the hallway.

That was about half an hour ago. I've been considering leaving ever since, as I want to get back to Buddy, who was hastily entrusted to Luca. I'm not used to being separated from the big guy, and I don't like it. But it feels awkward abandoning Samantha here, as silly as that might seem.

Now, all three of us – the Sasquatch cop from the party, Samantha, and I – are waiting in the corridor, watching the doctor perform her examination through the observation glass.

The doctor dims the lights to where we can barely make out the skeletal feature of the bed and the patient sitting on it with her back to us, as if staring out of the window to the blackness beyond.

"So who is she?" I find myself asking.

Samantha – who's standing with arms folded – doesn't turn but says, "She is my husband's research assistant."

"Research assistant?" I echo, although I heard my sister perfectly clearly.

"She went missing a few days ago with Ewan. Didn't she, Sarge? When they ran off together." She's addressing the giant cop with the serious ginger beard and frowny face who, I assume, has that nickname on account of the fact that he has stripes on the arms of his uniform jacket.

"Now, hold on a minute, Sam—" the man begins to protest.

"That's what you said, isn't it?"

"No. I said—"

"You suggested that they were fucking. You know, when you highlighted how they'd both disappeared at exactly the same time."

"No. No. Sam, you know it wasnae like that."

"Wasn't it?" my sister clips, turning to the man. And I'm on the other side of her, so I can't see her face, but by the tone of her voice, I can reasonably assume she's glaring at him. And if it's anything like my glare, it's probably a bit scary. Or so I'm told. "You all just assumed that because we'd had a few arguments, he decided to abandon his marriage and his child to run off like a love-stricken teenager."

"Sam, maybe we should talk about this later," the man says, his gruff voice clearly restrained as he eyes me, probably gawping with my mouth open since this is all news to me.

"Why? You ashamed to talk about it now? My brother's heard worse," she says, turning back to the glass.

I try to follow her gaze, but the man seems to have locked on me. I could be wrong here – maybe it's just a trick of the light – but those lines etched on his face, which I doubt are from laughing, appear to have deepened. And yeah, especially after my altercation with Junior, I'm pretty sure he wants to murder me. There. I said it.

Silence follows but for the moan of the wind outside as it tries to squeeze its way through a gap under the door and the muffled beep of the heart monitor in the room beyond the glass.

And so, remember what I was saying about awkward before? Yeah, just a little worse now. And the atmosphere much frostier than I first thought.

Thankfully, the haughty-looking doctor with bobbed hair makes her way out of the medical room and into the corridor with us, the door sucking itself shut behind her. She glances up, "Family outing, Allistair?" She asks but doesn't wait for a response. Instead, she scribbles on a clipboard she's holding as if we aren't all standing here, eagerly awaiting her report.

I realise now that she, too, doesn't sound like a local but one of those posh birds from my neck of the woods, knocking on her sixties, maybe, with no time for anybody's shit.

Her comment hangs in the air, and I'm not sure whether to chuckle or roll my eyes. It's a bizarre gathering, all things considered. The contrast between us is obvious, like characters from different stories forced onto the same page.

The policeman ignores her remark, sighs impatiently. "And?" he presses, irritably.

"And... she seems alright. Mild frostnip. Some dehydration. A touch of hypothermia and hypersensitivity to light," the woman says, continuing her scribbling.

"Has she said anything?" Samantha asks eagerly.

"No," the doctor says.

"What, nothing at all?" the cop asks.

"That's what 'no' means, Allistair," the doctor quips, frowning at him like he just asked a stupid question.

The cop rolls his eyes again. "So can ah have a word with her?"

"You can try," the doctor suggests.

"What does that mean?"

"She's clearly been through something traumatic. You said you found her wandering the high street, naked?" she asks, although it takes me a few seconds to register that the question's directed at me.

"I, um, well... not exactly wandering—"

"She showed up at the community hall like that," the policeman interrupts, impatiently.

"What do you think happened to her?" Samantha asks. "To traumatise her?"

"I've no idea. I'm not a psychologist," the doctor responds flatly while scribbling more notes.

The cop shifts his weight and sighs deeply. "Great."

"Marco is," Samantha declares, turning everyone's attention to me.

I smile at her before promptly performing a double take. "Wait.... What?"

"Are you?" the cop demands, hooking giant thumbs into his belt, eyes roving over me as if truth-detecting whatever my response might be.

"Well, I um—"

"Um's not a bloody answer. Are ya or not?" the cop demands.

"I am. I'm just—"

"Great. Then ya best get in there," he says bluntly. "We need to know where she's been."

My heart thumps a protestation, prompting me to verbalise it. "Now hold on... this... that... this isn't why I'm here."

"Then why are ya here?" the man asks, stepping forward, eyes wide, big hands still resting on that belt like he's John Wayne squaring up for a bloody duel. "Just to cause trouble?"

I'm instantly treated to a replay of what happened at the community hall and the image of my nephew's distraught face.

Shit.

The burn of shame melts the chill from my cheeks. I feel like walking out. Not in a petulant, flouncy kind of way, you'll understand, but in a definitive fuck-you manner. I didn't sign up for this. Actually, now that I think about it, I didn't sign up for anything. It seems my sister has taken care of all that for me.

I look at the cop and then back at Samantha again. She doesn't speak, but she doesn't need to. Her wide eyes and wringing hands tell me everything I need to know. My sister is worried, and I suspect it may have something to do with the fact that this woman is believed to have run off with her husband – all evidence to the contrary.

Don't get involved, my instinct tells me. Yet, this is precisely what I've trained for. I have a duty, both ethical and personal. This woman may have vital information about a major development – my sister's missing husband. He could be lying in a ditch somewhere, taking his last breaths while I stand here, torn with indecision.

And yet my heart disagrees; it's still thudding in my chest, urging me to leave.

"... Remember, we need to know where she's been and what she knows about Ewan's disappearance," the cop is briefing.

I gaze through the glass at the silhouette of the woman. Then I look at Samantha. Any reservations I might be harbouring are immediately nullified by the now desperate look in her eyes. I recognise that look. I'm no stranger to loss. I still feel it now, clinging to me like the cold in this corridor.

Sasquatch is still talking, but his words are just background noise as I push open the heavy glass door and step inside before the thing pulls itself shut with a loud hiss.

It smells in here. Antiseptic and something else. It's bittersweet. Tangy, like overripe apples, only not as appealing. More like grass that's been left to compost.

"Amy?"

I watch the shape on the bed. It remains perfectly still. Quiet but for the mesmerising beep of the heart monitor.

"Amy? My name is Marco. Is it okay if I speak with you?"

Beep. Beep. Beep.

I look over my shoulder at the eager faces illuminated beyond the glass and instantly know how it feels to be a bloody lab rat.

I take a deep breath, roll my shoulders, and turn back to the shape on the bed, half expecting her to have turned around and be staring at me like something out of one of those bloody horror movies I now actively avoid – you and I both know why.

She isn't. The patient, now my patient, is exactly where she was the moment we arrived here. And that alone is ratcheting up my anxiety.

Most conscious people will shift their weight from time to time. Not so here. This person keeps her back turned to me and is still seemingly looking out of that window at the darkness, as if she can see something out there.

I move forward, eager to make eye contact with her. Much of the therapeutic process is about words and body language. The absence of both is disconcerting, but this isn't my first rodeo, despite feeling as if it were, and even I don't know why.

I step around the patient, making sure to give her a wide berth, as I don't want to crowd her.

Her hair is hanging loosely around her shoulders, falling onto the hospital gown she's wearing. She has angular cheekbones that reflect the light, making me think she might actually be sweating despite the relative coolness of the room. Her eyes, almost black in this light, are deeply set, as if she's been malnourished for some time, but doesn't sound like she's been missing for that long.

"Amy?" I move in front of her, enough to be in her peripheral vision but not too much to crowd her. I can see part of her face now; the rest is steeped in shadow. It doesn't look like she's wearing any makeup. Her skin has a waxy hue to it, yet despite the unflattering light, she's still pretty in a natural kind of way. She's young, late twenties, maybe.

Now that I'm closer, I can hear her deep and steady breathing, a rhythm normally associated with deep relaxation or sleep. Together with the monitor's beep, it's almost hypnotic, contrasting with the howling wind outside that seems to resent our presence here.

"Amy?" I call again, and this time, her head turns towards me. My heart skips a beat. "Amy? Can you hear me?" I repeat.

Encouraged, I hastily yet carefully pull up a chair and sit so that I am no longer towering over her. It's shorter than I'd like, which means she's now looking down on me, but it'll do.

"Hello," she says, her voice hoarse, but at least she's actually smiling at me now.

"How are you feeling?" I ask warmly.

She thinks about this and nods. Then, holds a hand to her chest and whispers, "S… sore."

"Would you like some water?"

She nods. So I move over to the bedside table where there's a jug and a couple of drinking glasses. I fill one and hand it to her. She downs it in a couple of gulps, so I refill it two more times, glancing up at the doctor who is still observing from behind the glass.

Eventually, the patient sighs and coughs a few times before looking around the dimly lit room and asking, "What happened? What am I doing in here?"

"You don't remember?"

She looks at me and shakes her head.

Well, at this stage, I don't have a clue. So I improvise based on what I've overheard so far. "We think you were in the dome with, um... Ewan. Do you remember?" She nods, which I think is positive. "Great. Can you tell me anything about what you were doing?" I ask but instantly regret the question because I don't know if Amy even realises she has an audience out in the corridor and that in it is my sister, the wife of her colleague.

Adding to the tension, the patient seems to ponder my question before turning back to the window. I instinctively follow her gaze, but I can't see anything but blackness beyond the glass.

"Amy?" I nudge, but she doesn't respond. "Amy?" Still nothing, so I touch her arm, and it startles her. "Amy... sorry. You became distracted. Can you tell me what distracted you?" She stares at me as if finally realising I'm the stranger here.

For a second, I dread her reaction, but she suddenly smiles and says, "We were analysing samples."

"Samples?" I ask, cocking my head.

"Yes. The samples from the ledge."

"The ledge?"

"Yeah. We—" she interrupts herself with a violent coughing fit, and I don't know what I can do for her, so I react instinctively and fetch more water.

I fill her glass; she takes a sip, calms down a bit, and then coughs once more, violent bouts in between spasmodic retching. Her eyes are bulging now, tears running in rivulets from the shadow of her face into the light.

The beep of the heart monitor speeds up, too, shrieking louder, shattering the quiet, and raking at my anxiety. "Amy? Amy?"

I look up at the glass partition, expecting the doctor to enter, but she doesn't. When I turn back to Amy, she's gulping water once more. Urgently, desperately, the water dribbling down her chin and onto her gown.

I jump to my feet. "Amy? Are you alright? Are you okay? Amy?" She nods while gulping more water as the beep of the monitor begins to slow. "Are you sure?" She nods again. "Okay," I say, looking over her shoulder and scowling at the doctor, who continues to watch from behind the glass.

I give the patient a minute to recompose herself, then hand her a paper towel from the bedside table. "Everything okay?" She nods, dabbing at her chin and face. "Some cough, eh?" I smile.

Another nod.

"Okay," I say, stalling for time.

My instinct is to ask more questions, but I sense that the woman could use some recuperation time, so I'm about to suggest that when I hear her rasp, "W... w…work."

"Work?"

"W...work," she points at the window.

"You? Do you mean you?"

She nods. "Ewan... w...waiting."

"Ewan? He's waiting for you where? At work?"

"Lunch break... is over."

I frown and glance up at the others, who remain unmoving beyond the glass before I turn back to the patient. "You're not on your lunch break, Amy," I say gently. She nods. I shake my head. "No. It's evening, and you're in the infirmary." She observes me for several seconds before shaking her head. "It's true. You haven't been on your lunch break, Amy. You've been missing... for at least a couple of days." I've no idea how accurate that is, but it's going to have to do for now.

There's genuine stupefaction in the woman's eyes that I can see are wide open and dark. Black, in fact. At first, I thought it was just a trick of the light, but it isn't. From what I can tell, her irises are devoid of colour, pupils abnormally dilated and unresponsive to light, which would explain her confusion. She's obviously under the influence of some kind of toxin.

Shit.

I turn to the glass once more when the patient has another coughing fit. At first, she simply puts her hand in front of her mouth as she waits for it to subside. When it doesn't, she tries to drink more water but is unable to because her hand is jittering all over as if she's lost all control of her faculties. So I move to help her, but just as I do, she jerks the glass towards her mouth, smacking it into her teeth. The clink is loud but nothing compared to the violent coughing fit that follows. It's then that I realise that the glass has actually broken, cutting her mouth. Dark crimson blood instantly mixes with the water in the glass, the vision panicking the girl into spilling most of the contents over herself.

I hear a click, then footsteps rushing towards us, but I don't look up. I can't. I'm transfixed by what I think I see in what's left of the glass shaking in her grasp. It's so revolting that for a split second, I think I might be trapped in one of my waking nightmares. But no, this isn't a dream. It's reality. And in this reality, I'm sure I just saw something wriggling inside that glass. Strands of something long and white. But that can't be. Can it?

I stare at the glass, heart pounding, monitor beeping frantically as I watch the thing slip from the girl's hands and smash to the floor. I barely get a look at it when Amy convulses in her upright position, as if something were violently shaking her from the inside. Suddenly, I feel hands pushing me backward, and the doctor yells, "HELP! WE NEED SOME HELP IN HERE!"

My line. That's my line!

I feel a vice-like grip on my arm so forceful I yelp.

Looking down, I see Amy, eyes wide, teeth clenched like she's being shocked by something, as her body shakes violently, causing me to shake with her.

Then I'm screaming in pain as I feel fingers digging into my arm. The cops surround me, the younger of the two attempting to pry her pincer-like fingers from my arm as the doctor tries to get the girl to lie back onto the bed.

Eventually, eyes watering in agony, the grip is released. Amy thuds back onto the bed, and I'm thrown to the chair as the doctor and nurse fuss around her. More convulsions follow agonised wails from Amy as her body arches, lifting and falling from the bed before the room descends into absolute chaos.

11

THE PERMAFROST

THISTLE ISLAND INFIRMARY. LATE EVENING.

An hour or so must pass before we're all convened in what can only be described as the infirmary's multipurpose room. The space is equipped with medical supplies and a makeshift kitchenette alongside a long table and chairs. It's a utilitarian room with walls painted a sterile shade of cream, devoid of decoration. The scuffed plain table is littered with a couple of notepads and coffee cups in various stages of neglect.

A whiteboard streaked with the ghosts of past meetings stands at the foot of the table as if we're all here to attend one of those quarterly sales meetings. Beyond the board, a large rectangular window punctuates one wall, framing a nocturnal view of Thistle Island's moonlit snowscape. In any other circumstance, I'd be awestruck, but not tonight. Tonight, that view is nothing but a silent testament to the isolation that enfolds us out here, perched on the edge of the world.

I am seated on one of the chairs that looks like it's been scavenged from a different decade, wedged between the two coppers, the younger of which I've learned goes by the name of Eric. He is still looking a little pale.

The doctor, who is sitting opposite me and next to Samantha, looked at my arm, by the way. She told me it was bruising but that I'd live. Someone really needs to have a word with her about her bedside manner.

There's a long pause upstaged by that haunting howl of the arctic gale. It's like a bloody beast locked out in the cold, reminding us of the wildness surrounding our little bubble of light and supposed safety.

"Can I ask a question?" Yes, it's me breaking the silence. And I don't wait for an answer. "Amy said that they were analysing samples at the ledge or on the ledge. What did she mean by that?"

"She's obviously mistaken," Sasquatch, or Sarge, says dismissively. Personally, I prefer my nickname.

"Mistaken?" I retort. "She seemed pretty lucid to me."

"Who are you again?" he asks with an irritated scowl, as one might when there's an annoying fly buzzing around the room.

As you'd expect, that sends a flare of irritation burning through me. "I'm the psychologist you were happy to push in there to talk to her, remember?"

Obviously sensing the tension, Samantha jumps in. "What Sarge means, Marco, is that it's unlikely that Amy and" she takes a breath here, "... that Amy and Ewan were analysing samples from the ledge because that area has been designated off-limits."

I cock my head, curious.

Samantha continues. "Last year, a group of hikers made a discovery on *Creag-Thriste*, or Thistle Peak. The climb is popular with tourists. It's a bit like Wales' Snowdon, only smaller.

"There are clear paths up and around the peak, but these hikers were experienced. They decided to go off the beaten track at a section of the spire known as the ledge due to the natural shape of the plateau. This section, because of its height and the fact that it generally goes undisturbed, is often covered in snow and a delicate layer of permafrost.

"Anyway, these guys decided that they were going to abseil down to the ledge. One of them takes a tumble and nearly falls to his death. Thankfully, he doesn't. What he does, though, is dislodge sections of the protrusion that we believe were weakened by the gradual thawing of the permafrost, and he made a discovery.

"The protrusion turned out to be a spear of Norse origin frozen into the ice wall. Dated around one thousand years ago. The hikers reported their find, expecting a reward. The Treasure Trove Unit sent people, which resulted in an official dig and an actual treasure trove of ancient artefacts.

"The site made the news and was instantly deemed to be of significant historic importance. Great for tourism but not so great for the island.

"The area has since been designated off-limits both to visitors and islanders. Which is why it's highly unlikely that anybody would have been conducting any research there," my sister says, sitting back in her chair.

I take a few seconds to consider what I've just learned, which, by the way, I think is quite impressive. And yet I still find myself asking, "So why would she say that?"

"Mental fog" is the doctor's contribution. "The girl had been wandering around in subzero temperatures."

I lean forward in my chair because, after what just happened in there, I'm in no mood to skirt around any sensitivities. "Look, people. I'm just a visitor here—"

"That's right, you are," the doctor agrees.

I glance at her but continue. "... And as such, I may have a somewhat different perspective on this. But it seems to me that when you have two people disappear, one of them still missing and no leads to speak of—"

"Now hold on—" Sarge begins.

But I plough on. "But no leads to speak of, then any lead is worth pursuing. I mean, for all we know, Ewan could be hurt and still out there," I say, tapping my finger on the table and sharing eye contact with each and every one of them, because I'm pissed off. They all seemed way too quick to dismiss what the girl said. And while we're on that subject. "Did you check what was in that glass?" I ask the doctor.

"What glass?" is her response.

I can feel my hackles rising but take a deep breath, "The glass of water. I told you that something fell. I saw it moving in there."

The doctor makes a show of turning to the young cop. "He says that there was something in the glass. Did you see anything in there?"

"Hey! I'm sitting right here," I snap.

"I'm sorry, do you have some kind of jurisdiction that I need to know about?" the doctor counters.

I squint at her and am about to ask what her problem is when Sarge jumps in. "Okay. There was nothing in the glass, Mr Battista." Sarge directs his statement at me, but I have only mentioned it to the doctor, which makes me think those two have been talking. "And as for the ledge, Battista is right. There's no harm in taking a wee look. We need to pursue any and all leads. So, we'll be taking a look at first light. In the meantime, I still want to talk to Amy. So, Doc, the moment she's awake, I want you to give us a call," he says. "In the meantime, I don't want tae unnecessary gossip, so keep everything you've seen and talked about here to yourselves, aye?" He ends that line by looking at me for some reason.

Cheeky shit.

12

DEPARTURE

TUESDAY

THISTLE ISLAND. EARLY MORNING.

The trek back to my cottage wasn't anywhere near as creepy as when I left. I suppose that's because my overactive imagination was preoccupied with other thoughts. Like, what the eff? Even for me, that was a whole other level of weird shit.

The best part was definitely coming back to my prehistoric cave, which I discovered is actually quite cosy – provided you don't let the stove die. Otherwise, you risk waking up in the middle of the night to find that your testicles have shrivelled to raisins. I couldn't be bothered to wrestle with it, so I just layered up instead and went back to bed.

Big mistake. I woke up in the middle of the night because, guess what? That's right, neurotic Marco Battista thought he heard something scratching at his door. And for one panicky moment, I thought I'd actually left Buddy outside. But then I wiggled my toes – numb, sure, but warm where the big guy had wedged himself.

At home, Buddy has his own bed, but I decided to let him share mine last night because, well, let's put it this way – if he'd slept on the freezing cold stone floor, there's a good chance the poor pup would've turned into his own archaeological dig.

Which is why when someone rapped on my door this morning – yeah, I thought those days were over, too – I was reluctant to leave my cocoon but eventually had no choice but to rise, dragging the quilt with me.

Buddy was not impressed and promptly jumped into my warm spot. "Yeah, thanks, mate."

When I pull the door, it sticks like it's frozen, but I'm more inclined to think it's because even this little place isn't keen on allowing the bloody cold inside. But I tug on the thing, and it eventually gives, revealing Samantha, dressed for the freeze in a puffer jacket, gloves, and woollen hat. She's holding two flask mugs and wearing a smile.

"Good morning," she says cheerily.

"Morning," I mumble from inside my quilted shroud. I'm returning the smile, but it must seem more like a grimace because I can't help but squint at the glare of the morning sunshine on snow. It's bright out there and cold... so fucking cold!

Yeah. I have both Dolce Vita and Frost Lake Manor to thank for this sensitivity. A shiver ripples through me – I've no idea if it's the cold or just the thought of those places. Probably both.

I step aside.

"Don't tell me," Samantha says. "You let your fire die."

"Um," I make a show of thinking about it, but she's already looking at the dead, cold, traitorous thing.

"Number one rule," she says brightly.

"Yeah. Probably information I could have used yesterday."

"It's in the welcome pack," she says with a wink.

I give her a pointed look while taking a mug from her. "Thanks."

"Hot chocolate," she says, "the cure for everything."

I smile as I'm reminded of Sarah. "Not quite everything," I say gently, taking a seat on the couch.

I watch a cloud drift over my sister's sunny disposition. She nods and takes a seat in the armchair opposite.

"Why didn't you tell me about Ewan?" I ask.

"Why? What was the point? What could you have done about it?"

"It's not necessarily about what I could have done, but more about... I don't know... I would have been a bit more sympathetic. Less of a dick."

She laughs. "You've been just fine. I didn't invite you here to get you embroiled in all our drama."

I make a pained face. "I was talking more about what happened at the community hall last night."

"I know what you were talking about. But don't you think rescuing a naked woman trumps kicking the shit out of the brother you've never met?" she asks with a wry smile.

Ugh. She has a point, but all I can do is groan and hang my head at the mental replay of that before pushing it aside. "How is she? Amy. Any news?"

"No change, apparently. She's stable but not talking again. Sarge was in there first thing this morning. Thanks for yesterday, by the way. For what you did. I know I put you on the spot."

I nod. "I'm just sorry I couldn't help more."

"Oh, no, you helped. You really did. I just wish you could stay longer." I try not to read into that as I watch her fiddle with the lid on her mug while avoiding eye contact before quickly changing the subject, "Sarge was planning to go out to the ledge. You know, take a look, but with this new front coming in..."

"Front?"

"Yes. More snow. Heavier."

"Shit. Heavier? How bad, exactly, does it get out here?"

She rocks her head. "Bad is a relative term, but we can get cut off for weeks sometimes."

I swallow. The chocolate is hot. Tastes good, but the idea of being stuck out here for that long doesn't. "Weeks?"

"Yes. It's not a problem, though. We're well-provisioned. It's standard practice this time of year, and the ferry'll be bringing more supplies today," she says confidently. Something that, for some reason, reminds me she's the mayor of this island, the one keeping the place running, and I feel a twinge of pride. I've no idea where it came from, but I must have a look on my face because she asks, "What?"

I think about saying something but chicken out by taking another sip from my mug. "This is good," I say.

"Told you."

There's a pause. Crows caw somewhere on the roof. Seagulls respond.

"How's Luca this morning?"

"He's fine. Of course, he wants to come and say goodbye. I told him he can come and see you off at the dock."

"I'm surprised he wants to have anything to do with me after last night. Again, I'm sorry – not exactly a good role model."

"You're fine. He doesn't hold grudges, my son. Unlike Rob," she adds with a raised eyebrow.

"Ugh. How's he doing?"

"Nursing his wounds... pride mostly," she says, lips curled up at the corners. She's obviously enjoying this. Me? Not as much, as odd as that might seem. I hate losing control like that. It reminds me of the person I used to be. And while I may miss that bloke's unbridled approach to things sometimes, I know I'm much better without him.

I sigh. "So no Christmas card this year?" I ask.

She makes an exaggerated pained face before turning it into a smile. Then there's another pause as we both drink from our mugs.

"So I'm assuming Luca doesn't know about his dad? That he's missing, that is."

My sister shakes her head. "Up until yesterday, I suspected he'd run off with Amy. It wouldn't have been the first time," she adds, taking a sip from her mug.

Shit.

I feel like I should say something, but she heads me off with, "I've no idea what I'm going to tell him. He just thinks his dad's away at a conference."

"So what happens now?"

"I've called the mainland. They're sending someone."

"How does Sarge feel about that? I'm assuming he's the chief of police here?"

"Yes. Although, technically, you could say I am."

I lift an eyebrow and air toast her with my mug.

She forces a smile, but there's obviously much more to this. Hurt. Pain of sorts, but I'm reluctant to solicit anything that she isn't offering because I'm leaving today, and I don't want to stir up stuff that I'm not going to be around to support her with. That, and from what I can tell, she isn't particularly keen to discuss it. Remind you of someone?

And yet, "You must be worried," I say.

"Oh, well, you know. I spent the last few days coming to terms with the fact that my husband was cheating again, and that felt like the end of the world. But now, I realise that compared to Luca losing his father, it wasn't. Isn't. Shit!" she says, pushing her hat off her head and her hair off her face.

"Well, it's still early days," I offer feebly.

She looks at me in that way people do when they know you mean well. Or she's just thinking, What? And you call yourself a therapist?

"Please don't say anything to Luca," she adds quickly.

"No. Of course not," I say as I watch my sister drink from her cup while wishing I could fix this for her. "He's a great little man." Toby. "Smart. You must be proud."

"We are," she says, a smile blossoming on her face once more. "Anyway," she adds, snapping out of the thought. "You best get ready if you don't want to end up stranded here with us."

I groan inwardly at the thought of emerging from my synthetic chrysalis. That's until I consider the thought of being stranded out here a la Dolce Vita for God knows how long. And it's that thought that propels me off the chair and into the bedroom.

Half an hour later, we emerge into glorious sunshine. It's a beautiful day, punctuated by the call of seagulls. The crunch of snow underfoot cuts through the quiet as the morning's freshness pricks at my cheeks. It's that kind of cold that's more invigorating than biting, the kind that wakes up every sleeping cell in your body with a kiss of life.

My breath hangs in the air, a visible testament to the chill, as I gape at the spectacular view of the snow-covered wilderness and mountain. "This is incredible," I breathe, the scents of the island filling my lungs – that clean, sharp tang of snow mixing with the earthy aroma of pine and the distant sea. There's a rawness to it, something primal and untouched that I haven't experienced anywhere else. Gazing at the reflection of the pale blue sky in the calm mirror of the ocean, I utter, "It's moments like these that make me feel so insignificant."

My sister grins knowingly. "I felt exactly the same when we first moved out here – and still do."

I sling my hold-all over my shoulder before we slowly and carefully pick our way along the snowy track back to the village and dock. Buddy, on the other hand, appears to have abandoned all caution and is trotting ahead, seemingly impervious to the cold.

The island is already in full swing, not unlike when I first arrived here. And if I'm perfectly honest, there's something melancholic about the fact that life will go on at Thistle Island without us as we make our way home.

The snow's dusting is like confectioner's sugar over the rough wooden planks of the dock, and the sun, low and bold in the sky, throws long shadows that reach out like the morning itself stretching awake.

Buddy's breath puffs out in rhythmic clouds as he pants, excited by the bustle of the few locals gathered here. Samantha's alongside me, her eyes scanning the horizon where the ferry's cutting through the calm waters, right on schedule. It's not the crowd you'd expect for a mid-morning ferry – just a smattering of folk – but each one's presence feels like a story, a piece of the island's heartbeat.

I place my bag on a bench and watch the ferry approach. I'm just a visitor here, but I already feel like I have a good sense of the anticipation a boat must bring to a small dock like this. It's their lifeline, their connection to a world beyond this snow-covered sanctuary.

An old gentleman, wrapped in a heavy coat and woollen hat, stands beside a trolley brimming with boxes. Around him, several younger men lean on empty trolleys, chatting. Nearby, a mother and her young son greet the approaching ferry with waves as if welcoming a long-lost relative. And there are other assorted individuals gathered here. Each offers a warm greeting to Samantha and, by association, me, like they haven't seen us for weeks.

Nobody mentions the naked girl. It's as if it never happened. There isn't a hesitant look nor a roundabout question. The focus of conversation is the wonderful memorial, the celebration, and the day ahead. Something that I find both admirable and odd.

As the ferry drifts closer, I can't help but wonder what it's bringing in today, aside from the mail and chocolate. What stories, what news from afar? It's a daily gamble, a lucky dip into the larger world beyond these shores. And here the islanders stand, ready to claim their share of whatever it brings.

"Mum! Uncle Marco!" It's Luca, obviously, and we both turn to see him hurry to us, slipping and sliding as he goes, although judging by the grin on his face, I think most of that is for fun.

"LUCA! Don't run, Luca! Walk!" my sister yells. "WALK!" Buddy barks enthusiastically, but somehow, I don't think he's agreeing with her.

"Buddy!" my nephew calls, making a beeline for the big fella who bounds over to him, paws crunching in the snow. The two greet each other excitedly, and I won't lie – it's a sight that warms my heart.

Toby. Of course. There's never a missed opportunity to be reminded of my little boy.

The ferry's horn blares, echoing off nearby buildings – a distraction everyone seems to welcome.

The trolley men move forward. Water churns. Seagulls wheel overhead, their cries as bright as the sunlight on the water.

"Good morning, Uncle Marco," Luca says, going over to his mother and throwing his arms around her.

"Ooh... that's a strong hug. What's this in aid of?"

"Good morning, mate," I say, heart aching. My nephew is avoiding eye contact, which, based on what I've seen so far, is unlike him. So my first thought is that he's now wary of me after last night, but when Sam makes a pained face at me, I realise, and my heart melts.

"So," I say, "Luca. Listen, I was wondering. You know, when the snows have passed, if you and Mummy might consider coming down to visit? I know it's quite a long train journey, but if you feel up to it, there's plenty of room at ANEW, and I know Buddy would love to see you," I say, rubbing the dog's ears and looking at Samantha, who smiles at me.

I hadn't mentioned a visit before. It hadn't even crossed my mind until just now.

Luca's head snaps around instantly. "Oh, that would be brilliant! Can we, Mum?"

"Of course," she says.

Buddy barks as if he's understood everything. My nephew abandons his mother to throw his arms around him.

Sam mouths a thank you at me. I step forward, "Seriously. Would be nice to see you both," I say earnestly.

My sister nods, and I can see that there's a sheen to her eyes now.

People walk past us, chatting animatedly while crewmen and villagers busy themselves unloading cargo from the ferry.

"Are you going to be okay?" I ask. It's a spontaneous question.

My sister shrugs, "Of course. All in a day's work," she says.

"No. I don't mean running this place. I know you've got that covered. I'm talking about the family." I nod up the hill towards the hotel. "I know you went out on a limb to get me here."

She scoffs. "This isn't the first time I've clashed with them. Trust me. I'm just glad you came. It's been really good to meet you finally after all these years. You know, see what all the fuss was about," she adds with a smile.

There's a loud metal grinding sound as a winch is retracted on the ferry. Then the horn sounds twice.

"You better go," my sister says, throwing her arms around me and squeezing me tight. It's a peculiar sensation, one that I probably wouldn't even have noticed a few years back.

When Ellie and I got together, she became family, and Toby – he solidified that. But when I lost them, well, I just thought it would be me and the big guy forever. But now, over the space of a day, I've realised that maybe I'm not as alone in this world as I thought.

Samantha's embrace is long. Needy. And I return it because... well, I might just be needy, too.

"I hope everything works itself out," I say feebly because we all know I'm crap at goodbyes.

My sister. Yes, sister, breaks the embrace, nods, and presses at her eyes.

I turn to Luca, "Do I get a hug?" My nephew looks at me, and for a second, I think he's going to comply, but instead, he buries his face in his mother's side.

"Oh, it's okay, mate. We'll see each other soon. I promise," I say, and then pause because I realise that I truly have no clue how to sign off on this visit that's been as enlightening as it's been emotional.

The ferry's horn slices through the moment, a deep, sonorous call that heralds my departure.

I make my way over to the gangway but pause when Buddy stops to look back – Samantha is standing to one side, a comforting arm around her son – and barks twice.

Luca looks over with tears in his eyes and waves. I wave back, a lump in my throat. It's time to board.

"Not helping," I mutter under my breath. Buddy looks up at me, and if dogs ever had accusatory eyes, these are his. He seems to blame me for leaving. Like I have a choice. Like I don't have a home to go to and a book to finish... I mean, start!

"Seriously? Get onto that ferry," I say, walking across the gangway over the bubbling water. Buddy – tail down – at my heel.

The ferry is much busier than I thought it would be. I can only assume that's because many people are leaving the island on account of the weather or maybe even for the winter. I didn't discuss that much with Samantha, even though we talked about a lot. We didn't, of course, talk about why I'm standing here at the back of the ship where it's freezing when I could go inside, nor why I'm thinking about everything but what's in front of me.

A tightness grows in my chest as I consider the fact that I'm leaving this stunning place and what little family I have. It feels like I'm abandoning them, even though that doesn't make any sense. They live here. I don't.

Shit.

I look down at Buddy as crewmen yell information to each other, the hydraulic whine of the ship filling the air. The hound is already looking at me expectantly. "What? Do you want to be stranded out here for God knows how long?"

The gangway is about to be retracted. A crewman in a grimy fluorescent jacket moves towards it with purpose. All I have to do is wait, and then this will all be out of my hands.

13

THE ISLANDERS

THISTLE ISLAND. MORNING.

From the gentle sway of the water, the island rises majestically, its silhouette a testament to nature's artistry. The mountain, caressed by the morning's first kiss of sunlight, stands watch over the island. Its slopes are swathed in a cloak of white, dappled with resilient green trees, its profile drifting into the sea, a mesmerising blend of colours. From the deck of the ferry, the view seems almost ethereal, as if the island and its mountain exist in a realm of their own, suspended between the sea's azure embrace and the vastness of the sky.

Now, as I watch the island recede into the distance—

Oh, who am I bloody kidding? I got off, didn't I? Having incurred the ire of the crew, I left the bloody ferry. Now, I'm standing on the pier, watching it shrink to a white speck on the horizon, leaving me to the sound of the sloshing water and a family of seagulls perched on the railing, chatting like they're laughing at me.

Well, I'd defy anybody not to stay after being exposed to Buddy's judgemental glare. Like I'm responsible for any of the shit that's happened here over the past twenty-four hours. As if I can do anything about it.

"I hope you're happy now," I admonish the hound, but he just yawns in my face.

"UNCLE MARCO!" Luca comes bounding up to us, his radiant smile competing with the sunshine. "You stayed!" he exclaims.

"Yay!" I say excitedly, half throwing my hands up because, well, you know, I'm conflicted.

I look over and see that Samantha appears to be deep in conversation with somebody wearing a black coat and scarlet beanie hat. They have their backs to me, so I can't see who it is. "Who's Mummy talking to?" I ask as we approach.

"Oh, that's the detective from the mainland," Luca says with suppressed excitement as he makes a fuss of Buddy. "Mum says they're investigating that woman from the party. The one with no clothes on."

I can't help but smile at my nephew's candid comment.

"Marco?" Samantha says, noticing me, her face a mixture of surprise and elation, "Marco... You stayed."

"I did," I say. "Thought I'd stick around, you know. Help out whichever way I can."

"You realise that—"

"I do," I interrupt. I don't want her to say it out loud because if she does, there's a good chance I might jump off that dock and try to catch up with the ferry.

We're stuck here now until the next ride, and if that Arctic weather front Samantha was talking about earlier hits, it could be weeks, maybe longer, before we get home.

Yeah. Shit.

My sister touches my arm and smiles broadly. Then, remembering the person standing with her, she gestures towards me. "Oh, I'm sorry. Detective, this is the psychologist currently assigned to this case, Marco Battista," she declares, gesturing to me, prompting the person with the crimson hat to turn.

And I'll admit it – I'm momentarily lost for words. The detective is striking. Her beauty isn't classic, but it's the kind that whispers secrets you'd strain to hear. Beneath her scarlet beanie, strands of chestnut hair, ablaze in the sunlight, try to escape. They frame her face until a gust of wind tosses them aside. That's when I see the welted scar, a jagged line from her right temple to her ear – stories untold, adding to her allure. There's a smattering of freckles over her nose and a slight upturn to the corners of her mouth – wry amusement mingled with a hint of seen-it-all defiance. Yet, it's her eyes... hazel with flecks of green like the sea on a stormy day... that hold me captive.

"Marco?" Samantha prompts because I must look like a fart in a trance right now – whatever that looks like.

"Yes. Sorry," I say, holding out a hand while conjuring a smile.

"This is Detective Isla Macintyre," Samantha narrates.

The detective wraps her warm, gloved hand around mine, "Marco? Is that right?" she asks. I nod. "I'll need a full assessment. Everything you know, I want to know, and I don't want to get into the whole privilege thing since it's my understanding that your initial assessment took place in an observation room, am I right?" She looks at Samantha, but the question's obviously rhetorical.

"Well, actually—" I begin.

"I really don't want this to turn into a whole thing, if that's okay. You'll appreciate we don't have much time," she says, glancing at Luca, which reminds me that her investigation isn't just about Amy but also Ewan. "This girl is a material witness," she adds as if she just read my mind.

"Okay," I counter. "But I have no idea what you mean by whole thing. I was just trying to say that I haven't had a chance to fully assess her yet."

"No? What's the holdup?"

"Hold up? I'm not even—"

"What Mr Battista is trying to say is that he hasn't had a chance to perform his initial assessment, but he'll be sure to keep you in the loop with any and all information that doesn't break privilege," Samantha skilfully interjects.

"Mornin' Mayor," intrudes a loud voice like a boxing match bell.

We all turn to look at a man who seems as much a part of the Highlands as the heather and hills themselves. In his battered overalls and with a sweat-stained cap pressed down over his brow, he carries the unmistakable aura of the land—tough, unyielding, yet inherently connected to the earth beneath his boots. His face, lined with the map of countless seasons, carries a no-nonsense look that speaks volumes of his life outdoors, battling the elements.

Yet, he has a spark in his eye that belies his appearance. And I get the feeling that he interrupted, not with rudeness, but with the directness of someone used to commanding attention, whether from man or animal.

"Good morning, Douglas," Samantha says.

"Mayor, sorry tae interrupt, but I've been ontae Sarge about ma flock. He wanted me to let him know when it happened again. It has. This is the third time just this week. I cannae afford to keep losing ma girls like this."

"I'm sorry, Douglas. Sarge's been a bit busy with—"

"What's the problem?" the detective interrupts.

Douglas eyes the stranger, and for a second, I think he's going to tell her to sling her hook, but instead, he starts sharing. "Well, it's ma flock. Sarge seems tae think it might be a wildcat, but I'm no' so sure."

"Show us," the detective says eagerly.

"Actually, it's probably best we let the chief of police deal with it," Samantha says.

"You are the chief of police, aren't you?" the detective challenges.

Samantha looks at the woman, and for a tense moment, I think she's going to give her one of those ole Battista slapdowns, but she doesn't. Instead, she nods. "But just so you know, it's on the other side of the island."

I'm looking forward to seeing the bolshy detective trek across the island, but my anticipation is cut short when I turn and see a Land Rover parked behind us. Samantha notices my surprise. "These Land Rovers are electric and mostly for residents who need to travel back and forth across the island," she explains.

"Well, you guys have a good time," I say, stepping back.

"Aren't you coming?" the detective asks.

"I wasn't planning to. Unless you think there may be some animals out there needing therapy?" I say with a raised eyebrow and a wry smile.

The detective doesn't respond. Instead, she heads to the back of the vehicle and opens the hatch like she owns it.

Tough crowd.

"Why don't you come?" Samantha asks. "You'll get to see another part of the island."

"I've still got my bag with me," I say, watching the detective dump hers in the back and shut the hatch. I glance at my sister, who smiles. "And what about Buddy and—"

"I'll take care of him!" my nephew jumps in.

"... and Luca?" I finish my sentence.

"We can wait at your cottage until you come back," Luca suggests.

"Well, you just have it all figured out, don't you?" I say with an overtly artificial smile.

My sister grins before handing her son the keys to my temporary home, then kisses him on the head. "Be careful," she says.

"We will. Come on, Buddy!" he calls before hurrying off. Buddy hesitates and turns to look back at me. "No, I'm not coming, mate. But you go. Take care of him." My dog complies, and I watch the two run off together.

Toby.

I feel a gentle hand on my arm. It's Samantha. She smiles at me. "Thanks for staying," she says.

"Of course."

And so, because I'm just a sheep going to see sheep, I mirror the detective's action, place my bag in the trunk of the vehicle, and then join her in the backseat while Samantha sits up front with Douglas, our driver.

With the silent stealth that only an electric vehicle can provide, we're off, whirring through the busy high street, past the community centre, up the gravel road, by the hotel, and towards the other side of the island.

It's a great day for it. A lovely sunny day to maroon yourself on an island for God knows how long. Although, if today's glorious sunshine is anything to go by, it's difficult to think anything about bad weather.

In fact, as we bump over the snowy track with the sparkling ocean to our right juxtaposed with the iridescent snow-covered hillside to our left, it's hard to even imagine bad weather. But as I've heard multiple times now, the climate up here is as temperamental and changeable as it is in the southwest.

Oh, home... It feels and is quite literally hundreds of miles away. To think that we could be on our way back now, riding the train to my sanctuary. It makes me feel both homesick and sad in equal measure.

I don't know what possessed me. Getting off that ferry was madness even for me, yet I don't blame anybody but one person, and you know who that is... Well, not me, of course, but Doctor Ethan Holmes. That bloke may have opened my mind to so much, but he has reduced me to this wimp of an emotional sap.

Alright... okay... so maybe not complete emotional goo. My mind very kindly just replayed the image of me trying to pummel the life out of the half-brother I'd never met before, but, well, you get the point.

"... published author," is all I hear when I tune into the conversation taking place around me. Samantha has turned in her seat.

"Sorry, what was that?" I ask.

"I was just telling the detective that you're both a therapist and author, Marco."

"Ah, right," is all I can say because, well, it's embarrassing. See? That's one good thing about not having family: there's nobody there to try to big you up to the first hapless person to stand still long enough to hear it.

"What about you, Detective? How did you draw the short straw to come out here?"

The detective looks at my sister like she asked her to get out and walk. Obviously, not one for small talk. So she surprises me when she says, "I grew up on one of the islands. For some reason, my boss thought that's experience enough to send me here," she says, turning to look out of the window.

Samantha and I exchange looks as we bump down the track, eventually crossing Airmed's bridge – where my sister and I went through our respective releasing rituals.

The journey seems much shorter today for obvious reasons, and before long, the rusted ruin of the abandoned fish processing plant comes into view. "What's going to happen to that?" I find myself asking.

"There are no specific plans at the moment, but it might get knocked down. Thistle Island is going through some major changes. As you know, the dig on the mountain has generated a lot of exposure. We have a few investors courting us with a range of exciting leisure projects for the island. This includes the sympathetic restoration of key areas. It's a very exciting time. If these people commit, it will restore the fortunes of our home. Transform the lives of many," the mayor says.

"Aren't you worried conservation might suffer?" I ask.

"Not really. We've conducted our own extensive research. Ewan has..." My sister's voice hitches in her throat as she's suddenly reminded why, exactly, the detective is here.

I feel for her. I've no idea what could have happened to him, which only makes me more determined to get answers from the patient at the infirmary. She's the only clue we have.

"... ecologist. He oversaw everything to do with the flora and fauna on the island and was consulted closely on any plans for development since he was already working on a study – life on the island and all that. This has been and always will be our top priority," my sister says like she's giving an election speech.

"And what did your husband think about your development plans?" the detective asks.

Samantha frowns. "He was all for it, of course."

"Was that his official position as an ecologist or as a resident of the island?"

"I don't know what you mean."

"What do the results of his study say?" the detective rephrases the question, no doubt picking up on the fact that my sister appears to be stalling.

"I wouldn't know. The study isn't finished yet."

"I'd like to see it."

"See what?"

"The study."

"I just told you it isn't finished."

"That's fine. I'm happy to read everything you have so far. Where is it now?"

Samantha thinks about this. "I've no idea. On his computer, I suppose."

"Great. We'll take a look on the way back."

We've passed the cemetery now, approaching the woods. As if that wasn't atmospheric enough, there's a thin mist over the road and windblown larches on either side of the track – like the Land Rover is about to enter Jurassic Park.

The change in light is distinct. The canopy is dense, and I don't know if it's my imagination, but it feels like the temperature shifts, too.

For a couple of minutes, we travel through this shadowed world. Then, as suddenly as we entered, we burst into dazzling sunshine. A breathtaking vista unfolds, revealing a vast, emerald hillside towering above us, dotted with countless white sheep – a peaceful contrast to the wild forest left behind. Yet another of those powerful, sparkling streams carves through the hillside, slicing through our path, then rushing down into a shallow valley toward the sea. There's a dark grey building down there, with pylons at its centre, encased by a high fence. I imagine this is the power station.

Wow.

Don't get me wrong, I still wouldn't swap home for anything, but this is a natural beauty of a different kind and on a scale I have never experienced before.

A jolt notifies me we're crossing a bridge over the bubbling stream, heading towards more woodland. This time, we travel for about four or so minutes before the vehicle slowly whirrs to a stop.

"We're here," the farmer says, putting the vehicle into park and then stepping out. "They don't normally come this far in," he adds as we all leave the vehicle.

It's definitely colder in here. The air is pine fresh but with the metallic undertone of damp earth, decaying leaves, and bark. "... Which is why I wisnae expectin' tae find her here. If it wisnae for the dogs makin' a fuss, I might no' even hae noticed her..." The farmer gestures into the trees where dappled light is the only reminder of the pale blue skies beyond the woodland shroud.

We follow him in silence. Wings flutter. A raven croaks overhead. A cuckoo calls in the distance.

There's something creepy about this place. And yes, you could argue that I have a predisposition to this, but there's something off. Something that instantly puts me on edge, small hairs rising at the back of my neck. At home, being in the woods feels like a topiary hug, but here, well, it's like the trees are watching you.

I notice that the detective isn't missing a thing. Her eyes are looking all around us. I'd say she isn't enjoying the atmosphere in here either, but I think it's more than that. Almost like she knows something we don't.

Yes. Thank you. That's enough of that!

"Just over there," the farmer says, pointing to a clearing where a fallen tree lies, exposed twisted roots studded with moss and cloaked in snow that shimmers under a shaft of sunlight. Bright clusters of yellow aconite flowers fill the area, their vibrancy a stark contrast to the feeble winter light. The scene's actually quite picturesque, magical even, like it's been built by a set designer... but that image disappears as soon as I spot the body lying at the base of the tree.

Shit.

The sheep is big. I'm no expert, so I've no idea what kind it is. But it's larger than I expected, and it's lying on its side with its tongue protruding from its mouth, eyes faded to a brown murky hue.

I've never seen a dead animal like this, and I have to say it's disturbing, but it's nowhere near as grotesque as the giant chasm in the animal's abdomen that has caused its innards to spill onto the leafy floor like dirty laundry from a basket.

I know it might sound pathetic, but I feel the urge to turn away from the bloody sight, although I notice that nobody else is. These people, clearly hardened to island life, aren't even flinching. Part of that, I suppose, is the fact that the corpse doesn't smell as I imagine it would, but that could be just because I'm upwind of the breeze that continues to patrol the area, albeit with some reluctance, as if it, too, is afraid of venturing too far in here. The cold must also be slowing decomposition, too, because there are no flies. Not one.

Anyway, I swallow the lump of bile that is threatening to make an appearance and try to stay focused.

The detective, on the other hand, steps forward and crouches down to get a closer look.

"This cavity's what, ten inches wide," she says, hovering fingers over the sheep's wound like a makeshift ruler.

"Aye, probably."

"What are your thoughts?"

I think the question is directed at the farmer, but I find myself answering anyway. "A fox, maybe?" I offer because that's the only real barometer I have. I know what a fox tried to do to Buddy that day in the woods in Porthcove. It stands to reason that—

"Unlikely," the detective interrupts my thoughts. "I can't see a fox trying it on with an animal this size."

"Maybe it was lame in some way," Samantha suggests.

The detective doesn't respond but asks without looking up, "Did you say this has happened before?"

"Aye. A few days back," the farmer responds.

"Same location?"

"Nae. That was at the back of the farm."

"Similar wound?"

"The same," the farmer says, scratching his head under his hat.

"It's got to be a fox," Samantha says, "only animal brazen enough."

"Maybe it is a wildcat," the farmer concedes. "That's why I dinnae go anywhere without ma shotgun."

"Again, a wildcat's too small to take on an animal this size. Besides, the wound's all wrong," the detective says pensively.

"Wrong?" the farmer asks.

"Aye," the detective begins, pointing around the wound with her fingers. "If this were made by an animal, you'd see toothmarks all around here where it ripped through the wool and the flesh as it burrowed inwards..." Ugh. That bile ball has just grown. I swallow hard. "... and these tears would be folded in, but this seems to be folded out as if it exploded outward." The detective scans the area as if looking for clues.

"So you don't think it's an animal?" Samantha asks.

"Hard to say," the detective responds.

"If it isnae an animal, then what did this?" the farmer asks.

The detective doesn't respond; she's too busy plucking a twig from the snow and dabbing at what looks like a black sticky substance around the wound, on top of the red goop on the ground, and in contrasting patches on the snow.

"What is that?" I ask as I watch the detective lift the twig and a sample of the substance to her nose and sniff it. Instinctively, I put the back of my hand over my mouth as my stomach spasms.

"I've no idea," she says casually before suddenly standing up and asking, "You said that the sheep don't normally venture this far into the woods; is that right?"

"Aye."

"Then what was this one doing here?" she asks. It's a rhetorical question.

"Maybe it was dragged here," Samantha suggests.

"It would take a strong predator to drag an animal this size this far. And there'd be tracks, assuming it happened after the snow."

"Maybe it chased it in here," I contribute because if I don't do something, I'm likely to yack, and please don't judge, but for some reason, I really don't want to do that in front of this woman.

"That's possible," she says. "But again, it'd need to be something fairly large. Powerful. Did I see bottled water in the back of your vehicle?"

The question is directed at the farmer, who frowns and nods. "Aye."

Without comment, the detective strides purposefully back to the vehicle, retrieves a bottle of water, and empties its contents onto the snow-dusted ground. She gives the bottle a sharp shake, ensuring no errant water droplets remain. She meticulously selects another twig, then, with practised movements, she uses it to coax samples of wool, flesh, and the gooey black residue from various sections of the wound into the bottle. Finally, she secures the cap tightly and holds it aloft, scrutinising the contents in the distilled sunlight.

"If we can get this back to the mainland for analysis," she announces, "it should give us some idea of what we're dealing with. Of course, we can't rule out the fact that other animals may have got here before us and contaminated the area, although there's no sign of that."

Again, she scans the trees as if she's expecting something to jump out from behind one of them, which I have to say is doing nothing for my nerves. "What? What is it?" I ask, because, yeah, she's starting to freak me out. My hand twitches, and I reach out for Buddy before I remember that he isn't here.

The detective takes her time, eyes still scanning all around us. "Well, I can't be sure, but... how long do you think she's been here?" The detective puts the question to the farmer.

"A couple of days?"

She nods. "That's what I suspected. And yet, she's still intact."

I frown. "Intact? Doesn't look that way."

"Aye," the farmer clues in.

She looks at me for the first time, and I'm actually taken aback by her sudden gaze. "Well, middle of the woods, open fields. Small predators, scavengers, even some birds. To them, this is a veritable banquet. And yet, I could be wrong, but it looks like most of the animal is still here. It's as if there's something about it that's repelling all the carnivores."

"Like it's tainted in some way?" Samantha asks.

The detective nods thoughtfully. "Anyway, we'll know more once we get these samples analysed," she says, lifting the bottle. "Now, I'd like to get back to visit the patient, and then I have some follow-up questions for you," she says to Samantha before making her way back to the car, leaving the rest of us to exchange looks.

And so, five minutes later, we're all piled into the vehicle once more, heading back out of the woods and into the sunshine. And not a moment too soon. I think the whole dead sheep thing was disturbing enough without the detective's ominous last words.

She's looking out of the window again now. And I'm finding it really hard to get a read on her. I don't know if she's closed off because she's focused, if there's something else, or if, like me, she's a reluctant visitor.

"That was pretty impressive what you did back there, with the bottle," I say. She glances at me and conjures a faint smile. "Ah, so you do know how to—"

The rest of my sentence is cut short when, without warning, there's a thunderous crash that sounds like the sky is splitting apart as something slams into the right side of the Rover, forcing it to crumple inward as if made of paper. The sickening crunch of metal jolts us all. I feel my head snap, and then my body jerk sideways, the seatbelt biting into my shoulder as it attempts to anchor me against a world that is tilting off its axis before spinning violently, Farmer Douglas losing control as the vehicle succumbs to the wild forces of physics.

The Land Rover, once a reliable beast on the rugged track, is now a toy in the hands of an unseen force. It spins, a dizzying whirl of green and grey as the Scottish landscape blurs past the windows. I hear the detective's sharp intake of breath, a mirror to my own, while Samantha screams as the world inverts.

Then, we're airborne for a heart-stopping second before the Land Rover begins its brutal descent down the hillside. The earth comes up to greet us in shudders, rolling end over end with the terrifying grace of a wounded beast as the serene symphony of the island is replaced by the cacophony of destruction, shouts, grunts, and screams as glass shatters, showering us with a rain of diamonds that cut and glitter as loose items become unguided missiles within the confined space.

The tumble of terror feels endless, mercifully ending in a loud crunch and splash that explodes around us.

Water rushes, and birds chirp as the engine ticks over in a stuttering, haunting rhythm. For a few endless heartbeats, we are all prisoners to shock.

Samantha's breaths come in shallow gasps, a stark counterpoint to the sudden silence. Douglas is unnervingly quiet, his rugged features still. The detective is also motionless beside me, her silhouette etched with tension against the backdrop of the inverted world.

It takes several seconds for the sound to register, and when it does, I am filled with familiar dread. We're upside down in the stream, our vehicle's belly exposed to the sky as freezing-cold water rushes in through the broken windows beneath us, in stark contrast to the heat of adrenaline that floods my veins.

I've been in a similar situation, only my landing was much softer. Right now, I realise, I'm yet to land as I'm still hanging upside down in my seat, the world eerily still as my pulse thunders in my ears. "Is... is everyone alright?" I manage, my voice sounding foreign in the confined space, filled with the scent of damp earth and industrial lubricant.

Samantha is groaning, trying to unclip her seatbelt. The detective lets out a frustrated sigh – a swear, actually – girl after my own heart. But Douglas remains unsettlingly silent.

The stream's roar drowns out the battered vehicle's final groans as it settles into its watery grave. The water's a creeping threat, rushing to the frantic drum of my heart. "We need to move, now!" I shout, my hands shaking as I fumble with the seatbelt buckle. Then, click! Finally, I splash into freezing water that steals my breath for a shocking moment.

Somehow, someway, we emerge like drowned rats from the wreckage, each squinting and shivering into the sunshine as if we've just emerged from a watery lair.

The Land Rover lies defeated in the middle of the rushing stream, its wheels still spinning in a pathetic attempt to regain lost dignity.

"Is everyone okay?" the detective asks. Each of us murmurs a response, our breaths visible puffs in the air. Thankfully, that includes Farmer Douglas, who had me worried moments before.

"Sam?" I ask, turning to my sister.

She nods at me but is obviously still shaken.

"What the hell happened?" I say to nobody in particular, but they don't get a chance to respond because we all turn at the sound of someone calling. It's a man, hurrying up the hill towards us. I'm the closest to him, and for a split second, I wonder what he's doing out here and whether he might have had some hand in what just happened to us, but then I realise that he must be coming from the power station. He obviously saw the accident.

He's about fifty feet from me now. "Is everybody alright?" he calls out. "Anybody needin' medical help?"

"We're fine. Thanks, Derek," Samantha responds, and I'm reassured to hear that she knows the man.

"What happened?" he asks as he draws near, and just as I'm wondering the same thing, I see his expression change from concern to immediate horror. "Oh, shit!" he exclaims, looking back up the hill behind us. But before I have a chance to react, there's a rumbling sound, and then what can only be described as a blur rushes at him. There's a scream before the man is launched into the air and thrown several feet back down the hillside, where he lands in a heap.

There's a collective gasp and scream from the rest of us as it takes several seconds to process what we're seeing. Well, it probably takes me a little longer because I can't reconcile what I just witnessed, but there's no denying it. Just like there's no denying that the so-called blur is, in fact, an animal. A gigantic ram, it would seem.

"Jesus Christ," I gasp as I witness the beast's head pivot from the motionless man towards us, towards me! And then it stands there, the tips of its large, spiralled horns dipped in crimson blood, glinting menacingly in the sunlight. Its breath puffs out into the cold air, and it observes me with dead, black eyes.

In any other circumstance, I'd think this is a magnificent creature, its coat a rough tapestry of earthy hues, blending seamlessly with the rugged terrain. Its muscular body is taut, and its hooves, I imagine hardened by the rocky landscape, dig into the ground, kicking up small chunks of earth.

Someone calls my name, but I'm unable to respond because I am rooted to the spot, seemingly frozen numb by both the cold and terror as the animal fixes on me, unblinking, with an intensity that sends a chill down my spine. It's a primal, unspoken challenge, a declaration of its intent.

Someone's calling to me in a loud whisper once again, and I think it's Samantha, but I'm not sure. I can't really hear her over the rushing water and the thundering of my heart, and no matter how hard I try,

I just can't take my eyes off the creature that is now lowering its head, aligning those formidable horns with my chest. Then there's a moment of stillness, a brief pause in the world, as if nature itself is holding its breath before there's an otherworldly guttural bellow that echoes off the surrounding hills as the beast snorts loudly and—FUCK! IT'S CHARGING AT ME!

The ground seems to tremble beneath its weight, each stride bringing the beast closer and closer, and all I can do is brace for impact because no matter how much I will my feet to move, I can't. I fucking can't!

10 feet…

Closer.

6 feet…

Closer.

Then, the most peculiar thing happens. A massive clap of thunder reverberates, exploding right next to us, and the creature's head literally explodes, sending a cloud of blood and bone matter into the air and over me before the grotesque thing, like a prop out of the worst Saw movie, lands on me, knocking me to the ground, and the world turns black.

14

AFTERMATH

THISTLE ISLAND INFIRMARY. LATE AFTERNOON.

Okay. So not my finest hour. But then, as you already know, I've had worse, more terrifying, and equally humiliating moments.

I say that only because it turns out that while I was standing there, pissing my pants at the thought of that ram treating me with the same delicacy as it did that hapless power station worker, the detective – who is just one conveyor belt of amazements – fetched the shotgun she'd clocked earlier in the day strapped in the back of the upturned Land Rover and then rather expertly proceeded to blow the animal's brains out – to use an overused movie colloquialism – just seconds before it skewered me.

Impressive, eh? Me passing out from the ordeal – not as much.

Oh, and just in case you're wondering, I'm told that Farmer Douglas and the good ole Samaritan power station worker guy are going to be just fine. In fact, for a short period, we were neighbours in the infirmary, but naturally, when I came to and was, ahem, found to have nothing wrong with me, the doctor released me.

But not before giving me a somewhat judgmental gaze. You know, like one of those parents who discovers their child has fallen when they had no business climbing up that tree. In this case, what the hell was I doing out there if I couldn't handle a bit of blood? *It wasn't the blood,* I want to yell at her. *It was facing imminent bloody death!*

Anyway, I didn't because, well, between you and me, I actually find that woman quite intimidating.

You may be interested to know that the somewhat formidable detective didn't let any of this slow her down. She arranged to have Amy – AKA the naked woman – moved to her own room, apparently. I don't know why. I imagine it was because she didn't really want her talking to anybody else before she'd talked to her. Then, she debriefed Samantha. I wasn't privy to their chat. More's the pity because you'll appreciate that I've reached that stage where I'm like, *What the fuck is going on?*

"Marco?"

"Yeah?" I look up.

We're sitting in that makeshift meeting room at the infirmary again. Honestly, I'm beginning to dislike this place.

"Are you okay?" It's Samantha asking the question.

"Am I okay? You mean besides being thrown down a hill and then nearly being gored by a fucking sheep? Yeah. I'm just fine. What the hell is that all about, anyway? Why did that thing attack us like that?"

Samantha shrugs. "Rams can be territorial."

"What, you mean like that? Attacking the Rover and then coming after us in that way?"

"If provoked, yes."

"But we didn't provoke the bloody thing! We were just passing by."

My sister smiles, and for the first time since I've met her, it's one of those patronising smiles like I'm still the idiot from the city who hasn't got a fucking clue about anything to do with the countryside.

"Don't do that," I say, clenching my jaw, anger bubbling through me.

"Do what?"

"Don't condescend."

"I'm not," she says. "I'm just telling you what I know."

"Really? Really Sam? Are you *really* telling me everything you know?" I demand, sitting forward and leaning on the table. "What are you not telling me?"

"I don't know what you're talking about," she says, expertly maintaining eye contact.

"What aren't you telling me about this place?" I demand.

"I told you—"

"No!" I say, slamming a fist on the table. The action visibly startles her. "Not good enough. It doesn't make any fucking sense to me, Sam. Your husband's gone missing, and all you can think about is playing happy families with me, strutting about the place like you haven't got a fucking care in the world."

I see storm clouds gather in my sister's eyes. "You're a prick," she seethes before standing up, chair scraping loudly on the wood floor, leaving the room and slamming the door behind her.

Silence reigns for several seconds, punctuated by the sound of the ticking radiator.

"You know, it's perfectly normal," the detective – who is sitting across from me – says. I'd forgotten she was even here.

I don't look up at her. I'm too busy looking at my hands, the heat of my irritation slowly giving way to a cold wave of shame. "What is?" I ask eventually.

"For you to feel this way. Angry, that is."

"Don't tell me – you've got a psychology degree, too," I throw out.

When there's silence, I look up. The half smile on her face says it all. I scoff and shake my head. "Of course you have."

"Look, I don't do touchy-feely stuff, especially when it's none of my business, but you know as well as I do that coping mechanisms differ. Just because your sister isn't wearing everything on her sleeve, it doesn't mean she isn't feeling it. That said, one thing that's become abundantly clear is that she cares about you. She was really worried when you blacked out."

I take a good look at the woman opposite me. She looks different. Her face is softer.

"You don't know the half of it," I say, frowning at the dull ache at the back of my head. I touch it tenderly, and it bloody hurts. I think I must have hit it when I fell.

"True. But I think I know enough. She feels responsible for you. For asking you to stay."

"She told you that?"

"Kind of. Everything else is implied," she follows that up with another feeble smile.

"So, what, it takes me having a meltdown for you to crack a smile?"

She cocks her head. "Don't be too hard on your sister. She's going through a particularly tough time right now. Or yourself, for that matter. What happened was beyond our control. But we survived it."

"Yeah. Thanks to you," I say, trying my best not to sound petulant but no doubt failing.

"You're welcome," she says. Her words are gentle, not arrogant. Like it's all in a day's work for her. And I guess it was.

"I feel like such an idiot."

"You'll know this. You've been through a traumatic event. It's perfectly normal for you to question your reality. Test the strength of your relationships."

"You're shrinking me now?"

The detective holds up her hands. "Oh no. That's your job. I know better."

"Is that so?" I say, holding her gaze.

She isn't wearing her hat now, so her hair is hanging over part of her face, hiding that scar, and down to her shoulders. Her freckles are faded in the harsh neon light of the room.

"Your sister is worried about her husband. More than she's letting on, but I think that's because she feels like she has a responsibility to keep it together, you know, for her son, the family, the island. She doesn't want people to think she doesn't still have a grasp on things. But I'm worried that it's only a matter of time before it catches up with her."

I nod. That shroud of guilt is now hanging on me like a wet blanket.

"And right now, we only have one viable lead," she continues.

"Don't tell me. That's where I come in."

She rocks her head. "I need to know everything that research assistant knows. And you're the only one who's managed to get her to talk so far."

"No pressure then."

The door opens. Samantha enters carrying two large paper bags. "Lunch is served. Or early supper. Whichever works for you," she says cheerily.

She places the bags on the table and starts unloading drinks and sandwiches. "They're freshly made," she adds. And I see it now. My sister. It's not that she doesn't care. If anything, she's overcompensating. I would have seen that if I hadn't been busy indulging my neurosis.

Shit.

After everything that happened at Porthcove and Fawndale, I've been primed to look for the bad in everything, including people.

"Sam," I begin, but she catches my hand, looks me in the eyes, and says, "We're good." And I'm taken aback by this because the act is alien yet so clear to me.

I'm actually starting to feel overwhelmed when the detective conveniently shatters the moment. "Sam, Ewan's lab. I'd like to take a look."

"Of course. But just so you know, Sarge has already been over the place several times."

"Still... I'd like to look for myself."

"Of course. I can show you the way, but if it's all the same, I won't be coming inside," Samantha says.

"That's no problem."

"I can take the detective," I offer. "It's the big dome place, right?"

"If you don't mind."

"It's the least I can do," I say, returning the squeeze of my sister's hand.

"Okay," she says. "But first, you both need to eat something."

15

THE DOME

THISTLE ISLAND. EARLY EVENING.

Night's long shadows are already smothering the land by the time we leave the infirmary. The sun's waning rays put up one last stand against a canopy of thick grey clouds as a chill wind, born from the depths of the Atlantic, screams through the narrow lanes of the village, rapping on doors and barging its way in through any available crevice.

I lead the detective out of the village and up the coastal path towards the pine forest until the silhouette of the lab's structure appears in the distance. It reminds me of one of those biodomes that's carved its way into the hillside between the village and the trees, overlooked only by the snow-dusted mountain towering in the distance.

Agreed, this isn't your average vista. Doesn't make the place any less creepy, though.

Yes. Alright. I'm sanguine enough to accept that much of this could be due to my own neurosis. But hey, just because you're paranoid, it doesn't mean they aren't out to get you. I'm sorry. But as breathtaking as this place is – literally because it's so bloody cold all the time – there's something about this island that makes me feel uneasy.

Of course, one could argue that this is a perfectly natural reaction to the day we've had. The only problem with that theory is that I've felt like this ever since I first stepped off that ferry what feels like a lifetime ago.

We follow the stone path that branches off the main thoroughfare to the hotel and the other side of the island, leading us directly to the front door of the giant glasshouse with soaring slabs of glass set into a metal frame.

The light seems to fade particularly fast around here, which is why the detective magics up a flashlight seemingly out of nowhere. I've always wondered how people in her profession manage to do that. I mean, where, exactly, do they secrete these things on their person? Okay, probably best I steer clear of the thought because it makes me think about her clothes and pockets in places my warped mind has no business entertaining right now.

My fingers are numb, which means there's some fumbling with the keys... Samantha said it was the one with the—

A creak notifies me that the detective simply pushed on the door, and it opened.

"That's obviously an island thing," I say. "Nobody in their right mind would leave a place full of equipment unlocked in the city."

The cop doesn't respond. She's already reverted to type and has disappeared inside. That sympathetic character's exposition in the infirmary is simply another tool in her formidable arsenal.

I take one last look towards the sanctuary of the village as if we're about to undertake a perilous mission from which we may not return. Amber lights, bright and warm, are already glowing behind closed windows. I look over to my cottage and temporary home perched on the hillside, where I think I can just about make out the feeble lantern light. I imagine Samantha is there with Luca, keeping Buddy company. Oh, how I miss the big guy. I feel like I haven't seen him in days. I can't help but wish I was there, wrapped in a duvet, munching on a fat burger and chips.

When I turn back and enter the dome, it's to see that, true to stereotype, the detective hasn't tried to turn the lights on. I, on the other hand, fumble around for a switch and grunt satisfactorily when my fingers land on something, but we're both startled by a loud crunch and whir overhead that encourages the belligerent gale to howl louder.

"Shit! Sorry... sorry..." I hiss, flipping the switch once more and prompting what I assume is some kind of skylight to close with a loud slam that echoes around the space.

I try again, fumble for another switch, and reluctantly flip it up. After a moment, an array of low-hanging lampshades flickers to life, illuminating two rows of long benches, a series of glass cabinets, and individual plants. While it's a little brighter in here now, the place is still steeped in deep shadows that, coupled with the howling wind blowing through the structure, do nothing to calm the inexplicable tension in my nerves.

There are plants everywhere – in all shapes and sizes. They sprout from floor troughs, dangle from the ceiling, and line shelves in orderly rows. The air is cold, musty – scented with freshly dug earth and something else I can't quite place.

The detective, who's a few feet in front of me, aims the beam of her torch over a bench as if the lighting provided isn't enough and asks, "So you're an author. Are your books about psychology?" I notice her accent now. There's a Scottish inflection, but it isn't very strong. Almost like she has a voice for official questions and another for everything else. Still, now? She wants to make small talk now? We had that whole awkward ride across and then *down* that hillside today.

I pretend to study the tendrils of a plant dangling inches from my face, stalling for time because I've no idea just how much I want to share right now. I'd rather we just focus on the matter at hand, but then, maybe this is her method.

I survey the room so I'm not looking at her when I say, "Um, yeah, sort of."

"Sort of?" she asks, moving forward.

"What, exactly, are we looking for?" I say, changing the subject.

"We'll know when we see it," she says, the beam of her torch spotlighting a series of plants that appear to have wilted, which I suppose makes sense given that nobody's been tending to them.

A loud squeaking sound draws our attention upward into the metal rafters that are creaking and bending as the freezing wind we left outside squeals in anticipation of breaching this place. And by the way, the whole structure appears to be shaking; I feel it'll only take a huff and a puff to blow the whole thing down.

"So did you know Ewan well?"

"I didn't know him at all."

"You didn't know your sister's husband?"

"I didn't know my sister until yesterday. So, no, I didn't know him, but then, Detective, something tells me you already knew that. What's with the questions? Are you suggesting I had something to do with Ewan's disappearance?"

She stops and turns to me, the beam of light finding my face. It's bright, irritating, but I don't flinch. "Dude, relax... I'm just trying to establish some basic facts."

"Fact. I met my half-sister for the first time yesterday. Fact. I never met her husband. Fact. That light's really annoying, so if you've finished with the inquisition..." I leave the sentence unfinished because, well, that's how I roll. I'm irked. I know why. This whole mystery thing is getting a bit too real for my liking.

The light leaves my face. "Sorry. Just checking if the rumour had any legs," she says, turning back to the matter at hand.

"Wait. There's a rumour?"

"You seem to have bonded well with your half-sister but not quite with your half-brother."

"Oh, right. This is about last night. Have you met my half-brother?"

"He thinks your presence here might be making things difficult."

"For whom? For him?" I ask in a loud whisper as if the plants can hear as we move past a bench decked out with what looks like scientific gear – Petri dishes, microscopes, pipettes, and an assortment of other gear.

On the opposite wall, shelves house more plants submerged in liquid – which, in this light, I'm sorry to say, look unsettlingly like props from the set of *Aliens*.

"He says you tried to choke him out last night. In front of a room full of witnesses."

"Are you..." I begin the question loudly, then, as if I might be disturbing someone, I add in a loud whisper, "Are you bloody serious? He started it," I say, as though I'm back in the schoolyard. "I was there minding my own business, and he..." I don't bother finishing the sentence because the detective isn't even listening to me. She's already moved on, clearly finding something at the end of the bench far more interesting.

I follow her. There's a computer here, a mug of freezing cold black coffee, desk paraphernalia, and several large pots containing more dead plants. One of the pots has fallen from the bench, lying on its side, soil spilled in a small arc on the floor. The detective is shifting it around with her foot under the beam of her flashlight.

This must be Ewan's station. And the detective has obviously found something in the soil because she's crouching down now.

I join her and, in my favourite loud whisper, ask, "Is this the silent scream you were looking for? A hint, perhaps, at some hasty departure or struggle, maybe?"

"Shhhh," she says, silencing me. Then she lifts the flashlight, and its beam cuts through the gloom, but there's nothing there but the ceaseless, mournful howl of the wind.

Slowly, she shifts the circle of light from in front, to the side, and then behind us. And I, like a curious bloody cat, follow the thing with voracious interest as it moves faster and faster until it eventually finds a ghostly face—

"Oh, fuck!" I yell, losing my balance and collapsing against the bench, banging the ache in my head once more. Behind us! There's someone standing behind us!

"Stop that!" the voice orders, holding up a hand to fend off the glare of the flashlight. Then they're moving forward, fast, boots clunking loudly on the wood floor until that unmistakable gruff voice demands, "What's goin' on here?"

It's the bloody sergeant.

The detective stands to meet him. "We came to take a look around."

"Aye, I can see that. On whose authority?"

"My own, sergeant. I know it's easy to forget, but I'm here to investigate a missing person."

"Well, far be it from me to tell you how to do ya job an' all, detective. But me, I'd prioritise talkin' t' the last person who was probably in contact with him."

"She's sleeping."

"And you know this how? If you're out here?" the big grumpy carrot-head retorts.

"I'm fine. Don't worry about me," I say, getting to my feet and... ugh, what's that? I hold my hand under the light. It's covered in black sludge off that dead plant, and it bloody stinks.

The detective and I exchange a knowing look.

"Are ye okay there, lad? Wannae tissue?" Sarge asks.

"I'd love one," I say, holding out my hand, but the only thing he gives me is another of his trademark scowls.

"Right, you were being sarcastic. Walked straight into that," I say.

"Was it like this the last time you were here?" the detective jumps in, aiming the beam of light at the toppled plant pot.

"Like what?"

"Was this on its side?"

"Aye. And?"

I tune out of the conversation and look around the room for a rag or something but spot a sink on the other side of the bench.

I hurry over, turn the tap on with my elbow, and rinse the black goo off my hand before using liquid soap, washing and then rinsing again.

But that stench persists. In fact, it seems much worse now. It seems to have gone from something organic to something more... rotten, like that sour stink of meat that's turned.

I stand back from the sink. It's bathed in a pool of light from the overhead lamp, but its edges visibly fade to the grey of shadows and black of darkness.

I glance across at the flashlight in the detective's hand. I notice that the sergeant has moved closer now, his face half lit by the lamplight. He looks down on her, and I can't help but think that either she's much smaller than I noticed, or he's particularly tall. "... everyone on the island is," I hear him say. "I know that's not quite how ye folks from the mainland are, but here, we look after our own." There's a faint smile on the policeman's furry lips that doesn't quite reach his eyes.

I watch the detective respond, but I can't hear what she's saying on account of the fact that the squealing wind seems much louder over here, so much that I can feel the breeze blowing against my face, pushing at my hair.

I shiver and peer into the gloom. There's definitely a draft coming from somewhere. Like there's a window open or something. "Detective..." I begin, but the two cops are still jabbering on at each other and don't hear me.

So I step forward on the edge of the pool of light, hoping to see into the darkness beyond. But nothing.

"Detective..." I take another step. There's definitely a draft, and it's doing a disgustingly good job of carrying that stench to my nostrils.

"Detective?" Another step... out of the light, into the shadows now, the wetness of my hands feeling like the bite of ice on my fingers.

"Detective!" I yell. Louder now, desperate as I advance on the dark, both terrified and compelled by it. "Detect—" I feel a hand touch my arm. "JESUS CHRIST!" I snap my head around to see that pretty face look up at me and shrug.

I turn and point at the blackness. "I think there's a window open over there." The cop aims her light beam in that direction, banishing the dark. "And something smells really bad," I add reluctantly, as images of the sheep replay in my mind.

"You're right," the detective says. And, of course, this would be the perfect opportunity for me to make a joke about how she's the first female in a while to say those words to me, but I'm way too keyed up for that.

She's about to step over when – CRUNCH! She freezes as a harsh scraping sound echoes through the room. I follow the light beam of her torch down to the floor – broken shards of glass – then up the side of the building to a jagged hole – where something has smashed through. And I've no idea why, but that sends a renewed bolt of apprehension through me. I won't say fear because, well, that implies that I'm allowing myself to be conditioned—Oh hell, alright. Fear. Something or someone smashed a hole in the side of what is effectively a giant glass house. Why?

The sergeant joins us. "What's the matter?"

"Did you notice this the last time you were here?" the detective asks, pointing at the hole in the wall.

The sergeant hesitates. "Nae. I don't think so."

"Are you sure?" the detective prompts.

"Listen, lassie—"

"It's just a question, sergeant. I'm not impugning your masculinity. Was this glass broken when you were last here, yes or no?"

I glance at the man's scowl, being sure not to make direct eye contact.

"No," he says through gritted teeth.

The detective steps closer to the gap. I watch as the concentrated current of cold air pushes the loose strands of hair about her face as if it's panicked by what it is seeing.

"Something definitely smashed through here," she says, crouching down to the gap in the glass, which is a few feet wide and at knee level. She trains the light over the jagged glass, and I see it, too. What looks like blood and something else.

"What's that?" the sergeant asks.

"I... can't be sure. I think it's... fur," she says. "By the looks of it, dark brown fur."

"Rats, maybe?" I suggest, revulsion instantly rippling through me because, well, if you were with me that night at Porthcove, you know why.

"No. Something bigger," she says, cringing. "Can you smell that?"

"Aye" and "Yes," the sergeant and I say in perfect synchronisation as the detective moves the light beam around like a searchlight. "Smells like..." she begins but trails off when the light beam reveals a dark, glossy substance on the floor that kicks my heart up a gear.

The circle of light follows the slick for what feels like a long time before it picks up a paw, a head, and a sight that sends a cattle prod of a jolt through me.

"Shit," I hiss, because for a horrifying moment, even if all evidence is to the contrary, I saw Buddy lying there. It isn't him – thank God – but it's still a dog. And my heart goes from heartache to horror when the light reveals something else.

"Jesus wept," Sarge mutters.

The detective stands and moves in to take a closer look, as do I.

We both gape at the thing.

"I've never seen aught like this before," the sergeant says.

"We have," the detective and I chorus this time.

"Any idea who it belongs to?" the detective asks.

"I do," I say, surprising even myself. The detective looks at me. "Sam said that their dog went missing a week or so ago. She said it was a senior. She thought it'd wandered off somewhere."

"That's right," Sarge agrees.

"You think it's theirs?" the detective asks.

"Cannae be sure," the sergeant responds, "but I think so."

"When were you last here?"

The cop thinks about this. "Few days ago."

"So it broke in here? Why?" The detective's question isn't directed at anybody in particular, but I don't think any of us can answer it.

She crouches down now with the same professional curiosity she exhibited earlier in the day when inspecting the sheep's corpse. Like it, the dog appears to have a large tear in its abdomen as if it's been sliced open and its innards scooped out and left to marinate in a slick of its own congealed black blood. And I mean black. Of course, it could just be a trick of the light, but I'm confident that—

Shit!

The wind has really picked up now, wailing through this place like a rageful banshee hellbent on ripping it from its moorings. It's clawing at the panes, rattling the metal frames like skeletal fingers scraping bone. And now, in a somewhat bizarre twist, it's hurtling snow through the smashed glass, causing it to whizz and whirl before settling on the dark pool on the floor.

"Snow's 'ere," Sarge declares, like we can't see it for ourselves.

"We need to take samples and get them to..." the detective begins but trails off, shining the torch behind us.

Of course, this instantly puts me on guard and has me following that light beam once more. "What?" I ask.

"Did you hear that?"

"Hear what?"

She doesn't answer. The wind moans. The structure rattles.

"What is it?" I demand, heartbeat moving up a gear.

"I thought I heard something," she says quietly.

"You mean besides the blizzard—" I begin but cut myself off because I hear it, too. It's barely audible. Not quite a thump, not quite a drag, but an undeniable intrusion, a presence where there shouldn't be one.

The sergeant freezes, scanning the room for the origin of the sound.

Wind howls... snow ticks softly as it settles....

Then... there! A scraping, scuttling, and thump against the glass ceiling. We all look up.

What the hell is that?

The sound intensifies, followed by a low, rhythmic thudding, like something is moving overhead, hidden in the darkness outside.

On cue, the detective lifts the flashlight, the beam momentarily illuminating her breath in the gloom. The dome's glass is thick, opaque in the section we're looking at, but I'm sure I can see something out there. Nothing obvious. Just what appears to be a dark shape, its edges blurred by the glass.

"Do you see that?" I whisper.

"See what?" says the cop.

"There's something up there."

"I cannae—" the sergeant begins, but his words are cut short when there's a loud squelching and squeak, followed by the thump and slide of something scuttling across the roof.

"SHIT!" I yell as the detective follows the sound with the light beam in a series of erratic, jerky movements to the edge of the roof. Then, with a sudden, unnatural agility, the *thing* leaps – not down from the roof, but outwards, a good ten feet into the darkness of the pine forest, leaving nothing but the sound of the gale in its wake.

No one speaks. We're all transfixed by the torch trembling in the detective's hand, casting grotesque, shadowy twins of us over the walls. Then we all yelp as the radio affixed to the sergeant's chest crackles to life. "Sarge, you there?"

He swears, then speaks into it. "Yeah, go 'head."

"Sarge, we need you down here urgently."

"Whit's it?"

"Best ya see for yourself. We're at the infirmary."

"Okay. On ma way."

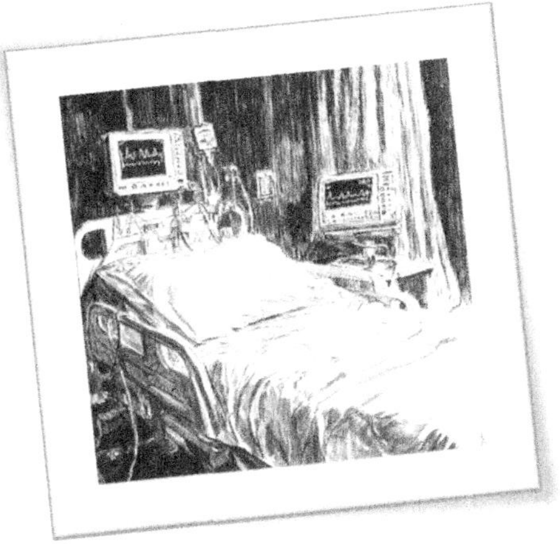

16

VITAL SIGNS

THISTLE ISLAND INFIRMARY. EVENING.

Our journey back from the dome to the infirmary was nowhere near as straightforward as our journey there; it was more like an Antarctic expedition. The snow dump was unlike anything I've ever experienced before.

The whole no-vehicle policy at Thistle Island might be fine during the summer months, but in winter, they could at least provide a sled and a pack of huskies.

Apparently, this level of snow is relatively normal for this time of year. I'm sorry, but there's nothing normal about falling snow that reduces visibility to just a few feet. Each step forward was a leap of faith on a path that disappeared before our very eyes.

Reaching the infirmary felt like a triumph – at least for me, anyway. Next time, I'm definitely checking the weather forecast before agreeing to star in yet another freakshow.

Shit.

Yes, of course, I can hear myself. I'm sounding like a moany old fart – and yes, more than usual. And I know why. I'm scared.

At first, I thought I disliked the cold, clammy sense of isolation that haunts this place because I viewed it as a trigger, never missing an opportunity to take me back to that place perched on the cliff by the ocean. But now, I see it's something far more sinister. Here, time isn't just lost; it's devoured by the relentless tide of darkness, each day swallowed so quickly it feels like one endless night. And in that night, something is always stirring—

What the fuck was that thing back there anyway? We didn't get a chance to talk about it on our way here. You know, on account of the fact that we were traversing the polar ice cap.

Damn you… Doctor Holmes! We could be back home by now, but instead—

"Marco?" It's Samantha. "Everything alright?" My sister is observing me curiously. I'm not sure how to answer that question since I'm still somewhat windswept from our trek over here. "How did it go?" she presses as I peel off my coat, shaking snow and freezing water onto the floor.

On the plus side, the reception room of the infirmary feels warm and somewhat cosy.

"Are Buddy and Luca still at the—"

"They're here. In the meeting room," my sister anticipates. "Is everything okay?" she repeats, concern etched on her face as she looks at each of us, in turn, for a response.

The detective glances at me, and it's almost telepathic.

"What?" my sister asks. "What is it?" Frustration clearly mounting in her voice.

"Nothing," I say quickly, touching her arm. "It's fine. Everything's fine. Apart from the weather," I add. "The weather is shit."

"I know. Apparently, it's going to get worse before it gets better," she says casually.

"Yeah. That's not helping."

"Sarge." It's the Sarge's sidekick.

"Eric... What's the mystery?" Sarge demands.

"It's the girl," he says.

Automatically, we all follow the policeman down the short corridor to the main ward and retake our positions behind the observation glass.

Amy, the naked wanderer, is now sitting up in bed, eating what looks like jelly, while chatting and laughing with the doctor and nurse.

Eric reaches forward and taps on the glass. The doctor looks up and exits the room, allowing the door to suck itself closed with a loud hiss.

"What's goin' on?" Sarge asks.

"Nothing specific. Jackie checked in on her about an hour ago, and she was awake."

"And?" Sarge asks.

The doctor frowns. "And... she has her eyes open," she says as if the Sarge has asked yet another stupid question.

The policeman rolls his eyes, then growls, "Whit's her condition?"

The doctor nods, glancing at the clipboard in her hand like she needs a reminder despite the fact that the girl is her only patient here. Even the power station guy doesn't seem to have hung around. "Good. All of her vitals are good. She's lucid, in relatively good spirits, considering, and is now happily having something to eat."

"Has she said anythin'?" Sarge asks.

"She's said plenty. Nothing I think you'd be interested in. Unless heavy metal is your jam. She doesn't remember anything, if that's what you're getting at."

"What, nothing?"

The doctor shakes her head.

"Can we talk to her?" the detective asks.

"Yes. But you need to take it easy. While she seems okay physically, there could be an undercurrent of something else."

"Like what?" Sarge asks.

The doctor shrugs. "Again, not my area of expertise. All I can tell you is that she's physically fine. In fact, I'm perfectly happy releasing her once you're done with your inquisition. Now, I'm going to get myself a cup of tea. You've got until I come back, okay? Enjoy yourselves," the doctor adds with a smirk before making her way up the corridor.

"Right. Let's see what she's got tae say," Sarge says, putting a hand on the door.

"Actually, Sarge. I'd rather go in there with Marco if that's okay with you," the detective says, stepping forward.

The sergeant freezes in his tracks, drops his hand from the door, and slowly turns to loom over her, bushy eyebrows lifted as if they have a life of their own and want to hide from what's to come. I notice Eric averts his gaze, and I follow suit.

"Listen here, lassie. This is ma island, ma investigation," the man glowers.

"Agreed. But I think you'll find I'm the senior investigating officer on this case."

"I'm the chief of police," the man bristles.

The detective rocks her head. "Well, technically, on Thistle Island, the chief of police is the mayor," she says, turning to Samantha. "So, if we're done measuring proverbial dicks, I'd much rather just get in there and find out what she knows."

Several seconds tick by, filled by the ever-present lament of that gale, and I just want the floor to open up and swallow me whole. Thanks, I want to say to the detective. The man already hates my guts. Which is why I keep my gaze lowered as I watch him step back from the door, those big hands forming fists, clenching and unclenching.

Shit.

Unfazed, the detective pushes on the door and glances at me to ensure I'm following her, which I reluctantly do. I'm already having second thoughts about being here. I wasn't expecting to be in the middle of a bloody turf war. On the other hand, I have to admit the way she dealt with a bloke twice her size was pretty impressive. And you know, I really can't make up my mind if I'm turned on or scared of her.

"Marco?"

"Yep. Here," I say, following her inside.

Amy and the nurse are laughing, but that stops the moment we enter the room.

"I'll leave you to it then," Nurse Jackie says, and with a look at the detective and a smile at me, she leaves the room with a loud hiss and clunk of the door.

Amy looks much better today. Last time, well, you know how she looked last time: haunted, sallow, and about ready to check out at the end. But this young woman has blue eyes that are wide open now. Her hair looks like it's been brushed, and if I'm not mistaken, she might even be wearing a hint of makeup.

The other obvious thing is that the wall-mounted lights are glowing brightly now. Last time, the doctor had them dialled down, so I assume this means the patient is no longer sensitive to light. She's wearing a hospital gown and is huddling under the bedcovers like it's cold in here. It isn't. It's actually quite toasty. Something the frozen popsicles of my ears and nose are welcoming after our Siberian excursion.

I can smell raspberries. I imagine it has something to do with the jelly that the patient is eating. There are already a couple of empty pots in front of her, and she is starting on her third now. I'm interested in establishing if that's her appetite or a direct reaction to our being here.

"Hello, Amy. I'm Detective Isla Macintyre. This is my colleague, Marco Battista."

"Hello, Amy," I say.

She nods and flashes a curious smile.

"How are you feeling? The doctor told us you're on the mend; is that right?" the detective asks.

She nods. "Much better, thanks."

"We don't want to keep you long. We just want to ask you some questions. Is that okay?"

Another nod.

The detective looks at me. *Oh right. Looks like I'm up.*

I take a step forward and put on my best smile. "Amy, do you remember me?"

She shakes her head. "No."

"You don't remember talking to me the other day?"

Another shake of the head prompts me to exchange glances with the detective because that's odd. It would be natural for her to repress memories after a potentially traumatic experience, but not remembering our chat in the ward the other day... that might suggest she was under the influence of something. It could explain her condition and the memory loss.

Need to check with the doctor on a potential toxicology report.

"Okay, Amy. Can you tell us what you do remember?" the detective asks.

The research assistant thinks about this. "I just remember going to work as normal. I remember Ewan was really excited."

"About what?"

"It was a big day. One of the plants he'd been cultivating was coming to maturity." The detective and I must have some kind of look on our faces because she adds, "It's a big thing. The seeds were rare. Most came to nothing, but one actually managed to germinate.

Ewan was thrilled at the prospect of it flowering. He brought champagne, cakes... the lot. He even brought a pie for Rusty."

"Rusty?"

"His dog."

"Okay. So, what happened?" the detective continues.

Amy frowns, producing lines on an otherwise smooth face. "I can't remember much after that."

"You can't remember much after him being excited?"

"No. Not really." She looks up at us. "Is Ewan alright? I haven't seen him, and nobody seems to want to tell me anything about him," she says.

I exchange glances with the detective. She then steps forward and says, "Ewan is missing, Amy."

The research assistant sits up. "W...what do you mean, missing?"

"Exactly that," the detective responds, closely observing the patient. "It's been a few days now, and we were hoping you might be able to help us find him." Amy shakes her head, those blue eyes wide with what appears to be genuine alarm. "That's why we need you to think carefully. Try to remember anything. Any detail could be useful."

"I've told you everything I know."

"And you can't remember anything else about that day?"

"No. I told you."

"What about you? What about where you've been?"

She shakes her head. "No... I don't... I don't remember anything about that either."

"Nothing?"

"No. Nothing," she says sharply.

"Okay." The detective pauses here before changing tack. "Why don't you tell us about the first thing you do remember?"

The patient looks around the room. "Waking up here?"

"Here?"

"Yes."

"In this room?"

"Yes."

The detective looks at me again. Amy must notice because she asks, "What? What is it? Why do you keep looking at each other?"

"Nothing to worry about. It's just that you and I, we've chatted before," I say softly.

She frowns, placing a hand on her forehead. "I... um... I don't... I don't remember that."

"Yes. Although we were in a different room." I step forward. "Is everything alright, Amy?"

"Yeah... yes. I'm fine. Just my head, it's aching. The doctor said it'll pass in a few days."

"So Amy, I just want to check that you don't remember talking to Mr Battista," the detective pushes.

"Oh, how many fucking times do I have to say it? No. I said NO!" she snaps, all traces of a smile erased. "Jesus Christ," she mutters, turning her attention back to her jelly and spooning some into her mouth.

Silence falls over the room, broken only by the scrape of that spoon against plastic.

Okay. I wasn't expecting that.

We both watch the research assistant eat eagerly, hungrily, in the way people do when they're eating angrily or trying to hide something.

I decide to wade in. "Okay... Amy. Why don't you tell us a little about your job? About working with Ewan. What's it like?"

This gets her attention. She looks up at us, and just like that, she's smiling again. "Oh, it's good. It's great," she says.

"What in particular is great about working with him?" the detective chimes in.

"We're good together. We think alike," she says.

"And Ewan's a good boss?"

"Yeah."

"Nothing else?" the detective prompts, obviously reacting to the girl's erratic behaviour and switching straight to testing her emotional triggers. I can't say I agree with the tactic.

"What do you mean?" Amy asks, returning her focus to the pot and scraping the dregs of jelly from it.

"I think you know what I mean, Amy," the detective says.

"No, I don't."

"I think you do."

The research assistant doesn't respond but continues scraping, faster now.

"Amy..."

Scrape... scrape... scrape.

"Amy?" the detective presses tentatively.

The scraping stops suddenly. The patient looks up but says nothing. She doesn't need to. I've seen that look before, in the mirror mostly: it's called guilt.

She looks across to the door, and although I can't see Samantha out there since the hallway lights have been deliberately turned off, I can still feel her eyes on us. Amy must, too. She shifts on the bed, her eyes darting to the shadows like she's expecting them to come alive, the spoon trembling slightly in her hand.

"Can you answer my question, please, Amy?" the detective insists, her tone sharp and pressing. I look at her because it's obvious where she's going with this, and I don't think we need to do it right now, especially with the audience outside.

"It's not what you think," she blurts. Her words are fast, desperate – as if seeking our approval. She looks at me, her eyes wide.

I don't approve, but I think that's because it's a reflection of me, of the memories it stirs. And I feel sadness for my sister and shame for the person I once was. I sigh, conflicted and frustrated that I'm complicit in raking this stuff up.

"... What was it then, Amy? Why don't you tell me?" The detective's voice continues, relentless. I watch Amy stiffen, reacting to the words.

I look across, "Detective..." My voice is a warning, but it falls on deaf ears.

"We were close, but—" Amy starts, her voice trembling.

"Yeah, you said that. How close?" The detective's persistence is a needle prodding at a festering wound.

"Detective. Can I have a word?" I interrupt, trying to defuse the situation.

"Not now," she says quickly, unwilling to let go of the moment. "What if I told you he's done this before? With another colleague?"

Amy's breath hitches. "What?" Her voice is barely a whisper.

My heart skips a beat. I look at the detective, who's still avoiding my gaze because I assume she's making this up just to goad the girl, isn't she? I glance at the corridor and then back again. "Detective!"

"I know you heard me, Amy."

"Why are you making this stuff up about him? Why are you lying?" Amy growls, her voice low and dangerous, eyes narrowing to slits.

"It's true. Another research assistant. At his old job. It's why he moved out here with his wife and child – to start anew. But then you came along."

"No. It's not true," Amy says, shaking her head more vigorously now, her movements jerky and frantic.

The detective steps closer. "You know it is, Amy. So you may as well tell us."

"It's not true."

"Amy—"

"That's a lie! You're wrong! It's not true!" she shouts, suddenly lunging forward, hands like claws, fingers curling into the detective's hair, yanking her back towards the bed. "YOU'RE A LIAR! YOU'RE A FUCKING LIAR!"

I jump forward. "AMY! Let go!" I demand, struggling to untangle the girl's hands. "Let go!" She does almost immediately, her grip loosening as she gasps for breath, chest heaving.

The detective stumbles back, her face pale with shock, but I barely have time to glare at her when Amy starts wheezing, hands darting to her throat as if she's unable to breathe. The action is closely followed by a coughing fit. Deep. Convulsive.

"Amy? Amy? Are you alright?" I ask as the girl doubles over, face flushing an alarming shade of red as she struggles for each and every breath.

"I... I'm fine," she says, waving me away while still attempting to clear her throat.

"Are you sure, Amy?" I ask, stepping forward.

"I'm fine," she hisses, head snapping up at me like I just said something else to piss her off. It's all I can do not to flinch because her eyes are watery, bloodshot, and veiny, as if all that coughing has burst blood vessels. "I... I... f...fine...," she insists through more splutters that rapidly turn into more barking, phlegm-infused coughs.

The room seems to shrink, the air squeezing out like it's being sucked into her lungs.

I take another step forward to help but pause when I see her remove her hands from her mouth and gawk at them – they are full of blood. This is followed by another coughing fit that sees her spray a crimson, jelly-like substance down her gown and across the white bed linen. "Oh, sorry about that," she says casually as if she just spilt water.

"Jesus Christ... DOCTOR! GET THE DOCTOR IN HERE!" I yell at nobody in particular.

"I'm f...fine... I'm fine," the research assistant insists, but the veins pulsating in her neck are telling a different story as more crimson phlegm dribbles from her mouth. "DOCTOR!" I call again as I watch those throbbing veins spread like earthquake fissures – up through her neck, over her cheeks, and to her eyes, resulting in her pupils disappearing into whites before she shrieks, the sound so loud, so raw like she's being burned, it cuts right through me, reverberating around the room.

I am startled when she grabs my coat sleeve and starts pulling me towards her while choking up more of the phlegm, and as much as I try to pull away, her seemingly inhuman strength pulls my face closer and closer to hers.

That's when I hear yelling behind me. "OUT! Get out!"

But I can't. No matter how hard I try, I feel myself being pulled inexorably forward, closer to the bulging white of those eyes and that distended mouth, now frothing with blood, which is growing wider and wider like it wants to devour me.

Closer...

I'm just inches away as I feel hands pulling at my other arm.

Closer...

Yelling. Chaos.

"GET OUT! Get him out of here!" I think it's the doctor ordering, but I can't pull away. I can't seem to untangle myself from the vice-like grip and that mouth, which is squelching now, retching.... Suddenly, the grip releases, and both the detective and I fall to the floor in a heap.

"GET OUT!" the doctor is still screaming as she and Nurse Jackie wrestle with the frenzied convulsions of the patient, her animalistic wailing reverberating all around.

I turn back to look at the thing on the bed just in time to see more dark blood pouring in rivulets from the woman's mouth. "Shit... she's biting off her tongue... GET ME 2CCs OF MIDAZOLAM.... NOW!" the doctor says, holding onto the patient's arm.

"Do you need us to—"

"GET THE FUCK OUT OF HERE!" the doctor orders.

The detective complies, tugging my arm and pulling us out of the room.

As the door sucks itself shut, we turn and watch through the glass partition. "What the hell happened in there?" Sarge demands. But both the detective and I are too shell-shocked to respond before he bellows, "ANSWER ME!"

"We don't fucking know!" I yell, gawking at the spectacle of the doctor and the nurse struggling to inject the woman as Amy's agonised shrieks continue.

"My God, what's happening to her?" Samantha asks, but nobody is able to answer, for we are all frozen in horror as we watch the once pretty research assistant's face wriggle and contort impossibly, almost as if something is living under her skin.

The sight must stun the medical team also since both of them have frozen to process what they are seeing. Then, the patient retches one more time before we watch clumps of something black and fleshy catapult through the air and pelt the doctor.

"Oh, God..." is the nurse's incredulous cry.

"What... is... that?" I hear Samantha ask, and I think she's talking about whatever was launched at the doctor. But then, to my absolute horror, I realise she's referring to whatever bloody thing is actually hanging out of the patient's mouth.

From our position behind the glass, it isn't easy to see what the medical team is seeing because the nurse is partially blocking our view. But now, she is slowly backing away from the bed, and as she does, the true horror of the scene is brought to us in shocking detail under the overhead examination lamp.

A sudden ripping sound fills the air, accompanied by an inhuman, agonised scream. "AHHHHHH... IT HURTS! IT HURTS! IT BURNS! HELP ME! HEEEELP ME!" Amy screams. "HEEEELP ME!" Words that I know will haunt me for the rest of my days, for it sounds as if the poor woman is being flayed alive.

"Oh, sweet God," the nurse gasps while the doctor – who has been nothing but the epitome of composure ever since I first met her – watches in astonishment. And it's this that sends a chill rippling through me, for nothing could have prepared me for this.

The sodden red stain on Amy's chest begins to spread, ripping the fabric as if there's something moving from underneath, something bursting out from the cavity of her chest and pushing through the fabric of her gown. Not blood nor viscera, but what can only be described as the giant bulbous head of a... oh, sweet Jesus, I don't even know.

Whatever it is, its head rises with an unnerving semblance of a cobra poised to strike. Its stem, thick and sinewy, unravels until it's standing erect, towering four to five feet over the gurney and Amy's twitching body with a dominion that feels almost sentient. Then the thing sways back and forth, from side to side, as if sizing up its audience before the folded tips that make up its head begin to unfurl with eerie grace. Section by section, each leaf, slick with a bloody substance, unfolds into a grotesque bloom atop its serpentine stalk.

The colour of the thing is otherworldly – swirls of deep purples and sickly greens that shimmer with an internal luminescence, casting an unholy light. The bloom is layered with the complexity of an orchid but is the size of a giant sunflower. At its core, the stamen and pistils form a glistening, golden spiral, drawing the eye inward, compelling in its beauty yet sinister in its implication.

Each of us is shocked into stunned silence while the atmosphere in the infirmary is charged with an almost palpable sense of foreboding as both doctor and nurse stand transfixed, their eyes locked on the extraordinary thing holding them in its trance.

CLICK! CLICK! CLICK! HISS! HISS! HISS! The stillness is shattered suddenly as the core of the alien plant quivers with a force that seems to defy the fragile beauty of its petals before it explodes! Stamen, pistils, and a cloud of fine, golden spores are propelled into the air, turning the room into a snow globe of floating, luminescent powder.

Caught in the beams of the lights, the spores dance like fireflies, a mesmerising display of light and motion. Yet, there's an underlying terror to their beauty, as the doctor and the nurse instinctively recoil while the spores drift lazily, carried on unseen currents, their golden glow stark against the darkness, as if each particle carries a fragment of some alien sun.

We can only watch in horror as the doctor and the nurse succumb to fits of coughs while the patient lies still on the gurney, the plant like a spear in her chest.

Then, I hear the doctor ask incredulously, "Where are you going?"

The nurse doesn't respond; she simply shakes her head and turns towards us. That's when we can see the front of her uniform is slick with blood and coagulated matter as she makes a run for the door.

"STOP!" the doctor orders, but the nurse isn't listening. Eyes wide, hands aloft like she doesn't want them tainted by what's dribbling down her front, she lunges for the door. As she does, she slams up against it, her face pressed against the glass.

Samantha screams as the doctor appears behind the nurse. "You can't go out there."

"LET ME OUT!" the nurse cries, eyes wide with terror, breath fogging against the glass.

"Sarge, lock this door!" the doctor orders.

"NO!" the nurse screams, cheeks hot with tears. "NOOO! LET ME OUT! LET ME OUT!" The two women then jostle, pulling and pushing each other as one attempts to leave and the other tries to keep her in the room.

"L...o...ck... the... f...f...ucking... door!" the doctor repeats through clenched teeth as she tries to hold the nurse, who is now screaming hysterically.

"PLEASE... PLEASE... PLEASE let me out!"

The scene is momentarily upstaged by a loud beep and click. The light on the door handle, which I hadn't even noticed before, switches from green to red.

"NOOO!" the nurse cries. "NO!"

SMACK! The doctor belts her subordinate across the face. "Pull yourself to-fucking-gether," she orders.

That slap may as well have smacked us all across the face – such was its power. We were all frozen in stupefied shock until that sound which, not surprisingly, causes the nurse to dissolve into floods of tears as she slowly slides down the glass to the floor and out of sight.

When I finally drag my eyes away from the spectacle beyond the glass, I find that it wasn't Sarge but my sister, Samantha, who locked the door. Now, straightening her shoulders and taking a deep breath, she pushes to the front of the glass and asks with a formal measure of composure that I don't even recognise, "Helena?"

The doctor doesn't respond; she's gawking back into the room.

"Helena?" Samantha repeats.

My heart pounds as I watch the woman turn to us once more. She is spattered with blood, awash with perspiration, and covered in the gold dust from that thing on the gurney.

I watch her take a deep breath, and then, with a composed demeanour in surreal contrast to what we just witnessed and her very appearance, she says, "You know what needs to be done."

17

PARANOIA

THISTLE ISLAND INFIRMARY. EVENING.

So, I bet you can't guess who I'm thinking about right now. I am thinking about Aaron Sinclair. Can you guess why? Well, why else but to curse that bloody American and his silver tongue?! If it weren't for him, we wouldn't even be here now, cooped up in this room that I've come to loathe but nonetheless appears to have become my second bloody home.

So anyway, yes... We're back in this meeting room, come dumping ground. It's been the best part of an hour since that mindfuck in the infirmary.

Yeah, I'm sorry. I'm back to swearing, and you can probably expect a lot of that because what the fuck?! Even now, I still don't know how to process what happened back there. In fact, now that the hideous tableau is no longer in front of me, I find there are moments when I actually try to convince myself that it wasn't real, that I'd somehow broken with reality once more, and that everything that happened and is happening, including the antiseptic stench that seems ever-present in this place, is yet another figment of my imagination.

Only it isn't – I'm not the one who's gone insane; it's the world around me. As I sit at this table and look at the grim, ashen faces of my fellow survivors, there's no mistaking that what we witnessed earlier this evening was anything but a nightmare.

To make things worse, the weather is deteriorating. That wind is hellbent on transforming this place into a glacial tundra.

Which means we haven't been able to send Luca home to his grandmother and uncle. We can only thank God that he didn't decide to venture down to that treatment room earlier. Now, he is lying on a series of chairs that I pushed together with my coat over him, sleeping.

Buddy is at my feet. I gave that boy such a squeeze when I saw him because he knew something was up the moment we walked in here.

I've missed him. I know that may sound pathetic, but I have. And I'm worried. I'm really worried that he and these new people that I have come to care about may now be in danger, and I've no bloody idea what I can do about it.

Oh, and me. I'm worried about me, too!

Samantha is sitting beside me, nursing what must now be a cold cup of coffee. The detective, Sarge, and the policeman are sitting opposite us.

Good ole Eric ran out into the snow earlier to throw up. There was definitely no judgement from me because I was keen on joining him. It was only the concerned look on my nephew's face that stopped me. He, like my dog before him, had obviously clocked our stupefied faces and was wondering what was wrong.

Where would anybody even start to explain what we saw in that room?

"We need to tell people." It's Eric. He's still looking washed out. Something that is only emphasised by his mop of soot black hair. This, coupled with his sunken, haunted eyes, is giving the uniformed man an incidental emo look.

"That's a terrible idea," Samantha says.

"People have a right to know," Eric retorts.

"Aye. They'll also have the right to panic. D'ye think we're equipped to deal with that?" Sarge retorts. "How many exactly are we talkin' about?"

The question is directed at Samantha, who responds confidently, "Last ferry tally puts us at six hundred and three."

"What about evacuation?" the detective asks.

"Yeah," Eric chimes in.

Samantha shakes her head. "In this weather? It's going to be at least a couple of days before they can get anybody out here."

"That's okay. We can tell everyone to stay in their homes until-"

"We can't," Samantha interrupts.

"Why not?" Eric demands.

"Because you seem to be ignoring what happened in there."

"Ignoring it? It's because of that shit that we need to get people out of here."

"We bloody can't," Samantha presses. "Why do you think Helena locked herself in there? She's quarantined the two of them. That room was built for that very purpose," she adds. "And we have no idea what we're dealing with or if it's contagious, and because of that..." she trails off.

"Because of that, what?" Eric asks.

Sarge, who I've noticed has been quietly observing the conversation, finally turns to his young subordinate and chips in.

"Because o' that, and until we know more, we have tae lock the whole island down," Sarge says slowly, his weathered hand unconsciously rubbing his chin as if to erase the words that are now hanging in the air like a death sentence, sending a creeping chill down my spine, unlike anything the weather could conjure.

"That's fucking crazy, man!" Eric explodes.

And if I'm perfectly honest, I'm thinking the same thing. I mean, the rational side of me knows that what my sister is saying makes sense, but the other side of me, the one focused on self-preservation, wants to get me and my new extended family off this rock.

"Eric—"

"No. That's fucking bullshit!"

"Eric..." Sarge continues.

"She just wants us to sit here—"

"ERIC!" the sergeant snaps. "That's procedure. It's fuckin' procedure, which is why the doc did what she did."

The cop scoffs. "Procedure? You're telling me that there's a procedure for what the fuck happened in there?" he asks incredulously.

"HEY!" Yes, it's me this time. "There's a child in here," I say with suppressed anger. "And he doesn't need to hear this shit, nor does he need to know that the bloke who's supposed to be protecting him is already falling apart."

"Who the fuck are you again?" The man glowers, leaning forward.

"I'm the bloke who's gonna come over there, drag you outside, and rub your face in that pile of puke you left by the front door if you don't pull your shit together."

"Like to see you try," he says, standing up.

I rise to meet him, but Sarge intervenes. "Alright, enough, ENOUGH! Sit down, both of you." When neither of us complies, he repeats, "I said, SIT THE FUCK DOON!"

Shit. My heart is thundering in my chest. Hands shaking. I don't even know where that came from. It's as if I'm standing outside of my body watching this fucking madness on television or something. This can't be happening to me. To us.

I sigh and run a hand through my hair. Buddy's whimper brings me back to myself, and I slowly sit back down. The cop follows suit.

Sarge turns to his subordinate. "Eric, he's right. I know you're scared. We all are. But ye're a cop. Ye've got a job tae dae. So do it. And you," he says, turning and pointing a chubby finger at me. "You threaten one o' my team again, an' ye'll be spendin' the rest of your time in a different kind of solitary confinement. Ya hear?" I don't answer. That adrenaline is still coursing through me. "Ya hear?" the man repeats. I nod.

I feel Samantha's hand on my arm. I don't know what came over me. Not my dark passenger. This was different. I just thought about Luca sleeping just a few feet from us and him hearing this stuff and not feeling safe. I mean, I'm pissing my pants. What the hell must it be like for a child? What's he even doing here anyway? We should have escorted him back ages ago.

The room falls silent, so that wind takes over, moaning through a gap in the window like it's taunting us, reminding us of our isolation out here.

"There's no way we can keep this quiet." It's Eric again. On the plus side, his voice isn't as loud or hysterical as earlier. So, yay for that. "Jackie lives with her mum. She's probably already wondering where her daughter is on account of the weather."

"Eric's right. There's nae way we're gonna be able to keep a lid on this if two people suddenly go missin'. Everybody knows there are no ferries, so we can't say they're off the island. Questions'll start flyin' soon enough."

"Ya know, it's fascinating to me how everybody's been focused on the islanders rather than on the problem." It's the detective suddenly talking as if she hasn't just witnessed everything else that just happened.

"That's because this isn't like the city. Here, we care aboot people," Sarge retorts.

"Is that right? Well, surely, if that's how you feel, then your priority should be on establishing what exactly we're dealing with here unless you already know, of course," the detective says, looking around the table.

And the room falls into an awkward silence in the way that gatherings tend to when someone is holding out.

"Okay. While it would be easy to indulge any conspiracy theory right now, we actually have a duty to ourselves and our neighbours to focus on the facts," Samantha says with true measured diplomacy.

The detective nods. "Of course." And yet, now everybody around the table is looking at everybody else. And even I, as much as I really don't want to, am now wondering why she said that. Does she know something I don't?

"Hold on. Hold on. Why did you just say that?" It's Eric, of course.

"I'd rather we not get distracted," Samantha jumps in.

"Why did you just say that?" Eric repeats, looking down the table at the detective.

She shakes her head. "No particular reason. It just seems odd to me that you're focusing so much on everything but what happened back there. Almost like it's no surprise to you."

"Ya know," Sarge begins, lifting that chubby finger once more, "you've done nothing but undermine our authority since you arrived—"

"ENOUGH!" Samantha brings her fist down on the table while simultaneously looking over at her son to make sure he's still sleeping. Then she looks at everybody in turn. "We're all scared. We're all confused, and it's only natural that emotions and opinions diverge. But no matter what you may think, Detective, nobody here has any idea what that abomination is back there. Nobody. Which in and of itself is plenty of reason why we want to focus on the safety of islanders before we start speculating about... whatever that is and what we're going to do about it." Samantha's voice falters on those last few words.

It's my turn to place a hand on her arm, since there's no doubt in my mind that she must be feeling *under immense pressure right now.*

Yeah, I know. I heard that, too. Doctor Holmes, much.

The detective holds my sister's gaze for several seconds before moving on in that trademark way of hers. "Okay," she says suddenly. "Why don't we look at what we know? A few days ago, your husband disappeared, along with his research assistant and the family dog. Today, we find that sheep on the other side of the island. Then, we're attacked by one – which may or may not be related. Then, both the dog and the research assistant return, but are both now dead in peculiarly similar circumstances."

Samantha looks at me but doesn't get a chance to react because, once again, it's Eric taking centre stage, eyes wide, nostrils flaring. "Hey, that research assistant was a *human being*, not an animal. A *human being* with a name. Her name was *Amy*, and you could at least show her some respect." It's Eric again. Nostrils flared. Eyes wide.

The detective looks at him, and for a second, I think she's going to apologise, but she doesn't. Instead, she simply picks up from where she left off. "My point is that they all died under similar circumstances."

"Not exactly," I say. "The sheep and the dog, there was no trace of that... um... *thing*."

The detective rocks her head. "Yes, I was thinking about that while you were all... um, squabbling. What if – and this is just a theory – that black stuff we found on the sheep and the dog... What if that is a byproduct of the, um... *thing*? What if, after it emerges from its host, it releases its spores or whatever, and then, having fulfilled its purpose, the thing wilts, dies, and becomes that black sludge? I would need to talk to the doctor to be sure, but I don't think it's much of a leap."

Ugh. I rub my hand. I forgot about that. I was grossed out at the time, and that revelation only renews the squirm factor.

"You've got it all worked out, haven't ya?" Sarge says.

"Well, if you have any other theories, I'd be glad to hear them," the detective responds.

"If what ye're sayin' is true, it'd mean anybody anywhere on the island could already be infected," Sarge says.

"Then our priority has got to be finding out how, exactly, this thing is spreading," Samantha says.

"My guess is we already know," the detective says. "We all saw what happened in that room. It's why the doctor wanted us to lock the place down. She knew they'd been exposed."

"Aye, but to what?" Sarge asks.

The detective shrugs. "That's what we need to find out. The good thing is that thanks to the doctor's quick thinking, we appear to have the thing contained."

"Not necessarily." It's Samantha. All eyes turn to her. "There's one major omission from your theory, Detective." My sister pauses, seemingly for effect, but the mist in her eyes tells a different story. Snow taps at the window. "If Amy and the dog came back, why didn't my husband?"

The detective moves to respond but is interrupted by the dimming of the lights and a nerve-jangling alarm that drills through the walls and my eardrums.

Luca is startled awake, his bleary, wide eyes instantly frightened. I immediately put my arm around him. "It's okay, mate. It's okay."

"What is that?" the detective asks, but nobody in the room seems to know.

"Is it the fire alarm?"

Alert. Containment breach. Attention all staff, this is not a drill. There is a breach in isolation chamber B1. Attention all staff, this is not a drill. There is a breach in isolation chamber B1. The recording appears to be playing out in the hallway. And I have absolutely no clue what this means, but it doesn't sound good.

Buddy starts barking.

Luca abandons me and runs over to his mother. I don't know what possesses me, but I tell him and my sister to "Stay here" before following the cops and the detective out of the door and into the hallway, where both the alarm and the recording seem much louder. And worse, to add to the terror of the moment, a red light on the wall is now flashing intermittently.

You know, nobody in this little troupe has any idea what's happening. But it's truly uncanny. We're rushing towards that room where, just a couple of hours ago, Amy was alive and well.

And when we get there, I realise that I must have somehow regressed and, once again, am seeing things that can't possibly bear any relation to reality because if they did, it would mean that somehow – and I have absolutely no idea how – the doctor and her nurse have managed to smash their way out of the reinforced glass of the window and make their way out into the night leaving nothing in their wake but swirling snow.

18

THE DARK

THISTLE ISLAND. LATE EVENING.

Okay, so as you've no doubt already concluded, things have taken a turn for the worse. By that, you know I mean for the terrifying, right?

When I saw that busted window, my stomach dropped. It felt like it wasn't two people who had just broken out of what was supposed to be a secure room but two lepers with a highly contagious disease that has placed every one of us in clear and present danger.

Oh, fuck.

That's exactly what they are. I keep trying to rationalise it, to tell myself that there's absolutely no evidence of that, but each time I do, I just get a hideous mental replay of that *Alien* chest-burst moment.

So now I'm really scared. Bricking it. Which is why when Samantha said she was going to contact the mainland, I was all for it. I just feel that the more bodies we can throw at this thing, the better right now. And that's absolutely no pun intended.

We also agreed she'd take Luca and Buddy back to the hotel where they'll be more comfortable – or safer – depending on how much into denial you actually are.

So anyway, they headed off with Sarge and Eric as escorts. The hotel isn't that far from here, but Sarge insisted, and again, I was all for that. Finally, the big guy and I agreed on something.

Of course, our mutual admiration spell was short-lived and ended the moment the man suggested that we split up. I actually laughed at the time because, well, split up? That's exactly what you *don't* do in situations like this. Every bloody horror movie, slasher thriller, and survival guide tells you: don't split up; stay together because there's bloody safety in numbers.

Naturally, my Indiana Jones of a detective was all for it. So I couldn't exactly say no. I couldn't exactly say it was a shitty idea because... well, you know, I'm a bloke, and I'm supposed to be tough, and she's..., oh, alright. I'm not a bloke; it would appear that I'm actually a misogynist who is shitting himself while she's, well, a bloody terminator, unafraid of anything.

For example, when we all did the obligatory post-mortem outside the isolation window with our flashlights – flakes of snow falling around us atmospherically like an overzealous snow machine – she did a Navajo crouch-down thing like she could also read footprints in the snow. Then, after inspecting the area for several dramatic seconds, she said, in words way too ominous for an average bloke like me, *These prints don't make any sense. It looks like there was someone or something else out here.*

Someone or *something* else? What the fuck are you talking about? I wanted to scream, but luckily, Eric did that for me. And she just casually panned that obligatory light around. *Take a look for yourself.* I was like, no thanks, I don't want to look. I don't *want* you to be right for a bloody change. But I did look. And guess what? She was right. The prints didn't seem to belong to two people leaving the building but were much more chaotic, like a dance floor after a brawl.

Shit.

So here we are, out in the heart of the night on an island that has been transformed into an Antarctic landscape. It's as if that gale has blown away all the colour of this land and left behind nothing but an eerie facsimile of snow and ice.

On the plus side, the storm seems to have abated. Now, the moon, a pale spectre in the sky, is casting a silvery glow over the place, turning the snow into a sea of luminescence. It would be a scene of haunting beauty were it not for the horror I believe has visited this peaceful island at the end of the world.

Yeah, I know, a somewhat pretentious description, but hey, I know it's easy to forget that I'm supposed to be a bloody writer who is supposed to be bloody writing. Instead, I'm traipsing across the glacier in the dead of night, hunting – at this stage – God knows what.

And it's so bloody quiet out here. Not a bark of a dog. The hoot of an owl. Even the tide that's supposed to stop for nothing and no one seems to have rushed out and refused to return to this place. All I can hear is the pounding of the blood behind my ears and the crunch of our footsteps in the snow.

"This must all be eerily familiar to you," the detective says suddenly, her voice quiet yet loud in the still as we make our way up the main high street towards the edge of the village where, we're told, Nurse Jackie lives with her mother. Not that we need the directions since there's a set of footprints leading the way.

"Familiar?" I ask, focusing both on the track and on where I put my feet because the last thing this woman needs to see is me falling arse over tit.

"Yes. After Fawndale," she says.

Which, of course, now has my complete attention. I smile. It's an awkward one because I don't know whether to be flattered or creeped out by her comment. "You've been checking on me," I say.

"Not exactly," she responds with a rock of the head, breath fogging out in front of her. Then, she must see my expression and qualifies the remark. "You were pretty hard to miss after what happened at Porthcove. The news. The papers. The book."

"Oh, right. And you remembered me. I'm flattered."

"Well," she says, rocking her head, "That's my job. Noticing details."

"Right. And you didn't think to mention this detail sooner?" I ask, suppressing a flare of irritation because, for some reason, I'm suddenly feeling at a disadvantage. She's been secretly observing me. Why? I know, a different kind of paranoia, but it would appear that's what this place does to you.

"I haven't really had the chance," she says.

I nod. "No?"

"No."

"Right. I just think that if it were me, I'd probably have mentioned something the moment my sister introduced us."

"I didn't think it was appropriate then."

"And you think it is now?" I say, indicating the fact that we're trekking through the snow in the dead of night.

"I came here to investigate a disappearance," she says.

"Right. And you didn't know if you could trust me. Is that what you mean?"

"That's correct. Did you know that the collapse of your father's business has left your new family in serious financial trouble?"

"Um, yeah. It's the first thing Sam told me."

"How much do you know?"

I think about this and shrug. "Just that the company struggled to regain its market share."

"Is that all?"

I look at her. "Yes, pretty much. That they were forced to diversify, and things are looking up now that they've attracted the attention of some major investors."

"Huh," she says, but she doesn't look at me.

"Huh? That's it? You're going to mysteriously park this conversation there? What? Not going to tell me that my stepfamily is secretly conducting weird human experiments to make ends meet or something?"

She frowns and looks at me. "What?"

"Never mind. What, exactly, are you trying to get at, Detective?"

"What did you and your brother fight about last night?"

"What, you mean you don't already know? You seem to know everything else."

"Could you just answer the question?"

"No. I don't want to answer the question."

"Why not?"

"Why? Why? Because—" I cut myself off as I'm forced to do a little jiggle to avoid that whole falling arse over tit thing.

"Are you okay?"

"I'm fine. Just slippery here, that's all," I say, regaining my balance.

"No. I mean generally, as I'm detecting a tone."

"A tone? Ya think? I can't imagine why."

"Right. So you *are* irritated."

"Of course, I'm fucking irritated! You know, you may be on some kind of spectrum thing where nothing rattles you, but me – I've been in situations like this before, and I don't like it. In fact, I'd go as far as saying I fucking hate it! So while I'm processing all of that shit, you can imagine that I don't respond well to you dredging up stuff about me, my family, and—"

"Stop."

"No. I think you need to hear this. Someone needs to tell you that you—"

"No. I mean, stop – I think we're here," she says, glancing past me. I follow her gaze to a stone cottage at the end of a row of trees. "The tracks end here," she adds.

I look down. Sure enough, the footprints turn here and, from what I can see, lead through a small, wonky gate into what I imagine is a front garden underneath this blanket of snow.

"Right," I say, the heat of my irritation with our conversation instantly extinguished with the cold chill of apprehension. We don't have any idea of what we might be walking into.

And yet, that doesn't seem to stop my fearless companion, who is already pushing her way through the creak of the gate that sounds like a squeal in the quiet.

So just in case you've already pictured this scene, let me just point out that as much as I would like it to be, this is not one of those American movies where the plucky detective and her hapless companion make their way down the garden path safe in the knowledge that should the need arise, she'll just reach into her holster and pull out her trusty handgun.

There's no such thing here. Neither of us has so much as a bloody stick to beat myself over the head with for ever agreeing to this excursion. I mean, I get her eagerness, but mine can't be anything but unadulterated madness.

And yet, I follow the detective to the front door. The lights are out, and something tells me that knocking will not help, and yet we do it anyway.

There's no response. A peek into one of the downstairs windows reveals... nothing. Just the faint glow of a light through an open doorway leading into a hallway, maybe?

The only way to know is to take a look at the back of the house, but I can see, shocker, that the detective has already had the same idea. She doesn't speak; she merely mouths *the back* and points around the side of the house with two fingers in that military kind of way, which does absolutely nothing for my nerves.

Now, I would be more than happy to say that *We came here, we tried, but there was nobody home*, so we turned around and hurried back to safety to wait for the cavalry. But with the detective, of course, no such thing. She's already reached the corner of the house and has just disappeared around the side.

Shit.

I follow her, my steps hesitant. The first thing I see is a large swath of amber light pouring out of the open back door onto the snow, accompanied by the faint sound of music. It's an old number about the end of the world, which only makes this scenario even more chilling.

Nobody is going to leave their door wide open in this weather. It's bloody freezing!

The detective looks down at the chaotic medley of footprints outside the backdoor. There's nothing distinguishable, just like it was outside of the infirmary window, and my heart desperately tries to convince me to turn back by thumping at my chest.

And yet... guess what I do? That's right, I follow the detective inside.

I've barely stepped over the threshold when the sweet scent of cinnamon engulfs me. There's warmth, too, beautiful warmth escaping into the night like prey fleeing a predator. Then, a scream unlike anything I've ever heard pierces the warmth and the pounding in my temples, revealing the whistle of a kettle on the hob. The detective hastily kills the thing by moving it off the heat.

The music is clearer now. Louder.

The detective looks at the small kitchen table. I follow her gaze. There are chairs pulled out like people have been sitting here. Two empty mugs, a sponge cake, and a knife resting on a wood chopping board, all dramatically lit by a feeble light bulb hanging from the ceiling.

Nothing about this feels good, and I want to tell the detective that we should leave. Just turn around and run screaming from here.

But I daren't make a sound, and she's at least four feet in front of me. I reach out to tap her on the shoulder, but she moves out of reach towards the hallway.

Fuck.

... Don't they know it's the end of the world?

She's just about to step into the hallway when I hear something. A sound barely noticeable above the music.

But it definitely happened because the detective stops and turns. I shake my head at her. *It wasn't me.* But then her gaze shifts and my stomach lurches – *There's someone standing behind me!*

No. She's actually looking across the room. Reluctantly, I follow her line of sight – to a door I hadn't even noticed until now.

When I turn back, she's looking directly at me. There's no need for words; she's expecting me to check it out because I'm the closest, but all I want to do is get the hell out of this place.

I shake my head and jerk my thumb at the door. But she refuses with her own shake of the head before starting forward. I scowl at her and hold up an angry hand.

Fuck!

I turn in that direction – throat constricted, beads of sweat tickling my scalp – and to my astonishment, make my way around the chairs, the table, and to the gloomy side of the room.

It could lead upstairs, down into a creepy cellar, or nowhere at all. Given the size of the door, my bet is it's a pantry, and that's weirdly the most horrifying scenario of all... much more terrifying. The threat would be so immediate, trapped in this small space, nowhere to run. You know, that kind of thing.

Oh, shit! Can you hear this shit?

It's fine. It's okay. There's going to be nothing in there. This is all in your head. Autosuggestion. Think about it. This is going to be just like one of those horror flicks. One of those subversive scenes where you think something horrible is going to happen when, really, it's just a cat or some other innocent plot device item that's decided to spontaneously throw itself off the shelf for a cheap scare.

Oh, God.

I arrive at the door. Small latch. Pantry. Has to be.

I turn to the detective, who is watching intently.

My heart is pounding so hard I think it's going to burst out of my chest. No, not the best analogy. I just think I've been holding my breath too long.

The music stops.

Lifting the latch with a loud clack, I brace myself as the door swings open with a nerve-jangling creak – of course. Then I hold my breath once more as my eyes adjust to the gloom, revealing the pantry.

The space is much deeper than I expected. The shelves on both sides are like runways full of jars, tins, paper towels, tableware, and... flour. There's a giant white explosion of it on the floor. A bag obviously fell somehow, and—hot and cold shivers rip through me as I first see the tip and then the rest of the... medical clogs – the rubbery material is unmistakable – and then, *Oh, God*, the outline of a person.

It's the nurse! She's standing at the back of the pantry where even the overspill of kitchen light refuses to venture. Yet, there's enough creepy illumination to highlight the woman's ghostly grey features covered by a tangled mess of wispy hair. Her face is glistening with sweat, dark circles staining the collar and armpits of her scrubs, causing them to cling to her body. But it's her eyes – oh, God – those bloodshot eyes bulging from their sockets, wide and frantic, like those of a cornered animal, that send a thunderbolt of terror through me.

I want to turn and run, slam the door shut behind me, but something tells me that would be the wrong thing to do, akin to running from a rabid dog because that's what she reminds me of – breaths shallow, fast, animalistic.

"Jackie?" *Fuck!* The words just slip out, my mind-numbingly afraid body slipping into therapist mode. "Jackie, hey. It's okay. It's okay," I say, holding out a steadying hand. "We're just here to help. Just here to help." And to my absolute delight, I see something. Nothing major, just a flicker. Something in those eyes, like she registered my words.

"I...i...t's h...e...re." She whispers, her whole face contorted into a mask of terror. At least, I think it's that before she throws her hands to her head and starts wailing....

"Jackie?" I say, moving one step closer. "Jackie... talk to me... tell me what's wrong. What's wrong? Tell me..." I hold out a hand towards the screaming woman before she falls silent once more and flatly declares in words that make me want to piss myself, "We're all gonna die out here."

I barely have time to register the horror of those words before she's careening forward, colliding with me, launching me backward onto the kitchen table, twisting my back, sending me sprawling over the cake and flying through the air until there's a sudden thwack to the back of my head as I land on the cold floor in a sprawling heap.

Pain crackles through my spine as I lie in a fog of agony. Yet ripping through this is the worst agonised wailing I have ever heard and a sight that pushes instant bile to the back of my throat – the nurse desperately tearing the clothes from her body, revealing her bare chest, and then clawing and digging into her skin as the detective rushes over to her.

I can only watch as the woman's flesh undulates as if something is crawling beneath it, something that pushes at and distends her skin before ripping through and reaching out into the room like a bony claw. The detective's attempt to administer aid is abruptly halted when she witnesses the grotesque transformation, prompting her to jolt backward and gawk in stupefied horror as I have been, until now. Now, I've moved on. I'm thinking of something else. I'm thinking of what took place in the infirmary, of what we witnessed in there, of what happened to Amy.

With a hand to the back of my head, I mutter, "No... Isla... get... out...get out," I say as I watch the nurse stagger back towards the pantry once more.

"P...p...ush her... in... there." I say, "P...ush her inside." But there's no way the detective is going to hear me over the woman's agonised screams.

I pull myself onto my knees – lightning bolts of pain shooting through me – grab hold of the table for support and attempt to get to my feet. "G...et ...out!" I groan. "Isla, get... OUT!"

But the detective still isn't hearing me as she resumes her attempts to help the nurse.

I push myself up onto my feet as I watch blood dribble down the nurse's breasts. "Ou...t..." I murmur, putting weight on my feet as the room begins to swim.

Oh, shit.

There's cracking, ripping... of flesh!

"Out..." I say, staggering over to the detective, grabbing her arm, and yelling, "WE... WE NEED TO GET THE FUCK OUT OF HERE!" I scream, yanking her backward towards the hallway, grabbing the door handle, and pulling as those gut-wrenching screams reach an ungodly loud pitch. Then, glancing back, a snapshot of an image that will forever haunt me sears itself into my mind – the nurse, standing naked under that lightbulb, while what can only be described as a tree branch bursts through her chest, spraying black matter all over the table.

I yank the door shut with a slam, and the detective collapses onto me just as there's a loud thump against the other side. This is closely followed by another thud before the world falls silent but for our rasping breaths.

We stay that way – on the hallway floor; the detective slumped against me, my arms wrapped protectively around her – for what must be seconds but feel like minutes, waiting for the toll of our exertion to subside.

As our panting begins to level out and I become aware of the heat of our proximity, I ask, "Are you okay?"

The only response is a groan. "I... think I smacked my head," the detective mumbles.

Her words barely register as my attention is snatched away. Overhead, the hallway's lightbulb is still swinging back and forth – I must have hit it when I dragged us in here. Now, with every sway, shadows stretch and distort across the hallway. It's in this unsettling light that I become aware of a sound as subtle as it is recognisable – muffled gagging.

A chill runs down my spine. I turn towards it... towards the stairs, and as the light swings back, I watch it glide across the linoleum floor to the first two carpeted steps and then onto a sight that pushes me right back into denial. A sight that makes me think that when I fell, I must have blacked out because this can't be real.

And yet, the detective's proximity, the cold in the extremities of my body, and the pain still humming through me all conspire to convince me that this *is* real. I am watching the grotesque spectacle of an old lady I don't recognise, dressed in a pink nightgown, lying upside down on the stairs. My breath hitches in my throat, and I squeeze my eyes shut, trying to will the image away. But when I open them again, she's still there.

She is looking at me, eyes beseeching, tears streaming down the creases in her face. She has something clamped over her mouth and nose – something as colourful as it is terrifying. Something that looks just like the alien flower we saw in the infirmary, only bigger. Much bigger. And this thing, with its flower tips made of needle-like teeth, has attached itself to her face and is monstrously pulsating. Nausea rises in my throat, and a cold sweat breaks out on my skin.

But before I can fully process this horror, a long tendril leading up into the darkness of the landing yanks the old woman upward by her face, twisting her into an inhuman sideways contortion until all I can see are fluffy beige slippers disappearing out of sight.

19

THE PLAN

THISTLE ISLAND. LATE EVENING.

We ran out of that house. We ran as fast as our feet would carry us, without looking back. And do you know what stuck with me the most, giving me some bizarre level of comfort? The detective ran, too.

I know there's absolutely nothing about it that should make me feel better, but it does. Until now, I've felt like just a passenger in all of this. Now, it feels like we're in this together, and that it isn't just me shitting myself here.

Yeah, I know you were probably expecting something a little more from me. Profound even. But, come on, you were there. You saw what we saw.

And what the fuck?!

The plan before we left the infirmary was to regroup back at the hotel, but the police station was closer.

And I can tell you, we nearly had another victim on our hands when the detective and I burst through the front door of the station and gave the receptionist, Tracy, such a fright we made the woman scream.

Of course, when she asked what was wrong, neither of us wanted nor was able to share. Instead, we wrapped ourselves in blankets meant for the occasional resident of the tiny two-cell establishment and sat drinking coffee for the best part of half an hour without saying a word, each lost in thought. It was only when Sarge and Eric made an appearance that I found I could still form words.

They did not find the doctor. Her tracks disappeared into the woods. Obviously, neither of the intrepid cops felt compelled to follow them in there. Normally, I'd find that alarming, but in this case, I think it's perfectly understandable.

Of course, when Sarge asked about our mission, we had a different story to tell. I let the detective recount most of it because, well, I still don't have words for what we saw back there.

Naturally, the big Scottish bloke struggled with the idea, yet when Eric threatened to start another of his obligatory hysterics, he managed to silence the man with just one glare. Yeah, there's something about that big, imposing islander I find both terrifying and reassuring in equal measure.

Interestingly, he sat fiddling with the ridge of his coffee cup for several seconds, which I thought was unusual for such a sceptic until I realised that it was probably all an act. He is scared, too. And after everything we've all seen tonight, who can blame him?

So now, talk has turned to action. Given that there is a clear and present danger to life, Eric is keen on warning the villagers, and Sarge, who was previously against panicking residents, appears to be on board, too. Isla – yeah, after what we've been through, we're on first-name terms – agrees, as do I, to a point.

It makes sense that we should warn people about the threat, but the real question is what we are going to tell them. The truth? Nobody is going to believe that. It's basic psychology. Even if everyone was open-minded enough to entertain such a nightmarish possibility, there's a good chance some would panic while others would go into denial – basic human behaviour. Something that would ultimately lead to a fracture instead of unity in the community, which is what we need the most right now.

Interestingly, my theory got Sarge's attention. At first, I caught him observing me with such intensity I thought he was going to chew me out for citing psychobabble bullshit or something, but instead, he grunted, and when Eric tried his usual contrariness, the giant shut him down again.

Yeah. Won't be long before we're the best of buddies. Okay, that might be stretching it.

Of course, one of the other ideas tabled by Isla is that we wait it out until the mainland gets in touch. They'd have protocols in place precisely for this type of scenario – no, I didn't get into the whole *when you say this kind of scenario, I'm assuming you're discounting the whole infirmary/house of horrors mind trip*. Either way, I was happy to hand the thing off, assuming we could all last that long.

But then receptionist/female cop Tracy, who was loitering nearby, jumped in to piss over everything. She said if there was any chance of anybody coming to the island, it would have to be within the next hour or so before the next front came in.

When Sarge asked what the woman was talking about, she very unkindly pointed at one of her screens.

Not surprisingly, island life is somewhat dictated by nature's meteorological movements, which means that keeping an eye on weather formations is par for the course. She – way too enthusiastically, if you ask me – showed us a radar rendition of a band of particularly thick and intense-looking cloud formation set to besiege the whole northern part of the country as an unprecedented ice storm.

I made the mistake of laughing when she said that an Arctic front was on its way, wrongly thinking for a split second that she was adding some levity to the situation by dramatically reenacting that scene from *Jurassic Park*, and, well, it turns out she wasn't.... There really is an ice storm on the way, and we're going to be smack bang in the middle of it.

You have got to be fucking joking?! is what I said when I saw the giant swirl. But she just shrugged and said it wasn't particularly unusual for this time of year. Oh, of course, that old chestnut. This meant that even if the cavalry made it to the island in time, there's no way they'd be able to evacuate all six hundred and however many residents in time. Assuming those people would even want to leave.

FUCK! That was my response. Yes, I warned you there'd likely be more swearing, but you can hardly blame me.

So now, we're all arranged around the small open-plan office of the police station like members of a pop band – some sitting at desks, others leaning on them.

Samantha decided to join us despite the fact that we'd all agreed to meet at the hotel. Sarge reprimanded her as if she was a teenager, and when she gave him a look, he went on to explain that things had escalated and that it was no longer safe for anyone to be roaming around alone. When she asked him what he was talking about, there was a long pause and he... looked at me!

Thanks, mate.

Anyway, I told her, and she just held my gaze but said nothing, which is understandable. What can you say to something like that?

Apart from, "We're going to need to tell everyone."

"I agree," I say quickly.

"Now, hang on, weren't you the one who said that they were all gonne t' shut down or whatever?"

"Denial is actually what I said, and there's still a danger of that, but it's better than the alternative."

"Yes, but we don't truly know what the alternative is, do we?" Samantha says.

I squint at her. "I just told you."

"Yes, but you also said it was dark and that you couldn't see much."

I gape at her. "We didn't need to see much else to know that there's fucking weird shit happening here, Sam."

"Is that your professional opinion?" she retorts.

"Are you serious right now?"

"Well, Marco. You and I both know that you have a certain propensity for..." She leaves the sentence unfinished, and I see that it has caught everybody else's attention.

"For what, Sam? Finish the thought. For what?"

"It doesn't matter."

"No. Go on. What is it that I have a propensity for?"

"I think we're getting off track," the detective jumps in.

"No. We're not," I come back. "Go on, Sam," I say, as I can feel everyone's eyes burning into me.

"Marco—"

"Go on," I say through gritted teeth.

"You've had a propensity for seeing... things in the past."

"And there it is," I say with a shake of the head. My own sister. My initial reaction is hurt – because I can't help but feel betrayed by her in some way. Then anger, because she isn't exactly lying. That, and I did kind of push her into it.

"What are you talking about?" Eric asks.

"It doesn't matter," my sister says dismissively.

"It does. I think it does. You introduced this man as some kind of expert. What is it about him that we don't know?"

"I don't understand why this is relevant—"

"He had a psychotic break a year or so ago after his son died," the detective interrupts my sister, and her words feel like a knife to the gut—not just because she's saying them, but because of the mention of my son.

Toby.

"Jesus Christ," Eric hisses.

"... He's been seeing things ever since. Things that aren't there."

I nod, angry now. "Yep. That's true. Kind of, because you weren't actually there, Sam," I say to my sister, "and nor were you, Isla," I turn to the detective. "However, you all were at the infirmary. You all saw what happened in there. Just like you saw that thing at the nurse's house," I say, turning back to the detective, which means that now, all eyes are on her. And for a dreaded second, I think she's going to bail, but then... shit, she is.

I watch that small nose crease up as if she's wrestling with her own thoughts. "I don't... I don't really know what I saw there. It was just too dark."

"Are you fucking joking right now? You were right there with me," I say.

She nods. "I was, Marco, but I was out of it. I'd banged my head when you yanked me through the door. I don't really know what I saw."

I shake my head, incredulous. I could smash something right now. I could pick up one of these computers and shove it through that fucking window. Or better still, down someone's throat!

But I swallow down the red-hot embers of rage and hold out my hands. "Look. I know where this is going. And you can think whatever you want about my past, but it doesn't change what you saw in that infirmary."

"He's right," Samantha jumps in. "But, by your own words, we can't tell them about that. We don't even know the extent of the problem. It may well be an isolated incident."

"Aye," Sarge adds.

"Isolated incident?" I echo. "I think the spatter pattern at the nurse's house would beg to differ."

"Be that as it may," my sister responds, "we can't tell the islanders the details of this. The panic it would spark could have the opposite effect. We need a cover story."

I shake my head. "Spoken like a true politician." She looks at me but says nothing.

"Well, there's the storm," Tracy speaks up.

Samantha thinks about this. "Perfect. We can cite danger to life and urge them all to stay indoors. Most will anyway."

The rapid tolling of a solitary church bell pushes into the conversation, and everybody turns toward the door as if they can see it.

"Good."

"Ye called a meetin'?" Sarge asks. "Already? I thought we were gonna discuss it a wee bit further.

"We have discussed it," my sister says, pulling on her gloves and walking over to him. "Time's of the essence. You know that. That storm's going to be here in less than an hour."

"What about the mainland? What did they say?"

"They said they're going to get a team out here as soon as possible, but with the storm on its way, that may not be for a while. Until then, it's down to us to keep everyone safe."

The policeman thinks about this and sighs.

"Samantha?" I say, walking over to her.

"Marco," she begins. "I know you're upset—"

"Upset? Me being upset is the least of your worries. You better hope that I have lost my bloody mind again because if what I saw in that place is true, then you're serving up your precious neighbours on a fucking platter."

My sister holds my gaze for several seconds, and I think she's going to say something, but she doesn't. Instead, she zips her coat up and makes her way towards the exit.

20

AS THE BELL TOLLS

THISTLE ISLAND COMMUNITY HALL· NIGHT·

It doesn't take long for the villagers to respond to the church bell's summons. One by one, wrapped in coats and makeshift shrouds of blankets and quilts, they all make their way like lemmings from the warmth of their homes to converge on the village hall. Their breaths, along with urgent chatter, fill the frigid night sky – a mix of concern and curiosity in their voices that's hard to miss.

Leaning against the cold stone of a nearby building, I watch from a distance, scanning the area, half-expecting something to jump out of the shadows at any moment. But, of course, nothing does, and as always, even I start to doubt if things really happened the way I think they did.

On the plus side, this uncanny call to worship should summon my nephew and, by association, Buddy. And I can't wait to see the big guy. It feels like we've been separated for days, and while I want Luca to be happy, I'm ready to have my companion back – especially since, right now, he feels like the only living, breathing thing that gets me.

I shiver. And this time, it isn't due to the cold but the god-awful feeling that through all my self-doubt, I still believe that there's something hideous out there, biding its time.

Movement behind startles me, and I turn around.

"Only me," says the detective.

I don't respond but turn back to the gathering crowd.

"Keeping watch?" she asks.

"Why would I? There's nothing out there, remember?"

She thrusts her gloved hands into the pockets of her coat. "I know you're disappointed," she says, "but my head was spinning. I really didn't see anything in there."

"Right," I say. And I know it seems childish, but there have been fleeting moments since I arrived here when, to my surprise, I actually felt like I was part of something. But now, it just feels like history is repeating itself, and I'm back on the outside.

"It's nothing personal," she adds.

I scoff. "You know, I really hate that expression because it's often appended to some of the most despicable acts. Anything you perpetrate on someone else is happening to them. That, by its very definition, makes it personal."

"I was just telling the truth. That's why I'm here."

"I thought you were here to find a missing person."

"I am."

"How's that working out for ya?"

She doesn't answer. Instead, we watch as more people file into the community hall. "Do you think something happened to him... Ewan?"

"I'm almost certain it did."

"Do you think it had something to do with what we saw in the infirmary?"

"I don't know. I still need to talk to your sister about Thistle Loch."

"The company? Why would you talk to her? It's my stepbrother you need for that, isn't it?" I ask. When she doesn't answer, I turn to her to find that she's looking at me. "What?" I ask.

"You don't know, do you?"

"Know what?"

"Roberto Junior stepped down as CEO over a year ago."

"Stepped down?" She rocks her head the way I do when weighing thoughts. "What?"

"Well, he didn't so much step down as he was pushed."

"Pushed, by whom? The board?"

"Yes. A vote of no confidence... Led by your sister."

"Sam?"

"Oh, I thought she told you."

"No."

"Yeah, Samantha is the CEO of Thistle Loch now."

Right. And those hits just keep on coming.

21

BLACKOUT

THISTLE ISLAND COMMUNITY HALL· NIGHT·

The community hall's layout has changed somewhat since I was last here. The space that was the dance floor is now filled with rows of chairs. And, as if for a press conference, two tables have been pushed together on the stage with chairs behind them. I don't know whose idea that was, but it doesn't inspire confidence. They should really be standing out here with everyone else if they want to project that all-important island camaraderie, but what do I know?

It's been ten minutes since my chat with the detective, and I still can't seem to shake off the latest revelation about Samantha. I don't think I misunderstood her. She very much made it sound like Roberto Junior was in charge. She must have taken over when things started to hit the fan. I had no idea. Why wouldn't she just tell me?

The hall is packed. All the seats are full, and the standing room at the sides and back where the detective and I are located is filling up, too. It's a major turnout that feels both comforting and scary since I'm liking the whole safety in numbers thing but can't help but think that these people would be better off at home behind locked doors.

There's a lot of chatter in the room, but a familiar sound slices through it and sends a warm buzz through me. I turn and watch people part as Buddy bounds over and almost knocks me off my feet.

"There you are, big guy! Oh, easy!" I say through chuckles as he jumps on his hind legs and paws at my chest. I bend down and stroke his head, and he covers me with cold, slobbery kisses.

"Yes. I've missed you too, mate. I've missed you, too," I say, hugging and kissing the big fella on the head. And of course, while doing my best not to make it too obvious, I squeeze that furry golden wonder like a long-lost relative.

Luca is standing nearby. "Hey, you. How's he been?" I ask.

"He's been great, but..." He steps closer and lowers his voice. "I don't think Grandma likes having him in the house."

I look up to meet my stepmother's gaze. She's watching us through the crowd.

"I can imagine," I say, without taking my eyes off the woman. Then, turning back to my nephew, I add enthusiastically, "We've got a space reserved for you right here with us."

But Luca bows his head. "I can't."

"Why not?"

"Grandma says she spoke to Mum and that I need to sit at the front with her and Uncle Rob." And as if on cue, I hear Claudia's obnoxious voice ring out through the crowd in that repressed, frustrated way of hers.

"I've got to go," my nephew adds with obvious disappointment.

"Oh, okay," I say. "Maybe we can hang out later?"

My nephew doesn't respond. Instead, he hugs Buddy and then turns and makes his way back through the crowd.

Oh, shit... I didn't like that. What's that all about? He's my nephew. I barely know him, and yet I hate the idea of him leaving. Buddy doesn't seem that keen either, by the way he's watching and whimpering.

"It's okay, Buddy. We'll see him later," I say, stroking my boy's fur while attempting to shrug off a cold shroud of dread that's just wrapped itself around me.

"Are you okay?" It's the detective.

"Yeah, of course," I say, "fine," as I watch my stepmother walk my nephew to the front where Roberto Junior is already seated.

Then, the buzz and chatter in the room quietens, and I look up. My sister, the mayor – and CEO apparently – takes her seat behind the table on the stage along with the police sergeant. The other two cops – Eric and Tracy – are standing on either side at the front of the stage as if they expect the speakers to need security.

Samantha clears her throat, drawing the room's attention with an ease that speaks to her experience in leadership. The murmurs fade to silence, all eyes fixed on her as she leans slightly towards the microphone, her expression solemn yet reassuring.

"Good evening, everyone," she begins, her voice steady and clear. "Thank you very much for coming out tonight despite the worsening weather. As always, your safety and well-being are our top priorities, and we wouldn't have asked you here if it weren't important."

She pauses, glancing briefly at the sergeant and the officers for a moment of silent solidarity before continuing. "As most of you will be aware by now, we have a major winter storm rolling in. Meteorologists predict that it's probably going to be one of the worst seasons for islands like ours. The severity of this storm cannot be overstated – it poses a significant danger to life if precautions are not taken."

The mayor – because that is the character my sister has now become: back straight, hands set out on the table in front of her – lets her words sink in, ensuring the gravity of the situation is fully absorbed by her audience. "In light of this, and after taking advice from various experts, I've decided to issue a strong advisory for all residents to stay indoors until further notice. This is not a suggestion – it is a necessity for your safety and the safety of your loved ones."

A ripple of whispers courses through the crowd, a mix of concern and questions unspoken. Samantha holds up a hand, a gesture for patience and attention. "I know this is a lot to ask, especially with the sense of cabin fever many of us are already feeling. But the risks of venturing outside in the coming days far outweigh the temporary inconvenience of staying put.

"We're working closely with our community services to guarantee support for those in need during the storm. If you're caring for someone who needs extra assistance or know of a neighbour in such a situation, please let us know so we can offer help. Your efforts remain invaluable, but we're here to assist you further, if needed. Ultimately, we're in this together, and it's by staying united and looking out for one another that we'll weather this literal storm, too."

Samantha's gaze sweeps across the room as nervous chatter fills the space. Then I watch her take a deep breath and add, "I'll now open the floor to any questions you may have. Please, let's keep this orderly so everyone's concerns can be addressed."

Sure enough, the first person to put up a rugged hand is the older man from the church – with the stereotypical beanie hat and white beard – that I imagined to be a fisherman. His accent is strong, as is the direct question that comes out of his mouth. "What's this truly aboot, eh? We've braved the storms afore – dinnae recall ye ever summonin' a meetin'. Why the sudden decree to bide indoors?"

"And so it begins," the detective says under her breath. I glance at the door and squeeze Buddy's fur. When I look back, Sarge is answering the old man's question. "Aye, Fin, we've been through worse. But the mainland's reported that there's also a peculiar strain of flu doin' the rounds. We want to minimise exposure, ya know?"

A middle-aged woman, wrapped in a headscarf and quilt, jumps up and chimes in. "A flu? So is that the real reason why you want us to stay indoors?"

Samantha answers with a reassuring smile. "Maggie, we just want to ensure everyone's safety. You know how it is. Prevention is better than cure." I watch her glance at the Sarge, no doubt wanting to kick the bloke for going off script. He does have a point, though. Flu sounds better than bad weather in this context.

But the woman has barely sat down when another woman, wrapped in a hat and holding a baby in her arms, rises next. "I heard something happened at the infirmary earlier. Is that true? Does this have something to do with Amy? Does she have this flu you're talking about? Should we be worried about our kids?"

Loud voices start talking over each other.

"Ladies and gentlemen, please..." Samantha begins. "We won't be able to hear anyone if you keep talking over each other."

It's Sarge who responds, using that booming voice of his over the microphone to drown out any unruly chatter. "No need to worry, Elsie. We had a visitor who fell ill suddenly, but it's under control. They're in isolation now, just to be sure."

A man in overalls and a thick black coat asks gruffly, "And what does the doc have to say about this? Why isn't she up there with you?" Some voices cheer, supporting the question.

I watch my sister coolly lean into the microphone and say, "Thanks, Dougie, but I feel we're getting a little off track. We called the meeting to discuss the storm. The only reason Sarge mentioned the flu is just as a precaution."

"Answer the question!" someone yells.

Others agree, and just when I think there's going to be a mutiny, a touch on my arm startles me, and I turn to see the detective pointing to movement at the front of the stage.

Someone wearing a parka talks to Tracy, the cop, and then climbs the few steps up onto the stage. I can't see them yet, but Samantha and Sarge's expressions tell all and nothing. They both look as shocked as the thump in my heart is feeling. And that's only exacerbated when the person takes a seat.

"Shit," I gasp.

"Shit," the detective agrees.

"Sorry, Dougie," the person says, pulling the microphone in front of her. "I got held up at the infirmary. As Sarge has already said, we're keeping a visitor there, but it's purely a precaution. Everything is perfectly fine," she lies. "We just don't want this flu getting around if we can avoid it." She follows that up with a big smile.

The detective and I look at each other. The woman looks perfectly fine, and once again, for a split second, I'm questioning whether or not all of that shit really happened. And I know, if it wasn't for the detective's reaction, I would still be wondering right now. But it happened. I know it did. We were there. I remember her speaking those ominous words: *You know what you have to do.*

And yet... she's sitting there looking like a picture of health, grinning from ear to ear like some kind of family-friendly automaton, fielding questions.

I look at Sarge and Samantha. Both are obviously seeing what I'm seeing, and both are discreetly recoiling in their seats, but with a whole island of people hanging on their every word, they're going to have to keep their shit together if they don't want to cause a panic.

"... and of course, Jenny. If your mother still isn't feeling up to it, I'll be happy to stop by after the meeting," the doctor is saying uncharacteristically sweetly.

"What are the chances of her not being exposed?" the detective asks, seriously and quietly.

"We need to get these people out of here," is my unequivocal response, anxiety crawling up my throat.

"How?" the detective asks. "There's no way without causing a panic."

I look to the front. I can't see Luca, but I can just about make out the back of Claudia's head. Then I look around for one of the most popular plot devices of any movie where a protagonist needs to empty a building fast. And I find one. "The fire alarm," I say.

The detective nods, impressed that I should even come up with that.

And so, as the doctor hijacks the meeting, answering questions both pertinent and not pertinent to her profession, I slowly move to the side of the room and home in on the red "*Break glass in case of emergency*" sign. And I'm just gearing up to do that very thing, heart throbbing, breath holding, when—

The lights go out, prompting a chorus of collective cries and screams. And when I say out, I mean out. It's pitch black in here, and my heart is now in my throat.

"Calm! Remain calm! It's just a power cut!" Samantha's voice rings out in the darkness before one, then two of the cops flick on flashlights.

"Why's there a power cut?" someone asks. "The storm hasn't even reached us yet."

"Please remain calm," Samantha repeats, her voice much softer now without the aid of a microphone.

"STAY CALM AS WE ASSESS THE SITUATION!" Sarge barks from the stage. I watch Eric and his flashlight move to the window; I'm assuming to establish if the outage is island-wide. The darkness beyond the glass tells me everything I need to know.

I reach for my phone but realise I don't have the bloody thing since there's no point in this dead zone of a place.

Other flashlights flick on now from some villagers who had the presence of mind to bring one with them, the beams slicing around the room like demented searchlights. One of them finds me, and I flinch, holding up a hand to fend off the glare. "Marco..." It's the detective.

I follow the light to her.

"We need to get everyone out of here," she says gravely. Then, I watch as the beam of her flashlight makes its way over the throng toward the stage to find Sarge and Samantha on their feet, squinting out into the crowd while between them, there is a troubling void.

"The doctor's gone again," the detective narrates.

"Oh, shit," I gasp just as there's commotion at the front of the stage. All available light beams converge there, as do a cluster of people, their bodies tense.

"CALM! Please, everyone, just—" Samantha's efforts are swallowed up by a series of raised voices.

"What's happening there?" someone shouts, the strained tone mirroring the collective dread.

Eric, flashlight in hand, moves purposefully towards the commotion, his silhouette a sharp contrast to the intermittent flashes of light.

Tracy, on the other hand, seems momentarily frozen, her flashlight beam trembling slightly in her hand, betraying her uncertainty.

Eric's voice cuts through the din, authoritative yet laced with an undercurrent of concern. "Stay back, please! Let us check— JESUS CHRIST!"

Hot and cold shivers ripple through me as an instant replay of what happened at the infirmary flashes through my mind. "Get to the door!" I order. "We need to get these people out."

The detective doesn't hesitate. She turns and barges through the wall of people next to us, her light bobbing as she goes. It's a struggle in the dark that prompts a series of complaints. "THIS WAY!" she yells. "THIS WA—" But she cuts herself off as she pushes on the door and bounces off it. She tries again, pushing and rattling, but still nothing.

Then she points her light at it and gasps. "It's locked... the key's gone."

"Why would anyone lock the door?" somebody nearby asks.

I can only see one side of the detective's face in the torchlight, but I can tell she's alarmed. Not an expression I am used to on her, and it only dials up my anxiety.

"PLEASE! EVERYONE! JUST GIVE HER SOME AIR!" Eric's voice slices through the gloom, and it may as well be fingernails down my spine as I realise, "Luca."

"Get that door open!" I order, turning towards the stage. "Do whatever you have to!" Like I'm suddenly in charge of this shit show.

The room seems much smaller now, the crowd and the dark growing tight around me, and I can barely breathe. Buddy, ahead of me, starts barking and growling, which actually helps clear some semblance of a path. But I've no clue where I'm going; I'm just making my way towards the flashlights at the front of the stage. As I push through the crowd, the brush of limbs and the rustle of coats are oppressive, the mix of breath and fear palpable in the air. When the opportunity arises, I reach out and snatch a light of my own.

"HEY! That's mine!" Somebody complains, but I'm not listening because as I beg, barge, and push my way forward, I become aware that I am putting myself right at the heart of this rapidly unfolding crisis, manifested as a puppet show of lights and eerie shadows played out on panicked faces.

I reach the front row. Nearby, the doctor has collapsed onto the floor and is surrounded by a tightly knit circle of concerned onlookers, including Roberto Junior. Eric and Tracy are still trying to tend to her by pushing back the crowd. My stomach somersaults because I know exactly what this is a prelude to.

Buddy's bark brings me back to my objective here.

"Buddy!" Luca exclaims excitedly.

I shine the light over Luca's sweet face, juxtaposed with my stepmother's, sitting next to him in all her resplendence, doing nothing to hide her annoyance at the torchlight blinding her.

"Claudia," I begin, my voice a mixture of urgency and frustration. "You need to come with me, now. It's urgent," I say.

Her response is as cold as the temperature in here. "What are you talking about? Turn that light away from me!" she hisses, her voice laced with disdain.

The voices nearby are also loud and frustrated. ... *Give her air.*

... What's wrong with her?

I turn back to my stepmother. "We need to leave. We're all in danger if we stay here," my tone is insistent, imploring.

"What nonsense are you spouting now? We're not going anywhere with you."

Nearby, the situation with the doctor escalates. "Move back! I said move the fuck back!" Eric screams as panicked villagers begin to hurl questions into the dark.

Is this the flu? Is that what's wrong with her?

Is she dead?

Tell us the truth!

I turn to Luca. He's clinging onto Buddy, but I can see that his expression has changed now. He's caught in the middle of this maelstrom. I know that if I don't do something soon, he's going to get hurt, and I can't let that happen. *I can't.*

"Claudia, please," I try once more, my voice as soft as I can make it yet desperate. "For Luca's sake, we have to go." But the woman remains unmoved, her refusal hanging between us like a death sentence. "Claudia, if we stay here, we're going to die!" I snap.

The woman gapes at me. My nephew whimpers, tears filling his eyes.

There's screaming from the group nearby: *What's wrong with her? What's happening to her?* Then, there's a collective shuffle backward that prompts Claudia to jump to her feet. "Watch it! That's my toe! Stop! Stop pushing!"

"Samantha!" I call out, my voice slicing through the turmoil, desperate to find my sister in this bedlam. "SAM! SAMANTHA!" But there's no answer, only the rising hysteria of both the nearby group and the rest of the villagers, who are obviously becoming aware of the fact that something is amiss.

"Luca, come on, mate. We need to leave now," I insist, the torchlight flickering over his features, highlighting his fear and confusion.

"Get your hands off him!" Claudia yells over the commotion, slapping away my arm.

"Claudia—"

"GET AWAY! GET AWAY!" she shrieks, her voice borderline hysterical.

A tug-of-war, a physical manifestation of the emotional storm raging within me, begins. Luca's small hands clutch at mine, his fear palpable in his tight grip. "It's okay, Luca. I've got you," I say, trying to infuse my voice with a calm I'm far from feeling while my stepmother refuses to relinquish her grasp of my nephew's other arm.

Buddy's barking escalates, a soundtrack to the chaos unfolding around us. There's screaming from the group nearby and a loud pounding at the back of the building that is literally shaking and echoing around the space.

"SAM!" I scream. "SAMANTHA, WHERE ARE YOU?" Desperation claws at me. One final plea, my voice cracking under the strain.

The cacophony of a panicked crowd reverberates through the darkness, amplifying the terror that envelops us. I feel a cold sweat bead on my brow as fear and blindness merge, thick as the surrounding gloom. Confronted with an impossible choice, I feel the weight of the moment: the lives of my nephew and my dog hang by a thread, and I know that with each passing second, our window for escape narrows, pushing me deeper into desperation.

Heart pounding in my throat, I yank my nephew to me with one hand and – God forgive me – shove my stepmother back with the other, causing her to scream as she loses her balance and collapses to the floor. "I'm so sorry," I murmur before yelling, "BUDDY! HEEL! NOW!" as I set about leading us back up the aisle.

I shove, elbow a path through the silhouettes and intermittent flashes of faces illuminated by panicked torchlight, chased by Claudia's screams. However, these are soon upstaged by the chaos unfolding around us and something else – something altogether inhuman, as the doctor's condition reaches its harrowing climax. Even as we jostle away, there's no doubt in my mind that this grotesque symphony of horror will be etched in our memories for the rest of our lives.

The doctor's voice, strained and unnatural, morphs into a guttural cry that curdles the blood. It's a sound no human should ever make, a deep, wrenching howl that crescendos into an explosion of pain. The wail is primal, a stark testament to the alien horror consuming her from within.

Gasps of disbelief rapidly morph into shrill screams of horror, the kind that scrapes the edges of sanity. *Oh my God, what is happening? What is that?* someone shrieks, their voice breaking under the weight of witnessing the unthinkable. *Help her! Someone!* another cries in anguish, a futile wish against the unfolding nightmare.

Then, there's *retching… ripping…* and the wet, *splattering* noise of something inhuman taking form. It's accompanied by a chorus of horrified gasps and cries, a collective witness to a scene so gruesome it defies comprehension.

"Keep back! Stay away! Stay away!" Eric's authoritative voice cuts through the din in a desperate attempt to impose order on the chaos. But it's drowned out by the pandemonium, the collective hysteria of a crowd pushed beyond the brink of horror.

As Luca and I make for the open doorway, we are thrown off balance when a man trips over a fire extinguisher and falls across the threshold, forcing us to jump over him and out into the snow. Just then, a collective scream erupts – I imagine it's the moment the doctor's chest bursts open, and that grotesque growth hypnotises anyone who dares gaze upon it. This is shortly followed by the soft bursting sound of deadly spores and the screams of those ignorant of their fate, including my sister.

"Marco! Marco!" The detective calls from the other side of the lane, where just an hour or so earlier, I had watched this place with apprehension, never imagining that what might happen here could be so much worse.

The icy night air slaps the numb horror from my face as I lead us across the street, my nephew clutching my hand as if his life depends on it. I check that Buddy is padding by my side while the sounds of people struggling to escape the deathtrap of the community hall chase us out into the night.

It's a sound of endings, of lives forever altered by what they've witnessed. And as we run, the echoes of that horror follow us, a grim soundtrack to the nightmare that Thistle Island has become.

22

TRUST

THISTLE ISLAND. NIGHT.

We didn't hang around the community hall. I wanted to – God knows I did – because I hoped that, by some miracle, we'd see Samantha emerge from there. But we didn't.

Things got worse when, after recovering from the initial shock of being physically dragged out of that place, Luca started stressing about his mother despite not even knowing half of what went down in there. I mean, sure, there's no doubt in my mind that he had some idea, especially after the dramatic way I told Claudia we were all going to die if they didn't follow me.

Shit.

But what was I supposed to do? The woman wasn't listening, and all I could think about was my nephew ending up like that nurse, and... well, I just couldn't have that.

I have no idea how many people were infected tonight, but there's no doubt that most of the islanders were in that hall. This means I can't trust anybody except Luca and the detective. The implications are staggering, and I can't begin to wrap my head around what this means for the rest of our time on this island.

Which is why I brought us back to the cottage. I need a safe place to gather my thoughts and process all of this. Although, truth be told, that five-minute walk from the village felt more like a journey across continents under the weight of our dread because every movement, every sound set me off.

I had to lie to Luca in the end. No, I'm not proud of it, but I had to get us away from ground zero. I told him his mom was okay, that she had some things she needed to attend to, and that she would join us as soon as she was done. Thankfully, he seemed to accept it, for now, despite the fact that minutes before, I had been screaming her name into the dark like a fucking madman.

It's snowing again now. Giant flakes this time, careening to earth, the prelude to the ice wall that's forecast to imprison us here with our nightmares.

The good thing is that I've managed to get a fire going now. We were all shivering, both from the freeze that was gnawing at our bones and the shock of what happened back there.

Now, we all look marginally better, huddled around the stove, drinking hot beverages as if nothing had happened, as if none of the freak show I've witnessed over the past few days ever occurred. But I know it did. I can see it in every glance the detective and I have shared since our escape from the community hall. We haven't talked much otherwise on account of the fact that Luca has been with us the whole time, so you can imagine my relief when the *little man's* eyelids – yes, I heard that too. Don't read into it – started to droop. I think once the tide of adrenaline went out; he was done for.

Now, he's on the small couch with my coat over him and the promise that I'll wake him when his mother gets here. Oh, God, that lie makes me sick to my stomach every time I think of it. And I know I'm going to have to confront it at some point, but—

"You did good in there tonight," the detective says quietly.

I look at her. There's no power here, mostly by design, so the scene is much more atmospheric, with the flickering light of the fire dancing off her smooth face and puppeteering our shadows onto the walls.

I'm not sure how to respond to that comment because, of all the things I did tonight, feeling good is not one of them. I force a creased smile and sip from my cup.

"You didn't have a choice," she says. And I don't know if she's referring to the fact that I dragged my nephew out of there or because I lied to him. Probably both. But I have the presence of mind to think that, coming from her, that's as good a compliment as I'm ever going to get.

"We need a plan," she says. "The weather's only going to get worse. We need to get word out to the mainland; tell them they need to prioritise a rescue."

I lean in, talking under my breath. "Do you think that's really going to help?"

"Marco, someone locked that door. We can only assume it was the doctor," she says slowly, ominously. "And if it was her, that shows premeditation, intelligence."

"No, I don't mean that. Call me naïve, but this, I'm assuming, must come under the banner of contagion, right?" She squints at me. "Well, will their priority really be about evacuating people? You've witnessed what's been happening. Can they risk whatever this thing is reaching the mainland?"

The detective smiles at me. You may have noticed that this isn't something she's prone to, so it immediately puts me on guard.

"What?" she says, her tone dripping with bemusement, "Do you think they're going to launch rockets and obliterate the island?"

My initial reaction is to be offended. But then, isn't that exactly how this stuff usually plays out? Yes, I've seen one too many movies, but "Think about it," I say, ignoring her tone for now. "Doesn't it make sense to keep this thing contained on an island rather than taking it back to the mainland?"

She doesn't get a chance to respond because a hammering on the front door makes us both jump from our seats.

"Shit," I hiss.

We look at each other, both clearly wondering what the other thinks we should do. Any thoughts of pretending no one is home are quickly dashed when Buddy barks and rushes to the locked door.

I lower my head and shake it, contemplating whether to ask who is out there in the dead of night in the snow. But I don't need to when there's another loud rap at the door. "MARCO! Open up! It's me," the voice says, sending an icicle down my spine and a tsunami of shivers through me.

Samantha.

The detective and I look at each other. Buddy barks some more. And then, as if things aren't already bad enough, I hear that word. "Mummy?"

"Luca," comes the muffled voice. "Baby, is that you?"

"Mummy?" Luca is up from the sofa and halfway across the room by the time I intercept him. "Wait! Luca! Wait!"

"Stop!" he says.

"Marco! Open this bloody door right now," the muffled voice continues. "Luca!"

"Mummy!" my nephew cries.

Buddy continues barking as my heart thunders in my chest. I look at the detective, who is also standing, eyes wide, staring at the door.

"Get out of my way!" Luca cries as he attempts to get around me because, of course, my nephew has no bloody idea why I'm stopping him from seeing his mother.

"Marco? Marco, open the door. It's alright. I'm okay."

"How do we know that?" I yell back.

"It's okay," the reasonable voice continues. "I'm fine. We got out in time," she lies.

With my arms tight around my nephew's shoulders as he continues to struggle free, I turn to the detective. "Wait, Luca! Wait!" But my nephew isn't hearing me. He just wants to see his mum.

Meanwhile, the detective and I are holding each other's gaze. We both know that there's no way Samantha could have made it out in time. The detective had smashed her way out of the community room door, so she was already outside when I just about managed to pull Luca out. Samantha was nowhere to be seen. There's no way she made it out.

But then I hear, as if she's read our minds, "... There's an exit at the back of the stage. A fire exit. That's how Sarge and I made it out."

"You left without your son?" I shout at the closed door.

"Yes. Well, no. I didn't. I couldn't get to you. There were people in front of us, but I saw you had him and knew he would be okay with you. Please. Just open the door."

I'm breathing heavily now, and so is the detective. Luca's still struggling, the fire's crackling intensely, and it suddenly feels much warmer in the cottage because I've no fucking idea what to do.

"Let go of me!" my nephew growls right before there's a sharp pain in my arm, and I release him. He bit me. Luca bit me, and now he's running towards the door.

The detective bolts after him, but I put an arm out in front of her. It's too late.

Luca slides the bolt across, pulls, fumbles with the door, and then yanks it open. A bitter cold wind rushes in, bringing with it a cloud of snow.

"Oh, my baby," Samantha cries, literally. Tears stream down her face as she collapses onto her knees and squeezes her son, who whimpers, "Mummy," reduced to a five-year-old once more.

And I feel wretched, both for being so weak and for distressing the little boy like this. This is probably why all the detective and I can do is watch the reunion with scepticism and hearts full of hope.

If my sister is telling the truth and there is an exit at the back of the community hall, which sounds plausible, then this is absolutely fantastic news, and my nephew probably will never speak to me again. If it isn't true, then there's a good chance he won't speak to me again because he – we – will all be dead.

Minutes must go by during the doorstep reunion. By the time it's over, the little warmth we had managed to accumulate through the fire has been well and truly whisked away into the snowy night, leaving the room as frigid as it was when we arrived.

Samantha gets to her feet and looks at me for several seconds before rushing over. I flinch, thinking she's going to punch me, but instead, she gives me a long, tight squeeze. "Sorry if I worried you," she says. "And thank you for taking care of him," she adds, breaking the embrace and appraising me while I study her face for telltale signs of... what? I have no idea.

"So where's Sarge now?" the detective asks, pushing the door shut and locking it. It's obvious from the look on her face that she still isn't quite convinced by my sister's story, and she's maintaining a noticeable distance.

"I don't know. We became separated. Everybody was panicking, people falling in the snow. It was chaos. He stayed behind to help," Samantha responds, clinging to her son, and I suddenly feel shitty noticing the distance between us.

"But you didn't?" the detective asks.

Samantha looks at her. "I tried... but..."

"But?"

"I needed to get to my boy. Make sure he was okay," she says, pulling Luca closer.

"Come sit by the stove," I say, touching Luca's shoulder, but my nephew shrinks away from me, and he may as well have kicked me in the balls for the effect it has.

My sister accepts the invitation regardless, and they both go and sit by the fire.

Me? I hang back and decide to go to the stove instead. Why? Because I think everybody could use a hot chocolate. Well, what else do you do in a situation like this? I'd make tea, but given the Siberian hellscape that's being sculpted out there, I feel the need to diversify.

"... What, exactly, is his plan?" I hear the detective say from across the room.

"Plan? I don't think he had a plan. He was just doing his job."

"Didn't anybody think about contacting the mainland? Getting help out here?"

"I already did that, remember?"

"That's right. But things have changed now. They've taken a turn for the worse. The situation is much more urgent. Wouldn't you agree?" the detective asks, taking a step closer.

Samantha pauses, eyes on the detective, before answering. "Yes, I agree."

"Because of you."

"I'm sorry?"

"The situation is much worse because of you."

"I beg your—."

"You were specifically told that summoning the villagers was a bad idea."

Samantha turns to me, and I must look like the proverbial rabbit in the headlights because she quickly turns back to the detective and says, "With all due respect to my brother, he's not the mayor of Thistle Island. I am."

"And you knowingly put all of us at risk."

"Now, you hold on... all I *knowingly* did was follow procedure. Those people had a right to know."

"Well, they definitely know now, don't they?"

Samantha glares at her, and for a second, I think she's the one who's going to get a punch in the mouth, but instead, my sister sighs and says, "Look, Detective. If your goal is to make me feel awful, then save it. You can't make me feel any worse than I already do," she says, swallowing hard, and clinging to her son. "I did what I believed was right. What I thought would keep them safe."

The detective scoffs. "Safe?"

"... Detective."

"Safe?"

"Isla..."

"Safe would have been telling them to stay in their homes, doors locked, not dragging them out and—"

"Detective!" I shout, my voice ringing around the room for several seconds, allowing that whiny wind to take centre stage. "This isn't helping," I add calmly because it just occurred to me that, despite her behavioural peculiarities, the detective, just like me, narrowly escaped that place with her life and, just like me, now finds herself stranded here.

"We're all a little strung out," I say. "Understandably so, considering. But there's no doubt in my mind that the only way we're going to get through this is if we pull together." The detective frowns at me. "I know. I just heard that myself," I say, "but it makes sense. We need to work together."

I turn and pull mugs off a shelf and arrange them in a row. Then I finish making the chocolate and hand out the steaming mugs before taking a seat on a stool next to the stove. I gesture to the detective to join us. She hesitates. I insist with a nod of the head, and she eventually complies, sitting in one of the free armchairs.

"Great," I say, but when I can't think of anything else to add, the wind fills in again, howling around the building like a wild animal. God, this situation would be comical if it weren't so tragic – us, huddled around the fire with hot bloody cocoa.

Shit, I had no idea how domesticated I would become when placed in mortal danger. I do know that in such situations, I normally think about anything but the matter at hand. And yet.... So I suppose now's as good a time as any to ask, "Sam, what the fuck are we dealing with here?" I glance at my nephew, but he doesn't react, focused only on being close to his mother.

My sister looks at me. "Why are you asking me that?"

"Because, as you keep pointing out, this is your island. What is this thing? What are we dealing with?"

"I don't know."

"How can you not know?"

"I don't know," she insists. "I know as much as you do."

"Which is?" the detective asks.

"I told you that—"

"Tell us again," the detective insists.

My sister's eyes widen as she stares into the fire, no doubt attempting to find the right words. "Well, you saw... You were there. Amy, Ewan's research assistant, went missing and... some suspected that she and..." She trails off here because Luca is hanging on her every word. "We believed that she had gone missing, as you know. It turns out she wasn't, and somehow, we don't know how, she came back the night of the memorial party. She was taken to the infirmary and... well, you already know what happened next," she says, then sips from her mug.

"What happened?" Luca asks.

"Never mind."

"You know, you're not helping by withholding information from him."

Both Samantha and I turn to the detective, who visibly wilts under the intensity of our gazes, before coming back with, "Okay, alright. So what about this thing? What do we know about it?"

Samantha shakes her head. "The first time I saw anything like it was with you."

"No idea where it came from? Who brought it to the island?"

Samantha continues to shake her head, then says, "What makes you think somebody brought it to the island?"

"What makes you think somebody didn't? It must have come from somewhere since you're saying there hasn't been anything like it before," the detective observes, her gaze fixed on my sister, whose skin seems to wriggle in the flickering firelight.

Samantha shakes her head. "I don't know. I just hadn't considered that somebody had brought it here."

"One thing's for sure. It's highly contagious," I say.

"And it has an incubation period," the detective adds.

"That's right," I agree. "But it doesn't seem consistent."

"Agreed," the detective says pensively. "So, let's work it back. The farmer and his sheep. Ground zero? He said it had happened before."

"That's right. He did."

"What about the ram? The way it attacked us," Samantha contributes. "Could it have been symptomatic?"

I shrug. "Possibly. Then there was Amy, who could have been exposed wherever."

"The nurse and the doctor," the detective adds, "who were infected by Amy. You're right, though. The gestation period for each one was different. Why? Physicality, maybe?"

"No. Couldn't have been that," I counter. "They were both of similar build."

"Age maybe?" Samantha suggests.

"The doctor was older than the girl and the nurse," I point out.

"Mutation?" We all turn to Samantha, but not to look at her – rather at my nephew, sitting next to her.

"What did you say?" Samantha asks.

"It could be a mutation," Luca suggests. "Just like with other contagions. You know, like COVID. Each time it infects."

"Of course," I agree.

"And what do you know about this?" Samantha asks gently.

"Not much. I only know what Daddy told me."

"Daddy talked about it?"

Luca nods. "He was really excited. Said he'd found a new specimen. That it was millions of years old and that he was going to try to germinate it. He said he was going to use the pot I made him."

Something tells me that my nephew knows much more about all of this than any of us think, including the disappearance of his father, and that, in and of itself, fills me with sadness.

"So you're saying that this thing is what, some kind of plant?" the detective asks sceptically, but then pauses. As do the rest of us, because we all know that as fantastical as that might sound, it makes sense.

The wind whines under the door, rattling it as if excited about our discovery.

"And..." Luca begins, but trails off here, obviously thinking better of it.

"What? What is it, darling?" Samantha encourages her son.

The boy hesitates and then says, "It's Amy... she and Dad weren't, you know..." he says timidly. "I know that because... Amy isn't interested in boys."

There's a moment as Samantha and I absorb my nephew's words, but it's soon fractured by the detective, who is obviously in no way affected by Luca's revelation. "So where did your father find the seeds?"

Luca shrugs.

"The ledge?" I suggest.

"The ledge? Why would you say that?" Samantha asks.

"Well, Amy mentioned the ledge to me, remember?"

"Amy was also infected with this thing," my sister retorts.

"That doesn't mean she was lying," the detective chimes in.

"I already told you. The ledge is a protected dig. Off-limits to everyone from the island. Including Ewan. There's no way he would have flouted that order."

"He might have." It's the detective talking again. All eyes turn to her, and she adds, "If you'd told him to. After all, you're the only person on this whole island with that kind of authority."

Samantha opens her mouth to say something, and I think she's going to scream at the woman, but instead, she seethes, "There's something wrong with you."

"It's not much of a leap, though, is it?" the detective insists. "After all, your company, this island, is in trouble. Isn't that the very reason why you're diversifying? Just one of those artifacts would be worth a fortune to the right buyer."

"And you think I'd risk the lives of everyone on this island, including my son's?"

"You tell me. Someone locked that community room door, and it certainly wasn't Marco or me."

23

WHITEOUT

THISTLE ISLAND. DEEP NIGHT.

The atmosphere in the cottage only grew worse after the detective's comment. Every word from thereon seemed tinged with veiled accusations. And yet... the detective had a point. Somebody had definitely wanted to make sure we were all exposed in the community hall. The question is *Who?*

On the bright side, if one could set aside the literal meaning of that for just a moment, while my sister and the detective differed in their views on most things, there was one critical point we all agreed on: we need help – and fast.

This meant leaving the cottage and its illusion of safety, braving both the storm and whatever else might be lurking out there to reach the police station. There, we could join forces with Sarge and contact the mainland.

This is why, less than an hour later, shrouded in layers of coats, hats, and makeshift wraps of bedding, we launched ourselves into the blackest night.

The snowstorm's ferocity mocked our feeble attempts at warmth, each howling gust of wind a freezing slap to the face, every snowflake hurled at us like shards of glass against exposed skin.

Thistle Island has turned against us, transforming the land into an alien landscape. *Alien* – that word again. The one that's haunted me ever since the incident at the infirmary, along with the image of that thing ripping its way out of Amy.

Oh, God... There's no doubt in my mind that if we actually got the chance to sleep, I would be having nightmares about something anchored to my rib cage, slithering around until the excruciating moment it decided to gnaw its way through flesh and tissue to burst out of me in a shower of blood.

Yeah, I don't know how my mind works sometimes, either. All I know is that I'm fucking terrified – not just for me, but for those around me whom I feel so powerless to protect.

The snow, once our ally in tracking anyone who might have come before us, has turned traitor. It's obscured once-familiar paths, transforming them into treacherous gambles where each step might be a slide into oblivion.

At one point, my senses began to betray me. I thought I could actually hear the demon wind carrying the screams of other villagers to us – guttural, tortured cries that seemed to scrape at the very edges of the soul. Sounds that even my overactive imagination couldn't have conjured in its darkest musings before I stepped foot on this rock. Mercifully, we were all too busy navigating the inhospitable to dwell on them for too long.

The power is still out, which means there were no village lights to guide our way, only deepening this particular brand of hell. Thankfully, the storm hadn't completely swallowed the village. We could just about make out the faint glow of emergency lights and lanterns flickering in the distance – a testament, no doubt, to the islanders' readiness for such eventualities. Yet, the question remains: Is the outage due to the elements or something else far more sinister?

Somebody locked that door. Somebody wanted all of us to be exposed.

Is someone deliberately trying to infect us, or has this thing, this organism or whatever it is, evolved to such intelligence that it manipulated one of its hosts to lock us inside that place with our fates?

Of course, the idea of turning around and holing up in the cottage did occur to me. We could wait until daylight, hoping that by then, the horror of the situation might seem less overwhelming. But I agree with Isla. Isolating ourselves might technically make sense in the short term, but the reality is that we need help; we need to get out of this place. Our best chance remains to join up with Sarge and the other cops to confirm that rescue is on its way.

Now, imagine my relief as we finally make it to the snow-covered steps leading off the hillside and onto the high street, which is almost unrecognisable. Everything is covered in snow or ice. There isn't a soul in sight, and even the gale is momentarily calm, which only accentuates the feeling that we've been teleported to one of those old nuclear bomb testing towns.

We take a minute to catch our breaths as snow falls and swirls around us, but it's nothing like the blizzard conditions on the hillside.

I pull the scarf down from over my face and speak in a low tone. "Is everybody okay?"

My response is mostly gasps and recovering breaths, but I get the thumbs up from everyone. Everyone but Buddy, who, wrapped in one of my fleeces, reminds me of one of those thoroughbred racehorses. His response is to shake vigorously, releasing a cloud of snow over me. "Thanks, mate," I say before reaching down and petting his damp, cold ears. I'm scared for him and so wishing now I had left him behind.

Everyone else, except for Luca, to some extent, knows what we're dealing with here, but Buddy... there's no way I can tell him not to be his usual nosy or tart self and to keep a distance from everything and everyone. Which is another reason I'm bricking it – because if anything happened to him... well, you already know our history.

"Luca..." I begin, but my nephew is still pissed off with me; he moves behind his mother. "It's okay, buddy. You've every right to be pissed off," I say. "Just promise me that whatever happens, you won't approach anything or anyone." He nods. Well, his hood does. I can barely see his face. "That goes for all of us. We've no clue now who was or wasn't exposed. We have to be cautious," I say, my gaze lingering on the wrapped-up features of my sister because something tells me that of all of us, she's the one who is most likely going to feel compelled to help one of her neighbours.

After collecting unanimous nods, I lead us up the high street as if I'm a native, not someone who arrived here just a few days ago.

The predator gale is back now, stalking the high street, hunting for exposed flesh to bite. Each gust rattles shop windows, their painted signs defiant under their shrouds of ice. Snowdrifts, sculpted by the wind, choke the road, obscuring the familiar cobbles beneath our feet. Icicles, like skeletal fingers, hang from eaves. A lone newspaper, frozen solid, lies plastered to a boarded-up window, its headline obscured by snow. But for the loud, icy crunch underfoot, the place remains hauntingly desolate, which, to my surprise, I find even more unsettling than the screaming sounds of earlier. Now, it feels like those people, whoever they were, have succumbed to their ordeal and that it's just us isolated here now.

Further up the street, the skeletal form of the church looms, and I don't know if I can actually see its silhouette or if it's a figment of my imagination fed by a projection of my memory of it. Everything, every building, every street corner, speaks of a community temporarily subdued, huddling inside against the fear of the unknown and winter's onslaught. Here, in this desolate tableau, the gale holds its temporary dominion, its ubiquitous mournful song the only accompaniment to the silence of a village waiting for the presumed safety of daylight.

My stomach somersaults when we reach the intersection before the church, where turning right leads to the community hall and the road up to the hotel. Here, the once pristine snow is churned into a chaotic mess, spreading outwards from the double doors of the hall like a macabre flower, sending a fresh wave of nausea crashing over me. Frantic footprints, some deep and purposeful, others scattered and panicked, crisscross the defiled snow, their paths leading away from the building. It's these crimson trails, snaking haphazardly through the white, that chill me to the bone – a stark reminder, etched in blood, that something terrible happened here.

I hurry us left, away from the scene, pausing momentarily to reminisce about the last time we were here. About when I found myself, for the first time in a long time, thinking about my fallout with the mythical being purported to own this place. The same being who took my son from me and who has now sent an altogether unique brand of pain. And I can't help but wonder what I may have done to offend him so that he should inflict all this shit on me, on us.

The moment doesn't last long, though, as I'm distracted by Samantha's arm. She's pointing; up ahead is the police station.

24

ABANDONED

THISTLE ISLAND POLICE STATION. DEEP NIGHT.

Thistle Island's police station is an isolated stone building, separated from the rest of the village by about ten yards. The front door is reached by three wide steps, complete with metal handrails, which is fortunate because I nearly go arse over tit when I step on the second one.

The relief from the freeze is instantaneous as we walk through the door, though we don't have long to appreciate it.

The station looks nothing like it did the last time we were here. Like the rest of the village, the power is out, but a couple of emergency lights flicker creepily, intermittently illuminating the place in a pale shade of blue. We can clearly see that something has happened here. Two of the desks are upended; a computer screen lies cracked on the floor. Smashed glass glitters like ice particles, and papers are strewn everywhere.

The detective doesn't hesitate to retrieve her pocket flashlight and starts brandishing it as if it's a weapon. More's the pity. Samantha and Luca are already behind me, but that doesn't stop me from putting out a restraining hand to both of them. We have no idea what happened here.

Then, I step forward and... "SHIT!" something smacks me on the back of the head.

It takes me a few seconds to realise what has happened. It appears that what I narrowly managed to avoid outside has caught up with me in here; I've just slipped and slammed to the floor like a bloody felled tree.

"Are you okay?" the detective asks without looking at me, panning the flashlight around the room.

"Really?" I scowl as shockwaves of pain radiate around my skull.

"Are you alright?" It's Samantha now.

"I'm fine," I lie, pulling myself up into a sitting position. That's when I feel something on my right hand and then the left.

"Isla?" I say, but when she doesn't respond, I call more forcefully. "Isla, some light, please." Eventually, she turns, and I hold my hands under the beam. They're slick in crimson goo. "Oh, shit!" I hiss. "Blood!" And from what I can tell, I'm lying in a pool of it.

The very thought of that propels me to my feet, but not without skittering a few times like a fucking newborn deer. I can feel the cold tackiness on my hands, and I stand for several seconds, holding them aloft before grabbing some pages from the floor to wipe them clean, avoiding the sight of the stains. I don't even want to think about where that stuff came from. Although, not surprisingly, the detective is already hunting down the origin.

She aims the beam over the slick on the floor – as my heart cranks up a gear. There are tracks all over it, leading in from the entrance, circling around the room, and then back out toward the same door we came through. We probably didn't notice them on the way in because of the freshly fallen snow.

"Whatever happened here happened post-mortem," the detective says to nobody in particular, which, of course, does nothing to make me feel better. "They've walked over and then dragged something through this," she states flatly.

Shit. The detective's light beam highlights a scarf hanging on the back of a chair. I don't hesitate. I step over and use it to give my hands a better clean, cringing as I do.

"Mum..." Luca whimpers.

"It's okay, darling," my sister reassures, pulling her son close. He's obviously scared and shouldn't be seeing this stuff. Hell, none of us should, but I think we've reached the stage where we don't have a choice. I exchange looks with Samantha. Neither of us knows for sure, but it's obvious we both share the same theory about what happened here.

The detective crouches down, picks up a phone receiver from the floor, and presses it to her ear. "It's dead," she announces. She begins to stand when a peculiar rattling sound cuts through the quiet. She freezes, her body rigid with tension.

Chills scamper down my spine as we all watch the detective's light beam move through the shadows to an overturned desk. I don't know if it's just a trick of the light, but it looks like that thing is shaking.

My heart switches gears as Buddy growls. I hold up a silencing hand.

The detective stands and looks across at me. I can barely make out her expression in the gloom, but I know it's an invitation. Reluctantly, I hold up a restraining hand to Samantha and Luca before stepping forward, the detective rounding the desk from the opposite side.

The rattling grows louder as we draw closer, mirroring the frenetic thump in my chest. I wish I had a weapon of some kind – anything more substantial than my bloodstained hands. We approach the desk, and the world seems to hold its breath. The wind moans, eager for a peek, the security light flickers and ticks, and then we each reach a corner of the desk.

I glance at the detective, who gestures, three... two... one..., and with a swift movement, we both step around the stricken desk as the detective shines her light.

"Jesus Christ!" I hiss, expelling the breath I'd been holding. There, curled into the smallest ball possible against the desk, is the female cop. Her uniform is dishevelled, her badge reflecting a sliver of light. Her eyes are wide, darting between us, a silent plea etched within their depths. She's shivering, her breath appearing and disappearing in the torchlight.

"Tracy?" It's Samantha, who has left Luca with Buddy and joined us. "Tracy, are you alright, love? Are you okay?" She kneels down next to the officer, who simply gawks at her, the whites of her eyes glinting in the spotlight.

"What happened here?" the detective asks, but her voice only startles the officer.

"She's in shock," I offer.

"Tracy?" Samantha calls softly once more.

"H...has he gone?" the officer stammers.

"Who? Has who gone?" Samantha asks, moving closer, and I fight the urge to pull her back.

"S...S...Sarge? Has he gone?" the cop asks.

"There's nobody here, Tracy. It's just us," Samantha soothes.

"What happened here?" The detective repeats, shining the torch on the traumatised cop's face.

"I... d...don't know. I... was at the back. Coming back from the loo. E...Eric. Came in with his hand to his neck.... H...he... he was bleeding down the front of his jacket.... I... asked him what happened.... He... he...," the cop pauses here, tears of terror welling in her eyes, staring into the middle distance. "He said that Sarge had... b...bit him."

The wind hums ominously outside.

Samantha glances back at Luca. Yes, my nephew is listening to all of this, which could explain why he's actually sidling up to me. I place a hand on his shoulder.

Samantha reaches out to the officer and says calmly, "Tracy, why don't you come out from under there and tell us—" but her hand is slapped away. "Okay, okay," she adds. "It's alright."

"What happened next?" the detective interjects.

The cop looks at her like she's an alien before turning back to

Samantha. "I... I got the first aid kit. Tried to stop the bleeding, but it was pretty bad. There... there was a hole in his neck. I've never seen him so scared. So I tried to call for help, but the phones were down. I got the satphone and..." the officer chokes up again.

"And... what?" the detective presses on.

"And... Sarge. He came back. Eric pushed me down here, told me to hide. I didn't wanna, but then the doors flew open. I was scared... s...so scared," the cop sobs again, tears and snot dribbling down her face.

"It's okay," Samantha soothes. "It's okay."

The detective shines the torch around the room once more, searching. "The phone's gone," she says, picking up the empty pouch with *Iridium* stamped across the front.

"Did you manage to call anybody, Tracy?" Samantha demands. But the cop doesn't answer, eyes wide and fixed on the space in front of her. "I... I heard him screaming," she says suddenly. "He... he was begging for his life, and then it went quiet. It went so quiet, and then... then he... fell down there," she wails. "He fell right down there on the floor! And then I watched him slide away. He slid away!" There are more tears, and Samantha attempts to reach out to the woman, but given her location, the action is awkward. "Shhh..." she says. "Shhh..." and I don't know if my sister is trying to comfort the woman or get her to shut up just in case Sarge makes a reappearance.

The detective must be thinking the same thing because she keeps looking up and shining the flashlight at the door and then around the room.

"We need to get to the hotel," Samantha says.

"Hotel?" I ask.

"That's where the other satphone is," she adds reluctantly, as if she doesn't want to go home. And who can blame her? I certainly don't want to go out there. But then again, I don't want to stay here either.

"Is there an armoury here?" the detective barks at the sobbing wretch huddled under the desk. But she doesn't answer. So the detective turns to Samantha and insists, "Ask her where the weapon storage is."

"Tracy... Tracy..." Samantha begins, reaching out to touch the woman's shoulder, but she recoils once more, her sobs intensifying.

"Oh, forget it," the detective says, standing and hunting around the room. She scans around desk placements, then moves to the back of the building towards the toilet, where I watch the eager light beam lick over walls and surfaces before finally coming to a stop on a grey metal cabinet mounted onto the wall.

"... You need to come with us."

I turn back to Samantha. It's much gloomier over here now that the detective's flashlight has gone, but from what I can see, she's still trying to coax the distressed woman out from under the desk.

"Sam?" I call. When she doesn't answer, I try again, but when she continues to ignore me, I call her much more sharply. When she finally turns to look my way, I slowly shake my head. And yes, I feel like a shit, but the more I am aware of my nephew pressed into my side, the more I know what we must do. We've no idea what really happened here, why Eric finally fell still. We just can't take any risks.

Still, Samantha turns back to the woman, so I walk over and tap my sister on the shoulder, "Sam?" She shrugs me away. "Sam?"

She jumps up and hisses, "Leave me alone!"

"Mummy," Luca cries, going over and throwing his arms around her. She hugs him tight. And it's hard to tell in the hue of the emergency light, but I think my sister has tears in her eyes.

Then, I realise. "Hey," I say softly, stepping towards her and placing a reassuring hand on her arm.

"I'm not going to end up like him," she whispers defiantly, swiping at tears glistening in the feeble light.

"Of course we aren't," I say.

"Sarge was with m...me," Samantha murmurs, but her voice trails off, lost in the chilling silence of the room.

"We don't know what happened here," I say, pushing aside intrusive thoughts that have no business in my mind right now.

"Okay, the key was still in the cabinet," the detective says, her footsteps heavy as she rejoins us. "It's been cleared out, though. Just this left in there and four cartridges," she adds, lifting a shotgun. A barely suppressed tremor runs through her hand as she cocks the weapon, causing it to click sharply – slicing through the tension of the moment – before holding it away from us with the dexterity of a seasoned rifleman.

I gawk at the woman, who is now reminding me of one of those overconfident marines.

"What?" she asks casually.

"Who are you?" I ask incredulously.

"I'm the big sister of four boisterous farm boys," she says. "We need to get out of here," she adds firmly. "We need to find that other satphone."

I turn to Samantha, who nods reluctantly before glancing back at the police officer. But she's staring at a patch of darkness on the other side of the room. I know it's because she's in shock, and her brain is overworked right now. However, I can understand how, to everyone else, her staring might seem creepy, as if there's something else lurking deep in the shadows.

"Yeah. The detective is right. We need to go. Now."

25

CHECKING IN

THISTLE ISLAND HOTEL. DEEP NIGHT.

The storm appears to have loosened its grip for a moment, although I'm not fooled. I've been in this horror movie before: just when you think the freak show is over, it all comes back with a vengeance. The silence that haunts our little expedition is worse than the ever-present whine of the wind beast that stalks this land. Yet, mercifully, the only phantoms are the puffs of our breaths as we climb the hill to our next destination.

The island has transformed once again. It's like each time I latch onto some semblance of the familiar, everything changes in this frozen, alien world where the snow isn't white but bleached – devoid of life, reflecting an eerie, ghostly glow under the dim light of the moon and stars. Even the warmth of humanity feels a million miles away, a forgotten dream.

For me, the police station – a place that is supposed to represent safety and security – was instead yet another scene straight out of one of my nightmares. I can only imagine how it felt to everyone else, especially Luca, whose youthful shield of innocence appears to erode with every step we take.

The hotel, our supposed haven, seems to rise from the white expanse like a tomb emerging from its shroud. The side road leading to it feels more like a claustrophobic tunnel carved through the snowbanks.

I have to admit, the detective's shotgun offers a twisted sense of security. It's cold comfort, this knowledge of being armed. It throws the harsh reality of our situation into stark relief – stranded in a hostile environment where the line between safety and oblivion blurs with every swirling snowflake.

As the hotel looms closer, a stark silhouette against the white void, I cling to the hope that it might offer a temporary respite from our ordeal. Yet, a deeper chill settles in my bones, fearing this refuge might somehow morph into yet another prison from which we might never escape. Yes, I know that sounds dramatic, but after the last few days, I defy anyone not to succumb to a touch of paranoia.

Things take a turn for the worse – of course – when we reach the front door and Samantha thumps on it, only to find it unlocked. On any normal day, this would be perfectly ordinary, but today is anything but. After the horrors at the community hall, you'd expect the rest of my stepfamily to be holed up here with the door securely locked behind them. Yet... here we are.

Samantha enters with the hesitant confidence one might have at their own front door, but her advance slows when the only answer to her calls is the echo of her voice.

"MUM! ROB!"

Inside, the darkness is oppressive. No candles. No lanterns. It's as if nobody's home.

For this reason, the detective, armed with her shotgun and trusty flashlight, takes point.

The doors to the living room and library are firmly shut, doing nothing to soothe my frayed nerves. Part of me wants to peek inside each one, but the stronger urge is to grab that phone and get out of here.

We reach the deserted dining area. The detective lowers her weapon, turning to Samantha, who squints in the torchlight, holding tightly to Luca. "How many rooms does this place have?"

"Ten," Samantha replies, moving over to the window to pick up a lantern. It looks vintage, but the way she flips the switch on the side, I assume it's battery-operated. She sets it on the table, casting a warm, welcome light into the space.

"We're going to need to check each of them before we can settle," the detective declares. "Where's the satphone?"

"It's in the study."

"Where's that?"

"Back down there," Samantha points down the hallway.

"The door we just passed? Why didn't you say?"

My sister, now lighting another lantern, merely squints at the added brightness and her interrogator. Her family is missing, and, like me, she's shaken, not thinking as clearly or logically as she might under normal circumstances. "I'll go get it," she offers.

"No," the detective steps in front of her. "I'll go." Switching her flashlight for one of the lanterns, she asks, "Where is it?"

"It should be in one of the desk drawers."

"Should be?"

"I can't remember. It's not like we use the bloody thing every day," Samantha snaps.

The detective eyes her for a moment, her expression unreadable. "Okay, look. We need to secure this place if we're going to stay here. We're going to need to split up."

I scoff, thinking that's she's got to be joking this time; everybody knows that splitting up is the last thing you should do when in danger. And yet, I only need to look at the resolve on both women's faces to know that she's not. "Oh, come on," I groan.

"I want to change out of these clothes anyway," Samantha says, looking down at her coat stained with Tracy's bloody handprints.

"Right, then I'll come with you," I offer.

"No. You check down here. As the detective says, we'll get this done faster if we split up."

"But—"

"I'll have Luca with me, won't I, buddy?"

Buddy barks, startling us, before moving to Luca's side. "No, I think she was talking to her son, mate," I say.

"But can Buddy come with us?" Luca asks, petting the dog.

"No. He needs to stay with Uncle Marco; otherwise, he'll be all on his own."

"Oh, okay," my nephew replies, clearly disappointed.

"No, it's okay, I'm only kidding. I'll be alright. I'd prefer it if you had him with you anyway. Just remember..." I step forward, wanting to caution them against approaching or interacting with anyone but realising the implication itself is terrifying. Instead, I settle for a serious look and hope they understand. "Be careful." Crouching down, I give Buddy a kiss on the head and a tight squeeze. "And you... take good care of them."

With that, each armed with a lantern, we split up. The detective heads down one side of the hall to find the all-important phone to call for help. I take the other, and Samantha, Luca, and Buddy slowly make their way up the stairs, the lantern light eagerly rushing ahead of them.

26

UNCANNY VALLEY

THE THISTLE HOTEL. DEEP NIGHT.

They say what doesn't kill you makes you stronger. Well, as someone who's nearly died a few times, I can tell you that's absolute bollocks. Those experiences don't make you stronger, at least, not if you're me. All they do is remind you of all the weird shit that happened before – and that could well happen again now, or maybe, if you're a particularly unlucky bastard (like me), some other, more creatively weird shit could occur. Imagine being stranded at the arse-end of the world with some kind of killer – what??

Bug? Plant? – on the loose. It's like COVID revisited, only much worse. Remember the early days of the pandemic, when paranoia was so rife we'd cross the street to avoid a jogger or wash our groceries? That's how I feel right now; only it's worse because I've seen things – including what happened in the infirmary and that house. Now, my imagination is filling in the blanks, and we all know what a cesspit that bloody place is.

So here I am, like one of those many hapless morons hunting around in the dark with just a lantern for light. I couldn't be any more cliché if I tried. I shouldn't have listened to the detective. I should have stood my ground and insisted we stick together. Instead, what's left of some semblance of my family is upstairs right now, on their own, while I'm down here, looking for what, exactly?

Shit.

I know I'm whining. And I know why. You do, too. You've seen it before. I may crack the odd witticism in the face of adversity because that's how I cope, but inside, in these shorts that I feel I've been wearing for the best part of a week, I'm shitting myself.

I yelp when the lantern light reveals a collection of glassy eyes glinting at me – dolls. A whole collection of them lined up on one of the shelves, eyeing me with lifeless curiosity.

To my left is the miniature train set I spotted last time I was here, silent and motionless. The lantern's light glints off the metallic tracks, creating a ghostly shimmer. The tiny colourful cars now carrying an invisible cargo of silence.

In the centre of the room is a box with an array of other characters, including a scarecrow with a grin as wide as its face. And yes, a chill runs down my spine. By day, the walls of this place may be adorned with vibrant murals, but by lamplight, these overfriendly characters seem to watch with unseen eyes.

Yes, I'm in the play area, but it's more like the uncanny valley. If you haven't heard that expression before, allow me to explain. You know that feeling you get when you see abandoned dolls in an attic or those super-realistic humanoids in movies? They're almost human, but not quite, and it gives you the creeps? That's called the uncanny valley. It's that sense when something looks familiar, like it should be friendly, but there's just something off that makes you feel weird. Hence why that surreal grin on Worzel Gummidge over there made me want to run screaming from this place. What? You don't know who he is? Never mind.

Anyway, the closer they get to looking real, the stranger it feels. It's like they're trapped halfway between life and death. Part of you wants to connect with them, but another part just wants to back away. Your brain kicks into overdrive trying to work it out. Why does their skin look almost like mine but not quite? What stories are they hiding? Throw in a diet of scary films, and you can easily expect that harmless doll in the corner to spin its head and start grinning.

Okay. That's enough of that shit.

See? This is what happens in the dark. Your mind works overtime. First, you start to rationalise the fear when really, you're just compounding it. At least, you do if you're me.

Thankfully, the playroom is just one room; there's nothing in there large enough to hide anyone, so I've hurried out of that place and back to the corridor. Further down and to the left, I can just about make out the glow of Isla's lantern spilling out of the study doorway. And I won't lie – the urge just to join her in there is strong, but I resist.

Instead, I turn to the next closed door, gingerly open it and hold my lantern high; a pool table sits at the centre surrounded by giant posters of vintage Coca-Cola ads – Roberto Junior's choice, no doubt. I bet Claudia had something to say about that. There are couches and a table flanked by a shelf bowed under a selection of board games. The room is otherwise empty.

Thank God.

I move closer to the next door and listen for sounds beyond it... Nothing.

So I listen for other sounds. The upstairs contingent, perhaps... But again, nothing nearby, just the click and tick of timber and that obligatory wind attempting to whistle under the door, only it's much calmer than its earlier belligerence. No doubt exhausted.

I glance at the study once more. It's closer now. And I don't know if I'm imagining it, but I'm almost sure I can hear the detective's voice. It's hard to tell.

And so, I turn the handle and push the door open to the lounge area. I hold up the lantern: stylish floor lamps, wallpaper, giant windows with drapes pulled shut against the chill, shelves laden with books, an armchair, and... oh, fuck... a sight that makes my blood run cold.

27

THE KISS

THE THISTLE HOTEL. DEEP NIGHT.

In life, we often come across forks in the road – milestones where we're forced to make life-changing decisions. It's a bit like choosing a box on a game show. Pick this one – you could win millions; choose that one – you get zilch.

Right now, I'm at one of those junctures, and every instinct in me is screaming to backstep right out of here. Yet, the rational side of me – the supposedly sane part – is trying to convince me that there's nothing wrong with this scene I've just stumbled upon in a pitch-black room. Someone's sitting on the couch with their back to me. As I hold up this shitty lantern, more terror-inducing than atmospheric in this context, I can make out from the cut and style of the hair that it's my stepmother.

"Claudia?" My voice breaks the silence, so stark that it sounds like a shout.

The only reply is the creak and sigh of the old building, the wind making the glass rattle in its wooden window frames. I hesitate, then call out again, "Claudia?" taking a step forward. The movement invokes a legion of shadows that seem to slither and dance around the stationary figure at their centre.

"Claudia?" This time, my voice is much more forceful, my heart thumping against my chest as it tries to warn me – there's something deeply unsettling about this tableau.

And yet, I find myself taking another step forward. "Claudia, it's Marco. Is everything alright?"

Really, does it look like it?

What else do you say in such a situation? My stepmother doesn't turn or react to my presence. She just seems to be staring towards the black window, much like Amy did at the infirmary. That memory alone accelerates the pounding in my chest.

I take another step, the soft glow of the lantern pushing back the darkness. And then, as if a director's camera is panning the room, the side of the sofa comes into view and part of someone's shoes – Timberlands, by the look of it.

Oh, Jesus!

There's somebody on the floor! There's a body lying on the rug in front of her. My eyes dart up to my stepmother's unmistakable profile – the same one I saw countless times as a teenager when she flounced out of the room after another row with my father, usually about me.

"Claudia?" I try again, my voice a tentative whisper now because I'm starting to feel that my words are pointless; I am not going to get a response. I'm terrified that my stepmother might be... dead.

I inch forward, the lantern's light revealing the room in breath-holding increments. A dark stain over the rug becomes visible, jeans, a shirt, and – *Oh, fuck!*

My jaw drops, and my stomach churns as I try to process what I'm seeing. It's got to be a trick of the light, right? Those can't be his glassy, bloodshot eyes. That can't be a grotesque hollow in his chest, a nest for the nightmare that has burst through, spattered with tar-like residue. This scene belongs in a horror movie, not my life.

Oh, my God. Please let this be a nightmare.

But the stench in the air is real, as is the chilling cold inside and the grim reality that my stepbrother, Roberto Junior – the bloke I was arguing with just days ago – is lying lifeless at his mother's feet.

I look up at her and freeze; she's staring directly at me with a disturbingly wide smile that slashes across her face – cheek to cheek. Disturbing mostly because I don't think the woman has ever smiled at me in my entire life. Her face is ashen, her pupils dilated and black, yet she still maintains her stylish appearance.

"Claudia?" The word just crawls out of my lips and flops into the room. Yet, there's no acknowledgment. Not a blink nor a sigh.

The wind moans... windowpanes tremble...

Oh, shit!

The realisation hits a millisecond too late. I've barely moved when an animalistic screech pierces the air, and I watch, in stupefied horror, as my stepmother leaps onto the couch with the agility of a wild animal before launching herself at me. The impact sends me reeling and then sprawling onto the wood floor; the lantern clattering loudly nearby yet persisting in its projection of the shadow version of this horror flick over the walls.

I scramble to my knees and scurry forward, only to feel fingers like talons grab a chunk of my hair and tug me backward. I wail in pain as the momentum yanks hair roots from my scalp with a sickeningly familiar ripping sound.

But I don't stop. I jump to my feet and am making for the door when I feel a weight collide with my back and pull me down like a predator would its hapless prey. Then, I feel those claw-like hands once more, anchoring into my side, pushing and spinning me onto my back before scrambling onto and straddling me in a grotesque, horrifying position. I gag.

I reach up to push the frenzied creature off, but my hands are intercepted by powerful vice-like claws and are slowly pushed back beside my head. I growl through my teeth as I attempt to resist the assault, but I am no match for this thing that appears superhuman in strength.

Then, I see it, rippling under the artificial lamplight, a homicidal mask of a face that may seem familiar but is devoid of all humanity, and it's bearing down on me with repugnant intimacy. Close enough for me to smell its cold breath on my face, the fetid stench of rotting flowers.

I scream. And it's not a quick sound but a primal release of abject terror, not just because I feel helplessly pinned to the floor by this creature but because of what is now dangling from its slender nostrils. It's the same thing I thought I'd seen in the glass at the infirmary. White shoots, like emaciated maggots, extend and wriggle like grotesque strands of nose hair gone wild.

Then, I watch that letterbox mouth open, yawning into an unnatural distension that seems like a gateway to hell itself as rivulets of drool begin to pool, hang loose, and drip.

I turn my face aside, feeling cold droplets of saliva splatter against my cheek as I grunt and struggle to free myself from this horror. But my strength is ebbing; I'm no match for this entity, even when it releases one of my hands. It then clamps its painted talons into the flesh of my face, forcing me to look up into what looks like the contorted, maniacal features of my stepmother. Yet, there's something undeniably alien, not just in her expression but in the overwhelming strength that suggests some kind of monstrous alteration.

I groan and grunt as I attempt to resist, but it's futile. I feel the nails gouging at my cheeks as my head is anchored in place, and I am forced to watch helplessly as more spittle forms at the sides of its mouth and pools to drop straight into my face. And I prepare myself because I've seen enough to know that there's no coming back from this infection. There'll be no—

A sound, loud like a percussion grenade, explodes around the room. I feel a spatter of something warm across my forehead before the weight is blown backward off of me.

I lie there for several seconds, ears ringing, breaths panting, heart thumping, trying to process what just happened. Even though I know the thing is off me, it still takes time for my brain to believe it.

Once I do, I instinctively crawl backward as fast as my hands and feet can propel me before crashing into something – and I scream. Again, not exactly like a little girl, but enough to question my masculinity, especially when I look up to see what's impeding my way out of here: the detective looking down at me, shotgun in one hand and the other reaching down to help me to my feet.

Shit.

Isla leads me out of the room and into the corridor where I fall into one of those convenient antique chairs that look just as decorative as they do incapable of sustaining the weight of a parked arse.

I flop into that thing as my brain scrambles to catch up with exactly what just happened in there, because I still can't believe it. And I must still be reeling because the detective's hands are all over me. Touching my face. Feeling my body. My arms. My chest.

Oi. Stop that! Now isn't the time.

Don't get me wrong – you know me, you know my past, and you know exactly what I'm like, or rather, was like. That's something else that's changed about me, by the way. I mean, I haven't really talked about it – when the fuck would I have had the chance, exactly? But yeah, I don't feel that way anymore for some reason. Ever since Fawndale or, more specifically, ever since Holt burned down, courtesy of that crazy lady – and no, I'm not talking about my wife – I just haven't felt that compulsion anymore. I haven't craved intimacy as I used to. It's weird. Even worse, I haven't even thought about it –

until now. What do you think that means?

So anyway, as much as Isla and her Lara Croft scar – no wait, I don't think Lara Croft has any scars, does she? I wonder how she got that thing, anyway. I should ask. Oh... well, not now. There's a time and a place for that stuff. Anyway, I digress. Yeah, as much as the detective is attractive and everything, I'm not sure—

"Ow, what the fuck?!" I yell as a searing pain burns across my left cheek.

"Marco?"

"What?" I snap, blinking away the stars exploding behind my eyelids.

"Are you okay? Are you alright?"

I touch my cheek. "Um, I was.... Did you just slap me?"

"I had to. You were in shock and a little hysterical. I needed to snap you out of it," she explains flatly.

"Oh, well, I think you bloody succeeded. That bloody hurt."

The detective simply rolls her eyes at me. "We need to go. Now," she states urgently.

"Go? Go where?"

"We need to find your sister."

Dread ripples through me. "Why? What's wrong?" My question is cut short by Buddy's bark, hauntingly muffled, drifting down the stairs.

"Buddy?" I don't wait. I snatch the lantern from the detective's hand and start sprinting up the stairs.

"Marco! Wait!" she calls after me, but I'm not listening. I'm not fucking listening. I take the steps two at a time as Buddy's bark grows louder.

"Marco!" I can hear Isla's heavy footsteps pounding behind me, but I don't slow down. In fact, I push myself faster as I race down the hallway to a closed door.

I don't even take a beat; I barge into the room as if my life depends on it, holding the lantern aloft. At first, I'm startled by a scary pair of glinting eyes, then Buddy's familiar form materialises.

"Buddy!" I exclaim, rushing to my dog, falling to my knees, and pulling him close. "You're alright, boy. You're alright," I soothe, running my fingers through his fur, checking for injuries.

Isla arrives, panting heavily.

Seconds tick by before Buddy's whimpering forces me to break the reunion. "What is it, mate? What's wrong?" I ask him, and then it hits me.

I stand abruptly. "Sam? Luca?" My voice echoes slightly in the empty room as I wave the lantern around.

They're gone.

Buddy whimpers again and pads over to the window, looking out. I follow him. "What is it, eh? What do you see?"

I peer out; the clouds have parted, and the moon casts a weak light, barely outlining the silhouettes of trees and the coastal path.

"No," I whisper, disbelief tightening my throat.

"Marco?" Isla calls after me, but her voice is distant, so distant because I cannot believe what I am seeing.

I fling the double windows wide, and an icy breeze barges into the room. With the moonlight aiding the weak glow of my lantern, I spot scuffled footprints on the snowy ledge of the iron fire escape, leading down to the extensive garden, then trailing off toward the stone steps up to the coastal path.

"No," I mutter again, the word barely a breath.

But it's the detective who voices the dread swirling in my mind. "They're gone."

28

THE DARK SIDE

WEDNESDAY· JUST BEYOND MIDNIGHT·

I know what you're thinking; now would be the worst time for the detective and me to fall out, especially after she literally saved me from the kiss of death. Yet, that's exactly what happened.

Similarly, you might be thinking I've recovered from my whole ordeal in the lounge quite well. I haven't. Well, I have, but not in the way you might think. More in the way I would normally tell a client they shouldn't. It's the same way Doctor Ethan Holmes, in a roundabout way, lectured me about repressing my past trauma by, well, repressing it.

But come on. You've seen what's been happening here. There just isn't any time to fall apart. As much as I would like to go and rock myself in a corner, the few seconds – alright, minutes – I tried to do that, the detective quite literally slapped me out of it.

Besides, there's a whole conspiracy thing to deal with now. You know, as if every other bit of this mindfuck isn't enough, Isla, yes her, Miss Know-It-All, decided to share some news with me that, well, just can't be right because, well, it can't. And I'm not even going to bother sharing it with you because it's obviously just a pack of lies that this perfectly capable police officer is spinning because... because...

Shit!

I keep getting to that point and faltering because I just keep concluding that the woman has absolutely no reason to lie to me about this. My sister, on the other hand... well...

FUCK!

"Marco?"

"Give it a rest, Isla. I said I don't want to talk about it."

"Marco, if you want to stand any chance of saving your nephew, we need to leave now." Isla's tone is firm, a sharp contrast to my rising frustration.

I scoff. "Save him? From what?"

"You know what I mean." Her voice is steady, but there's an edge of urgency.

I turn to her, my eyes narrowing. "No. I don't think I do, Detective. Why don't you tell me?"

"You know," she repeats, more forcefully this time, her gaze unwavering.

I turn back to look out the window as if this might magically return what fragment of a family I have left. I don't know how long we've been here now. Five, ten minutes? What I do know is that I can't feel my nose or my ears anymore. Especially my ears. Which, of course, got me thinking about David. Wondering what, exactly, my friend is doing right now, probably snug in his bed.

I'm suddenly filled with such overwhelming homesickness that I think I'm going to puke in that virginal white snow.

What the fuck am I doing here? I should never have come.

Oh, well, hindsight and all that, eh?

My sister, Samantha Battista, lied. She never called the mainland. She never called for help. Which means there's nobody coming to save us. Correction, there is a rescue on its way now, but it isn't going to get here for at least two hours. Until then, we're on our own, the detective kindly informed me.

But why did Samantha lie? Why would my sister lie to me? I think those were my words. Probably a bit more shrill and somewhat hysterical, perhaps.

The detective said she had a theory if I was open-minded enough to want to hear it. Open-minded? Me? I'm the epitome of open-mindedness. Bloody cheek!

She thinks that the more Thistle Loch Foods, my father's company, started struggling, the more the board would have wanted to oust my stepbrother, Roberto Junior. Samantha somehow – and the detective admits she doesn't know how since there's a good chance my sister actually led the action to evict her own brother – managed to get herself nominated in his stead. And with her being Roberto Battista's daughter, she was approved.

She was forced to shut down all the company's manufacturing operations and farm all of that out in a drastic cost-cutting exercise. While she managed to save the company, she was unable to restore it to its former prosperity, with dire consequences for Thistle Island. Most of the island's inhabitants relied on Thistle Loch in some way for income, which meant that many were forced to leave for the mainland. All of this proved disastrous for an island so badly in need of inland investment.

It fell on Samantha, as elected mayor, to find a solution. She diversified by focusing more on traditional revenue streams, such as tourism. But this still wasn't enough.

Then, a stroke of fortune: the discovery at the ledge on the mountain. It raised the island's profile, boosted tourism, and attracted foreign investment. All very positive, but slow.

Samantha became desperate and turned to her husband. He illegally removed artifacts from the site, including these so-called seeds, and that's where it all started.

Now, Samantha knew it was just a matter of time before the mainland was contacted and it was revealed that she never called them. And she knew the moment that happened, it'd all be over for her.

"Nice theory, but can you prove any of it?" I say, defiantly, defensively.

"Not right now," she says through breaths, gesturing around us. "But I know the evidence is there. I just need to follow the trail."

The detective's theory swirls in my mind, colliding with the chaotic reality of our situation. Could Samantha really be that desperate? Is she capable of risking everything, even our lives? I don't want to believe it, but as the detective kindly pointed out, I can't possibly know her as well as I think I do. The thought gnaws at me, but I can't afford to dwell on it. We have to focus on getting through the next couple of hours.

"Alright," I finally say, exhaling a breath I didn't realise I was holding. "We need to find them. They can't have gone far."

The detective nods, her expression steely. "Let's move," she says, handing me a flashlight. "We'll figure out the rest once we're safe."

With that, we brace ourselves against the cold once more and head back out into the icy night. The storm may have paused, but the real tempest rages within us, driving us forward into the unknown.

I wish I could say that was a deliberate pun. A witticism inspired by this stranger who may have the social skills of a cactus in a balloon shop but has never failed to impress. But sadly, I know it isn't.

We've left the hotel and are at the top of the hill now on the track we took the day of my father's memorial, which seems a lifetime ago. At least, that's where I think we are. The track's gone, buried beneath at least five inches of snow. What is still visible are the twin sets of footprints leading the way.

Thank God, or whoever heads up the meteorological department, that the storm appears to have passed. This would be a whole different experience if it hadn't. Of course, the downside is that I'm instantly transported back to that night at Fawndale and that hideous time at Frost Lake Manor. While the scenery may be different, every loud crunch of snow beneath our feet and every breath of fresh air is a reminder of the night we nearly died.

I can't have that for my nephew or my sister – no matter how much shit she might be in. Because I have to face it: for all my blustering, I know the detective is right. I just don't want to see it. I just wanted everything to be alright. For them to be safe. But I get the hideous impression that this situation is neither. This is underscored by the fact that the detective is walking beside me, clutching that shotgun as if our lives literally depend on it.

Meanwhile, Buddy, tail high like there's absolutely nothing wrong in the world, is trotting up ahead, sniffing the footprints from time to time, obviously making sure we're on the right track to his new pal. Until suddenly, we see it, and everything becomes clear.

The trail is leading off the main path and down towards the abandoned fish processing plant.

We pause at the top of the hill, the dilapidated structure looming in the distance, a stark reminder of the island's struggling past. The building, once a bustling hub of activity, now stands as a ghostly relic, its windows dark and broken, the metal siding rusting away.

"Of course. It's here," I say quietly. "I hated this place during the day. At night... well, it's a whole other nightmare about to come true."

"I don't understand," the detective says. "Do you know why she came here?"

It would be easy to say I don't know, but unfortunately for me, I do. It became clear the moment I saw those footprints in the snow. Don't get me wrong, there were several heart-stopping seconds after I entered that bedroom and discovered they were missing that I thought they'd somehow been taken, but the moment I saw the tracks, I knew. And from that moment, I've been trying to decide which scenario was worse.

"She's trying to get them off the island," I say without taking my eyes off the structure.

"What?"

I nod. "There's no other way off the island without the ferry. But there are trawlers docked inside the plant."

"How do you know this?"

"Sam mentioned it when she was giving me the tour."

There are several seconds of silence filled only by the wind blowing snow dust across the icy expanse.

"You realise that we can't let that happen, right?" the detective says.

I don't answer. I can't. "Come on," I say instead before stepping forward and cautiously making my way down the hill.

29

THE NURSERY

BEYOND MIDNIGHT

The moon, though full, peeks out from behind its shroud of clouds, offering only a thin sliver of light as if it can't bear to watch. The diffused glow, though useful, isn't enough to push away the darkness clinging to this place like a second skin.

Yet, there it squats, the skeletal frame of the former fish processing plant, still standing proud at the edge of Thistle Island – a relic of rust and peeling paint with shadows etched deep into its bones. It's a ghost, a shade of what it used to be, and yet, there's a glint of life in one of those dead eyes – a light that shouldn't be there. A lantern, maybe? It's hard to tell. Whatever it is, the ominous glow through a jagged break in one of the windows is enough to make my heart skip a beat.

The place is still at least a hundred yards away, and yet it's giving off a vibe that sends a shiver skittering down my spine. It feels like a relic from another time, whispering tales of its heyday through the howling wind that sweeps across the barren snowfield surrounding us. It's like stepping into a photograph from another era, crumpled and forgotten until now.

The contrast is stark – the natural beauty of the island, serene under a blanket of snow, against the man-made decay before us. It's a scene that stirs the gut, a reminder of nature reclaiming what we've abandoned.

The village might as well be a world away; here, there's only the sound of our breaths and the occasional crack from the ice along the shore. The sea is a black mirror reflecting the uncertain sky. The plant's roof, peppered with patches of snow, looks as if it could come down any minute under the weight of years and neglect.

The air bites at my cheeks, a mixture of frost and salt clinging to each breath I take. It's so quiet out here. Too bloody quiet, and I can't shake the feeling that something's waiting for us in there, in the belly of this beast that once fed the island's life.

It doesn't take long for us to follow the footprints to what I imagine is the entrance to the building. This is, after all, a processing plant, and while I have no clue as to the layout of the place, I've watched enough documentaries about factories to know that these places are laid out in sections, each representing a stage of the product's journey. In this case, we're taking that journey in reverse: from despatch through intake.

The air inside is heavy with the stale, lingering odour of fish and damp, a pungent reminder of the plant's former life.

The detective steps in front of me and holds up her shotgun, which, of course, momentarily fills me with panic as I can't help but wonder who she plans to use that thing on. I may be repressing what happened in that study, but the sensation of that spatter will stay with me forever. I conclude that my companion is just being cautious, something I realise I'm actually grateful for.

It's easy to underestimate just how massive this place is until you walk through the entrance – or exit, depending on how you prefer to look at it – of the despatching area. Given the limited light, my first thought was that part of the walls had fallen away, but the track revealed by the beams of our flashlights tells a different story: we've just walked through hangar-like doors and entered a realm no longer of this world. By that, I mean a world of abrupt abandonment, where the remnants of haste and disuse are palpable in the frigid air. It's a cavernous industrial space lit by dappled silvery moonlight sifting in through grime-smeared windows.

The walls, once pristine and sterile, now peel back like old skin, revealing the bones of a structure that must have thrummed with activity. Conveyor belts coated in frost weave through the area like dormant steel serpents. They are flanked by pallets stacked with empty, soggy boxes branded with the Thistle Loch logo, their colours, edges softened by time.

Forklifts stand sentinel, silent in their obsolescence, and rusted tools lie scattered on workbenches amidst fish scales that still cling stubbornly to the surface. Ice has claimed the ground, with puddles from leaks long gone, having frozen over, turning the floor into a treacherous glass mosaic.

Overhead, giant circular fluorescent lights hover like dead alien spaceships condemned to drift through the eternally lifeless space of darkness. Near the loading docks, the heavy plastic curtains that once controlled temperature now hang in tatters, swaying slightly with the wind that moans through the gaps in the metal shutters, carrying with it the salty sting of the sea.

This section must have been a bustling nexus of efficiency where the day's catch would begin its journey to markets far beyond. Now, it is just a hollow shell of its former self, its purpose demoted to eerie gateway into the deeper, more shadowy heart of the plant.

"Can you hear that?" the detective whispers suddenly, her voice loud in the stillness.

I listen but can't hear anything. "What?" I whisper back.

"That droning sound."

I listen again, and at first, I still can't hear anything beyond the perpetual mournful howl of the wind through the structure, but then, suddenly, underneath all that, I hear it. She's right.

Background noise – the hum of a refrigerator, the whir of the central heating – is a way of life. It has become the soundtrack of our existence. But out here in the wilderness, the motorised din of a petrol generator is hard to miss. Unless you're me, of course. The point being that if there's a generator running, somebody switched it on. The question is *who and why?* Because it obviously isn't to power the lights.

Instinctively, we move toward the noise, through the tattered plastic curtain and into another barn-like space. The area is so wide that the detective's torch beam travelling ahead of us finds nothing but darkness.

It stinks in here, too. The odour is pungent, like rotted fish meets abandoned fridges. Which makes perfect sense since, when the spotlight lands on a row of thick metal doors reminiscent of institutional solitary confinement, it becomes clear that this must be cold storage. The irony, of course, is the fact that the roof's perpetual drip of frozen water appears to have sculpted giant icicles like stalactites. They are now clinging menacingly to the metal girders, threatening to plunge down on us at any moment while every inch of the place has been dusted in frosted white. Nature imitating technology.

We don't linger in the frigid mausoleum, and I'm grateful. My overactive imagination was already beginning to hear a click on one of those catches and imagining something emerging from the other side.

The next grimy curtain leads into what must be the heart of the plant – the processing area. Here, the underbelly of productivity lies exposed under the beam of the torchlight. Overhead, strip lighting hangs frustratingly lifeless, the dull metal casings reflecting a ghostly glow back at us. It's like stepping into a time capsule, preserved by the cold and silence.

The generator's hum is unmistakably closer here, a mechanical heartbeat in the quiet, drawing us further in, like moths to a flame.

The detective moves ahead cautiously, her shotgun at the ready, scanning the shadows that taunt the edges of the light beam, which has now found two conveyor belts running the length of the room, parallel relics of the plant's bustling days. They're covered in a fine layer of frost, untouched for who knows how long. I can almost hear the hum, clank, and chaos of a typical day here, the belts moving relentlessly, carrying the latest catch through their mechanical digestive tract. Now, they rest in silence, a stark testament to the abruptness with which life here ceased.

Off to one side, stainless-steel tables stand in rows, the surfaces dull under the patina of dust and disuse. This must have been where the fish were prepared, gutted, and filleted before being sent off to be frozen or packed. The tools of the trade, knives, and hooks, lie scattered, as if abandoned in haste. Salt crystals glisten under the torchlight.

Above us, the ventilation system looms, a network of ducts that once fought a losing battle against the smell of fish and sea, now silent and probably home to nothing but dust and I shudder to think what else.

I pull my coat tighter around me as the cold gnaws its way into my bones. We push forward, the detective's training urging her to pause from time to time and sweep her light across the vastness of the processing floor. The darkness is so palpable that it smothers me with a claustrophobic sense of desolation. This place is not only abandoned but forgotten by time, as if we are the only souls to venture here in ages.

Then, the detective stops abruptly, and this does nothing to ease the tension at the back of my neck. She pivots her light down to the concrete floor that is iridescent with frost, yet this isn't what makes my heart skip a beat but what's imprinted there.

Footprints. They must be recent. Samantha and Luca must have come through here. The sight spurs me forward. I'm just about to make my way through the next plastic curtain when I notice that Buddy isn't following. For a horrifying moment, I think he's wandered off, but as soon as I turn the beam of my flashlight, it finds first his furry butt and then that creepy look of his. He turns his head back to look at me with a blank expression that normally precedes a stare-off with an empty wall or ceiling, like he knows something I don't.

"No!" I hiss through gritted teeth. "Not now." But the dog doesn't move, doe eyes squinting into the torchlight.

I sense the detective move closer, her beam crisscrossing mine, probing beyond the dog into more blackness, which I assume is some kind of corridor. Her beam pans around the area and uncovers a sign on the wall: CAFETERIA.

"Seriously?" I hiss again. I have no idea why I'm whispering. I just get the distinct impression that we shouldn't be drawing attention to ourselves. "You're worried about food, now? Come on, let's go!" But the dog isn't moving, and I'm just about to lose it—

Jangle… jangle…

The detective and I freeze. Buddy growls, and in unison, both torchlights move over the dog to probe at the darkness beyond, but this place is so vast that even the fringes of light dare not venture too far into the black.

Oh, shit. I thought I was scared before, but I'm shitting myself now. Sorry. But that growl from Buddy is seldom the prelude to anything good. And so, what do we do about that? We wait, apparently. Maybe to see if we both imagined the sound, but...

Silence, except for the wind pushing at the structure, making it creak and groan.

Seconds tick by, yet as always in these situations, it feels like minutes, and, if I'm perfectly honest, I'm ready to move on, swiftly, through the curtain and to our destination. I have no interest in investigating what—

Tinkle... jangle... tinkle... jangle.

Fuck. We didn't imagine it. And Buddy confirms by growling at the dark once more.

The haunting sound, akin to the wooden jangle of a wind chime, drifts out of the black and crawls over me, then down my spine. Wind chimes, by their very nature, respond to changes in atmospheric pressure. But there's no wind in here. So what unseen hand is molesting them?

A touch on my arm makes me yelp. It's the detective. I release the breath I'm holding and widen my eyes at her. She uses the beam of her light to point downward. I follow, and... shit.

Footprints. This time, out of a puddle of water, leading away from the curtains and into the dark. For some reason, my sister and my nephew decided to abandon the main artery through the plant and veer off towards the cafeteria. And something tells me they didn't choose to stop off for a snack.

I move over to Buddy and pet his head as an apology, then turn to the detective, but she's already moving forward. Looks like we're going this way.

The hallway is short, dark, and wet. It's as if this section of the plant has remained impervious to the atmospheric elements. Correction, it's as if it was once painted with the same freeze as everywhere else but is now thawing. That, and the drone from earlier sounds much louder here, which means we must be drawing closer to that generator. The sound is nowhere near as creepy as it was before, simply because it's got to be one of the refrigerators from the cafeteria. Somehow, some of the machinery must still be running.

Our flashlights home in on two blue swing doors. Above them, a sign reads: CAFETERIA.

We each take a beat. I tell Buddy to heel, and then I push.

The cafeteria doors groan open, a reluctant invitation into a world that has no place in the land of the living. My boots scrape against the floor, the sound is a rude awakening in a room that's embraced silence like a long-lost lover. It's surprisingly warm in here, a striking difference from everywhere else, and it's most welcome. Unlike the atmosphere, which is anything but.

That generator is definitely nearby, the sound much louder now. I imagine it's somehow powering this place, although, like the rest of the plant, everything is still dead. The only difference here is the absence of frost, replaced by pools of dark water.

Across the room, patches of flickering red light, while obvious in the black, do little to actually illuminate the space. And then it hits me. Heaters. They seem more decorative than functional. Not really warming much, but enough to change the atmosphere, coaxing shadows from the gloom, projecting them onto the wall in a dance with the devil in the dim. The light paints everything in shades of blood – not bright and fresh, but dark and congealed, a reminder of what's happened and what's still menacing.

Upended chairs sprawl across the floor, some leaning against the wall at odd angles. The serving counter, once a hub of hasty lunches and hurried tea breaks, now stands abandoned. The food is long gone, replaced by a stillness thick enough to cut with a knife. The salad bar, a trough of rot and wilt, exudes a sour stench that stings the nostrils. Scattered napkins and crumpled wrappers litter the floor, remnants of meals long forgotten.

My gaze flicks to the vending machine in the corner, its glass fogged over. I can still make out the shapes behind it – rows of snacks and drinks, untouched, undesired, witnesses to the stillness. Above, the ceiling tiles are stained with age, and I can just make out the faint drip, drip, drip of a leak somewhere in the darkness. It's rhythmic, like a clock ticking down to an end I'm not ready to meet.

This place is a still life of the everyday turned inside out, a snapshot of normalcy that's been gutted, leaving just the carcass. And yet, in the red twilight, something about the way those shadows move isn't quite right. It's not the light that's alive; it's something else, something that shouldn't be.

A heaviness hangs in the air. A low hum that vibrates through the floorboards. Unseen eyes. Breaths held in anticipation. The half-light, the almost-darkness... That's where the real terror lies. Just out of sight but felt all the same.

I let out a breath I didn't know I was holding, the sound loud in the quiet, too loud. Because in here, noise is not just noise; it's a herald, a summoning. And I'm all too aware that we are not alone.

Buddy steps forward and whimpers, making me jump and almost instantly eliciting that *jangle* once more. The idea of something moving in the dark sends a surge of fear crackling through me.

The detective must feel the same because she instantly lifts the shotgun in front of her and uses the torch beam as a laser sight, sweeping it across the room until it finds something. Something that doesn't belong in here. Something that makes me want to turn and run from this place.

Tendrils. Plant tendrils, like serpents, slithering out of the open double doors on the opposite side of the room. It's as if they've grown outward, pushing the doors open, spreading out across the walls, and hanging from the ceiling, but only halfway, as if the leaves have met some kind of invisible demarcation line.

I've never seen anything like it before. It looks like ivy but isn't. I mean, I'm no expert – just the little I learned when we built ANEW. Oh God, how I long to be there right now. These things look bigger than ivy, with jagged pointed edges like nettles, glistening in the dark.

But what's most disturbing – and I imagine the detective feels the same because she's allowing her light beam to linger there – is the way some tendrils, like claws, appear to have somehow smashed, pushed, and burrowed their way into a vending machine by the door and slithered inside where – and there's no other way to put this – they've inserted themselves into the confectionery in there, as if sucking the life from it. It isn't obvious because the things aren't moving, of course, but it's just the way they've invaded the machine that's particularly disturbing.

Isla's light is moving now, venturing beyond the double doors that have been transformed into a leafy tunnel into the next room, which appears to be the point of origin. Buddy whimpers again, gazing in that direction.

Jangle. Jangle.

Again, those chimes, but much louder now. The sound is undoubtedly coming from inside the tunnel.

My heart is in my throat as all my instincts are telling me to leave this place, never to look back. But another part of me knows that my sister and my nephew are in here. This is reinforced by Buddy's whimpering, pulling against my hand on the nape of his neck.

"No," I hiss.

Jangle.

I turn to the detective, but she's already looking at me. And I know that look. She wants me to follow her, and reluctantly, I do.

We slowly follow the shotgun across the room, the detective occasionally sweeping it and the beam of her flashlight around, presumably to ensure there's nothing lurking in the dark corners.

Drip... drip... drip...

Water falls from the ceiling, plopping loudly in puddles all around us as we slowly make our way forward. I'm hunched over, my hand tight on the thick of Buddy's fur, keeping him close. I'm not taking any chances.

I don't know if it's my imagination, but it seems warmer over here. The generator is louder.

The leaves are much bigger up close, dangling down like ripped curtains. We make a conscious effort to avoid them, but they're getting denser. I move to avoid touching one and bump into a table, sending an abandoned mug crashing to the floor.

Jangle... jangle...

We're getting closer. Even over the drone of the generator – still hidden from sight – the wind chimes are obviously somewhere in the green tunnel that I imagine was once some kind of hallway, either out of the building or perhaps back to the main plant. I've no idea.

We're at the doors, tentatively moving forward. The detective first, Buddy and me close behind.

The crimson heater light in here seems stronger, albeit not strong enough to penetrate the inky blackness. The heat is much more palpable, yet I find it in no way comforting but stifling. It's thick, oppressive, and heady, with a stench so foul it's causing me to gag.

I cling to Buddy's fur, half expecting the poor dog to cry out in pain.

Then, the detective stops abruptly, her light sweeping over the hundreds of leaves that, like ants from a nest, have fanned out in symmetrical rows overhead and around us towards the cafeteria.

Jangle... jangle...

The sound seems different up close. Not melodic in the conventional sense of a wind chime but dissonant. And not just one, but many, echoing all around us.

I barely have time to process that thought when the detective begins to lift her light beam from the glistening wet floor, upward, revealing a pair of boots, a leg, and—*Oh, Jesus!* A torso with a large, bloody cavity at its centre. From this grotesque wound, thick green stems sprout, reaching upward like parasitic vines towards the ceiling. The stems culminate in a giant flower, but this one differs from the others we've seen. It's bigger – much bigger – with the monstrous makeup of a perverse sunflower. Its petals are an unnerving shade of crimson, curling unnaturally to sharp points like teeth, and at its heart are long, silver stamens that shimmer with a sickly, metallic sheen.

The sight is enough to churn my stomach, the stench of blood and decaying flesh filling the air making it almost impossible to breathe.

The thing has no eyes, but it's facing forward as if watching us. The very idea sends a shudder of revulsion through me, which only gets worse when the detective's flashlight slowly reveals the rest of the uncannily grotesque spectacle. It's like something out of the worst nightmare, arms... legs... heads, bodies contorted into inhuman shapes, acting like biological growbags for these *things*. They've lined both sides of the corridor like some kind of macabre gauntlet.

"Oh, my God," gasps the detective.

Jangle! Hiss! Jangle! Hiss!

I hold my light up and can't believe it. I just can't believe it, but all the flowers appear to have turned towards us like a room of angry, faceless heads, objecting to our presence with reptilian hisses.

What the...

This isn't possible. Is it? This has got to be a bloody dream. Wake up!

Whimper... Jangle! Hiss! Whimper... Jangle! Hiss!

At first, I think it's Buddy whimpering, but I soon realise that the sound is coming from further down the corridor. I aim the flashlight in that direction and see small boots, jeans, a heavy puffer jacket, and... Luca! His face is ashen, contorted in a mask of sheer horror, red hot and wet from tears. He is holding a trembling finger to his mouth, urging us to be quiet. Samantha is standing directly behind him, equally terrified. She has her arms around him, and I can see – yet I'm hoping I'm imagining it – her coat is slashed, tinged blood red in places as if somebody has taken a razor blade to it.

Woof! Buddy barks and follows that up with a growl.

Hiss! Jangle!

Oh, fuck! This is happening! The whole room of these things just swung towards us, faceless heads bobbing and swinging like reptiles.

Jangle... jangle... jangle.

Oh... I can see them now. Those stamens, vibrating like tonsils. It's them. They're producing that sound. Like a bloody alarm call. Communicating with each other.

Buddy growls again, haunches rising.

"Buddy! No!" I cry.

Jangle! Jangle! Jangle! HISS!

And before I know it, the nearest flower snaps forward and lunges for us. Buddy leaps backward, fortuitously taking me with him. I feel the literal displacement of the fetid air as the tendrils of that thing whip just inches from my face.

"JESUS CHRIST!" I yell.

HISS! JANGLE! HISS! JANGLE!

The detective squeezes off a round from the shotgun, causing the head of one of the nearby flowers to explode. The sound is so loud in the confined space, my ears instantly start ringing.

"FUCK!" I yell.

And I don't think those things took kindly to the action because they're literally quivering now, vibrating, stalks and flowers shaking and jangling, a loud cacophony that rakes at my eardrums and nerves.

But somehow, I know it's now or never. "RUN! LUCA! RUN!" I yell over the din, but my nephew is too terrified to move, which is why Samantha has to shove her son towards us.

Buddy adds his own encouragement with a series of barks, and my sister and nephew race through the tunnel of leaves. But the plants, as if enraged by the shotgun blast, suddenly snap towards them, tendrils whipping through the air with lethal intent.

One of those razor-sharp things slices through Samantha's coat, leaving a deep gash in the fabric. She screams and stumbles, pushing Luca forward as they dodge and weave to avoid the deadly lashes.

"Keep going!" I yell, panic surging through me.

To Buddy's frantic barks, my nephew manages to slide his way out to us with one final push by his mother. Samantha skids and crashes hard to the floor. Having made it out successfully, Luca instantly turns to look back at his mother, eyes wide, as another of those barbed tendrils snaps through the air, narrowly missing Samantha's head.

"MUMMY!" he screams.

Without thinking, I push Luca back towards the detective and dive forward as more air is displaced millimetres from my ear. I reach out to my sister, who is already attempting to scramble to her feet and grab her hand. "COME ON!" I yell, yanking her towards me and then out to the exit.

The plants are still jangling and shaking. I had expected them to continue their attack, but it seems they're too busy doing their creepy dance to attempt to reach out of the corridor to us.

Luca throws his arms around both of us. And it's strange because, in this moment, I decide that I don't care about Samantha. I don't care about what she did or why she did it. This is what's left of my family, and I'm just so bloody grateful they're both okay.

I instantly break the embrace and check on my sister. "Are you okay? Are you alright?" I ask, inspecting her body. Her coat looks shredded. Shining a light over it, I can see that it's quite thick, so the wounds aren't as bad as I first thought.

"I'm fine," my sister says, holding my face, tears welling in her eyes. And I can tell she wants to talk, no doubt about abandoning us at the hotel and God only knows what else, but now isn't the time.

"We need to get out of here," the detective jumps in.

I nod.

"There should be boats on the other side of the plant," Samantha says.

"Great. Let's go," I say, getting to my feet and freezing when I see the outline of a person standing in the doorway at the opposite side of the tunnel. Not unlike the detective before them, they are holding a flashlight like a laser sight, and it's aimed right at me. The next thing I know, I am being shoved sideways. There's a flash, a loud explosion, a pain to the right side of my head, and I'm seeing white-hot stars.

30

GUNS

THE EARLY HOURS

So, if I'm perfectly honest, I would be happy to lie on this wet, slimy, disgustingly freezing floor for much longer than what feels like ten or so seconds, but whoever it is – probably Samantha, I'm not sure – has other plans. They are calling and tugging at me like it is the end of the bloody world.

Of course, when I finally manage to get to my feet despite my wobbly head and see that familiar and equally terrifying bulk of Sarge charging through the corridor at us, I appreciate the immediacy of the situation.

"Come on!" I yell. "Let's go!" But then I notice the detective. She has her arm around Samantha's neck, and despite my fuzzy head, something about the scene feels off—until I realise the detective is limping.

Oh, shit! She's been shot. Oh, fuck! I think she's been shot because of me. I think it was she who pushed me out of the way.

"GO! NOW! Get to the dock!" I yell, "Take Buddy! GO!"

All comply.

At least, I think they do. I've already moved on to my next no-doubt bad idea, but, again, you'll appreciate that I have just milliseconds to process this stuff.

And yet, I'm still able to digest the fact that the bloke who I don't think ever took a particular liking to me, the same one who mysteriously vanished and was likely infected at the community hall – the burly guy who bit his own deputy – has miraculously reappeared. That is shocking enough but perhaps not as shocking as seeing him barrelling through that tunnel of those things, whatever the fuck they are, without them reacting to him in any way. In fact, they even stop their hideous, shaky dance and just start hissing in that bone-chilling sentient way of theirs.

So I'll admit, it probably costs me a couple of precious seconds before I react to the fact that my people have barely made it across the room to the exit when the not-so-gentle giant is almost upon me. I do what any self-respecting, scared shitless bloke does in such a situation – I pick up one of the nearby chairs, and when I see that freak point his flashlight and shotgun at the others, I swing it with every ounce of strength I can muster and smash it into the man's face. The impact sends the big oaf reeling backward and crashing to the floor, gun, and flashlight clattering and sliding loudly nearby.

I couldn't have hoped for a better outcome. And sure, I would love to give credit to my present yet somewhat humble anatomical guns, but I think it's mostly down to the element of surprise. The man was so focused on aiming at the others that he didn't even stop to consider me.

Either way, given that I achieved the desired effect, you're probably thinking I'd choose to stay and finish the job – pummel the bastard into the floor. If you are thinking that, well… you'd be wrong. I've no fucking idea what's going on here, and I have no intention of hanging around to find out.

So I grab my flashlight from the floor and run. Well, it's more of a slip, slide, and scramble on the wet surface before bursting out of those double doors and heading back in the direction we came.

Back at the main thoroughfare through the plant, I skid left through the heavy plastic curtains and find myself in a dark corridor that reminds me of an aircraft gangway, only wider. From what I can see, it has a conveyor belt at its centre and a walkway on both sides. If my heart weren't already thudding against my chest, this dark echoey place – a metallic kill box – would shove it into a completely different gear because—*Oh, shit* – it's starting to feel like these metallic, container-like walls are closing in on me. *And… Oh, no… Let me out! How do I get out of here? Let me out!*

I'm stuck in a cage with no way out, and I'm going to—

Oh, right. Finally, the light beam of my flashlight finds a door latch with a sign above it that reads TO DOCK – *Ensure doors open when conveyor belt is in operation.*

Okay. So the sign and door latch were there the whole time. And I think I may have just had a minor panic attack. *It's okay. It's alright.* It's perfectly normal considering the fact that, for several seconds, it felt as if I had been locked inside one of those isolation tanks without water. That, or I had been buried alive – both scenarios abhorrent to me. I could go into the whole episode I had when training for my degree, but, well, now's not the time.

I yank on the door handle, and the thing squeals open like it's being murdered, the sound tugging on my frayed nerves. But I don't have time to react because I am slapped out of any hysteria by a freezing gale. I thought that place was a giant icebox, but it's nothing compared to the funnel of ice blowing through this place, bringing with it the loud slosh of the ocean.

This is a megastructure. At least it is according to the light beam from my flashlight, which can barely make it across to the other side of this place. It's massive, like a giant porte-cochère, but for fishing trawlers. There's glass above and to the side, allowing some distilled moonlight to enter the space. I could hear it before, but now I can actually see the water a couple of stories below me. And on it, the best sight of all, is a fishing trawler. It's bigger than I expected, and for some reason, that makes me happy – but not as much as the sight of a flashlight bobbing towards it. *It's the others!* They're already down there, and the urge to call out to them is strong, but I resist it. I'm in no way eager to draw attention to them or myself. The only thing I'm keen to do right now is join them.

I look around. There's a large crane in front of me, rising from the dock. I imagine this is what they used to unload the catch of the day and haul it up to the conveyor belt in that room behind me. There's a metal ladder affixed to the side of the thing, presumably for service, so that can't be the way down.

I shine the flashlight around. I am standing on a gantry of sorts, a bitter cold wind whipping around me.

Okay... There's an elevator at one end, but that's obviously dead because there's no power. I turn. At the opposite end is what looks like steps down; it's hard to tell.

I move in that direction. Fast. The flashlight highlights the way as my boots clang too loudly on the metal beneath me, and... *yes*, I can see it now. There's a fork up ahead; left leads to darkness, and in front of me... I can see a handrail. I'm just a few feet away, the steps down materialising under the light, when I hear more clanging from the left – boots on metal, like mine, but they sound much heavier and *shit!* They're rushing this way!

I barely have time to lift the flashlight when *WHOMPH!* The figure collides into me, the impact so powerful it propels me several feet backward. I land with a heavy clang that makes the whole structure shake. The flashlight flies out of my hand and clatters somewhere behind my head. It rocks back and forth, projecting a terrifying strobe view of Sarge clanging towards me.

Winded, I turn and scramble to get to my feet, but a powerful hand grabs the sleeve of my coat, spins, and yanks me down onto my back once more before setting upon me. The weight of his body pins me down, the stench of rotting compost strong.

I grunt through gritted teeth as I attempt to push the mountain off me, but he's going nowhere. Then, I make the mistake of looking up. The flashlight behind me has stopped in one horrifying position and now, like the wheel of misfortune, is pointing at my head, the light deflecting and illuminating the maniacal bearded features of the police sergeant as he attempts to throttle the life from me.

He has a gash in his cheek, presumably where I hit him with the chair, but oddly, he isn't bleeding. It's as if he were an automaton, the artificial skin a mere façade. But it's not an illusion. What I see partially exposed, wriggling beneath that torn flesh, is anything but; plant roots, wriggling like albino worms, move around the man's face and forehead, the veiny things squirming as his features contort into a homicidal sneer.

His breath, hot and rancid with the sickly-sweet stench of rotting plant matter, washes over me, adding to the desperation of my situation, urging me to muster whatever strength reserves I might have to evade this thing, to push him off me and run screaming down that gangway. But there's no escaping this. Worse, as my brain is starved of oxygen, I can feel my consciousness dimming, and I know that unless I do something soon, this is where it'll end.

And that's when it occurs to me.

I fight the instinct to claw at the man's powerful hands around my throat, letting go with one hand as his thumb presses on my windpipe, making the cartilage click. I scramble as fast as my remaining consciousness allows until my fingertips brush it... push it away... then find it again. I grab the flashlight, turn it, and strike... SMACK! Once.

... SMACK! Twice.

... SMACK! Three times!

This time, I seem to get some kind of momentum behind it because the blow actually manages to turn the man's ugly, demonic face from me, only for him to turn it back seconds later. And if I could scream, I would right now. The sound would be so loud you'd be able to hear me from the other side of the island, but I can't. All I can do is gape at the long strands of white sinew hanging out of a gash in the man's face and dangling down towards me, wriggling unhappily in the moonlight. And that's it. Something switches. That red mist descends, and I just think, I'm not dying here. *I AM NOT DYING HERE!*

I lift that flashlight as far as I can, then bring its weight down with all the anger I can muster. Again... and again, until I feel that fucking vice-like grip loosen. Then again, and once more, all the time avoiding the hanging things that seem to reach for me. I kick and knee the man until his grasp relaxes enough for me to shimmy both hands underneath him and shove him sideways.

I gasp and sputter as the grip is momentarily released, but he turns back to me. I kick at him, but he comes back again, hands out like claws. I kick him in the face.

He comes back.

I kick him again... and again, driving him backward until he stumbles, the edge of the railing catching him at an awkward angle. One final kick sends him toppling, his body wedging between two vertical bars of the railing, legs dangling over the other side. Wheezing from the ache around my throat, I manage to crawl onto all fours, spluttering and gasping for air.

Sarge's face is almost unrecognisable, his beard alive with those wriggling things, and yet he's still trying to move towards me. And that's it. I lose it. I crawl forward to intercept him, aiming my shoulder at his chest, shoving him through the railing. One shunt... two, before the man is dangling over the side. Then, as I pause, retching, gasping, and sputtering, suddenly wondering what the fuck I just did to a police officer as gravity does the rest.

Sarge doesn't make a sound as he plummets to the dock two stories below. The only way I know he's crashed to the bottom is by the loud clanging thud his body makes upon impact and that reverberates around the structure.

31

EMBARCATION

THISTLE LOCH PROCESSING PLANT. THE EARLY HOURS.

I was reluctant to pick up my flashlight again after... well, you know. Luckily, I didn't need to. I'd barely got myself back on my feet when the detective's torchlight found me and guided me down to the dock, where I was promptly greeted by Luca and Buddy. And oh, that felt so good. Which was handy because I couldn't speak. My throat was already sore, and I quickly discovered that talking made it worse.

Oh, well, it's a little price to pay for everybody getting out of this thing safely. I'll be alright. As will the detective, apparently. Her wound is just a graze, which is also good because I had visions of having to perform some kind of rudimentary operation on her.

What? You're doubting that after everything else that happened? I tell you, the more I go through this stuff, the stronger my belief in expecting the unexpected. You know me, I would much rather go through this life ignorant of those things about me and the world that I was more than happy to relegate to the category of fantasy. But...

well, you were there, and you were here, too. You've experienced those things with me... some truths are unavoidable. No matter how much we choose to ignore or deny them, they'll continue to exist, regardless. I would know – I learned this the day I became consciously aware of the fact that my little boy was gone.

Toby.

I cling to Luca. I squeeze that boy and then the hound, probably a little tighter than necessary, but I'm so grateful they're okay. So grateful...

And then I emerge from the embrace to yet another of those bloody tableaux, and I'm like, *Man, are you serious with this shit?* Yeah, I know I'm sounding just a little too "street," but, come on.

So picture the scene. I'm euphoric, hugging Buddy, clinging to Luca. Elated for a variety of emotions I didn't even know I was capable of experiencing, not least for the warmth because, if I'm perfectly honest, it's freezing on this dock. It may be under cover, but the snow has still managed to find its way in here, as has that glacial wind.

I'm eager to get on the trawler and get the fuck out of here. But when I look up, it's to find my sister stepping backward towards us with her hands up because the indomitable detective is pointing her shotgun at her.

Yes. That's right. The detective is pointing a weapon straight at Samantha's chest.

"Isla... what... the fuck?" I ask incredulously. Well, I think I did. It was probably more of a gasp and a wheeze because my throat feels like I've just been deep-throating a cactus.

"We can't let her go, Marco," the detective says, gloved fingers clinging to the weapon.

"Mummy!" Luca exclaims, running into his mother's arms. And I won't lie, the sight of that sent a bolt of anger sizzling through me. The boy's been through enough already.

"You're scaring him," I growl.

"I'm sorry, Luca. I don't mean to, but... it's how it is," she says, her voice flat, emotionless. I'd love to tell you it's because she's been taken over by those things or something, but my instinct tells me this is just her. Ironically, this is exactly how I know she *hasn't* been possessed. Which is why I think she'd suck at being a doctor, but, hey, that's not the issue here. This is just me avoiding again.

I step forward. "P...put the fucking shotgun down," I wheeze.

"No. You know I can't do that."

"Put it down, Isla."

"Isla? First names, eh?"

"What's wrong with that?"

She just smiles at me. I imagine it's because she thinks I am trying to handle her, which I suppose I was, on some level. It is a tactic used by negotiators all the time.

"Look, Isla, Detective, whatever... I just want to get the fuck out of here."

"And that's fine. But we can't take her."

"You realise that's my sister you're talking about?"

"Yes, I do. I also realise that if your sister is infected and she manages to make it to the mainland, she could expose and thus kill millions of people. Do you realise that?"

"Yes, but she isn't infected," I croak, taking a step closer.

"She was with Sarge, Marco. You know that."

"So? That doesn't mean anything. He could have been exposed after the community hall."

"Do you really believe that?"

"I don't fucking know, Isla!" I explode. And then instantly regret the action because it feels like my throat is on fire. I take a breath. "Look," I say, taking another step towards her. She's standing several feet from me now. "I appreciate that you're just doing your job. But this, this isn't right. Look at her." The detective is already shining the torchlight at my sister. "She's fine. You can see that," I say reasonably. And for a split second, I think she's going to yield. But instead, she regrips the weapon, and I'm just about to lose it when—

"She's right, Marco." It's Samantha talking.

"Mummy! No!" Luca wails, and my heart aches.

"She's right. I mean, I know that I'm fine. But it makes sense that you all be cautious. Besides, I must account for my hand in all of this."

"Isla, you put that fucking gun down right now," I yell, my voice breaking.

"You know I can't do that," she repeats steadily.

"Put the fucking gun down!" I yell, taking another step forward.

"NO!" she insists, swinging the weapon in my direction.

"Stop that! Stop this!" It's Samantha again. "It's fine. It really is."

"Mummy!"

"It's okay, darling," my sister coos. "The detective is just being cautious. And she's right to be, my baby. I couldn't bear for anything to happen to you. This way, we can be sure," she says, fixing my nephew's hat and making sure his coat is pulled tight.

The detective still has the light trained on her, so I can see that my sister is putting on a brave face. But then, I don't need to see to know that. What parent would willingly be parted from their child in such a situation?

Oh, God. And just the thought of that burns through me.

I look at the detective and consider what it would take to make a run at her, but she must read my mind or something because she says, "You know I'll shoot you if I have to. One life, your life, mine, means nothing in comparison."

"The sacrifice of the few for the good of the many and all that shit," I say.

"You know I am right, Marco. I know she's your sister and—"

"Stop talking." It's Samantha interrupting, rolling her shoulders and lifting her head. She's back in professional mode, the same way she was that night at the community hall when giving her speech. "I'll stay here until help arrives and I can be cleared." She turns to her son. "Luca. I want you to go to your uncle now."

"No, Mummy! No! I want to stay with you," the boy says, clinging to his mother.

I turn and glare at the detective, but she's busy looking at the gut-wrenching scene. And once again, I consider running at the woman, but this time, it's my sister who intercedes. "Marco?"

I turn to her. "Marco. I know I have no right to ask you for anything after what I've done, but..." she trails off here, eyes misting with tears. And I know what she's asking of me, but I don't even know if I've got it in me. I felt so wretched last time.

"Luca. I need you to go with Uncle Marco. We'll see each other soon. I promise."

But my nephew, in true obstinate Battista style, refuses. Samantha looks at me, and that's my fucking cue. *Oh, God.* I'm shaking, but it isn't from the cold; it's because I ever agreed to come here.

And now, I find myself moving forward because I know that despite this gut-churning scene and my absolute loathing of the detective right now, I know she's right. I know that what she wants is absolutely right, given the circumstances, but it doesn't make this any fucking easier.

"Come on, Luca, mate," I say.

"NO!" my nephew insists.

"Come on. We'll see Mummy again soon, I promise."

"NO! Get off me! Get off me!" my nephew insists as I grab his arm and start unravelling him from his mother. And I pause. I pause because I don't think I can do this. But Samantha gives me a look. It's just our eyes meeting, nothing particular. But it's all it takes for me to know that the longer this continues, the harder it's going to be for all of us. So I grab my nephew by his side, and I pull him with me despite his protestations. I manhandle the boy and drag him, quite literally kicking and screaming, past the detective towards the trawler, but not before growling, "I hope you're fucking happy with yourself."

She doesn't answer. Instead, she looks back at Samantha, and I hear her tell her she'll be sending help soon. Meanwhile, I, now up for the award for shittiest uncle of the year, manhandle my little nephew onto the fishing trawler that, from the scrawl of faded paint on the bow, I can see is named *The Wanderer*.

It's a sturdy-looking, mid-sized vessel, approximately 60 feet in length, with a weathered, steel-grey hull etched with the wear of its many voyages. The deck looks spacious yet functional, surrounded by railings that are coated with flakes of rust. A small wheelhouse sits towards the rear, its windows glowing with a warm, inviting light against the cold night. The boat's main mast supports a modest crow's nest while several powerful spotlights are mounted on crossbeams, ready to pierce the night's veil.

On deck, the trawler carries the essential tools of its trade – nets and lines neatly coiled, crab pots stacked against the cabin, and what looks like a compact hydraulic winch system no doubt used to haul catches from the deep.

Despite its undercover location, snow has dusted the deck, no doubt brought here by the wind funnelling through this place. There are scuffed footprints leading towards the cabin, which I imagine were made when the others started the boat's engine, now humming relatively quietly, a sound that momentarily lifts my spirits along with the steam rising from its exhaust into the crisp air.

Outside, the moon, full and observant, casts a silvery glow over the world, turning the icy waters into a mirror of the starlit sky.

I dare to glance back. Samantha hasn't moved. The detective has made sure of that by keeping both the shotgun and the light beam on her. And I swear, it's all I can do right now not to jump off this fucking thing and pummel that woman's face – as unchivalrous as that might seem.

But it's weird. It's like I can feel my sister's pain. That excruciating and inimitable brand of agony in her chest at the very notion of having her baby taken from her.

A sudden jolt brings me back to the moment, and I snap. "Hey!" I yell angrily. "Hey!" But my nephew continues to struggle. "Hey! Listen! Listen to me! Listen!" I'm clutching him tightly by the sleeves of his coat. "Listen to me," I insist through gritted teeth. "Don't worry. We're not abandoning your mum. I promise. We're not. But you're going to have to trust me. Do you understand? Luca? You're going to have to trust me, mate," I say, shaking the boy so that he's looking at me. And he seems to calm a little. I swallow hard on a raw throat, then add, "Now," I nod at Buddy, who is standing nearby. "I'm going to need you to look after the golden wonder here for me. He... only seems to listen to you now," I say with a lift of the eyebrows.

My nephew hesitates, probably thinking I'm full of exactly how I feel – shit – but I think I may have reached him. I hope so, for both our sakes.

By the time I stand up, the detective has limped her way onto the boat – shotgun in hand.

I look at Samantha on the dock. And then back at the woman who would have me abandon my sister here in this godforsaken Arctic tomb. And I'm shaking. I'm literally shaking... with rage.

We all fought to get here, and the fact that this stranger, this automaton, insists that we leave a part of my family behind, is just too much, even for me. But then, I know she has a good reason for this. She is right. And as much as I don't fucking like it, I agree with her. This whole thing is so much bigger than we are.

That's why I swallow hard, take a deep breath, and release my nephew. I look up. "See the cabin over there." I point. "I want you to take Buddy, go in there, get out of the cold," I say. My nephew glances over at his mother on the dock and then back at me. "Go on," I insist. "Go. Now!" My last words are probably a tad more forceful than I intend, on account of the adrenaline still coursing through my body and the fact that my head is fucking killing me. But it does the trick. Reluctantly, my nephew turns and makes his way over to the cabin, dog trailing behind him.

I turn back, then walk over to the detective. "So what's the plan? Abandon my sister and sail off into the night?" I say as calmly as the anger simmering through my veins will allow.

Miss Hop-Along turns to me. "Look, Marco... I know you don't think—"

The rest of the detective's words are cut short as I snatch the shotgun from her with one hand and deliver a shove to her chest with the palm of the other. The impact – powered by all of that pent-up rage – propels the police officer backwards off her feet for a couple of seconds before she crashes onto the deck, skidding a couple of feet.

It must look bad because I think I even heard Samantha gasp from her position on the dock.

I stomp over to the stricken woman who is just getting up onto her haunches, squinting into the overhead floodlights as she looks up at me.

Then, I watch as the disorientation in her face soon turns to determination. Which is why I lift the shotgun and growl, "Uh uh. I've never fired one of these, but there's always a first time."

"Have you lost your fucking mind?" she demands, holding the back of her head.

I nod. "Probably."

"You're making a big mistake."

I think about that and nod once more. "Again, you may be right. But I just can't, in good conscience, leave my sister here."

"Can you, *in good conscience*, justify the deaths of millions if you're wrong?" she retorts.

I look at her on the freezing deck. I would offer her a hand, but it's probably best for both of us that she calms down first.

32

DEAD CALM

THE WANDERER FISHING TRAWLER

SOMEWHERE IN THE NORTH SEA. THE EARLY HOURS.

You know those movies where the characters try to escape the danger and just as they're about to succeed, something awful happens? That didn't happen here. Thank fuck for that. (Whatever that's supposed to mean.)

It's weird because the whole time I watched Samantha enter the wheelhouse, thrust the boat into gear – or whatever one does with boats – and get us the hell out of there, I really was expecting that last-minute jump scare shit. So much so that I kept the shotgun with me and everybody else in my sight the whole time.

And yet, we're good. We're okay.

Now, as my sister pilots the boat away from the jetty, the engine's low thrum feels almost soothing compared to the cacophony of horrors we've left ashore. The sea is eerily placid tonight, flat like a sheet of glass, reflecting the full moon with such clarity it's as if its twin lies beneath the surface, submerged within a darker sky.

Ice fringes the edges of the boat and rigging like a shroud, the winter's touch turning *The Wanderer* into a ghost ship charting a course through an ocean of ink.

The trawler's lights, feeble against the enveloping night, throw my shadow, long and thin, on the deck, an omen as we cut a slow path through the water. The quiet inevitably leads me to wonder about the other residents of the island and whether there are others like us who have survived this long day's night of horror or if each has succumbed to their plight.

And so, it's no surprise that as Terror Island slowly morphs into a mass of shapes, the amalgamation of all our fears blending into the frigid night, I feel a different kind of chill settle in my chest as I wonder if I could have done more to save others. But I suppose that's the price of decisions made; the cost of paths chosen.

I pull my coat tighter around me, my breath appearing and disappearing in clouds under the lights. As I watch the water churn in our wake, a realisation dawns on me: I've bloody conquered my fear of water! That's a positive. Right?

So if you ignore the fact that the detective thinks I'm an idiot and the minor detail that I seem to have spent most of my time here manhandling my nephew in such a way that I doubt the boy will ever want to come near me again, all is well.

Alright. There's room for improvement, but we're here. We're alive, and that's all that matters.

I'd also just like to say that I think fishermen have it pretty damn cushy. *Shit.* I've just had visions of those remains in the tunnel... Okay, maybe not all of them, but those who owned this rig definitely did.

My point being that this boat is kitted out really well. It's top of the bloody range. Cooker, oven, lounge areas. I mean, everything's compact, but the space usage is incredible. If I'd known half of this stuff over a year ago, I think ANEW would probably look completely different. I'd—

Oh, hell... I'm doing it again. Allowing my mind to wander everywhere but where it probably should be right now. The thing is, I don't even know where that is. Everything that happened? The families we probably left behind, or maybe even the fragment that I managed to bring with me.

This is all probably why I offered to forage for some semblance of a beverage, maybe even some food, for Luca, that is. But it turns out that no hunting and gathering is required. This place is fully stocked. From long-life milk to alcohol, this baby has pretty much everything a family of sailors needs for at least two weeks on the waves. It's impressive. What isn't as impressive is that these men were obviously slobs. The galley is a pigsty. More like the place was raided than lived in. Despite that, I managed to rustle up coffee, tea, and even some chocolate biscuits.

According to the satnav on the bridge of this nautical version of the Enterprise, it's going to take us just over an hour to get back to our destination, less now. And until we dock, given that Samantha is piloting this thing and the detective has been wounded, I'm designated cabin service.

I serve the hot drinks and cookies to Samantha and Luca and am now crouching down to the detective who is resting on one of the built-in seats at the back of the wheelhouse.

"How are you doing?" I ask, negotiating the drink and the shotgun that's still casually slung over my shoulder like I'm Indiana bloody Jones or something.

"I'll live," the detective says flatly, looking at the drink and me with equal contempt. "It's just a graze but stings like a bitch." I note that she's wrapped a scarf around her leg wound now.

"Look," I say, taking the shotgun off my shoulder and clumsily attempting to open the damn thing.

"Okay, first, point the thing away from everyone," she says with a sigh. "And always keep your finger off the trigger when handling a weapon."

"I know," I say with a faint smile. I don't, but she knows that. "The point is, I don't want us to fight. I know we..." I try to find words that won't prompt another snarky comeback, "had a disagreement. So what if..." I break off here as I can't remember how to open this bloody thing. The last time I handled one of these was clay pigeon shooting with Aaron, and that was ages ago. Oh, alright. Last year sometime.

"Push the lever at the top," she prompts.

"Alright," I say like she's rushing me. I find the lever and am about to push it when she adds, "and don't look straight at the thing unless you want a cartridge to the face."

I look at the woman like she's telling me what I already know, but she's not really. I push the lever, and both cartridges jump out, falling to the floor with a loud clacking sound.

"If you wouldn't mind," I say, holding out my hand.

The detective looks at my hand and then at me for several seconds before sighing, reaching into her pocket, retrieving the two cartridges, and then shoving them at me.

"Thanks," I smile, taking the cartridges from her and slipping them into my pocket. Then I close the empty shotgun with a loud snap before handing it to her. "Peace?"

She looks at me, my pocket, and then the shotgun in my outstretched hand, hesitating for several more seconds before finally taking it and placing it next to her.

Removing her hat, she tucks her hair behind her ears, her gaze finally settling on the forgotten mug. I hand it to her, and she accepts it.

I let out a sigh of relief, a small smile playing on my lips. "Those cartridges were empty the whole time," I say.

She doesn't respond. Her eyes meeting mine, a flicker of amusement in their depths. "You're just dying to know, aren't you?" she says.

I meet her gaze. "About?" I ask, though my eyes linger on the scar that now stands out against her pale skin.

"It's alright. Most people have the same reaction," she says casually before sipping from the mug. "This scar's been with me for a while. Grew up with it and older brothers who always thought they knew better. I wasn't just the scrawny runt of our brood but also the only girl. I was always trying to fit in with them. Prove that despite my diminutive size, I was just as tough.

"We lived on a farm – rugged land, as stubborn as we were. It and my dad demanded a lot of hard work.

"One summer, we were fixing up the roof of the old barn, as you do, because my dad insisted that his children learn every aspect of maintaining the place. He'd say, 'Self-reliance isn't just a skill. It's a way of life.' Well, at least it was for them. Not for me because, well, I was the little girl. That day, he left my older brother in charge. I decided to climb up and show all of them that I was just as strong and just as capable as they were. Thing is, I wasn't. I tried to carry a beam that even they wouldn't have tried to carry on their own. I slipped. I managed to twist out of its path, but not fast enough. A nail caught me here," she says, pointing down the side of her face, "just missing my eye."

"This scar isn't just a reminder about knowing your limitations but that the world doesn't give a shit about what's right and what's wrong, what is and what isn't fair. It just comes at you, and you've got to react. You've got to decide whether or not to stand your ground or move before it crushes you.

"People look at this scar, at me, at my attitude, and they think they know me. They don't know me. They don't know anything about me. About the things that I, that *we,* carry. Our choices often have consequences, but that shit doesn't mean anything if we don't learn from it.

"Back at the dock, I had to make a call. I did. And I don't regret it."

I swallow hard. She's holding my gaze now. I've no idea how her speech suddenly became about me, but I understand it. I recognise it. It is me. At least, it is the person I used to be. The person you first met. I was so full of rage back then. I mismanaged it in so many bloody destructive ways. It took years and months of therapy for me to see what I had become, to come to terms with what happened, but this woman seems to have her shit together in ways I couldn't even have dreamt of. She's unapologetic. And if I didn't already respect her, I'd say my admiration just shot up a few notches.

I smile and nod. That's in part because I was a little distracted just then. I thought I heard something.

I turn around. Samantha is at the controls, sipping her drink. Luca is huddled under a coat on one of the seats behind her even though it's quite toasty in here now. I'm the warmest I've been in a while, probably all week.

"Did you just hear that?" I ask. The detective squints at me. I think she's wondering if I'm going to make a sarcastic comment about her speech. And I don't blame her. If this were David and me—

Shit. David. My life with my friend literally feels like a lifetime away.

"Are you okay?" the detective asks.

Then I hear it again. I stand up and turn to see my sister, who has her back to us.

"What is it?" the detective asks again, but I don't respond. I'm hoping I imagined it. But then it happens one more time, and my stomach lurches. And I don't need to turn to know that the detective has tensed behind me.

"Sam?" My sister doesn't respond; she's too busy coughing. The sound, a harsh, rattling cough, resonates around the insufferably warm cabin, suffocating me with heart-pounding dread.

I take a tentative step forward. "Samantha?" Still no answer. My sister is doubled over now, sputtering and coughing.

"Marco?" comes the detective's wary tone, but I ignore her.

I take another step forward, calling my sister's name until finally, agonisingly slowly, she turns to me, eyes watering. And she must clock our horrified expressions because she asks, "What?"

Neither of us speaks, but then we don't need to. She instantly realises. "What? You think that..." She rolls her eyes. "Relax, it's just the biscuit. It went down the wrong hole!" She holds up the half-eaten cookie.

So I have to admit – it takes a short while, partly because I'm wanting to check that I haven't literally just shat my pants – but then a snicker turns into a chuckle, then a laugh, and before long, I'm joined by my fellow passengers in a chorus of no doubt hysterical yet well-needed laughter. Although it takes just seconds for me to tune into another sound that brings said laughter to a rolling stop.

I look around the space. "Where did Luca go?"

"Oh, he was falling asleep on his feet. I told him to go have a lie down on one of the berths. He has Buddy with him..."

I barely hear the end of that statement, and I'm moving as fast as I can over to the steps and down into the belly of the boat to find Buddy standing in the corridor, barking.

I skid to a halt. "Hey, you. What's up?" I ask, moving close to the dog and touching his fur, but he doesn't respond. He just keeps barking towards the end of the short corridor.

"Seriously? Dude... don't start with the creepy corridor shit."

It's fine, though. I'm not remotely affected. I've seen creepy corridors, and this isn't one of them. Besides, I already scoped this place out when I was down here making drinks earlier. Well, you can't blame me.

Anyway, there's nothing here. Just empty cabin spaces.

And yet, my dog is now barking like there's something else down here with us. But I know that isn't possible. I also know that the big guy enjoys creeping me out.

"Okay, Buddy. That's enough," I say. But he doesn't stop. "Hey! Buddy. Oi!" I try to get his attention, to get him to turn to focus on me, tail wagging. Confirm that this is all some kind of false alarm.

But he doesn't. He just keeps barking down that corridor, which, to be fair, is gloomy as hell, but it's easy to see that there's nothing hiding in the shadows.

"Is everything alright with Buddy?" Luca asks, coming out of one of the cabins.

I pry my eyes off the dog and smile at my nephew. "Yeah, all good, mate. He's just on one. Probably best we all go back on top."

"But Mummy told me to—"

"Let's go," I say. "You can sleep up top with us."

He looks at me warily. "Is there something wrong?"

"No, mate. Nothing's wrong. You know, I just want us to stay together."

"Yes, but why?"

"You're just going to make me say it, aren't you?"

My nephew cocks his head.

I make a show of sighing. "I just feel safer if we're all together. You know, with Buddy, too," I add with a shrug.

Nah, no Oscar for me. I don't think he's buying any of it, even for a split second, because he's already looking at me curiously. But still, it does the trick, although I have to physically turn the dog around. "Come on, you."

I send the two of them back up the steps first. Buddy, bless him, struggled with them at first, yet, like a child who wants to prove himself, he jumps the next few steps before I can interfere.

Beyond the dog, looking down, is Samantha. Her face is etched with concern. "What is it? What's the matter?" she asks, her voice cutting through the rumble of the engine, which seems louder down here.

"Nothing," I say reassuringly. "I just heard Buddy barking and wanted to come down and have a look."

"And?"

"And nothing."

"Are you sure?"

"Of course, I'm sure," I say, injecting calm into my voice while putting a smile on my face.

I've looked everywhere. There's nothing else here but us. And yet, I can still feel the atmosphere down here. No longer light but heavy with the memory of Buddy's discontent.

Suddenly, the dog's eager face appears beside Samantha, his left ear perked up, the right still floppy from that puppyhood injury.

He barks again, the sound drilling through me, making me jump. "Jesus Christ, Buddy! Stop it. There's nothing here," I say, turning to look behind me.

"Marco?"

"It's okay. I just want to check something," I find myself saying.

"Check what?"

I don't answer. Instead, I move fast, eager to get this over and done with. I snap the light on... first cabin – empty. Second cabin – empty. Third cabin – empty. Thankfully, these spaces are so compact, nothing could hide down here even if it wanted to.

Happy now?

"Marco?" Samantha calls loudly.

I'm about to respond, but as I move, I hear a clink underfoot. I look down to see what it is. It's the handle to the latch in the floor, which may as well be the handle to an ice shower for the shivers that wash through me.

Oh, shit. The engine room.

"Marco?" Samantha's voice hurries down to me, but I'm paralysed – terrified to move or speak as I feel the already narrow corridors lean in, bending and contorting like a scrap metal compactor.

Oh, how could I be so fucking stupid?

And to make it worse, I think I heard something. It didn't register before because, well, I didn't want to hear it, I suppose. But deep down, subconsciously, I must have been aware of it. It's the very reason I don't want to open my mouth right now: because if it's validated, I don't know what I'll do.

"Marco! Answer me! I need to know you're okay," comes Samantha's strained voice. Alarmed but repressed, no doubt, because she doesn't want to frighten Luca.

"I'm okay!" I yell back, closing my eyes in the way you do when you know your action might have repercussions over which you have no control. A bit like jumping off a cliff and hoping there are no rocks beneath the water's surface.

I strain to listen. Eyes tightly shut, focusing not on the thrum of the engine but beyond that, beyond the mechanical sound to something else. Something that doesn't belong here. Something... there! What was that?

I step away from the hatch.

"Marco?" It's the detective now. "I'm coming down."

"NO!" I yell, taking another step back, then listen. One... two... there! Oh, God. I'm sure I heard it, but there's only one way to be positive.

I retreat to the steps and call up. "Sam?"

"What? What is it?" is my sister's eager response.

"I need you to turn off the engine."

"What?"

"I need you to kill the engine," I repeat calmly.

"Why? We're almost there."

"Just turn it off," I say flatly, eyes still on that hatch.

"I don't understand. Why do—"

"JUST FUCKING DO IT!" I snap as beads of sweat tickle my brow. The warmth of the vessel, once a comfort, now stifling.

I keep my eyes on the hatch. Seconds later, the drone of the engine suddenly stops, and I, accustomed to the motion of the craft, lose my balance and stagger to the opposite side of the corridor.

And then, it's the most peculiar sensation – like astronauts in space – we're just drifting, floating through the water as our momentum dissipates, leaving nothing but the sound of sloshing waves, creaking wood, ticking metal, and—

"Marco?" It's Samantha again, her voice so loud now it startles me, rushing down the steps and echoing in the hollow before another sound slices through it, one that sends a skitter of terror down my spine.

Jangle… jangle…

The sound is muffled but unmistakable, as is the thud of my heart, the roar of blood behind my ears.

Samantha must have heard it, too, because she orders Luca to take a seat, and there's tension in her voice.

My mind is racing now. Part of me thinks that we're fine. We're perfectly fine. Just lock the hatch if there is a lock on that thing, get back to the mainland, and let the authorities deal with whatever is in there. If those things are anything like the others, then they're confined to the engine room.

We're fine.

But what if they're not?

Then we're fucked! Because we're on a bloody boat in the middle of nowhere. Drifting now, thanks to me.

"Marco?" It's the detective.

Jangle… jangle…

Buddy barks again. I hear Samantha attempt to quiet him.

"Marco, get back up here," the detective says quietly yet forcefully.

"We need to know exactly what we're dealing with," I say, not recognising and hating my own words.

"Marco, get up here," the detective repeats.

"We need to know, Isla. We can't just ignore it."

"We already do," she says ominously. "Sam's checking the surveillance system. You don't need to be down there."

Of course. There are cameras all over the boat. I spotted the monitors when I first entered the pilothouse. I was still reeling from everything that had happened, and I didn't even take them in, but I remember thinking that the whole boat was much more modern than I expected.

"Alright. I'm coming up," I say. But I've barely finished the sentence when I hear Samantha's distant voice breathe, "Oh, my God."

"What? What is it?" I ask.

But there's no response. When I look up, the detective has turned away from the steps, her attention now on whatever has filled my sister's voice with dread.

"WHAT IS IT?" I demand, much more loudly than I intended.

Jangle… jangle…

That hideous sound, albeit muffled, may as well be claws dragging down my spine for the difference it makes. "What is it?" I repeat, pointlessly quieter, as I watch the detective reappear at the top of the stairs, and the look on her face is something I will never forget. In all the time I've known her, I don't think I've ever truly seen her looking scared. Not even back at the processing plant.

"It's full of them," she says ominously, her face ashen.

"F...full of them. Full of what?" I ask, even though I obviously know the answer.

"Full of *them*," she repeats. "They're all over the engine. They must have planned this," she gasps thoughtfully.

Planned this?

Dread pushes down on me so heavily that my grip momentarily loosens from the handrail.

"Marc... get back up here. We're almost there. They're isolated. We'll just secure the latch from here," Samantha says.

I can see the lights of the mainland through one of the portal windows. We're just a couple of miles from help, and that fills me with newfound confidence.

"Okay. I'm coming up," I say, beginning my ascent.

But I've barely made it up two steps when the lights suddenly flicker and die. I freeze mid-ascent because I've no idea why that would even happen right now, but it bloody doesn't bode well.

"They cut the power," Isla whispers.

Cut the power? How can they cut the bloody power? They're

plants!

"Don't worry. The emergency lights will kick in," Samantha says, adopting a calm tone, no doubt intended for Luca.

Seconds drift by. Water sloshes. My heart thumps in my chest, urging me to continue the climb, when...

Beep! There's a click, a whir, and small red lamps on opposite sides of the corridor spring to life. This is shortly followed by another continuous beep, and a tiny LED light on the opposite wall pulsates, indicating a flashlight mounted there.

I look up. The detective has been reduced to little more than a silhouette now.

"Marco, get back up here!" Samantha orders.

And she doesn't have to ask me twice, but just as I'm about to reach the top step...

Clink.

Shit! I pause.

"What?" the detective asks.

"Did you just hear that?"

"Hear what?"

Slowly, I retreat a couple of steps, but the handrail is blocking my view – *I can't see!*

"Marco? What is it?"

"I thought I heard something," I say, tilting my head, but I still can't see shit from this angle. So I descend a couple more steps.

"Marc!" the detective hisses.

But I don't hear her. Well, I do, but I'm trying to work out if I'm imagining things. The end of the corridor is now filled with shadows, those red LEDs providing just the basic amount of illumination, but there's a blind spot at the end of the corridor where the latch is. *Bad design, if you ask me. Surely, it would make more sense if—*

Stop bloody avoiding!

I squint into the gloom. *And, oh, fuck...* I, um, think the latch to the engine room is open now.

That's not possible! That isn't possible! And yet...

"Marc!" the detective is hissing.

Beep.

I allow my line of sight to shift from the silver square shape in the floor and up, and... those hideously familiar chills ripple through me.

Oh, God. I think there's something over there. A shape.

But I can't tell in this light. If there is something there, it is standing perfectly still, watching me.

Beep.

I look at the opposite wall – the flashlight. Then look back down the corridor – nothing has moved.

I swallow on a parched throat. Heart hammering on my ribcage. I take a deep breath. Am I imagining this? I could be imagining all of this.

Autosuggestion, Marco! It's not like you aren't prone to it.

I look at the flashlight once more. It's just a few feet away.

I take the last few steps down and then over to the opposite wall, being sure to avoid any sudden movements. I have no idea why. Then, I pull the flashlight out of its cradle.

The beeping stops. Water sloshes outside.

I switch the light on and reluctantly aim it toward the latch, and my breath catches in my throat.

Oh, fuck. It is open. How is that possible?

Oh, shit... Slowly, I step backward while shifting the light beam from the hole in the floor to the dark patch at the end of the corridor as a cold sweat tickles my forehead.

"Marc?" It's the detective again, but I'm not hearing her. I'm focused on the other end of the corridor, eyes screwed up into a squint as I attempt to see through the gloom, and...

There's nothing there. There's nothing bloody there! The end of the corridor is empty! IT'S FUCKING EMPTY!

Relief floods through me as I release the breath I'd been unconsciously holding captive.

I turn back to the steps. "It's okay," I say, mounting the first one. "I thought I saw something down here."

"What? What did you see?"

JANGLE! JANGLE!

The sound of those things fills the corridor, much louder now that the hatch is open. Then, movement flickers in the corner of my eye. Instinctively, I lift the flashlight and aim it in that direction, and my breath catches in my throat as a pair of eyes glint back at me from the darkness.

"OH, SHIT!"

"What?"

"THERE'S SOMETHING DOWN HERE! THERE'S SOMETHING ON THE CEILING!" I scramble up the stairs, lifting myself with the handrail, when I suddenly feel something coil around my leg and yank... *once... twice*, dragging me down once more with a *Thump! Thump! Thump!*

"MARCO!"

I land on all fours, smacking my jaw against the bottom step as if I've just been punched, but I don't linger. The tugging at my leg makes me instantly flip over, and I immediately wish I hadn't.

I aim the flashlight – which I'm clutching as if it can save me from this ordeal – down to reveal the horror coiled around my leg. It's something that resembles a vine but is made of flesh, slick with a viscous, putrid slime that gleams in the torchlight. I scream as I watch the thing slowly slither up my leg, moving with a will of its own.

In my panic, I follow the tether of horror with the light beam. The fleshy, vine-like appendage slithers back to the gaping maw of a grotesque, humanoid monstrosity lined with uneven rows of thick, thorny teeth.

Another scream rips from my throat, raw and desperate. The thing responds with a hiss and chitter, accompanied by the rustling and jangling from beyond the hatch.

I feel like I should do something – pull away, run, scream – but I can't. My body stubbornly refuses to obey, trapped in a straitjacket of terror that restricts my pounding heart and squeezes my breath into a fogging mist in the cold air. I am the prey of something that should not exist, something from the shadows of the worst nightmare. But this is no dream, and I am in its grasp, gaping at a grotesque symbiosis I can't begin to comprehend.

Partially lit by the red emergency lights, the thing's features are distorted, flesh extended beyond its limits to accommodate the abomination it has become. Strands resembling twisted tree roots hang from its pitted bald scalp and the edges of the gash of its mouth, drooping like the weeping willows of a haunted swamp. Above the gaping slash of its mouth are two green, filmy eyes with tiny black pupils, observing me with predatory hunger. They are set deep within a face, human in shape but not in essence, skin bark-like and taut over protruding bones, with veins pulsating visibly beneath the surface. I can only watch as it cocks its head with a sickening, fluid motion, studying me, deciding if I'm prey or an obstacle.

The rest of its limbs are more like knots and gnarls of muscle and sinew, giving the impression of a humanoid shape twisted by some cruel artist's hand. It clings to the ceiling in an uncanny bat-arachnid–like fusion that conspires to make me scream and scramble away.

It hisses once more, its cavernous slash of a mouth widening, threatening to devour me whole. Instead, it drops to the floor with a loud thud, and to the rabid jangling of those demonic flowers in the engine room, it begins to retreat to the other end of the corridor, dragging me with it.

I scream, louder now, reaching for anything I can anchor myself to. I relinquish the flashlight and reach for the bottom section of the handrail, but I miss it and feel myself pulled down the corridor, past the first room.

... *Second room.* There are grab handles overhead, but they're too high for my outstretched arms.

... *Third room.* I desperately try to catch anything within reach, my fingers scraping against the metal walls as my heart pounds in my chest, each beat a countdown to an inevitable end.

I dig my nails into the floor, trying to find some grip, any grip, to slow my relentless slide towards the engine room, but it's all to no avail.

The monstrous appendage tightens, and the pain shoots up my leg like a burning fire. My screams echo through the narrow corridor, mixing with the hissing and jangling ahead.

The darkness closes in, the red emergency lights casting eerie shadows that dance around me, mocking my futile struggle. The excited jangling is louder now, deafening, as those things beckon me to the hole in the floor, a killing box from which I know I will never return.

We're just feet away, the creature yanking me ever closer. I writhe, scream in my futile attempt to stop the inexorable drag, but there's nothing down here for me to grab hold of. I am thinking it's inevitable. I am thinking this is my fate.

The creature is positioning itself now, weird bendy appendages crawling into the cavity—

"HEY!" a voice yells from somewhere up the corridor behind me, the sound reverberating around the space like a siren. *Coastguard? Police? Army?*

Isla!

The thing actually looks up at her. Then a loud click precedes the word, "Fuck!"

Again... *Click!*

Again... *Click! Click! Click!*

If the creature presumed danger, it must know that it has passed because it starts to tug at my leg once more. Only now, it's partially submerged in the cavity, placing gravity firmly on its side and causing me to wail in agony.

"MARCO! THE CARTRIDGE!" I hear the detective yell. "I need a fucking cartridge!"

Oh, shit!

JANGLE! JANGLE!

The thing has disappeared down the hatch now, dangling from me and yanking harder and harder, dragging me over to the void where I cling, screwing my face up and raging through gritted teeth as the determination of the beast cranks up to unbearable and intolerable pain.

You're going to have to let go!

"N...OO!" And as much as my instincts are screaming for me not to, I reluctantly relinquish my hold, let go of the latch with one hand, reach into my pocket, and feel my leg disappear into the hole, shortly followed by the rest of me.

I wail once more at the exertion while feeling for the cartridge in my pocket. I barely pull the thing out and throw it behind me with a clatter as the hinges of the trapdoor begin their own protestation to the cacophony of those things down there. And as I feel the door slowly relinquish its moorings, I begin to resign myself. There'll be no getting out of this.

But then a warm coat is thrown over my head. I hear the thing chitter loudly just before there's a deafening explosion and squelching sound, instantly followed by the release of the weight pulling at my body.

33

A NEW REALITY

THE WANDERER FISHING TRAWLER

ONE MILE OFF THE COAST OF THURSO, SCOTLAND.

THE EARLY HOURS.

Okay, so that was different, right? Not entirely, it would seem. After the initial shock of nearly being dragged into a literal cesspit of... shit, I don't even know how to describe them. *Man-eating plants?*

Ugh. I still can't get my head around it even now. And it's been... what? Ten minutes since the detective fired that weapon so close to me. I realise now why she threw her folded coat over my head – to muffle the sound. Yet, even now, my ears are still bloody ringing.

But I digress. As you can imagine, I've been going over this thing in my head again and again, and I just can't wrap my head around it, but I think I've seen that thing before. That or something similar. Back there, at Frost Lake Manor. Do you remember that night in the woods with Drew? We went back to the house, and I saw that thing climb up the building then jump into a tree. It's so weird because, as grotesquely alien as it seemed to me, I realise now, in hindsight, that there was also something grotesquely familiar. Could it be that these horticultural, for want of a better expression, things are actually some kind of natural aberration? Some sort of biological evolution? Nature's way of fighting back against man's aggression?

Oh, fuck… You can hear this shit, right? Whatever that thing was, it's now lying down there with those *other* things.

Of course, I haven't mentioned anything to anybody here because, well, they'd think I've truly lost it. See? This is the part where I would normally start to question whether or not I actually have lost it, but I don't need to. This time, there are others who can corroborate what I saw. And I'm both comforted and horrified by that. Because one says that I'm not a few sandwiches short of a picnic, while the other... well, that's validating the fact that these things, these horrors, happened to us. That this whole week wasn't just a figment of my imagination but a divergence from anything resembling normalcy.

On the plus side – if it's even possible to rummage for one of those amongst all of this shit – it would at least appear that both my sister and the detective are now seeing eye to eye. Can you believe that? Even after the detective wanted to abandon her on that rock, my sister has somehow come to her way of thinking.

Samantha was reluctant to get the engine turned back on and get us this last mile or so back to the mainland. She started questioning what was going to happen once we get there.

I don't bloody know! All I know is that I want off this boat for now. We'll worry about the rest of it when we get back.

"Marco?"

"Are we there?" I turn, expecting to see Samantha standing behind me, but she isn't. In fact, I'm alone here in the wheelhouse. And, um, worse, the boat isn't moving. It's still dead quiet in here.

"Sam?"

No answer, just that perpetual slosh of water, reminding me we still haven't reached *terra firma,* and ugh, I think I've just realised that maybe I still don't like the water after all.

"Marco?"

"Sam?" It was definitely her voice. I could hear it filling the cabin. "Where are you?"

"Marco. I'm down here."

And that's when I realise. My sister's voice seems so close because it's coming out of the large speakers built into the ceiling. And on the large monitor, I can see two views: the deck where a large floodlight is showing the detective and Luca pulling a tarpaulin off what looks like a life raft, and the other... well, the other invokes that loathsome fairground-stomach-lurch sensation in the pit of my gut despite the fact that my brain is still struggling to process what it's seeing: Samantha, close to the camera. Her tired yet still pretty face filling the screen.

"Marco, I know you're going to want to react, and I know you're definitely going to want to say something, but I need you to listen to me. I need you to listen to me now because we don't have much time. Okay?"

"Sam? Where are you?" I ask, but I don't need to because I can already see the caption on the monitor: *Engine Room.* I realise now why I was feeling sick to my stomach.

"Sam? What are you doing?"

"Marco. Listen to me. I need you to listen," she says calmly, dispassionately, as she moves away from the camera and her body fills the frame. Behind her, *Oh, my God,* I can see the rest of the engine room. She's holding something in her hands, and at first, I can't tell what it is, but then, as she shakes the thing around, I can see.

Oh, shit!

"Oh, fuck! Sam?! Sam. What are you doing?"

"We can't let them reach the mainland, Marc. You know that," my sister says as I watch her empty what can only be fuel over the leaves that, other than a weird vibrating shake, do not appear to be reacting to her presence.

"Isla was right," she continues, casually splashing the liquid around, moving in and out of the camera frame. "I have one inside me," she says calmly, and I can feel the blood drain from my face, leaving a nauseating, cold, clammy sensation in its wake. "I can feel it, moving under my skin. It's been still this whole time. I had no idea, but it seemed to come alive the moment I made my decision, almost like it could read my thoughts."

"Sam!" I thump the console. "I'm coming down there," I say, moving away from the display towards the hatch.

"You can't!" my sister says quickly, but the moment is fleeting before she returns to her steady, unnervingly rational demeanour. "I knew you would try to, so I've barricaded both hatches."

I stop and rush back to the screen, smacking it. "Then I'll smash it down."

My sister comes back into view and smiles. "I knew you'd try, but you can't, my love. You can't because I need you. I know it's a big ask, but I need you to grant me this wish. Will you grant me this?"

A lump forms in my throat. Tears prick my eyes. I touch the display. "Sam, please..."

"You are one of the most beautiful human beings I have ever met." A warm smile spreads across her face. "In some ways, you remind me of Ewan. Fiercely loyal. Protective of me, of our son. That's why he did what he did to help me, to support me. And that's why this has happened to us. All of those people, Marco... I'm responsible for all of it." She swipes tears from her eyes. "So now I need you to do what you do. I need you to take care of my son. I need you to take care of my boy."

My gut churns, and I feel like I am going to spew all over this dashboard. Hot and cold chills ripple through me. *This isn't true. This isn't happening. I am dreaming this... Wake up! You're dreaming this! Wake up!*

"... You know... You know what it's like when you have a child, your own flesh and blood. You can't imagine ever entrusting them to anyone else, but I trust you. I trust you, Marc. I trust you to nurture, support, and protect my little boy so that he'll remember his mother and grow up to be a man like his father – a man like you, Marc. Strong, loving, and fiercely loyal."

"Sam..." I whimper, considering how long it'll take me to smash through both hatches, get to my sister, and talk some sense into her.

"You know what this thing is," she says, her voice full of disgust. "You've seen what it does. I can't... *I won't* let it do that to me."

I wrestle with that. I actually fucking wrestle with the image of what that thing does to people versus the idea of at least trying.

"Sam, we should at least try.... We don't know anything about this thing. Maybe there's a treatment."

"There's no treatment, Marc."

"You don't know that."

"That's right. And nor do you. I'm not going to be a lab rat. Besides, there's no coming back from this. I'm responsible."

"No," I shake my head. "NO. I can't, Sam. I can't let you do this," I say, rage blowing through me. "I CAN'T!"

She places a hand on the screen and smiles. "My handsome brother. You don't have a choice," she says softly.

"NO!" I rage, tears bubbling over. I turn towards the latch when I hear something – a rumbling sound. I look around the cabin, out of the windows but can't see anything. Then I glance at the monitors. Nothing. Yet, the sound becomes progressively louder until it transforms into the thud-thud-thud of my heart before exploding into a whoosh that sweeps over the boat and has me instinctively ducking for cover.

Helicopters. Two of them. Large. Bigger than any I have ever seen before. Military. I can just about make out that obligatory olive colour as they glide past us at great speed, dissolving into the new dawn, tail lights flashing.

I rush back to the monitor. "SAM! They're here! Help is here!" I say excitedly.

"They're not here for us. They're heading towards the island. Nobody even knows we're here. Besides... It's... too... late," my sister groans, clutching her chest, and lifting what looks like a gas lighter.

"Sam. Please... please... please don't do this," I beg, touching the screen and then punching the console. "Please."

"Marco... did I tell you I read your book?" She says with a smile.

I seize the opportunity. "Yes. Yes, you did. Can't remember though if you said you liked it."

She coughs. Subtly at first, she clears her throat before it recommences and turns into a barking spasm that makes her eyes water. The sight stabs at my heart.

I look at the latch and then back at the screen, unable to decide. My sister recovers, clears her throat, and with a now hoarse voice says, "I loved it. I only have... just... just..." she clears her throat again. "One bit of feedback."

"Go on," I say as tears fill my eyes once more.

"I think you're wrong. It... wasn't your fault, Marco. Forgive yourself... Forgive me." With that, I hear that dreaded clicking sound. The same one that has haunted me ever since that day at Holt. And then the camera feed cuts to static.

At first, I can't even move. I struggle to absorb what just happened. But then, I feel it, just like those helicopters before – a rumble. It starts in my legs and vibrates through my body, pushing me to the other side of the cabin where the steps down to the next level have been blocked off by some kind of door.

But I don't hesitate. I stomp into it with my boot, kicking and stamping until splinters of wood fly in all directions. The door isn't breaking. Like a wild animal, I look around the room for something to help smash it. I find a fire extinguisher. It's small, but it'll do the trick.

I've barely retrieved it when an alarm blares, a strobe LED light on the ceiling flashes, and an automated voice intones, *"Attention all crew members. This is an emergency announcement. A fire has been detected in the… engine room. An evacuation order is in effect. Please move to the designated assembly point… on deck."*

"Marco?" The detective appears in the doorway. "What the hell is going on?"

"She's down there! She's down there!" I wail, smashing at the door. It's working. I've managed to create a hole.

"Marco. That's the fire alarm. We need to leave."

"Not without her. I'm not leaving without her," I say, clawing at the wood as the stench of smoke reaches my nostrils, burning my eyes.

"Marco! You can't do anything for her now. We need to evacuate."

I swipe at the tears on my face and look at her incredulously. "Did she tell you about this?"

"No. Of course not," she protests.

"Then how did you know? How the fuck do you know, Isla?"

"Because she's the one that sent Luca and me to deploy the life raft. She said there was something wrong with the engine. She obviously planned it this way."

I glare at her. "Well, I don't give a shit," I say, attempting to push through the hole in the stairwell but gagging and spluttering at the smoke that has already filled the hallway and is using the hole I just created as a funnel.

"Marco. That engine room is highly flammable. This whole boat could explode at any moment."

"I d...don't... c...are!" I grimace, attempting to push my way through the hole. But I feel hands pulling at me. "G...ET OFF! GET THE FUCK OFF!" I scream before submitting to another coughing fit. The smoke is thicker now, acrider. I can't fucking breathe! I turn away.

"Marco! WE NEED TO GO! WE NEED TO GO NOW!"

"NO!" I cry. "I CAN'T! I CAN'T! I WON'T! NOT WITHOUT HER!"

She tugs at me angrily, "THINK ABOUT LUCA, Marco! Think about your nephew!"

I turn back to the hole, but it's impossible – bitter black smoke is billowing out of it. It's like putting my face to a chimney.

"NO!" I cry.

"We need to go. Come on!" The detective pulls at my arm and yells, "MARCO! COME ON! COME ON!"

And this time, as much as I don't want to, I let myself be led out of the wheelhouse and back on deck because all I can think about now is Luca sitting in that raft all alone. My little nephew who has lost everything, and I was powerless to stop it. The least I can do now is make sure he gets out of this safely.

Other than that, I'm numb. Numb as I descend the ladder to the life raft and pause momentarily to watch the orange glow of the flames wriggle through the portal windows and dance on the surface of the water, celebrating the tragedy that just unfolded here. Numb as I watch my nephew's eager little face look around me and hear him ask after his mother. Numb as I tell him she's gone. And numb when, once again, I am forced to overpower that little boy to stop him climbing back out of the lifeboat, as he refuses, just like I did moments before, to accept this as his new reality. And yet, as the raft drifts away from the inferno that is now *The Wanderer*, that is exactly what both of us must do.

EPILOGUE

ANEW, CLIFFHAVEN.

SIX MONTHS LATER. MID-MORNING.

I'm cursed. And I don't mean that in the figurative sense - I mean it quite literally. I believe it now. I don't have any evidence to corroborate it, of course. In fact, all evidence is to the contrary: that woman - the former housekeeper at Frost Lake Manor, my patient - did not set herself on fire at my best friend's wedding. That, it would appear, was just a figment of my imagination.

"Ciemne światło. Spełnij moje życzenie" - *Dark light, grant my wish. "Usłysz mnie! Usłysz mnie!"* - *Hear me! Hear me!*

I can still hear her hideous voice now. That's why I can't dispel this feeling in my gut that somehow it happened. A sense that somehow - and I don't know how - out of that woman's blind hatred, something else was born. Something not of this realm, but from somewhere far beyond the natural, something that dwells deep in the shadows of the supernatural. Something that has taken the worst thing to ever happen to me - the death of my son - and is using it to inflict further heartache by taking Samantha and leaving Luca an orphan.

I know how this all sounds, but something happened to us. Something that can't be explained. At least, not easily. God knows I tried. First to Detective Isla Macintyre's colleagues, and then to colleagues of her colleagues. Shifty characters, with one chief interviewer and a bunch of eager voyeurs who witnessed everything but said nothing. Government agents? No idea. All I can tell you is that they had the same unnerving traits as those characters you see in movies – the ones who smile while twisting the knife. Maybe not as polished, if I'm honest.

This whole interrogation took place after we'd been subjected to a battery of medical tests. *Just for our health, of course, to ensure our well-being,* they said. It had nothing to do with what we found on that island. They barely acknowledged that. What they did share was that most of the islanders had been evacuated. Others, well, they succumbed to some mysterious chemical infection, which is why Thistle Island is now strictly off-limits. For all intents and purposes, it's a ghost island. We weren't even allowed to collect our belongings. Not that I would have ever gone back, but I wanted to arrange for some of Luca's things to be retrieved, and they refused. *Just a precaution.*

Of course, when I tackled the issue head-on, told them I knew what they were doing, that they were trying to bury this whole thing, the chief interviewer decided to ask me how I was feeling. *How I was feeling? Seriously?* That's when I realised what he was doing. He was using the question as a segue, a way to subtly remind me of my past, my reputation as the man who suffered a psychotic break, was institutionalised, and then wrote a book about it. The bloke who went on TV shows to tell the world he believed in ghosts. Well, technically, that last bit wasn't true. It was kind of foisted on me.

He took his time with it, this weasel of a man who reminded me of my literary agent, peering down into the digital tablet in front of him like it was a bloody crystal ball. I remember the fluorescent lights buzzing overhead, the faint scent of stale coffee lingering in the air, and the way his eyes flicked up at me, assessing my reaction. When I corrected him – pointed out that I never actually said I believed in ghosts – he just cut me short, veering off onto questions about Luca. How he was settling in, about my petition to become his legal guardian. How the boy had been through a lot already. He delivered that last line with a practised smoothness, leaning forward in his chair with a thin smile, like he'd been rehearsing it for that very moment.

I was seconds away from jumping over that scuffed table and throttling the life out of him. You don't have to be a psychologist to know that the whippersnapper – who couldn't have been half my age – was trying to manipulate me, and doing a shitty job of it. I could feel the red mist descending, my jaw clenching, my fists tightening. But just as I was about to lose it, he decided to let me go. I don't think for one second it was because he was afraid of me. It was because he knew he'd made his point.

And he had. I could put up with hours of that crap, but the moment he started talking about Luca, hinting at potential problems with custody, my heart started pounding in my chest, reminding me that any actions I take from here on out extend far beyond me to that boy down on the beach, playing stick with Buddy. I can't risk it. And I'm sorry if that sounds like I'm selling out, but my nephew has and will always come first. That's the vow I made months ago. It hasn't been easy, and it will only get marginally better in time, but Buddy and I, we're going to be here for him.

I'm not even going to get into the whole thing about whether or not I'm ready and capable of taking care of a boy who in many ways reminds me of Toby. No. I'm already going through that with Doctor Holmes, and, well, you won't be surprised when I tell you that the urge to punch him, too, arises more often than I care to admit. Well, what can I say? You can take the boy out of Tottenham and all that.

Bong. Bong. Bong. Marco. There is someone at the front door. Would you like them to leave a message?

"On screen," I say, turning to look at the display mounted on the inside of the balcony doors.

Oh, right. "Please direct her to the lounge balcony."

As you wish.

I check the beach, squinting into the sunshine. Looks like Luca is building a sandcastle, and Buddy, the canine excavator, appears to be digging a moat for it. I have to say the sight of those two together always brings a smile to my face. I'm not going to say what it reminds me of because you'll just think I'm weird. Alright, even weirder. You get my point.

"Some greeting," says Detective Isla Macintyre, joining me on the balcony. "I was expecting little electrodes to cattle prod me if I deviated from the path here."

I stand up. That's right, because chivalry isn't dead. Not quite. Just lying bleeding from the head. "Detective. What a surprise. Haven't seen you since you didn't say much at your hearing." I move to greet her with a two-cheek kiss, but it just turns into an awkward ballet, her stiff posture, and hesitant demeanour making it clear she's not the touchy-feely type. So I give it up as a bad job. "I think you'll find I said enough," she claps back.

"Really? How did that go for ya?"

"I was reassigned, remember?"

"Right." I indicate the table in front of me. There's juice and a cafetière with freshly brewed coffee. "Can I tempt you?"

"No thanks," she says, looking over the balcony at the garden and cove, bathed in the azure of the ocean and the trees languidly swaying in the breeze. "Wow." I watch her take in the salty ocean air. "This place." I smile, mostly because I like the fact that there exists something on this earth that appears to move the detective's sensitivities. "I know, right?" I say proudly, as if I conceived of all of this beauty.

"How's he doing?" She asks, clocking Luca who's in fits of laughter because Buddy's frantic excavation is showering him with chunks of sodden sand.

"Oh, you know. One day at a time."

"Are you still considering it?"

"Adoption? Of course," I say brightly, yet there's an ache in my chest whenever I even think about it and what the future holds. Doctor Holmes and I have been through this, but I struggle with it each time. I don't show it, though. "But," I add, "something tells me you didn't come here to ask me about that."

She turns to me with a half-smile. "No. I didn't. I'm here because I need your help."

"*My* help? That's a first," I say with a grin.

She doesn't respond. Instead, she reaches down into the bag beside her, pulls out a file, hesitates, and then hands it to me.

"Okay," I say. "This isn't one of those prank things. You know, like those greeting cards where you open it, and it squirts water at you?" I'm grinning, but the detective just furrows her brow. "Okay. Tough crowd."

I open the file and skim-read part of the first page before looking up at her. "Why me?" I ask.

She shrugs. "Because you have, shall we say, a certain expertise in this area."

"Ya think? And what? You want me to be the Mulder to your Scully?" She frowns. "You're kidding? You've never seen *The X-Files?*" She shakes her head. "Are you serious? Oh, bloody hell, you are; we're going to have to rectify that."

She groans, "I'm not really into that supernatural shit."

And I think about that because, in a way, she sounds like me. While I used to enjoy watching that stuff, I didn't really believe it. Some would argue that was the very reason I enjoyed watching it.

But now... well, now everything has changed. I've stopped watching it, and I know why – it's because I've started to believe.

That doesn't make that stuff any less scary; it actually makes it worse. The only difference is that from now on, whenever the natural strays into the supernatural, I'll be ready.

And it would appear that time starts now.

BONUS CONTENT

ANEW

SATURDAY

Dawn's first light peeks through the trees as I run down the woodland trail, the world around me slowly awakening in hues of gold. My breath fogs out in front of me as I ease into a steady rhythm, matching the cadence of my beating heart.

There's something about these early hours that makes me feel so alive, so connected. This is the time when the cacophony of the world is reduced to the whisper of the wind through the bare branches of winter's trees and the crisp rustle of dead leaves beneath my feet. The air feels fresher, tastes cleaner, carrying the scent of damp earth and the promise of awakening life.

This experience fills me with a deep peace and a humbling reminder of the fleeting existence of humanity within the grand cycle of life and death that surrounds us all. It's a perspective that reaffirms our place in something much bigger – a vast and vibrant tapestry woven by nature.

Buddy is a blur of golden fur by my side as we weave through the trees where daylight filters through, creating a dappled pattern on the ground. It's like running through an Instagram filter. #NoFilterNeeded. His energy is boundless, and there's no doubt that he loves these morning runs as much as I do.

We emerge from the sheltering woods, and the coastal path

unfolds before us. The vast canvas of the Atlantic Ocean stretches far into the distance, its aquamarine surface streaked with the golden rays of the rising sun. Waves crash against the shore in a rhythmic counterpoint to the cries of early-rising seagulls overhead—the soundtrack to this perfect moment. I don't think I'll ever tire of this view.

We make our way through an avenue of cypress trees, their trunks bent to the will of the strong wind that haunts this coastline, before reaching the gravelled courtyard and driveway – our finish line.

I throw my hands up into the air and skid to a halt, narrowly avoiding a collision with the black BMW SUV parked here. Buddy bounds past, a blur of brown fur, before skidding to a halt and looking back at me with a triumphant wag and lolling tongue. *Is that all you've got?* his wag seems to say.

I ignore the playful taunt and place my hands on my hips, letting the cold salty breeze push against me as I suck in lungfuls of fresh air, seeking to recover. I check my watch. Not my best time, but not the worst either.

Then I look up and pause, as I always do after a run, taking in the vista before me as if seeing it for the first time. It's a painter's dream: serene waters stretching toward the horizon and the small town of Cliffhaven nestled against the far side of the bay. It's a typical southwestern town, seemingly untouched by time, its charm rooted in its detachment from the modern world.

The bay curls around like a protective arm, sheltering a series of secluded beaches below, disturbed only by the occasional footprint and the ceaseless dance of the tides.

Above these beaches, the land rises sharply, cloaked in vibrant greens. Trees dominate the landscape here, their dense canopies occasionally broken by houses that peek out like hidden gems tucked away in private nooks – man and nature coexisting peacefully.

I sigh and descend the stone steps, passing a large boulder bearing a gold plaque that reads *ANEW.*

This is one of my favourite areas because it feels like stepping down into a secret garden, away from the real world.

Towering evergreen trees stand guard, a majestic mix of Monterey pines and Holm oaks, their branches swaying gently in the caress of the ocean breeze. Interspersed between these giants are large, sculptural Cornish palms, adding an unexpected tropical touch to the landscape.

The undergrowth is a vibrant tapestry of winter bloomers – fiery red dogwood stems erupting from the ground, pops of pink heathers and red holly berries mingling with the deep purple blooms of viburnum. Clusters of Daphne bholua perfume the air with their sweet, heady fragrance. Even in the heart of winter, this natural yet sculpted landscape explodes with colour.

A stone path winds through the garden, guiding me past the cascading splash of a small waterfall down a mossy rock face, leading under a bridge and directly to a building that comprises two rectangular volumes of glass and black steel – clad in weathered cedar that mimics the surrounding trees – stacked atop and overlapping each other. I barely reach it before a section cracks and swings open.

I kick off my trainers and step inside.

Welcome back, Marco, a softly spoken male voice echoes around the foyer. *You were just over a minute behind your best time today, yet you managed to maintain an optimal cardiovascular heart rate.*

I smile as if the AI built into this house can see me, although technically, it can. "Yes, thanks for rubbing it in, Holt," I say, seemingly to the walls.

And so, I suppose this is as good a time as any to fill you in before you question whether, for a change, it's you losing your marbles.

Don't worry. You're not. You've seen a place like this before. It once stood about a hundred fifty miles northeast of here before it was reduced to ashes.

It's been almost two years since that nightmare at Frost Lake Manor, that night that could've been ripped straight from the pages of a Stephen King novel. Almost two years since Sarah lost our child and left for Porthcove, never to return.

Not that I blame her. You were there, weren't you? Would you have stuck around with the walking disaster that I was?

Don't answer that.

Of course, my first instinct was to fix things, to make good on all the damage I had inflicted on our relationship. But after a gut-wrenching visit back to Porthcove to see her, it became instantly clear that there was no fixing this. Sarah had had more than enough of me and my particular brand of crazy. And I, no matter how difficult, had to learn to respect that.

Buddy and I spent the rest of that year licking our wounds. It took several months of physiotherapy and minor surgery for the big guy, but against all odds – and despite the vet's grim prediction that he'd suffer a lifelong limp – he's bounced back completely.

Me? I've recovered, too, mostly. My arm has now regained most of its mobility, but there was a time when I accomplished less than a sloth on a sleeping pill holiday. And writing? Forget about it. My two-finger typing technique, already a marvel of avian inebriation, became a one-armed tap dance with a drunken flamingo – and trust me, those birds have zero rhythm.

But you'll be pleased to know that I adapted and overcame. I made the most of the downtime – thanks to the wonders of modern technology – and after a frustratingly awkward start, was able to dictate most of the first draft of my first novel, *Psychosis* – an autobiographical account of everything that happened at Dolce Vita before Ellie made her special appearance.

No, it wasn't easy revisiting all of that, but after a while, I realised that Doctor Holmes was right; it became cathartic. Expressing everything I experienced in that place – as well as the parts we both know I didn't (i.e., the figments of my imagination) – really helped me come to terms with everything. I found myself looking forward to the sessions, and before long, the words were just pouring out of me.

By autumn, the book was published. And you won't believe it – it's doing rather well. Fancy that, eh? More people doomscrolling through the tragedy that was my life. Who would have thought?

But it's okay, actually. I've come to terms with the fact that it was all really a means to an end. Especially when I received the balance of my fee from the publisher and the subsequent royalties. And who said you can't polish a turd?

My agent – yes, as you know, I have one of those now, pretentious as that may sound – wanted me to get started on the sequel. That's right, he immediately wanted me to dredge up all that shit about how my wife tried to gaslight me. As well as all that other stuff, the fodder for my nightmares, about how we nearly followed what was left of Dolce Vita to the bottom of the bloody ocean, just so we could make a few more quid.

But that same agent also assigned a publicist to me to promote book one. She had me giving interviews and making appearances left, right, and bloody centre, to where I felt like I was permanently on tour, like I was losing control of my life. And being based in London again, well, that wasn't helping.

The publicity for *Psychosis* only reinforced all the exposure that had come before, most of it unflattering, as you know. One moment, I was the survivor; the next, I was the nutter turned psychologist. People started recognising me. Not all the time, but more than enough for it to become embarrassing. Especially when one of the most popular ways of acknowledging me was to shout shit from across the street.

Yeah. So I started re-evaluating living in the city. I know, try not to roll your eyes. I wasn't ignorant of the fact that this seemed to have become my MO – seemingly incapable of settling in one place, constantly running from something. Doctor Ethan Holmes was sure to remind me of that at every opportunity. But then he – unlike the big guy and me – hadn't been cooped up in the city for the better part of a year, most of which was spent confined to quarters at my best mate David's pad. And yes, I know we weren't exactly slumming it, but it was getting to the point where either the hound or I was going to end up biting someone.

Oh, alright – me.

Either that, or I was going to end up reverting to type and smacking someone in the mouth. It even got to where I found myself envious of the lad's country retreat in Hertfordshire.

Don't get me wrong – I love London and everything. It's a beautiful place, but it just doesn't feel the same anymore. Not without Toby. Not without my son.

I was ready... to start... anew.

So... okay, I'll admit it up front. The scene was reminiscent of a few years back. I hired a vehicle, bundled the overanxious golden retriever and myself inside, and drove us the hell out of there. Again, I had no idea where we were going, but it didn't matter. After all, I had planned to tour Italy, but that didn't happen, so this was the next best thing.

At first, I thought we'd head north for a change, but as I joined the motorway around London and saw the road signs, I felt an inexplicable pull – one that led me, once again, west. We passed the New Forest, and in my mind, we'd keep driving until we reached Wales. Yet, I found myself detouring south. As we followed that familiar stretch of motorway, it hit me: I could try outrunning the terrors of Porthcove or the horrors of Fawndale, but they'd always be with me. No matter where I went or what I did, those memories were part of me now. Therapy had drilled this into me; those events may have shaped me, but they didn't define me. And the reason I was driving southwest once more wasn't because of some cosmic autopilot but because, despite everything that happened, I loved the beauty of that peninsula at Porthcove and the tranquillity among the trees.

I realised that I wanted that back – minus the hair-raising horror, of course. That part, I was more than ready to consign to the past. And again, I knew that was down to me.

So I began searching for a new place to call home. Somewhere that embodied the beauty of the past but offered a more hopeful future. Somewhere we could truly start anew.

But... nothing.

I couldn't find anywhere. We spent over a week driving around the entire southwest – north, south, and everywhere in between – making sure to give Porthcove and its surroundings a wide berth.

Nothing.

I even scoured the internet for old properties. I was looking for somewhere special. A project that would become my own labour of love. And yet, despite actually having a decent amount of cash burning a proverbial hole in my pocket, I kept drawing a blank – wrong place, wrong location, wrong price.

Oh, didn't I mention that? The cash part.

As you know, the sale of Frost Lake Manor went through. But then, there was Battista Properties... I had considered keeping the business running, maybe striking a deal with Irvin, perhaps a partnership. But I knew he wasn't that keen; he understandably missed the country.

And just as I was contemplating this, the perfect opportunity arose, and I took it. In the final analysis, Battista Properties didn't look so shabby on paper. I sold it to a national conglomerate that made me an offer I couldn't refuse.

I gave Irvin and the lads a generous bonus, and the rest sat in the bank, gaining interest while waiting for my next crazy scheme. Only, as you've already learned, even with the best will in the world, I seemed incapable of finding one.

But then, we stumbled upon Cliffhaven. Buddy and I had stopped off there during one of our many scouting trips. I'd never heard of the place before but was immediately drawn to its cobblestone charm. Yes, much like Porthcove – incidentally, about an hour or so south.

One thing I really like about Cliffhaven is that while it retains all the rustic charm of a small seaside town, it also boasts the amenities of a small city.

We stopped off at the Tide's End Café – an old boathouse perched on the harbour wall – drawn in by a charming portrait of a Labrador outside, captioned with an inviting *We're Welcome*!

Inside, the place doubled as an art gallery, with the walls serving as a canvas for an eclectic collection of paintings. Each artwork, varying in size and style, breathed life into Cliffhaven's history, the brushstrokes capturing moments and memories woven into the very soul of the building.

One painting, in particular, really spoke to me – yeah, I know that sounds poncy, but it's true. It depicted a group of smugglers from centuries past, gathered on a moonlit beach. There was something about it that drew me into its world, a glimpse into an adventurous, long-lost past. I seriously considered buying it, but with us still living at David's and no clear destination in sight, I hesitated.

As I sat there, eating a tuna melt and sipping tea, surrounded by vivid depictions of the town's seafaring legacy – when the ocean was both a threat and an ally – I was reminded, in a way, of my own connection to the sea. But it wasn't until we were driving the coastal route out of town, with spectacular views of woodland, beaches, and coastline, that we stumbled upon something unexpected.

A dirt track caught my eye, marked by a makeshift paper sign flapping in the wind. Part of it was ripped and held together by bits of Sellotape on a plywood board. I drove past it at first, dismissing it as unimportant. I wasn't looking for land; I wanted an old property, something that needed love – a project where Irvin and the lads could help me make it my own. But then, the ever-present *What if?* that had haunted me since my life took that heartbreaking turn a few years back forced me to reconsider.

I stopped the car, reversed back to that sign, and watched the piece of paper flutter forlornly in the wind. It kept waving one word at me:

LAND – *For Sale*

I turned on the hazard lights, pondering for several seconds, before glancing at Buddy in the backseat. "Well, what do you think?" I asked the golden wonder. He lifted his head, wagged his tail, and gave me that single bark that tells me everything and nothing at the same time.

"Okay," I said with a smile, steering the car off the main road and onto the semi-gravelled drive.

We followed the road downward, through what I imagined was a meadow in summer, for less than a minute before the world seemed to fold inward. The open, pale blue sky vanished, replaced by a dense canopy of interlocking branches. The car's tires crunched a rustic symphony on the gravel and earth, a rhythm that quickened my pulse.

It was like entering a different realm. Shadows and dappled sunlight flickered in a staccato rhythm as we journeyed through this arboreal tunnel, the scene instantly transporting me back to the day we first visited Holt.

As we passed the age-old tree sentinels, their massive trunks silent witnesses to centuries past, I felt the weight of my history lessen, becoming just another story whispered among the leaves. A glance in the rearview mirror revealed Buddy's excitement. His nose was pressed against the window, fogging the glass as he eagerly sniffed the new scents wafting through the vents – a mix of earth, sea salt, and the faintest hint of wildflowers. His wagging tail made his entire body vibrate with anticipation, a language as clear as words: this was a place of adventure, of possibilities.

And then, just as suddenly as we had entered the woods, we emerged. The trees parted like curtains, revealing a cove – a crescent of solitude kissed by the ocean. It was a hidden jewel, stunningly beautiful, the kind of place you'd whisper about, fearing its magic might vanish if shared.

The land sloped gently towards a beach adorned with smooth pebbles and sand that whispered of secret midnight walks and sun-drenched days. Lush greenery framed a rocky cove where waterfalls tumbled over moss-covered stones, their music joining the symphony of the waves crashing against the shore. The vast ocean before us – a canvas of blues and greens melting into the horizon – held a wildness that spoke of nature's untamed heart, a rawness that both captivated and soothed.

I brought the car to a rolling stop, transfixed. This forgotten Garden of Eden, hidden amongst the trees, literally stole my breath away.

It took Buddy's eager groans to snap me out of my reverie. I pulled on the door handle and stepped out into the fresh air and the film score of nature: the operatic birdsong, the melodic rush of water, and the dramatic crash of waves smashing against the rocks.

Buddy's excited barks filled the air as he bounded back and forth, seemingly incapable of deciding which part of this haven to explore first.

The dog's enthusiasm stretched a grin across my face until I became aware of her. She was standing right of frame, alone. Solitary. Mournful. Majestic against the backdrop of a serene autumnal landscape.

I was in love the moment I saw the weeping willow. Its branches, heavy with a crown of auburn and gold leaves, dipped low, their tips tracing languid circles on the surface of the gurgling water below. A gentle breeze whispered through its leaves, casting a dappled, melancholic light that shimmered on the water. The tree, a quiet guardian, seemed to lean closer, its cascading foliage sharing the wind's secret stories with the flowing stream. Each droplet of water, I imagined, carried tales of both grief and resilience, a testament to the enduring spirit of nature.

It was there, in the presence of that majestic willow, that a sense of calm settled over me. It felt like a silent guardian, a natural monument not just to my sorrows but also my joys. And as I gazed across the sprawling landscape, a vision blossomed in my mind's eye – the perfect house. Not an imposing structure, but one nestled seamlessly within the embrace of the land, a true haven to call home. A blank canvas upon which a new chapter could be written, one filled not with pain but with the vibrant promise of hope.

I breathed in the fresh air, the scent of earth and salt filling my lungs. A sigh escaped my lips, a long, slow release of tension I hadn't realised I was holding. "Looks like we might have finally found our new home, Bud," I murmured, my voice thick with emotion. Because deep down, nestled amongst the roots of this newfound peace, flickered a feeling I hadn't embraced in a long time – a sense of belonging. This was the place. This was our chance to start... anew.

HOME

ANEW· EARLY MORNING·

I made an instant offer for the land – subject to survey, of course.

Holt, that original house in the New Forest, soon became the embodiment of my dream home. While I didn't have the means at the time to buy such a place, things were a little different now. So I sought the building's original designer and construction company while simultaneously commissioning a comprehensive investigation to understand the site's geological history, soil sampling to check for stability, and a battery of other laboratory tests for additional detailed insights. Oh, and I consulted a flood risk specialist, just to be on the safe side, because – well, you were at Dolce Vita that night – you'll appreciate that I was in no hurry to repeat that experience.

Everything came back green with some reasonable recommendations, so I commissioned a separate company to run the same checks. Green again.

My dream home is almost a carbon copy of the one I fell in love with in the New Forest. I say "almost" because there were some specific changes to the standard plans that I knew I wanted right from the start.

The build was supposed to take five to six months but, in true construction fashion, ended up taking eight. By the time ANEW was finished, it had almost emptied my bank accounts, which is the reason I'm feeling somewhat pragmatic about baring my soul in that book deal.

Oh, but it was worth every penny.

I am reminded of this as I step into the atrium, its decorative circular hood washing the space with golden early morning sunshine, illuminating a small indoor garden that's a slice of Eden right here in my home.

A stone pathway winds through a copse of small trees – lemon and dwarf apple, already hinting at future harvests – leading to a welcoming wooden bench. It's an invitation to sit and soak in the sound of the cascading water feature that feeds into a pond where koi glide beneath the surface like living jewels.

Lush ferns unfurl around flowering plants, the air is fresh, and everything is perfectly tempered, as if the garden itself breathes in the peace of the morning.

Here, among the quiet rustle of leaves and the soft murmur of water, is where past and present meet, where every element is a nod to the journey that's brought me to this moment.

To my right is an open-plan dining room with a large banquet table made of natural, reclaimed wood, with room for ten. It leads to a state-of-the-art kitchen – not unlike the one at Holt, but with a few additions and gadgets. And while I still may not be weaving culinary magic just yet, I'm forever expanding my repertoire, inspired by that very room.

Down the hall is the switchback staircase leading up to the four bedrooms and beyond to the roof, where there's a living garden of herbs and vegetables, as well as a couple of giant solar panels that contribute to the power needs of the building.

On the far-left side of the atrium is the door to the study, with that unique dual perspective – this time over the garden, trees, and coastline towards Cliffhaven – and the other over the front garden, the rocky waterfalls, and the stream out to the cove and ocean.

On the far right of the atrium is the door to the den, flooded with more beautiful natural light thanks to the glass wall that offers a stunning and unobstructed view down the front garden and stream. The room's minimalist design, with sleek, modern furniture, mirrors the contemporary architecture of the house. It's furnished with comfortable plush sofas in neutral colours that add warmth to this otherwise cool palette of steel and glass – yes, I learned a thing or two during my stint as CEO of Battista Properties. There are also glass coffee tables sitting in front of the sofas, their reflecting surfaces echoing the glass walls and helping to distribute light throughout the room.

I went back to that café by the ocean and secured that *smugglers on a moonlit beach* painting and a couple others. Now, hanging on the walls are a series of carefully chosen pieces of art – depicting the history that is the bedrock of my new home – adding a personal touch to the space while complementing the room's colour scheme and modern aesthetic.

Although, if I am completely honest, as much as I adore these pieces, there is one that I am particularly fond of. You'll remember this – it's that solitary photo I found backed up in the cloud account. The one of Toby and me, the selfie we took by the river. Toby, with his chestnut brown eyes wide and sandy blonde hair gleaming in the early morning sun, proudly holding up to the camera his first catch of the day while I have an arm wrapped around him, fingers folded into a shaka sign, grinning proudly with my tongue hanging out.

I love that photo. I love this canvas. *And I love you, Toby. My pride.*

My joy.

Adding a touch of nature to the room are several indoor plants – their greenery creating a seamless transition between the indoor space and the beautiful outdoor view. A plush area rug underfoot adds texture and warmth.

The den, of course, like most of the rooms at ANEW, extends to a spacious outdoor balcony furnished with comfortable seating and tables. It's a favourite spot for enjoying the ocean view – whether I'm sipping my morning coffee or entertaining carefully selected guests.

I take a second to catch my breath. On a day like today, without the playful obstruction of clouds, one might mistake this view for an artist's rendition of a seascape – yet it's anything but artificial.

This is my sanctuary. My Eden, where the stream doesn't merely pass by – it dances, leaps, and pirouettes over rocks, giving life to waterfalls and reflecting pools that coax the surrounding greenery and flowers into a vibrant display of beauty. It's a scene that finds a delicate order in its wild rush to the cove below. And the ocean, oh the ocean – it's a living canvas, daubed with every conceivable shade of blue.

There are various other modern marvels built into ANEW, such as the micro-hydropower system that converts the kinetic energy of the stream into power. Both this system and the solar roof panels can generate enough energy to power the home for a week. Similarly, the natural spring water is filtered for use here, which means that as long as the stream keeps running, we'll continue to enjoy ample water without the need to tap into the local supply.

Again, if you followed our stay in the New Forest, you pretty much know all about this place, although there is one major exception: the study. While it follows a design similar to Holt's – in that it features a dual aspect over the waterfall and woodland as well as the garden and the ocean – there is one notable difference: it remains a strictly private space.

ANEW has a self-sufficient annex attached, functioning as both my office and a potential guest house. Well, you didn't expect me to take any chances again, did you? After everything that happened last time with Frost Lake Manor's creepy squatter, there's no way I'm ever going to invite complete strangers into my new home.

THE LITTLE MAN

ANEW. MID-EVENING.

Right, so regarding that whole *No strangers in the house* policy – a little retraction, if I may.

If I'm perfectly honest, I didn't think this was actually going to happen, but ANEW is welcoming its first official guests this evening.

By official, I mean strangers I wouldn't ever consider entertaining – except for a good cause. And, for me, there's no cause more deserving than the Little Man Foundation.

You'll probably remember that a while back, I received a payout for my former wife, Ellie, which turned into a whole saga because the insurance company paid out on her death. Only, it turned out she wasn't actually dead but very much alive – and then, well, she wasn't. Yeah, it was a confusing time, both legally and emotionally.

Anyway, as you know, while I believed Ellie was gone, I couldn't bring myself to use that money, so I started the Little Man Foundation. The intention was clear and heartfelt – to support bereaved parents like we were, offering both counselling and relief from the burden of financial stress.

But when Ellie reappeared... well, let's just say legal complications ensued. By the time the dust settled – and no, there's no macabre pun intended here – after Ellie fell from that roof in a shower of dust and glass, the foundation's funds were already allocated. And, after some back and forth, it was determined that the initial payout had been made in good faith, allowing the foundation to keep its funds.

It turns out, though, that when you start a charity, your contribution doesn't end there. It's generally good practice to fundraise to ensure the charity doesn't run out of money.

If I'm perfectly honest, the whole book promotion thing has been instrumental in this. My relative notoriety has elevated the charity's credibility, which, in turn, has encouraged additional donations. This is yet another reason why I don't think becoming an author was so bad after all.

Which is why I'm standing in front of the full-length mirror right now, giving myself – and the tux I'm wearing – the once over. Apparently – and I don't see this, but I seem to be in the minority – I am looking younger these days. The sea air obviously agrees with me, or so I'm told.

My hair's a bit longer than I normally like it, but right now, it's in a neat side-comb, and, as much as I don't want to admit it, there's an ever so slight recession at my temple. My beard is thicker but neatly trimmed, and, by the way, this tux is moulded to me. I'd say I'm in the best shape I've been in a long time, thanks, no doubt, to the early morning runs and the occasional pull-up. This is more for maintenance, you'll understand, than vanity because, despite what people keep telling me, I'm very much aware of the fact that time marches on and I'm not getting any younger. And, well, motion is lotion, and all that.

As I descend the stairs, Holt's playlist – a blend of classical melodies and Rat Pack–era tunes – fills the air, creating an elegant yet sophisticated ambiance I hope will resonate with my guests.

The house, now in *evening mode*, is a symphony of light and shadow. Lamps cast cosy pools of warm light throughout, while low-level LEDs add a subtle glow to the nooks and crannies of ANEW. It's a contrast I'm hoping speaks of care and thoughtfulness – a setting designed not just to impress but to welcome.

But it's the atrium that truly steals the show. Stepping into this space is like walking into a curtain of light, a dreamscape crafted from the simplest of things. The dwarf trees, each adorned with a constellation of tiny LED lights, create a magical forest in miniature. These lights twinkle like stars caught in a slow dance, casting a gentle, ethereal glow over the entire room.

Beneath my feet, the stone pathway – meandering through this indoor Eden – leads to the familiar comfort of the handcrafted wooden bench. It's more than just a seat; it's an invitation to pause, to breathe in the beauty of this place.

And then there's the pond. In the soft light, its surface is a mirror, reflecting the glow of the LED lights nestled within its depths. It adds an element of fluidity and calm to the space, a reminder of nature's serene presence amid modernity.

This atrium – this light-filled haven – is more than just a centrepiece for ANEW; it's a testament to new beginnings and the hope that even amidst the darkest times, there can be light. And tonight, as I host this fundraiser for the Little Man Foundation in honour of my son, I feel that light not just around me but within.

Yeah, I can hear it, too – the undercurrent of change. Is it the burgeoning writer in me, or is it something more profound? Ever since I arrived here, it's like I've been on my own road to Damascus. All those twisted paths I've wandered have led me to this place. To this haven. And for the first time in a long time, I can breathe.

Don't get me wrong. I've still got issues – who hasn't? – but they no longer feel like a noose around my neck. I feel lighter, unburdened, and surprisingly mellow. And before you ask – no, I'm not on anything. The only high I'm riding is life itself. So don't be shocked if I start sporting sandals and growing my hair down to my arse.

Now, here come the nerves. The atrium is buzzing, packed with Cliffhaven's finest, and while I've had my fair share of public speaking, this is different. These are my neighbours, local business leaders, council members, and even a few global pioneers. They're all here, in my house, tonight.

I weave through the crowd, exchanging smiles and handshakes, the buzz of conversation a backdrop to my escalating heartbeat.

When I'd first imagined this fundraiser-cum-housewarming, I thought it'd be a small affair. This turnout? It's beyond anything I'd expected.

David's hand lands on my shoulder, giving me a start. "You alright, mate?" he asks in his blue tuxedo, looking more Bond than friend.

"Yeah, mate. Of course," I reply, though my pounding heart might suggest otherwise.

He glances around and then meets my eyes again. "Good, because you looked like you might bolt at the thought of speaking to this lot."

I force a scoff, pulling my best *Who, me?* face.

He gives my shoulder a reassuring squeeze. "You've got this. Just be your usual captivatin' self, and they'll love ya – as much as we do," he says with a grin.

His confidence is infectious, almost enough to make me believe I can actually do this without embarrassing myself.

"Go on, then. I'm starving," he urges, and I can't help but smile.

With squared shoulders and resisting the urge to smooth down my hair, I turn to face the sea – a moonlit spectacle beyond a curtain of lights and glass.

"Holt," I call out, my voice steady. "Announcement, please."

The familiar airplane-like cabin chime of Holt's system preludes his smooth announcement: *Ladies and gentlemen, please join us in the atrium for a special message from your host.*

Most guests are already here, including Aaron at the front, who winks and starts a ripple of applause. Then there's the architect of the night, the orchestrator of this full house – Charlotte Radcliffe. Her smile tells me I'm in for an evening to remember.

They step forward and hand me a reassuring smile, along with a flute of champagne. I nod gratefully as they clap, too. And no, I haven't taken up drinking again. I've managed to avoid the booze for some time now, but tonight is a special occasion. That, and I could use the help.

I take another deep breath to speak but find that it catches in my throat. Okay. So, I'm a little more nervous than I realised. And I know why. It's because this whole thing isn't about me but my little boy and... A murmur ripples through the crowd, closely followed by laughter, and then I watch people part as Buddy makes his way over to me, tongue hanging, tail wagging.

I smile at him. He barks once as if to say, *Are you going to get on with this or what?*

There's laughter. And I take my cue.

"Good evening, everyone. Wow. Thank you so much for joining me here at ANEW for this very important evening.

"You know, when Charlotte told me she knew a few people, I didn't realise she meant most of the town." There's a faint buzz of laughter. "But really. Thank you all for being here for this event, which, as some of you know, means so much to me."

I take a few seconds, wishing that I had written cue cards after all, but I had told myself I was just going to speak from the heart, and that should be enough. But now, standing in front of these people... Well, it's a different kettle of fish.

"You know, I used to think that a house was just four walls and a roof to keep the rain off. But after my, um, recent... life experiences, I've learned that it's so much more. A home is where memories – good or bad – linger, where friends and loved ones converge, and sometimes, it's a refuge after the worst days."

I let my gaze drift over the sea of faces. "For me, home was where my family was. Where I had a wife, a son... but not anymore." Buddy settles down with a groan, his paw touching my overly polished shoes.

"We lost our son in a terrible accident. I, as some of you may have read, didn't handle it well. And, um, my late wife, Ellie... she had to cope alone after her refuge, her peace, was snatched away when she needed it most.

"The Little Man Foundation was created to lend support to parents facing such unimaginable pain because no one should have to worry about the mundane aspects of life when their world is falling apart." Memories cascade through me – *Toby on the pier, the walls of Dolce Vita collapsing, the wail of that wind on the rooftop of Frost Lake Manor. Ellie, please!*

I take a moment, a deep inhale to steady the emotions that, even after all this time, feel as raw as if the wounds were fresh.

Feeling the weight of every gaze, I take another breath and rub at the phantom ache in my arm.

"Um... we used to call Toby little man because that boy..." I swallow the knot that's suddenly formed in my throat. "He... he carried wisdom beyond his years. Wisdom that often surpassed my own. He taught me so much of what I know – about the purity of unconditional love, about finding joy in the simplest things, and about the sheer wonder of the world we live in." I swallow again, my mouth suddenly dry, but I push on. "And there isn't a day that goes by without missing that little boy."

I love you, Daddy.

"And so," I continue, voice steadying, "I see some of you have already found the bench at the heart of this Eden – *The Toby Bench.* Crafted from the only thing I saved from a storage unit that was a time capsule of a life that feels like a moment and an eon away. All else from that time? It's out there now, donated, helping others. But that bed, Toby's bed, it's been reborn into that bench over there. A spot to sit, to reflect, and to remember a little boy whose fascination with dinosaurs was only matched by the depth of his father's love for him."

A smile breaks through at the memory of Toby, animated and vibrant, orchestrating a dinosaur family reunion in our living room bathed in sunlight.

"And speaking of dinosaurs, take a gander at the pond later on. You'll spot a brachiosaurus – Toby's favourite – emerging from the water. It's my way of remembering that life persists, endures, and transforms in the most unexpected ways.

Eventually, the applause dies down, and I clear my throat to shift gears. "Thank you so very much. And, of course, if you're looking to support a great cause and snag some stunning art, then you're in luck." With a flourish of my hand, I draw attention to the three impressive paintings on easels nearby. "These masterpieces were generously donated by Charlotte Radcliffe of the Tide's End Art Café. Yes, the very same Charlotte who not only convinced you all to join us tonight but also played a key role in organising this entire evening."

I beckon Charlotte over, and we share a continental greeting amidst warm applause. Charlotte's scent is particularly intoxicating tonight, a mixture of something floral and the ocean breeze. Her fiery red hair falls just right, framing sapphire eyes that sparkle even more against her figure-hugging black dress. And before you ask – no, she doesn't remind me of Ellie.

"Some of you might know that it was Charlotte who anchored Buddy and me to Cliffhaven. It all started with a simple stop at The Tide's End, and, well, we've been here ever since. When I first shared the story of the Little Man Foundation, Charlotte offered to reach out to a few friends." I gesture to the crowd, then back to Charlotte. "At the time, I had no idea that meant the majority of this wonderful community." I raise my glass. "To Charlotte, the heart of this community; to you, your generosity; and, why not, to your chequebooks!"

***

A couple of hours later, after obligatory mingling, posing for official press photos – again, courtesy of Charlotte – several selfies, and a few house tours, I'm about ready for everybody to go home. In the nicest possible way, of course, since it would appear that the evening was a success. All the paintings sold, raising even more funds for the foundation, and initial feedback from Charlotte informs me that my neighbours aren't short of a few quid.

Who would have thought such a sleepy town would harbour such wealth? And, as you can imagine, I'm absolutely thrilled. I mean, I'm a pauper compared to some of this lot, which, as you'll know, isn't something I'm alien to. And, of course, it'd be easy for this to fill me with a sense of inadequacy, but it doesn't. I've reconciled my life. Buddy and I have found our place in the world, and while I may no longer have a fat bank account, I don't think I've ever felt this content before.

That said, I think I may need to get on with this next book if Buddy and I don't want to live off porridge for the rest of our lives. But then, that might be preferable to listening to the owner of Carpet Cove – one of the county's largest carpet suppliers – wax poetic about the fascinating history of shag pile versus the existential angst of the modern throw rug. But then, mercifully, I hear a voice I recognise. It cuts through my artificial smile instantly. My heart is equally surprised because it seems to do a double tap.

In the tender wash of the evening's lamplight, she's looking nothing short of radiant. Her dark hair is swept to one side and over one shoulder, partially veiled by a long, tailored tuxedo jacket. Black, maybe navy, hard to tell in this light, but it's classy and fits like it was made for her. And there's something else about her, something different tonight. A touch of makeup, maybe, because she's positively glowing.

"Sarah? Wow," is all I can say.

"Marc," she says. And we pause because, well, it's surprisingly awkward. But she touches my arm, and it's like a prompt; I bend down to kiss her on both cheeks. She smells delicious.

"I, um—" I interrupt myself, then turn back to the group standing next to me. "I'm sorry. Please excuse me for a second." I don't wait for an answer, and touching Sarah's arm, we step away. "Wow. Sarah," I repeat. "I didn't know you were coming."

I watch her face crease into a broad smile, but then she crouches down. "BUDDY! Oh, I've missed you," she says warmly. "I've missed you." She hugs the dog.

I stop short of rolling my eyes at the golden wonder who never fails to upstage me. Especially when there are pretty women around.

I watch my ex-girlfriend make a fuss over the dog and am instantly transported back to Fawndale. To Holt. To the wedding. And, of course, to the cold and that night on the rooftop when this beautiful woman almost lost her life.

I shiver the memory away just as she stands up to her full size once more. I notice that despite her glamorously sophisticated attire, she's wearing flats. That's my Sarah. I smile inwardly, chastising myself for using that possessive noun. She isn't mine anymore.

"You look great," she says, taking in me and my tuxedo.

"You think?"

"Yeah. Healthy."

"Thanks. And you... you..." Oh shit. What happened to my words? "You look like you're... glowing." *Glowing? Seriously. What is she, a light bulb?*

She rocks her head. "Thanks. Amazing what a bit of makeup can do, eh?" she laughs.

"No. It's not that—"

"This place, Marc," she interrupts, looking around. "... wow."

"You like it?"

"I love it," she says, eyes wide.

"Well, happy to give you the tour if you like."

"No need," she says, turning to me with a mischievous smile and a twinkle in those beautiful hazel – in this light – eyes. "We had a quick nose around when we arrived. You'd just finished that wonderful speech."

"We?"

"There you are," a stranger says, walking up to us. He's dressed in a sharp suit and waistcoat like he's just got back from working at the stock exchange. He hands Sarah an orange juice, then spots me and breaks into a wide smile. "Marco Battista!" he exclaims, offering a hand that I reluctantly take. His grip is firm and vigorous. "Liam. Liam Turner. I've heard so much about you."

"You have?"

"Yeah."

"Sorry, I can't say I've heard much about you, Liam," I say, glancing at Sarah and then eyeing the blue-eyed man who bears a remarkable resemblance to that Craig bloke she used to work with, but I know it isn't him because this one seems more mature, more worldly.

"Loved your book, by the way," he adds, seemingly unaffected by my comment. "A real page-turner. Intense. I can only imagine what that must have been like for you," he says gravely.

It was one of the worst experiences of my life. Thanks for bringing it up, shithead! I allow a tight smile to play on my lips, but it most likely doesn't reach my eyes.

"This building, though..." he gestures appreciatively around the atrium, "is so far removed from Dolce Vita," he says like he knew the place.

"Liam's an architect," Sarah offers. "He was desperate to look around as soon as we got here. I hope you don't mind," she adds with a bite of her lip.

"Guilty as charged," Liam admits with a smile, holding up his hands.

And I don't know what to say here beyond the obvious, which is *Who the fuck are you, and why the fuck have you put your arm around Sarah's shoulder like that?* But somehow, I think I already know the answer, and I'm still trying to work out how I feel about it.

I glance across the room at David and Irvin. You know them – the traitorous two who obviously knew all about this bloke but didn't bother telling me. When I look back, my new pal, Liam, has an enthusiastic spark in his eyes, "... the interplay of natural light that must flood in here during the day... The way the fenestration is designed to enhance solar gain while maintaining thermal comfort is quite ingenious."

Is this bloke for real?

"And the use of sustainable materials here aligns perfectly with biophilic design principles. It's not often you see such a seamless integration of eco-conscious architecture with modern aesthetics," he continues in somewhat of a plummy accent, making me think the man can't be from the West Country.

He glances back at Sarah and makes a pained face. "I'm geeking out again, aren't I?"

"Just a little," she nods.

"I'm so sorry," he says to her, then to me, he adds, "I'm sorry to be such a bore. I'm just in awe of your home, Marco. Truly."

I smile. "Well, that's nice to hear." Because I have no clue how you respond to such a statement.

"You've done really well, Marc," Sarah adds warmly.

"Thanks," I say earnestly.

"Phew," I watch her blow her hair.

"Are you alright?" Liam fusses. "You're looking rosy. Another hot flush?"

"It's a bit warm in here," Sarah says, fanning herself.

I'm surprised by this since Sarah normally runs a bit cold.

"Here, let me take your jacket."

"No, it's okay," she protests, but Liam has already opened her jacket, and then it becomes obvious, especially when she places an instinctively protective hand on her belly. She looks at me, and we exchange glances, saying nothing and everything at the same time. And me, well, shit, I feel like somebody just punched me in the gut.

Sarah's pregnant, and I get the impression she didn't want me to know. And the selfish part of me wishes it that way. "... I'm okay, really," she says, "I'd rather keep it on."

"Well, if you're sure," Liam says.

There's an awkward silence, one I'm just about to fill with the first thing that pops into my head, when Sarah downs her drink and holds out her glass. "Liam. Would you mind getting me another?"

"No, of course not. Marco?" He looks at me.

I shake my head. "No thanks."

"I'll take some time," Liam says with a smile. "Give you two a while to catch up."

I watch him leave, then turn to Sarah and mime my head exploding.

She makes a pained face. "I'm sorry. I didn't mean for you to find out like this. I even considered not coming, but I was so proud of you, of what you've accomplished, and this place. I just wanted to—"

"Sarah, Sarah," I interrupt. "You don't have to apologise. I was just surprised, that's all."

"I know. Things moved fast. At first, I thought I was on the rebound after you, but... well, he's a good man. A decent man... Not that you weren't."

I place a hand on her arm. "I'm happy for you," I hear myself say. *Wait! What!?*

"You are?"

I smile at her. "Of course I am. You really deserve nothing but the best. I was... I was just surprised is all. I didn't even know you were seeing someone."

She drops her gaze and nods. "I know. Uncle Irvin. I think he was being protective again. Of me, of you."

I hesitate because part of me wants to speak the words, and the other thinks I've lost my bloody mind again, and yet, "It suits you." She looks at herself. "Being pregnant. You look fantastic."

She cocks her head and smiles bashfully. "I don't feel it."

And it's odd because I feel like I need to say something here. I want to say something, but there are so many thoughts jostling for my attention that I can't seem to single out any of them. But then there's one.

One thing that I'd like to ask, and I am just formulating the words when I feel a slap on my shoulder. "Fuckin' 'ell, Marco, mate, this is some party, ain't it?"

I turn to see Eddie Chapman, my agent, in a sleek midnight blue suit that's tailored to perfection. His unbuttoned white shirt adds a touch of irreverence to his outfit, and the burgundy paisley pocket square lends a pop of audacious flair. Brown brogues round off his look, a testament to his knack for mixing business with a dash of East End edge. There he stands, a perfect mix of London Street and literary elite, his bleached pearly whites competing with the lighting in the room.

"Eddie?" I say – while that giant, overinflated emotional balloon releases and screams off over the heads of the other guests.

My agent notices because he glances at Sarah and then at me, then back again. "Sorry, am I interrupting someffin?" he asks.

"Well—"

He doesn't wait for an answer. He takes Sarah's hand. "Sarah, isn't it? Nice to meet ya at last," he says softly, kissing her hand.

He's definitely had a few. Not that Eddie can't be a charmer when the mood takes him, and I'm not talking just females here. I'm talking about anybody, regardless of sex, that he needs to influence and or bend to his will. It's this very skill that makes him exceptionally good at his job.

How else do you think I caved? And no, he doesn't remind me of me.

"Is there something I can do for you, Eddie?"

"Actually, Marco, me old china, it's more about what I can do for you."

"Eddie, if it's about the book, I—"

"No, I'm gonna get to that. No, this is about the email I forwarded to ya. Ya know, in my new capacity as your personal secretary. Ya know, given that the sender thought to send it through me rather than looking up your details on your website."

"No. I haven't looked at my phone in a while. It's been on silent because I've been a little busy," I say, gesturing to the room.

"Well, you may wanna take a look," he says, patting me on the shoulder. "Don't worry about this lovely lady. I'll gladly keep her company in the meantime. I've got a glass of champers with your name on it."

"Well, actually—" Sarah begins.

But Eddie has already taken her arm and is leading her away from me and through the crowd.

Shit.

I pull out my phone so I can see what's so bloody important, then go and save her so we can finish our conversation, but then I open my email, and my heart skips a beat:

FW: IMPORTANT – ATTENTION OF MARCO BATTISTA

Please see attached.

Best regards,
Samantha Battista

If you enjoyed

NEMESIS

Please leave an Amazon / Goodreads rating
so that others may enjoy it also.

Generally, only a fraction of satisfied readers will leave a rating, so yours really will make a difference.

THANK YOU

FOLLOW TONY

If you can't wait for Tony Marturano's next thriller, subscribe to the blog, mailing list, or follow on social media for the latest news, special chapter previews and exclusive giveaways.

VISIT
www.tonymarturano.com

JOIN THE MAILING LIST
visit www.tonymarturano.com,
click on contact and subscriptions.

LIKE THE FACEBOOK PAGE
facebook.com/tonymarturano.author

BROWSE INSTAGRAM
instagram.com/marturanotony

FOLLOW ON X
x.com/tmarturano

or google tony marturano

ACKNOWLEDGEMENTS

As always, I am deeply grateful to everyone at A Different Angle who has supported me throughout this book's journey from manuscript to print. Special thanks to the following individuals who have contributed actively to its realization.

FOCUS / READER'S GROUP
My heartfelt thanks to all members of the reader's group for generously giving their time and sharing their insights. Your feedback has been invaluable!

(In no particular order)
Francesca Marturano-Pratt – Anna Pratt – Renee Owens
Rosa Littleton – Lisa Hall – Cheryl Green

MY EDITOR
Jamie, thank you for keeping me on the straight and narrow. You are living proof that some good things did come out of the pandemic!

YOU, THE READER
If you're reading this book, there's a good chance you bought it, and for that, I am obviously very grateful. Thank you!
But if you borrowed or were gifted this book by someone else, even better—it means they thought it was good enough to pass on.

Printed in Great Britain
by Amazon

58452592R20219